Measuring UP

Lily LaMotte ★ Ann Xu
Colors by Sunmi

HARPER
alley

An Imprint of HarperCollinsPublishers

Chapter 1

In a small town in Taiwan . . .

My life in Taiwan is sweet.

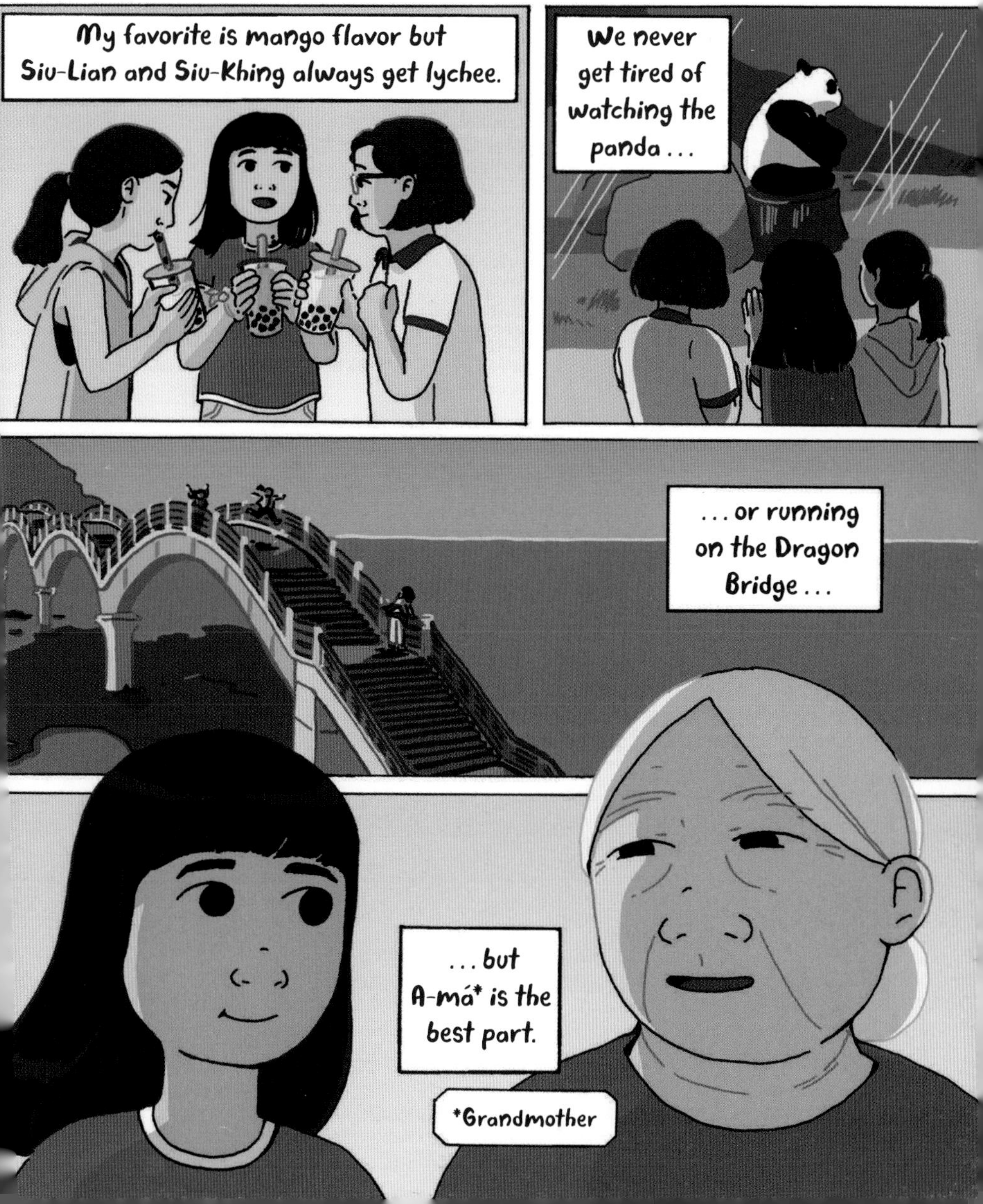
My favorite is mango flavor but Siu-Lian and Siu-Khing always get lychee.
We never get tired of watching the panda . . .
. . . or running on the Dragon Bridge . . .
. . . but A-má* is the best part.
*Grandmother

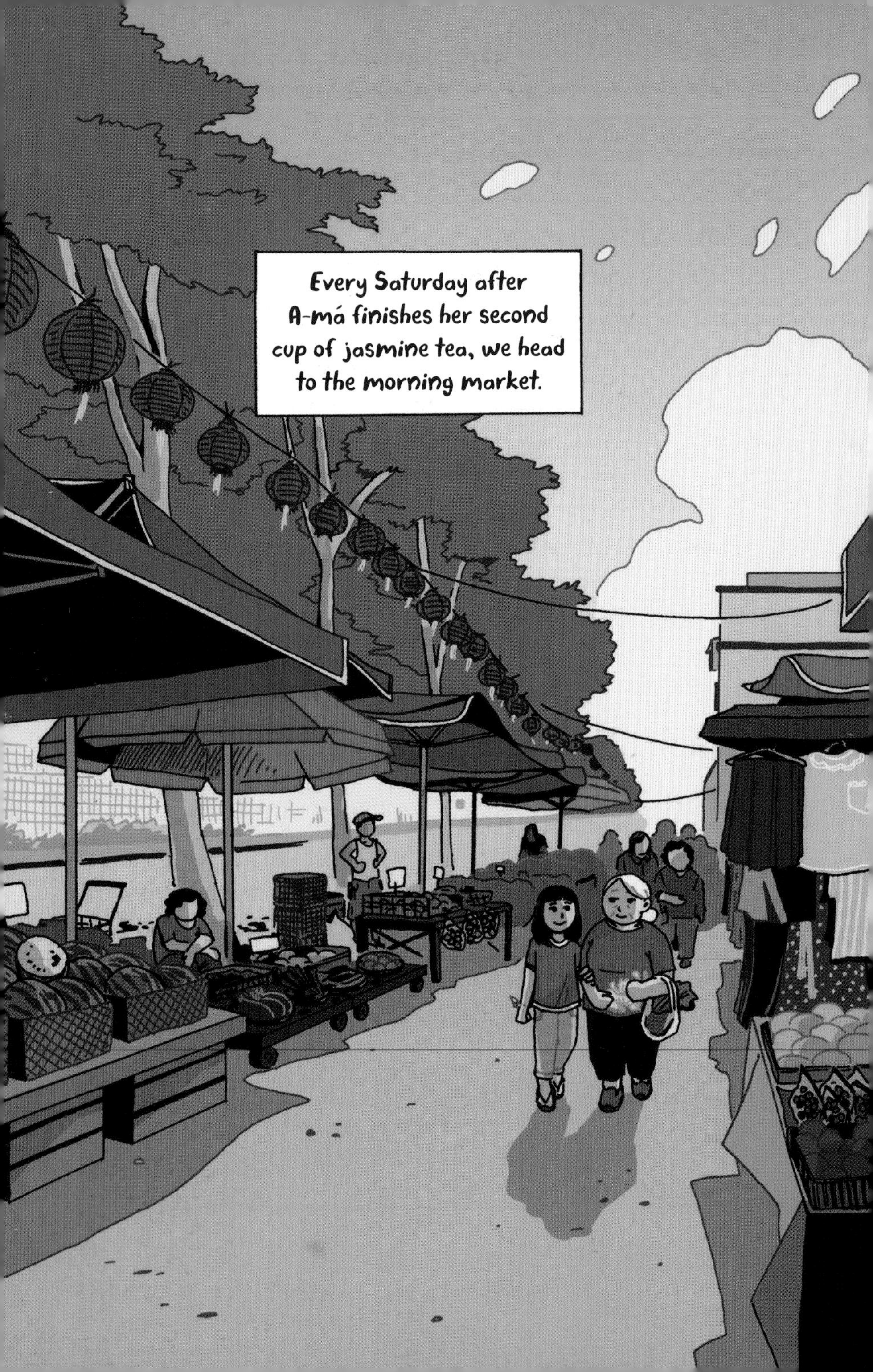
Every Saturday after A-má finishes her second cup of jasmine tea, we head to the morning market.

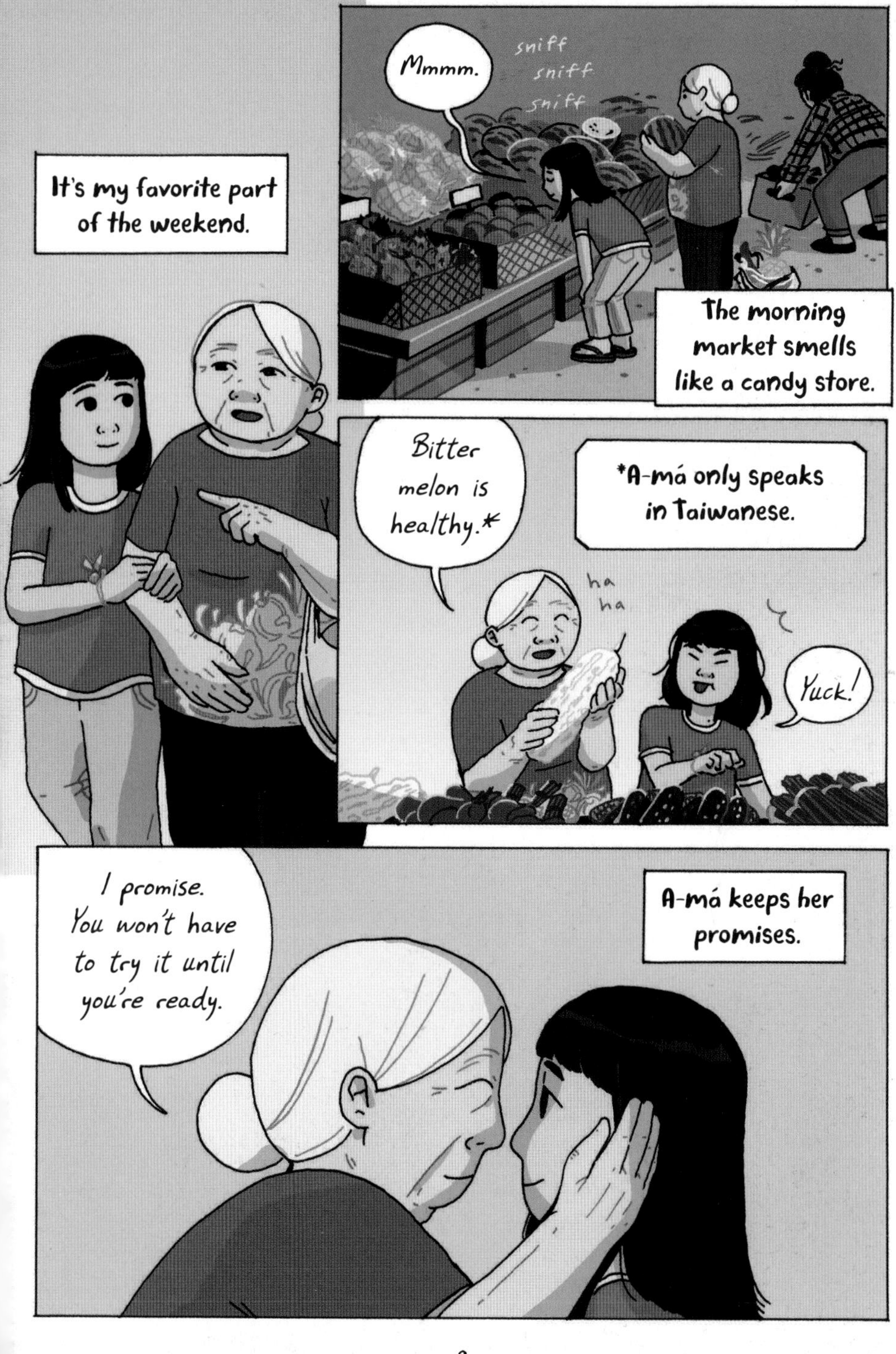
It's my favorite part of the weekend.
Mmmm.
sniff sniff sniff
The morning market smells like a candy store.
Bitter melon is healthy.*
*A-má only speaks in Taiwanese.
ha ha
Yuck!
I promise. You won't have to try it until you're ready.
A-má keeps her promises.

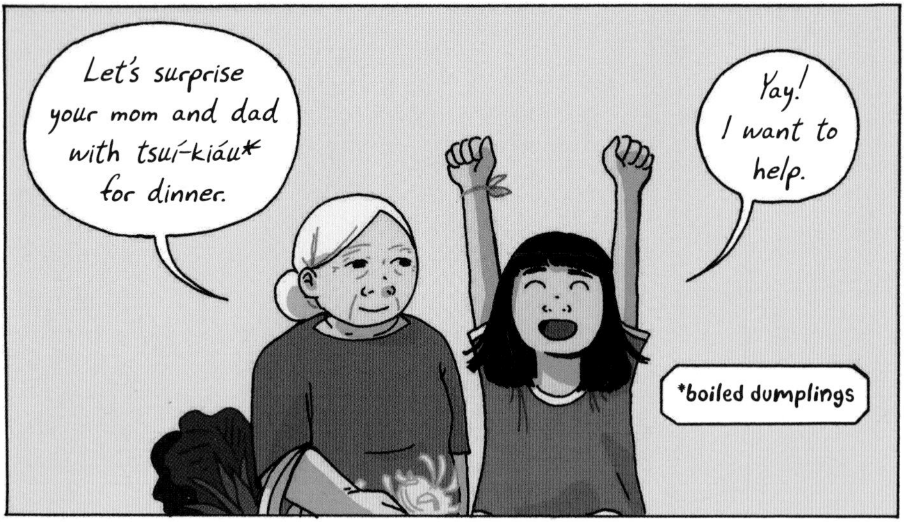
Let's surprise your mom and dad with tsuí-kiáu* for dinner.
Yay! I want to help.
*boiled dumplings

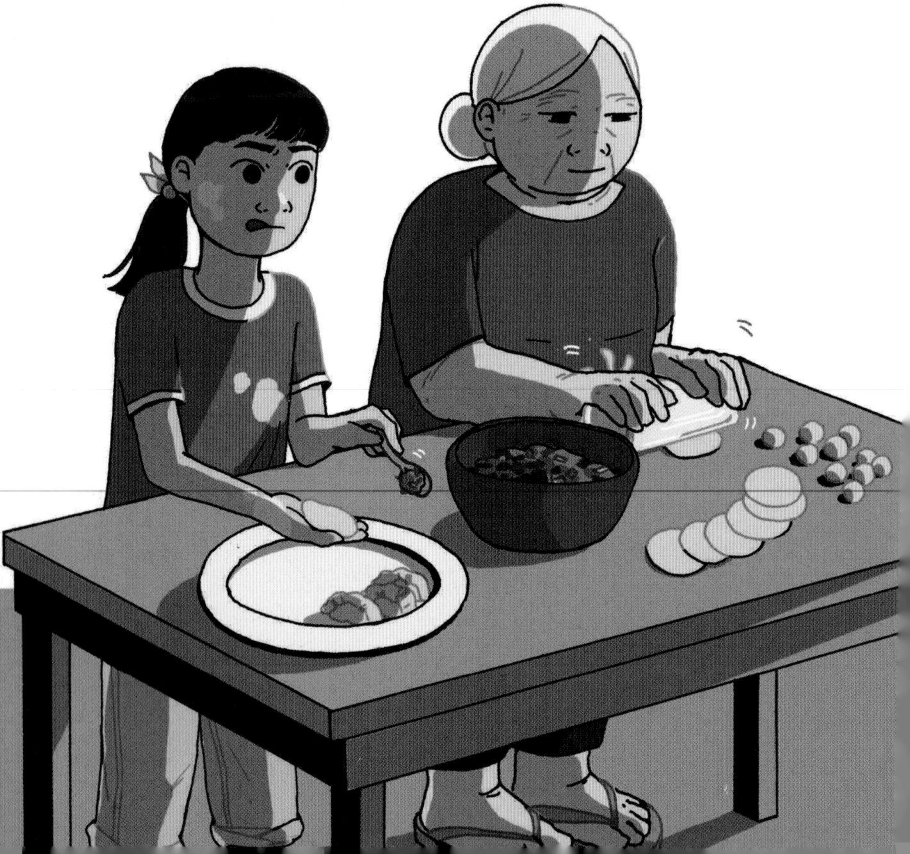

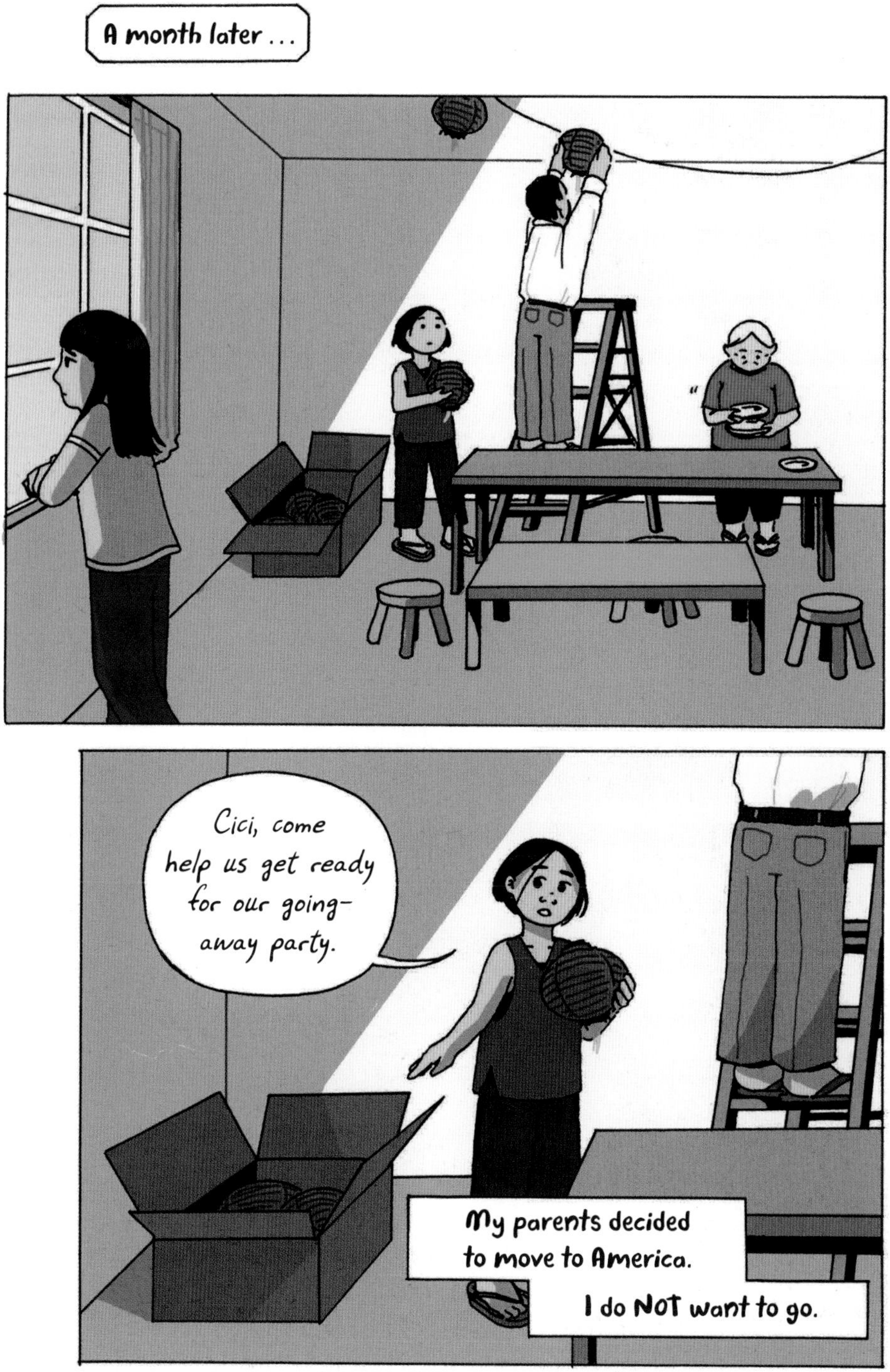
A month later . . .
Cici, come help us get ready for our going-away party.
My parents decided to move to America.
I do NOT want to go.

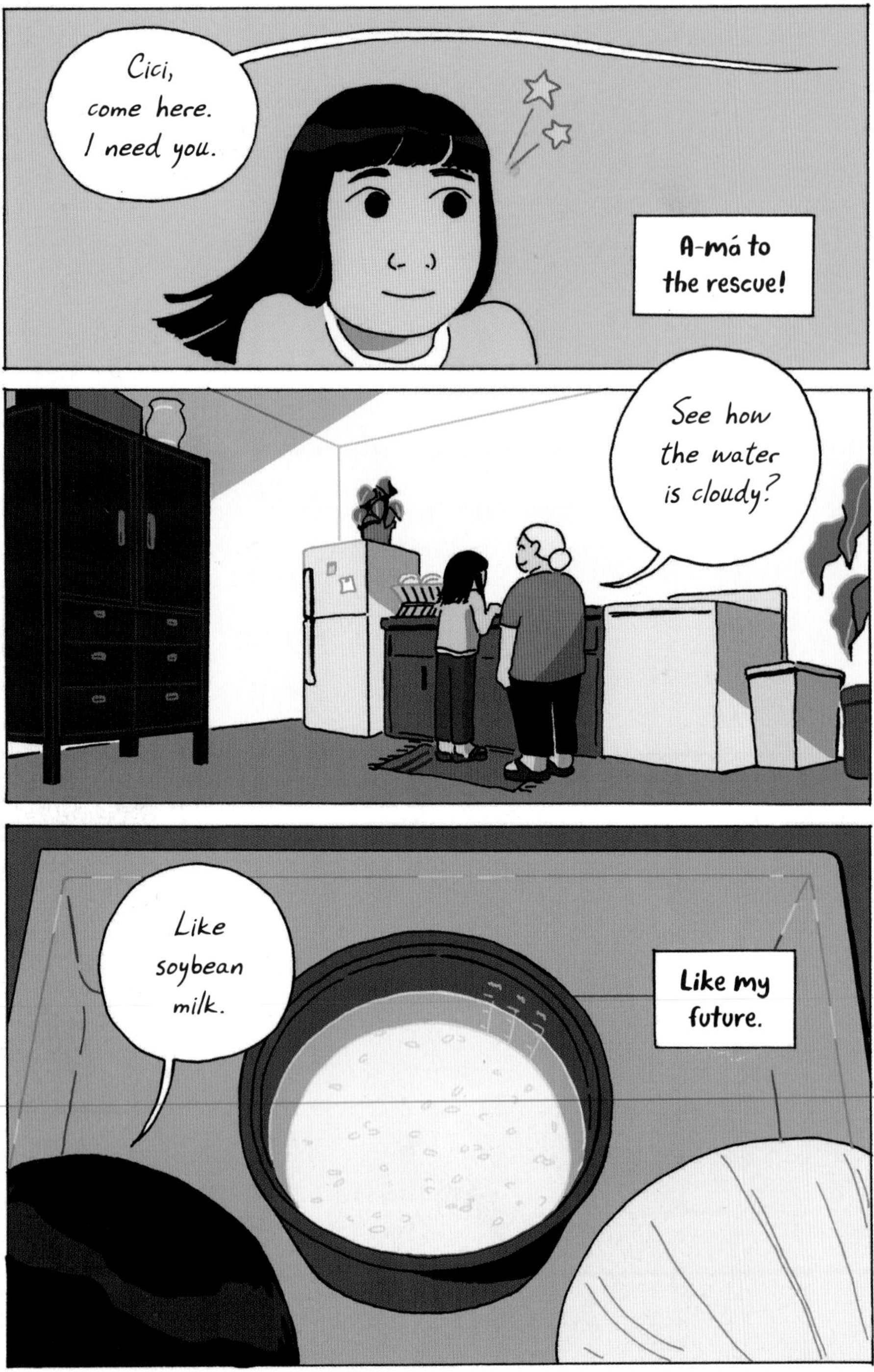
Cici, come here. I need you.
A-má to the rescue!
See how the water is cloudy?
Like soybean milk.
Like my future.

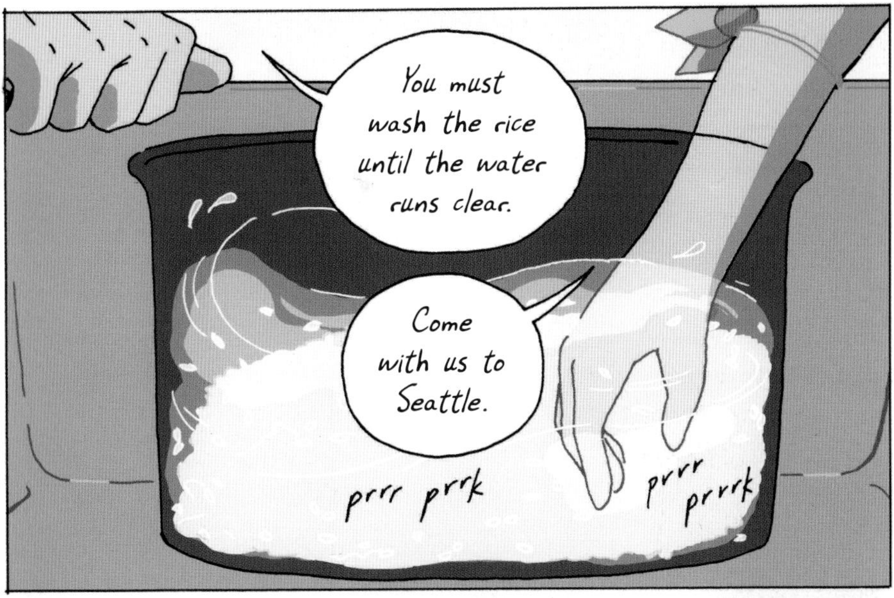
You must wash the rice until the water runs clear.
Come with us to Seattle.
prrr prrk
prrr prrrk

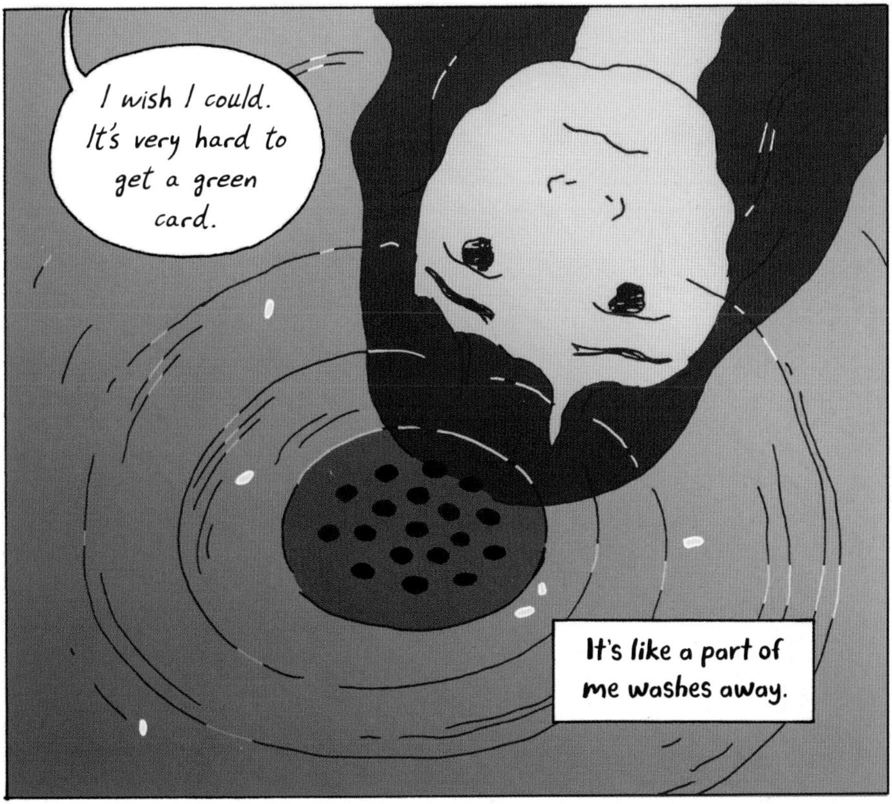
I wish I could. It's very hard to get a green card.
It's like a part of me washes away.

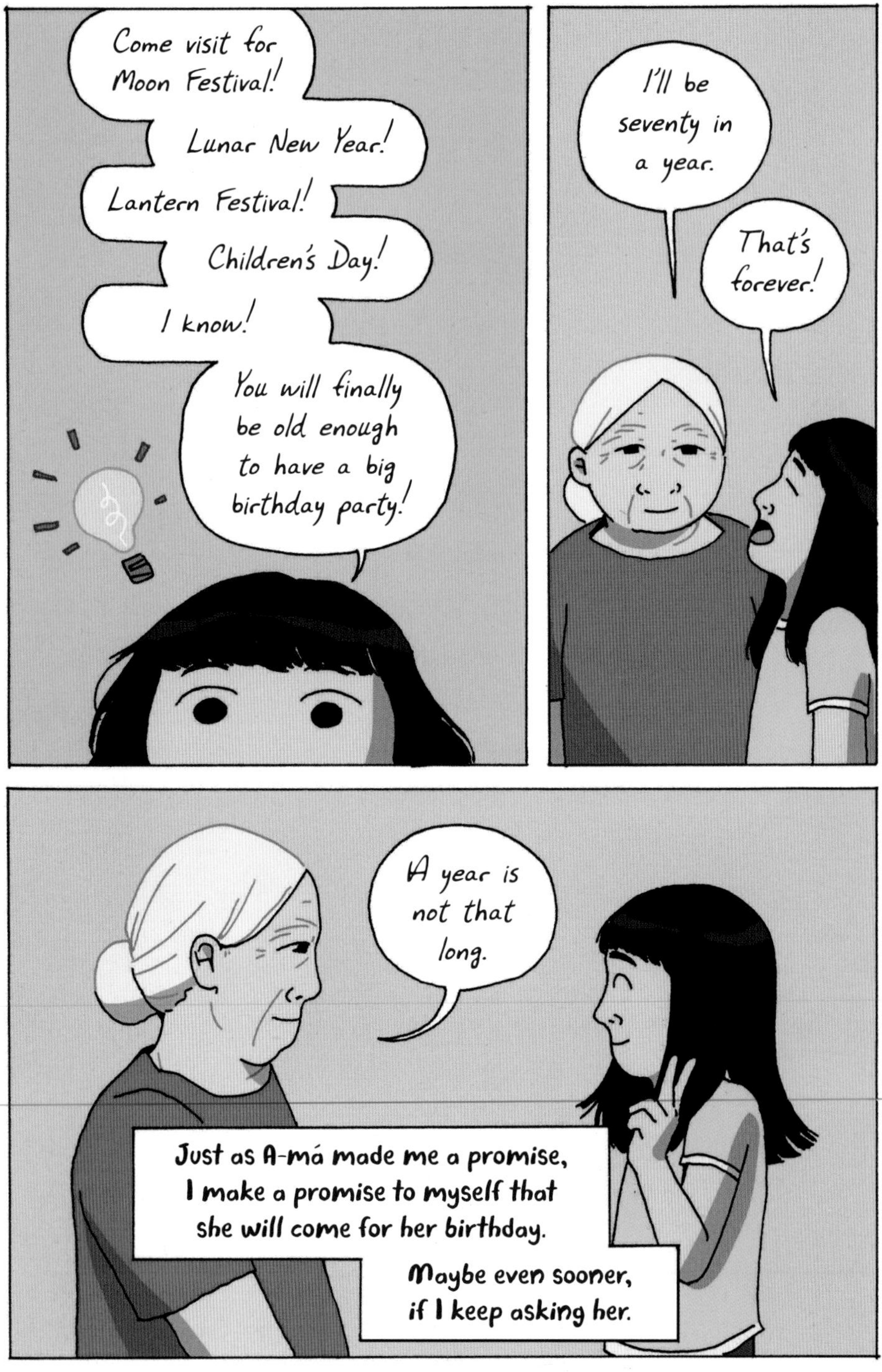
Come visit for Moon Festival!
Lunar New Year!
Lantern Festival!
Children's Day!
I know!
You will finally be old enough to have a big birthday party!
I'll be seventy in a year.
That's forever!
A year is not that long.
Just as A-má made me a promise, I make a promise to myself that she will come for her birthday.
Maybe even sooner, if I keep asking her.

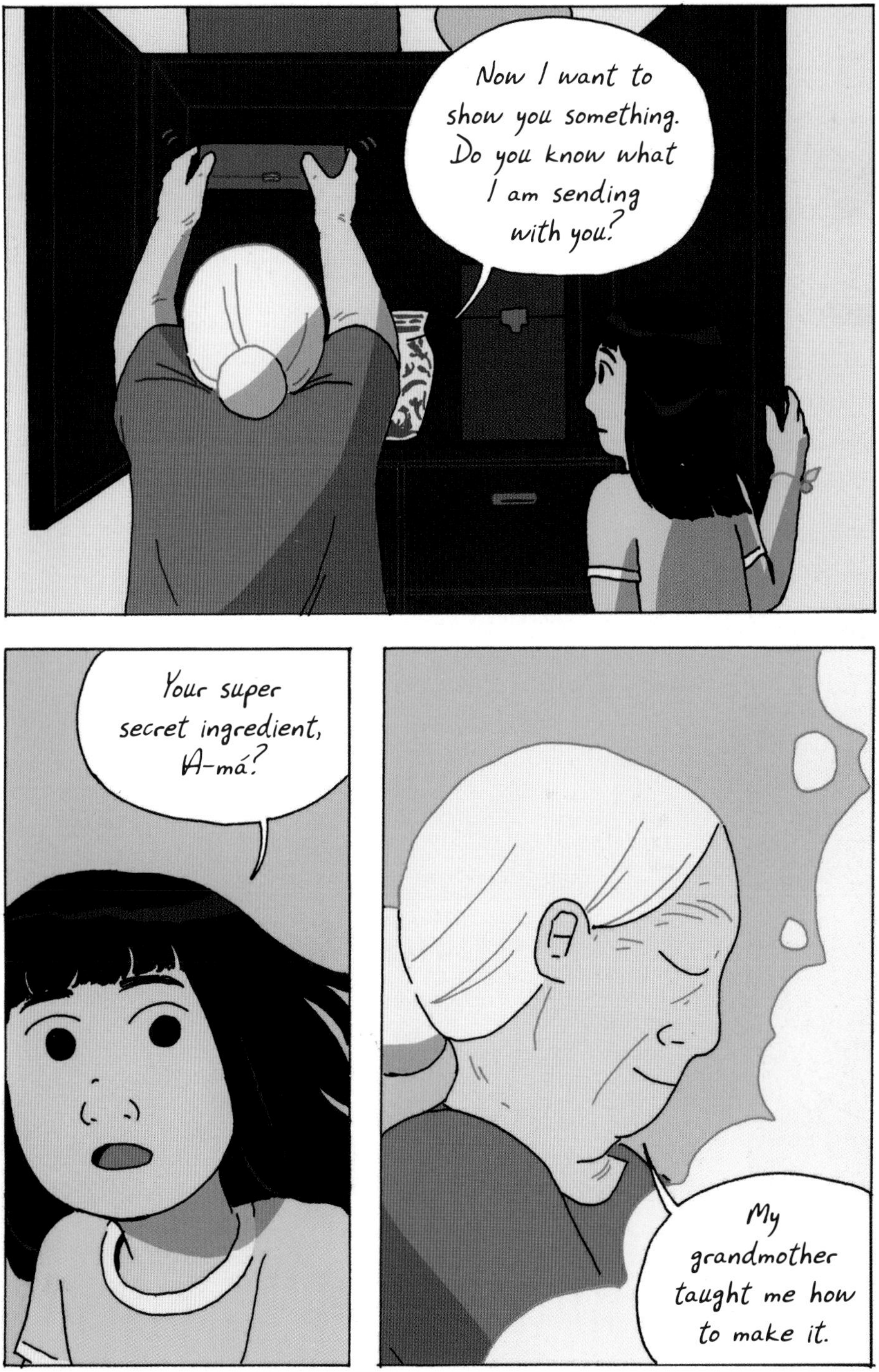
Now I want to show you something. Do you know what I am sending with you?
Your super secret ingredient, A-má?
My grandmother taught me how to make it.

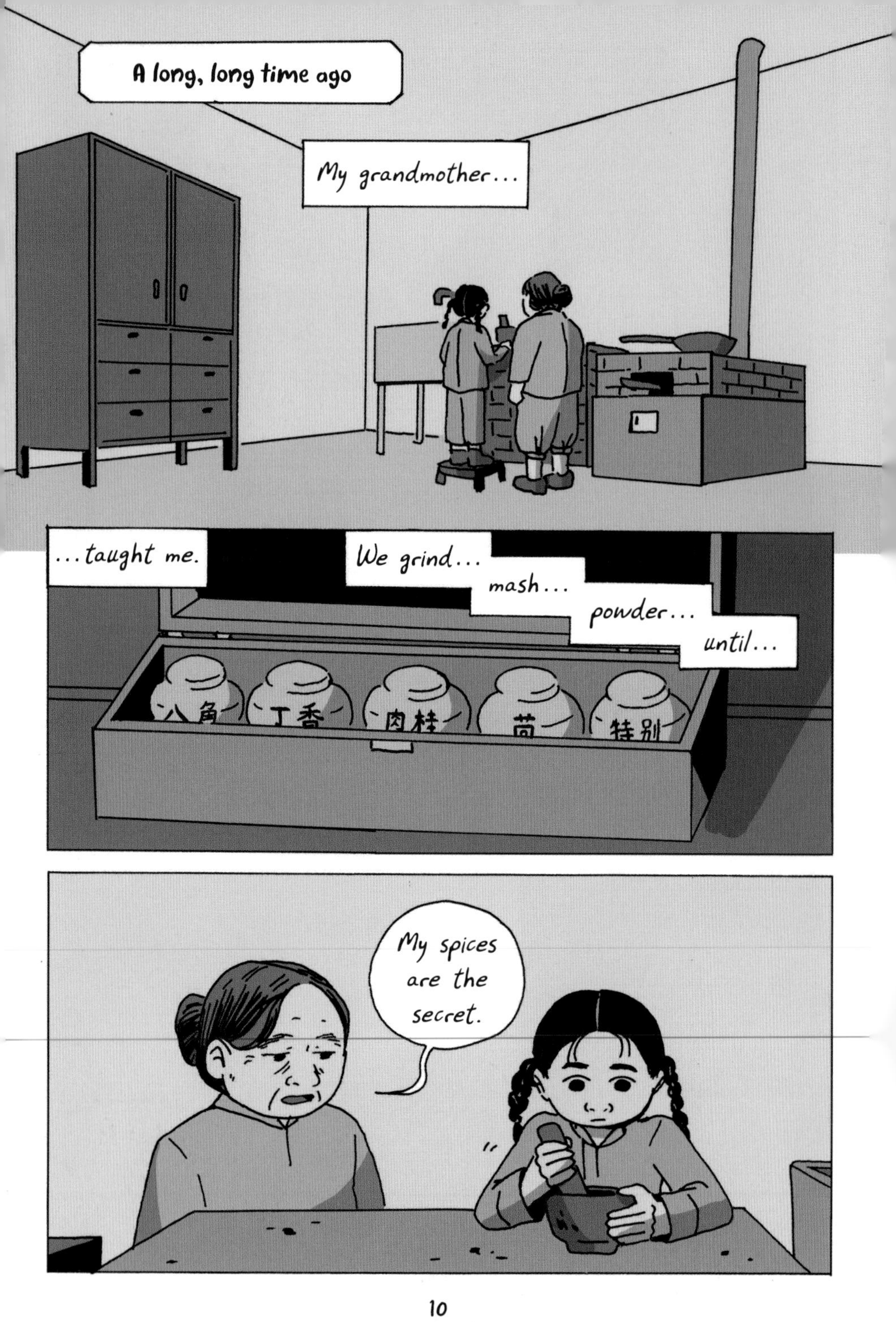
A long, long time ago
My grandmother...
...taught me.
We grind...
mash...
powder...
until...
八角
丁香
肉桂
茴
特别
My spices are the secret.

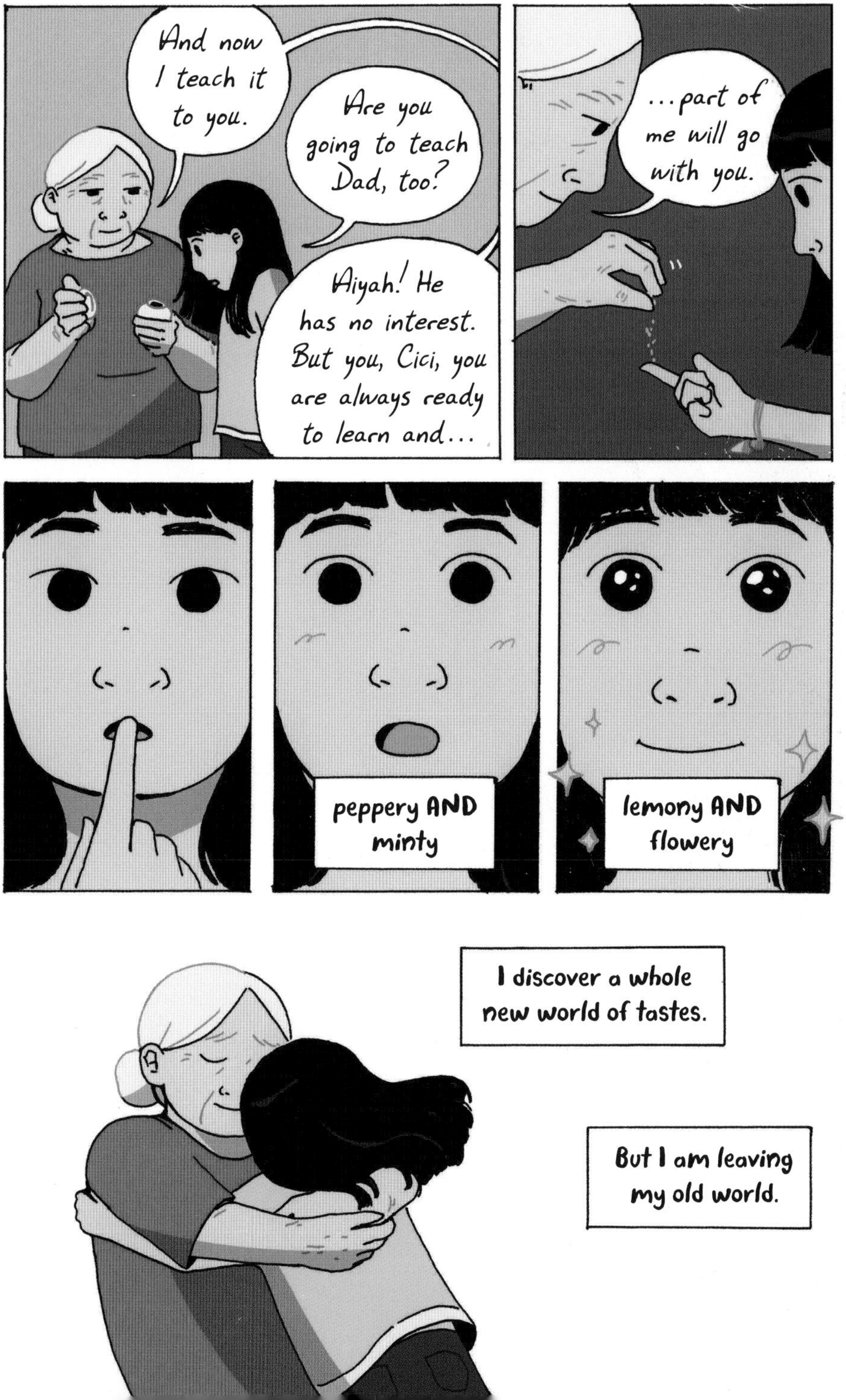

And now I teach it to you.
Are you going to teach Dad, too?
Aiyah! He has no interest. But you, Cici, you are always ready to learn and...
...part of me will go with you.
peppery AND minty
lemony AND flowery
I discover a whole new world of tastes.
But I am leaving my old world.

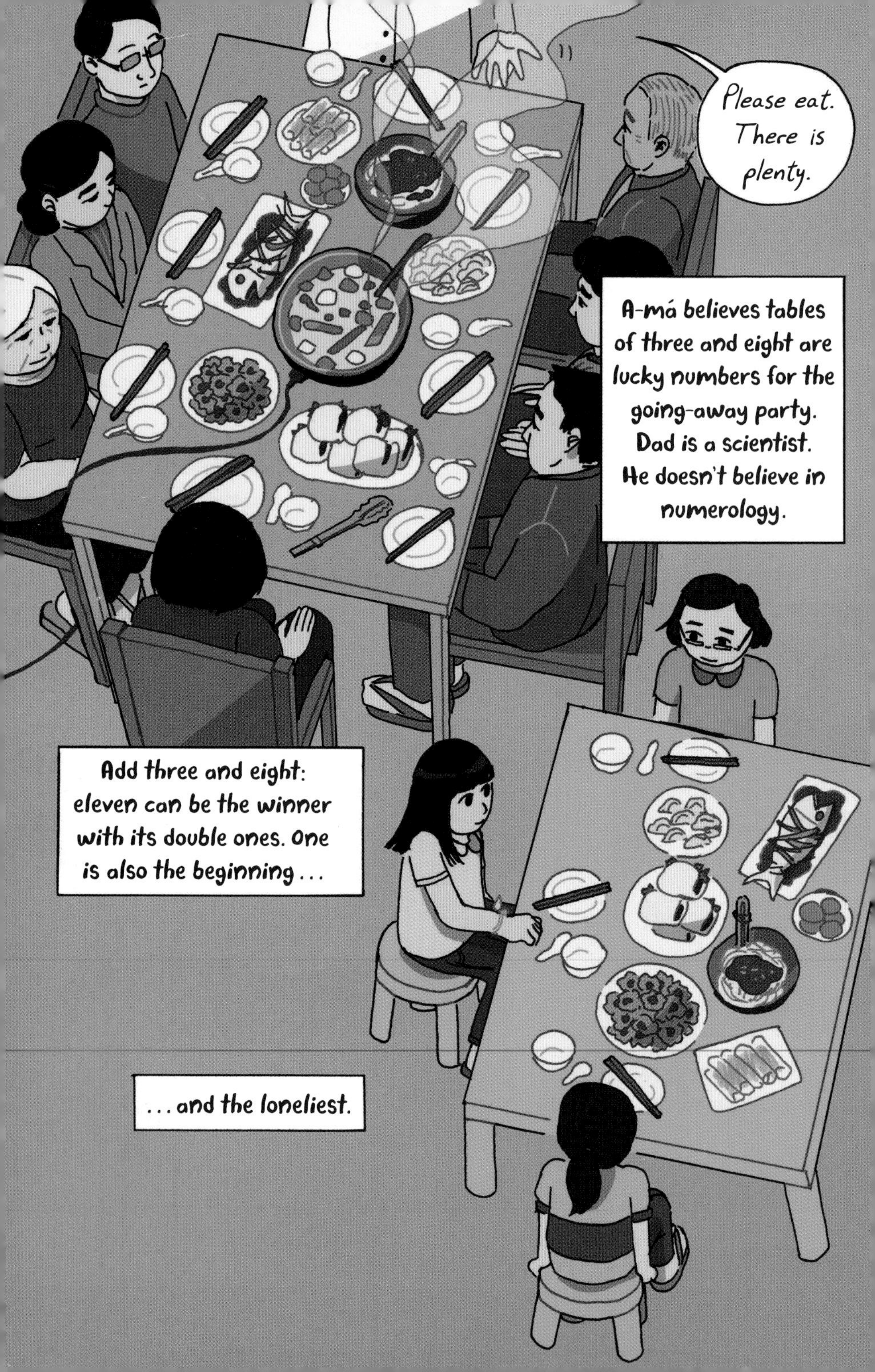
Please eat. There is plenty.
A-má believes tables of three and eight are lucky numbers for the going-away party. Dad is a scientist. He doesn't believe in numerology.
Add three and eight: eleven can be the winner with its double ones. One is also the beginning . . .
. . . and the loneliest.

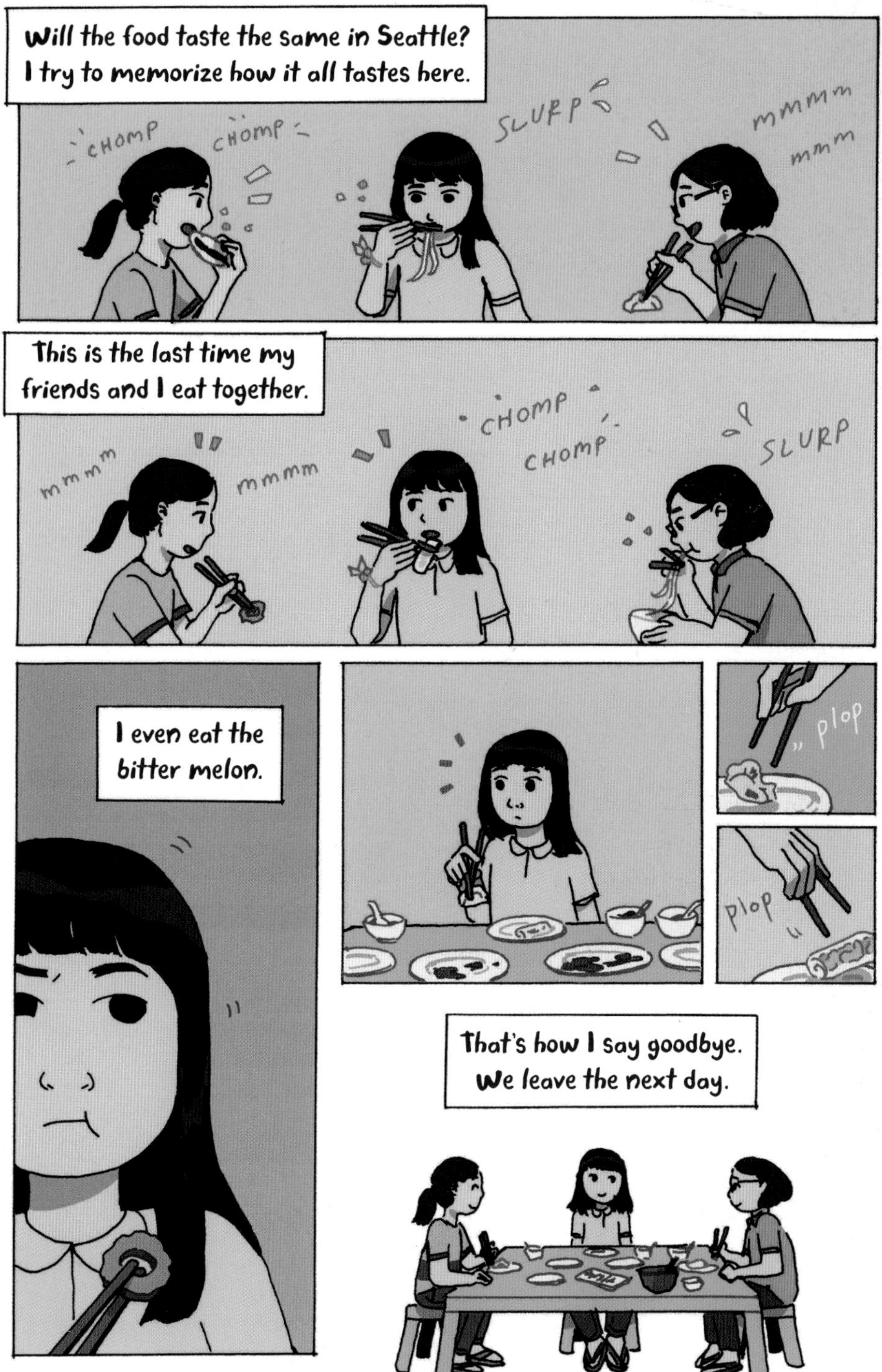
Will the food taste the same in Seattle? I try to memorize how it all tastes here.
CHOMP
CHOMP
SLURP
mmmm
mmm
This is the last time my friends and I eat together.
mmmm
mmmm
CHOMP
CHOMP
SLURP
I even eat the bitter melon.
plop
plop
That's how I say goodbye. We leave the next day.

Chapter 2

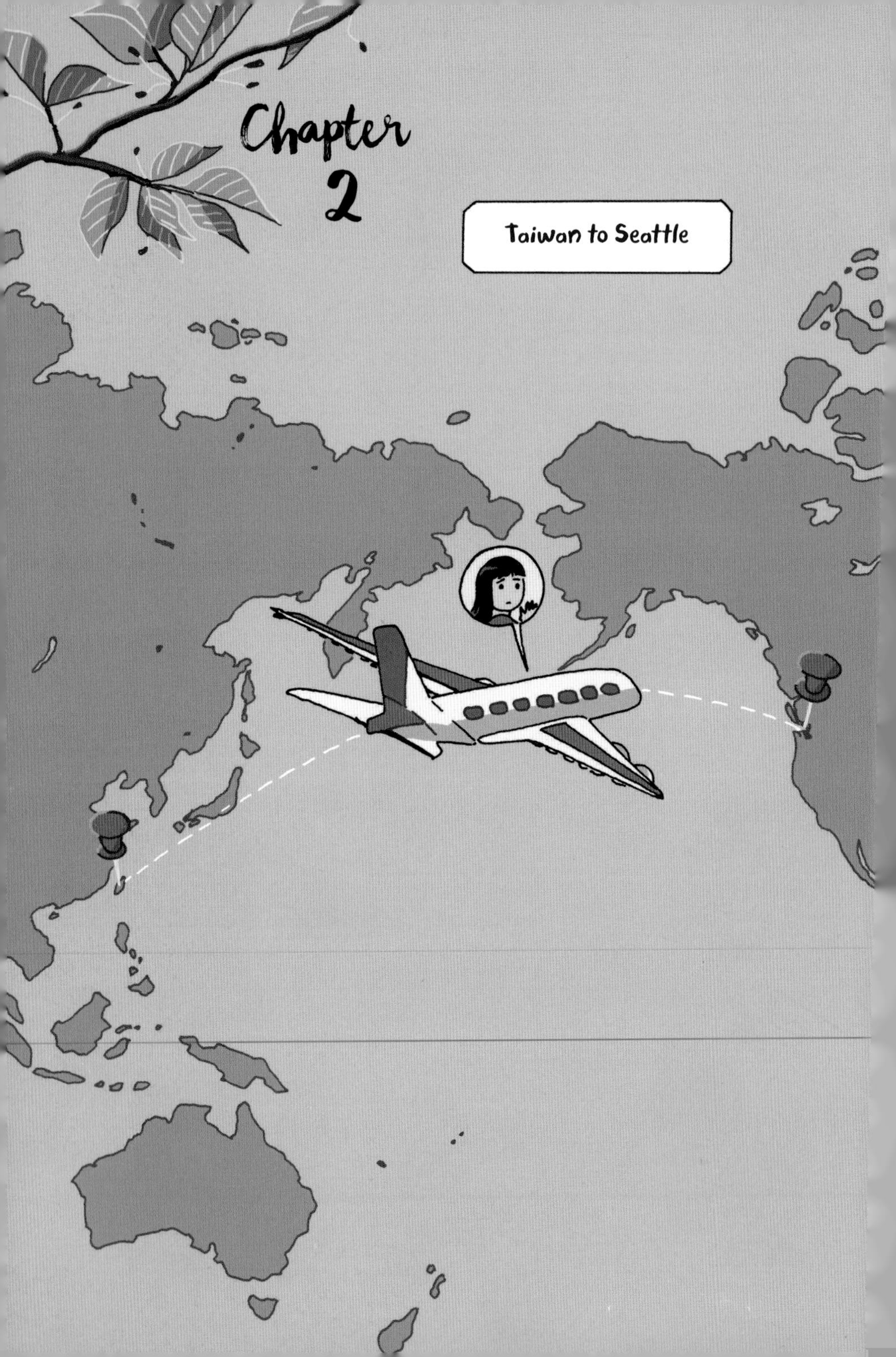
Taiwan to Seattle

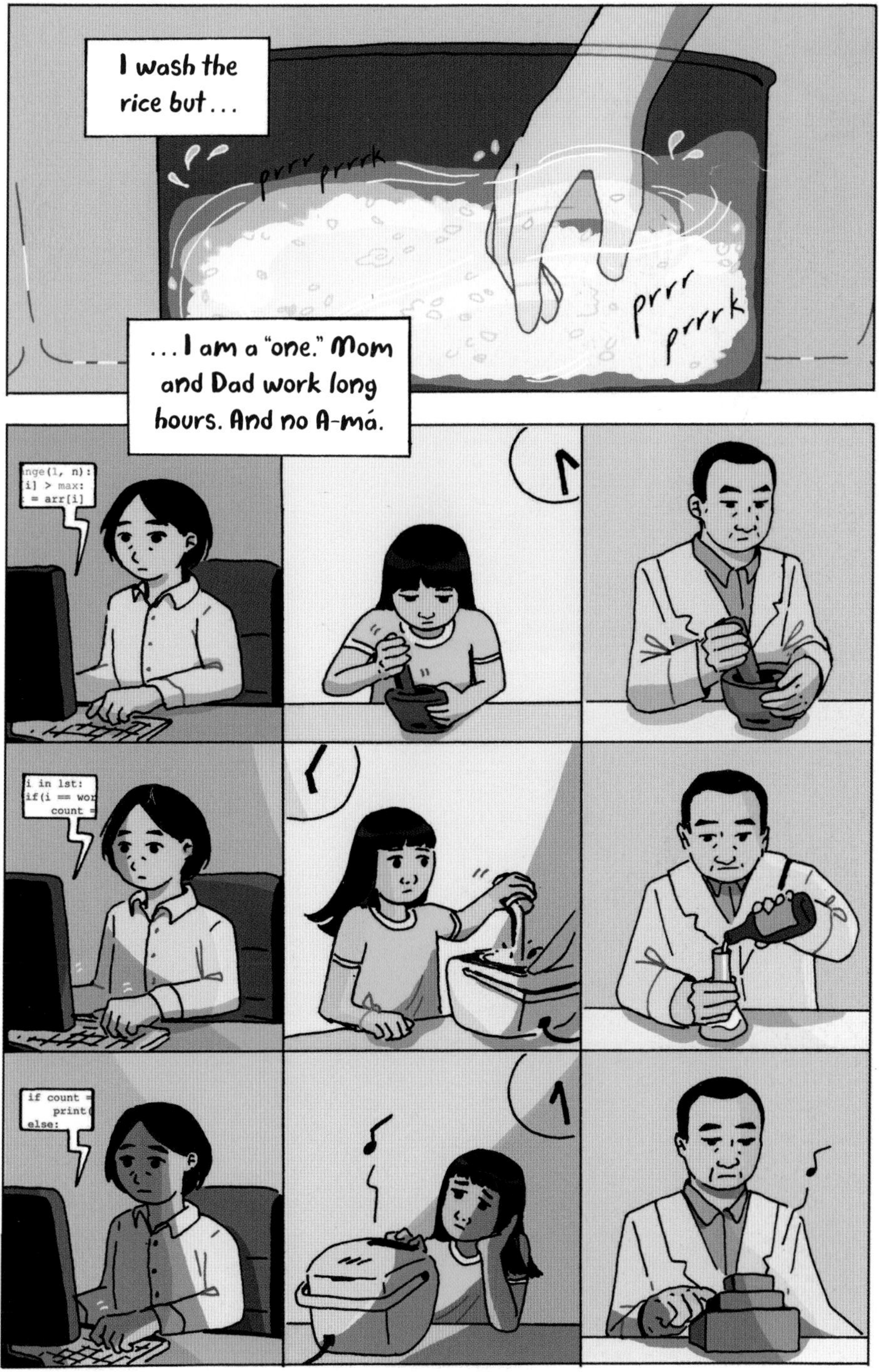
I wash the rice but...
prrr prrrk
prrr prrrk
...I am a "one." Mom and Dad work long hours. And no A-má.
nge(1, n):
i] > max:
= arr[i]
i in lst:
if(i == wor
count =
if count =
print(
else:

Chapter 3

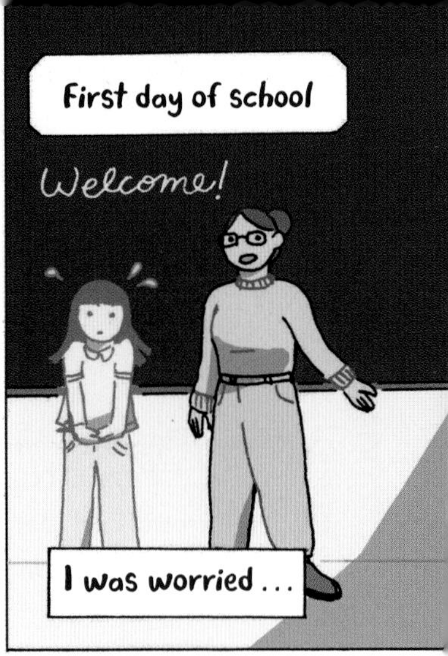
First day of school
Welcome!
I was worried . . .

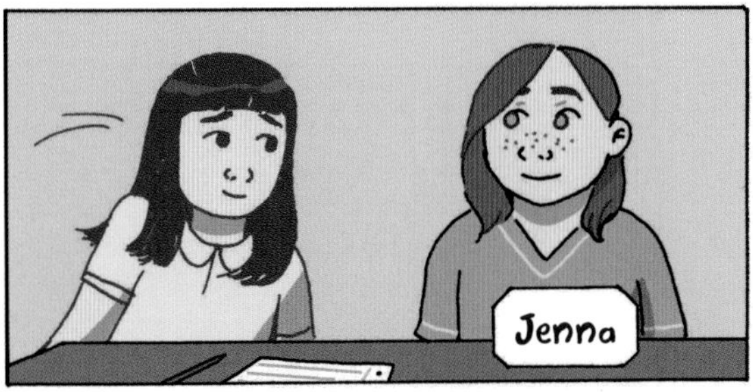
Jenna

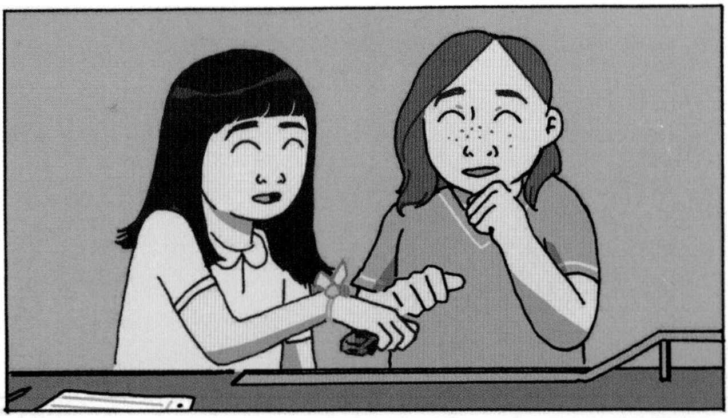

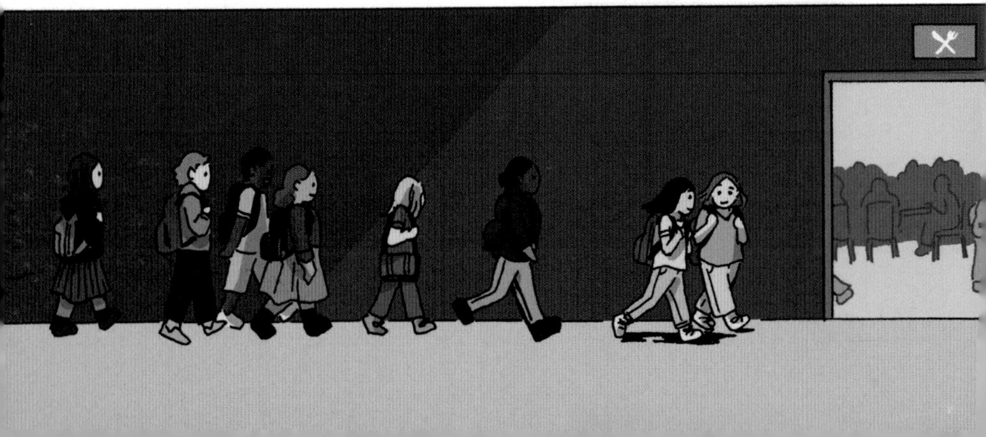

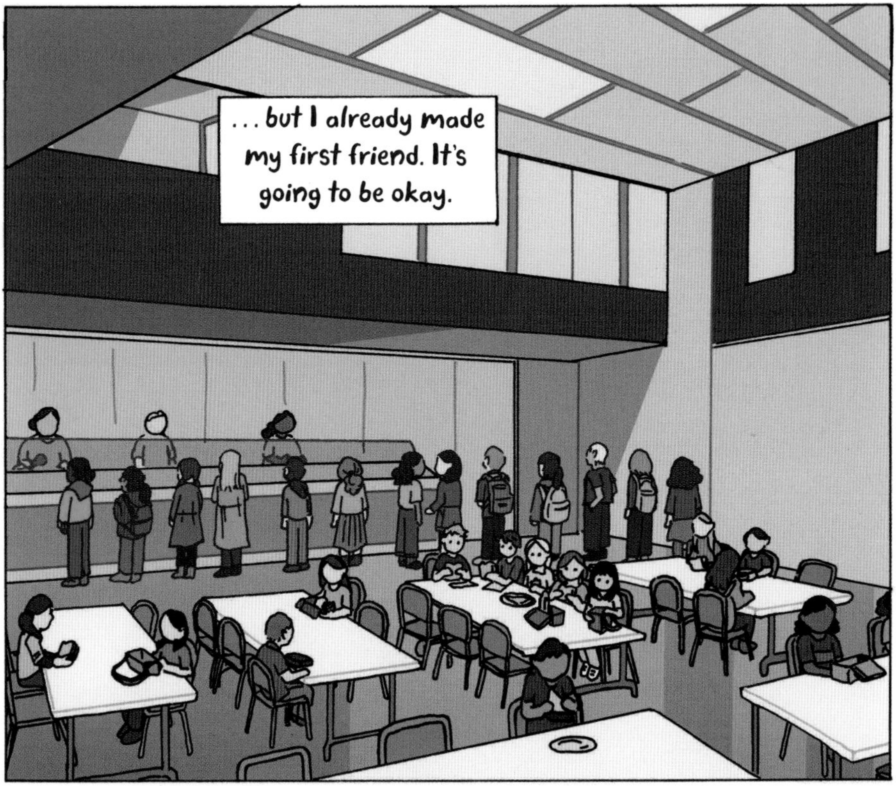
...but I already made my first friend. It's going to be okay.

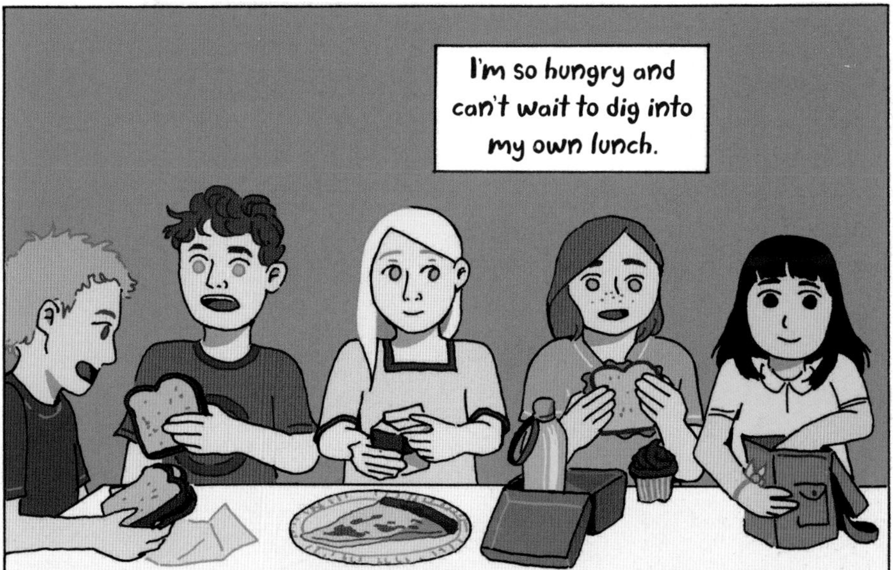
I'm so hungry and can't wait to dig into my own lunch.

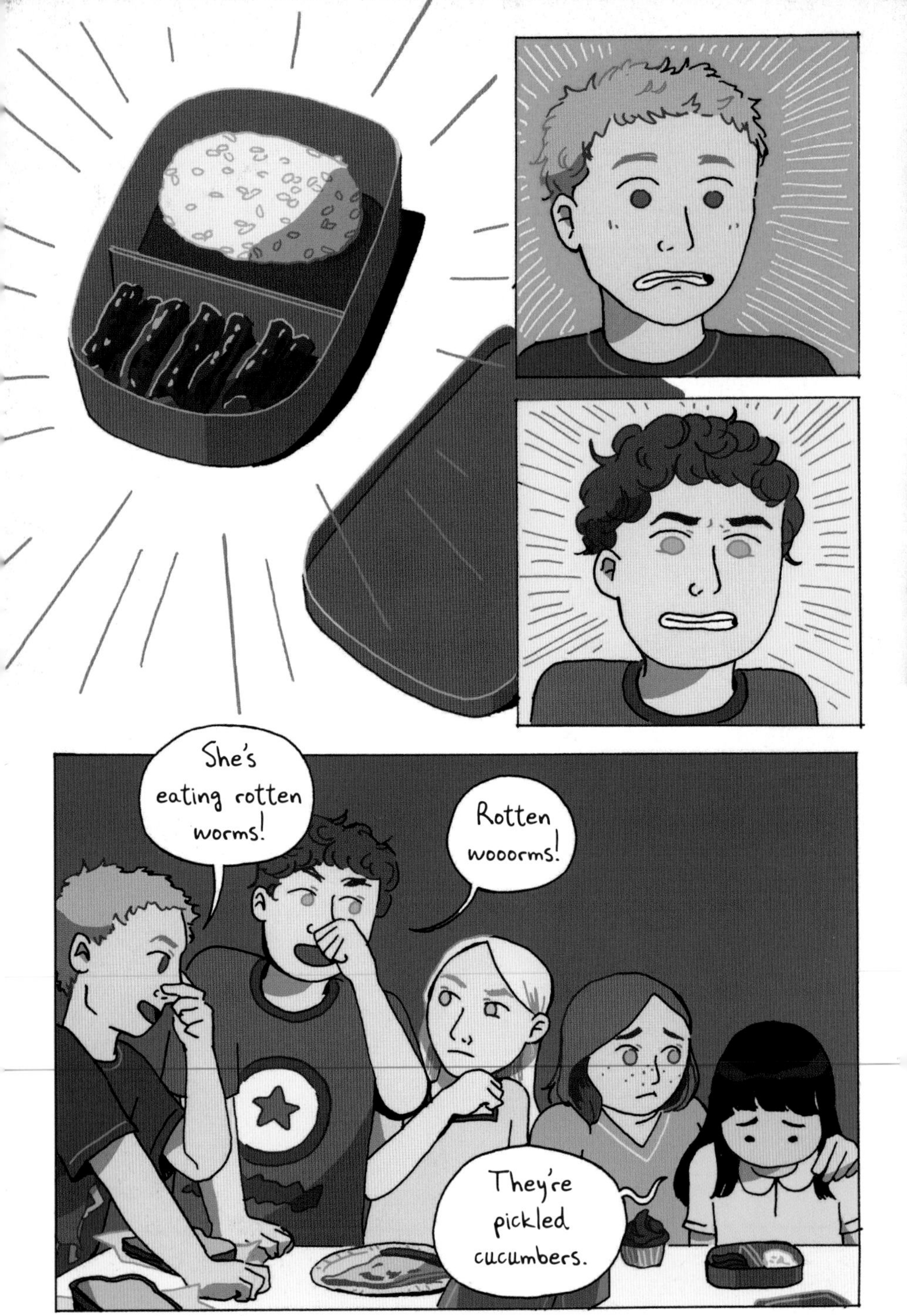
She's eating rotten worms!
Rotten wooorms!
They're pickled cucumbers.

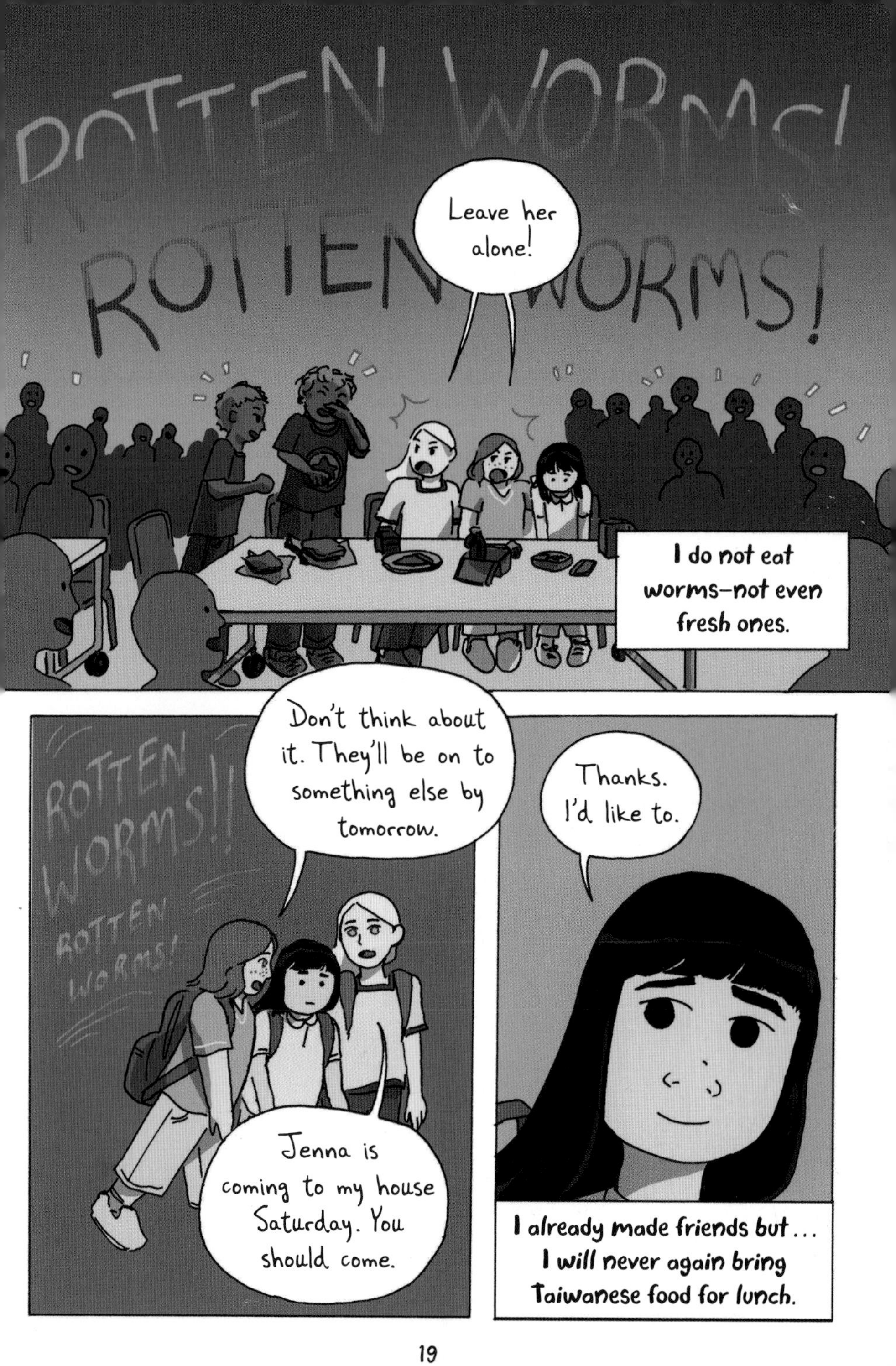
ROTTEN WORMS!
ROTTEN WORMS!
Leave her alone!
I do not eat worms—not even fresh ones.
ROTTEN WORMS!!
ROTTEN WORMS!
Don't think about it. They'll be on to something else by tomorrow.
Jenna is coming to my house Saturday. You should come.
Thanks. I'd like to.
I already made friends but . . .
I will never again bring Taiwanese food for lunch.

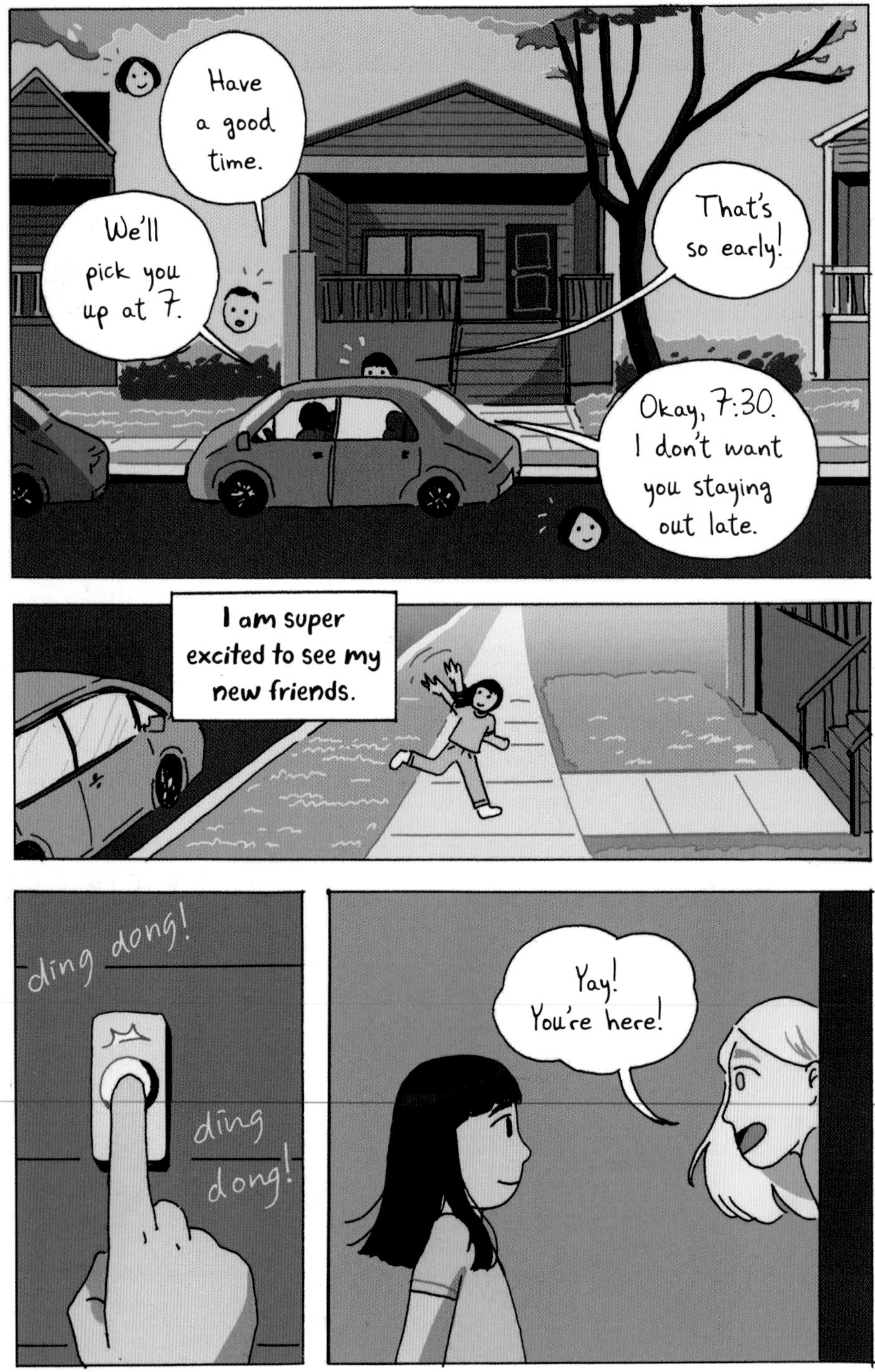
Have a good time.
We'll pick you up at 7.
That's so early!
Okay, 7:30. I don't want you staying out late.
I am super excited to see my new friends.
ding dong!
ding dong!
Yay! You're here!

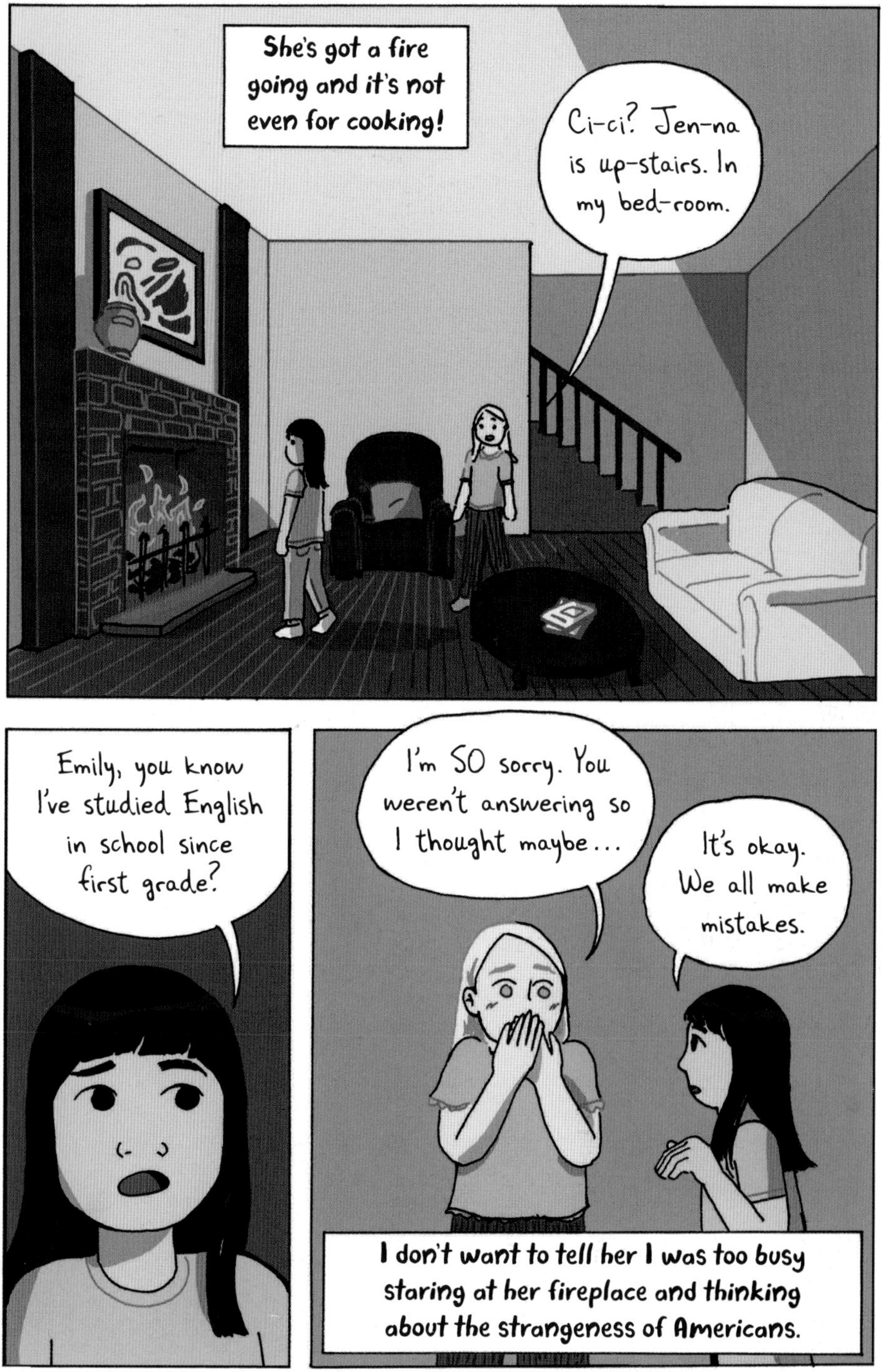
She's got a fire going and it's not even for cooking!
Ci-ci? Jen-na is up-stairs. In my bed-room.
Emily, you know I've studied English in school since first grade?
I'm SO sorry. You weren't answering so I thought maybe...
It's okay. We all make mistakes.
I don't want to tell her I was too busy staring at her fireplace and thinking about the strangeness of Americans.

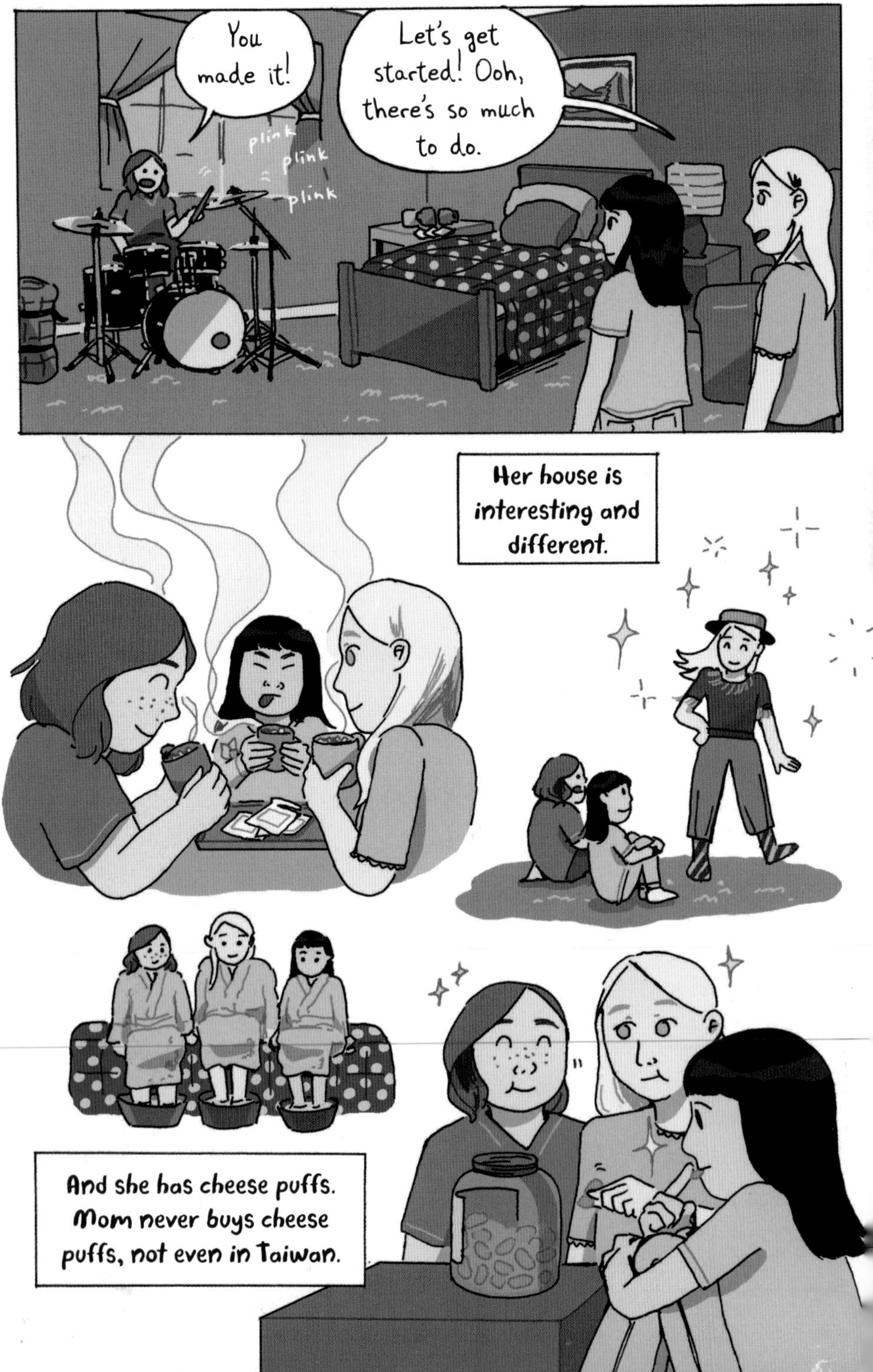
You made it!
Let's get started! Ooh, there's so much to do.
plink plink plink
Her house is interesting and different.
And she has cheese puffs. Mom never buys cheese puffs, not even in Taiwan.

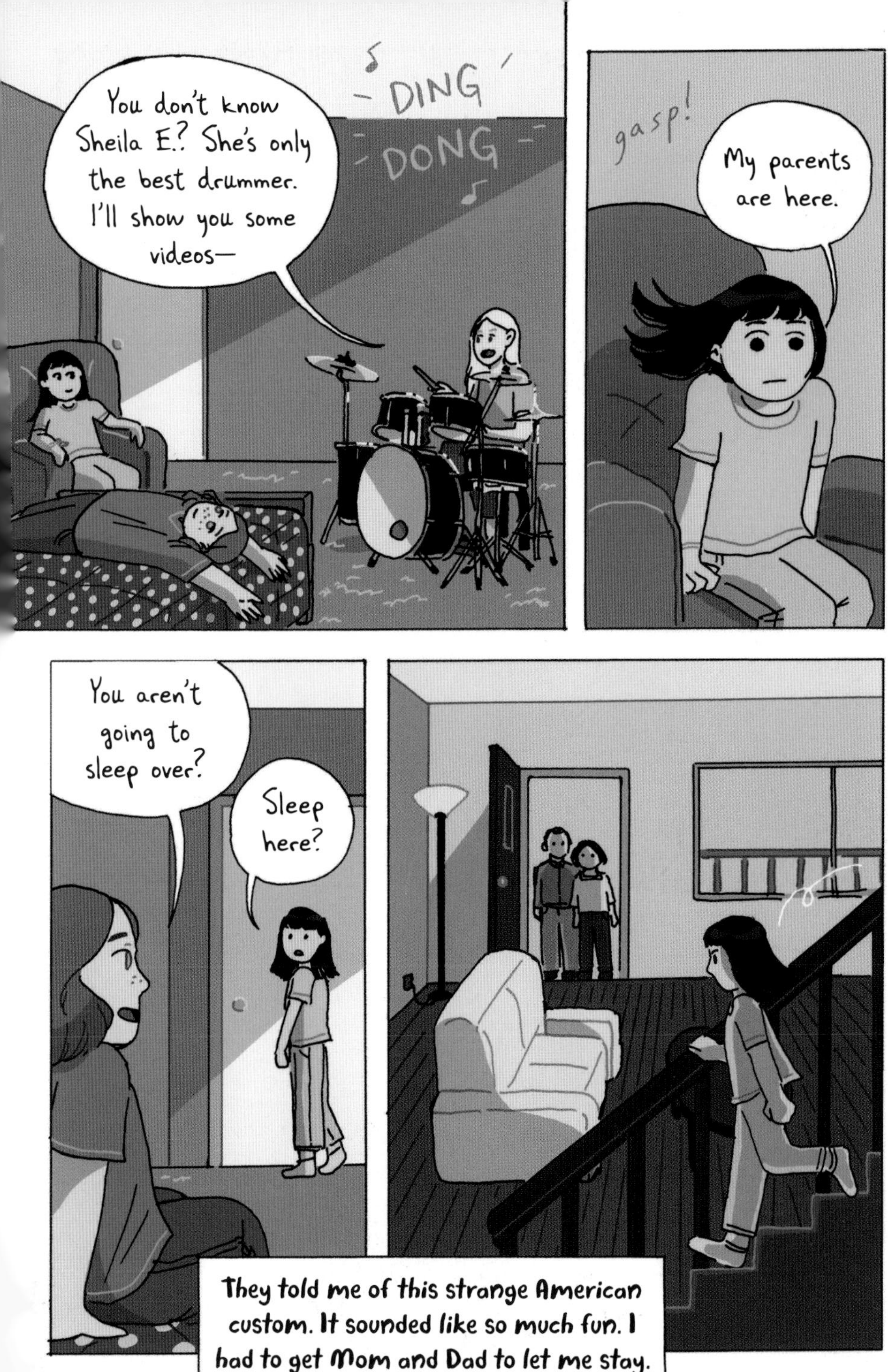
You don't know Sheila E.? She's only the best drummer. I'll show you some videos—
DING
DONG
gasp!
My parents are here.
You aren't going to sleep over?
Sleep here?
They told me of this strange American custom. It sounded like so much fun. I had to get Mom and Dad to let me stay.

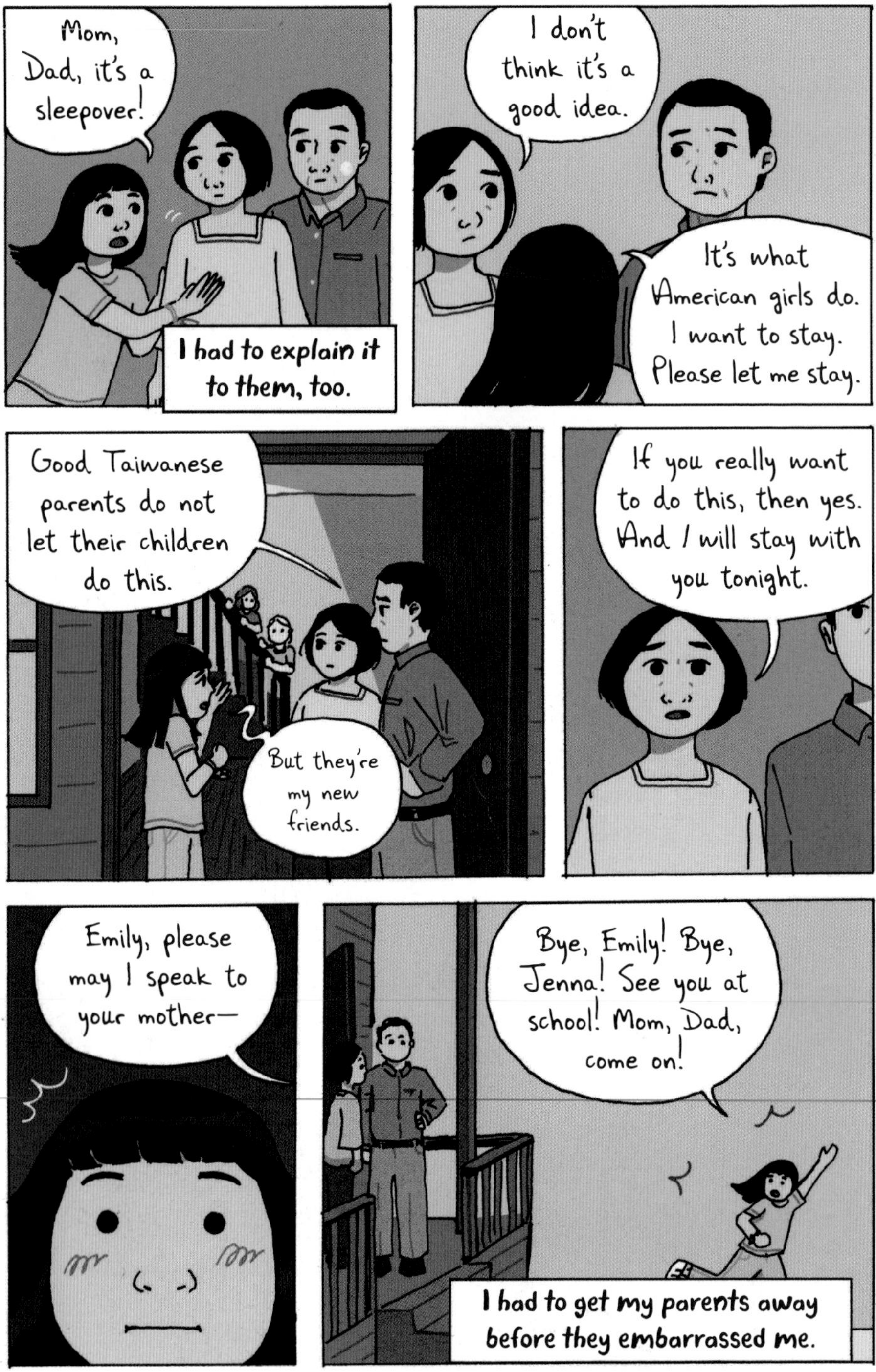

Mom, Dad, it's a sleepover!
I had to explain it to them, too.
I don't think it's a good idea.
It's what American girls do. I want to stay. Please let me stay.
Good Taiwanese parents do not let their children do this.
But they're my new friends.
If you really want to do this, then yes. And I will stay with you tonight.
Emily, please may I speak to your mother—
Bye, Emily! Bye, Jenna! See you at school! Mom, Dad, come on!
I had to get my parents away before they embarrassed me.

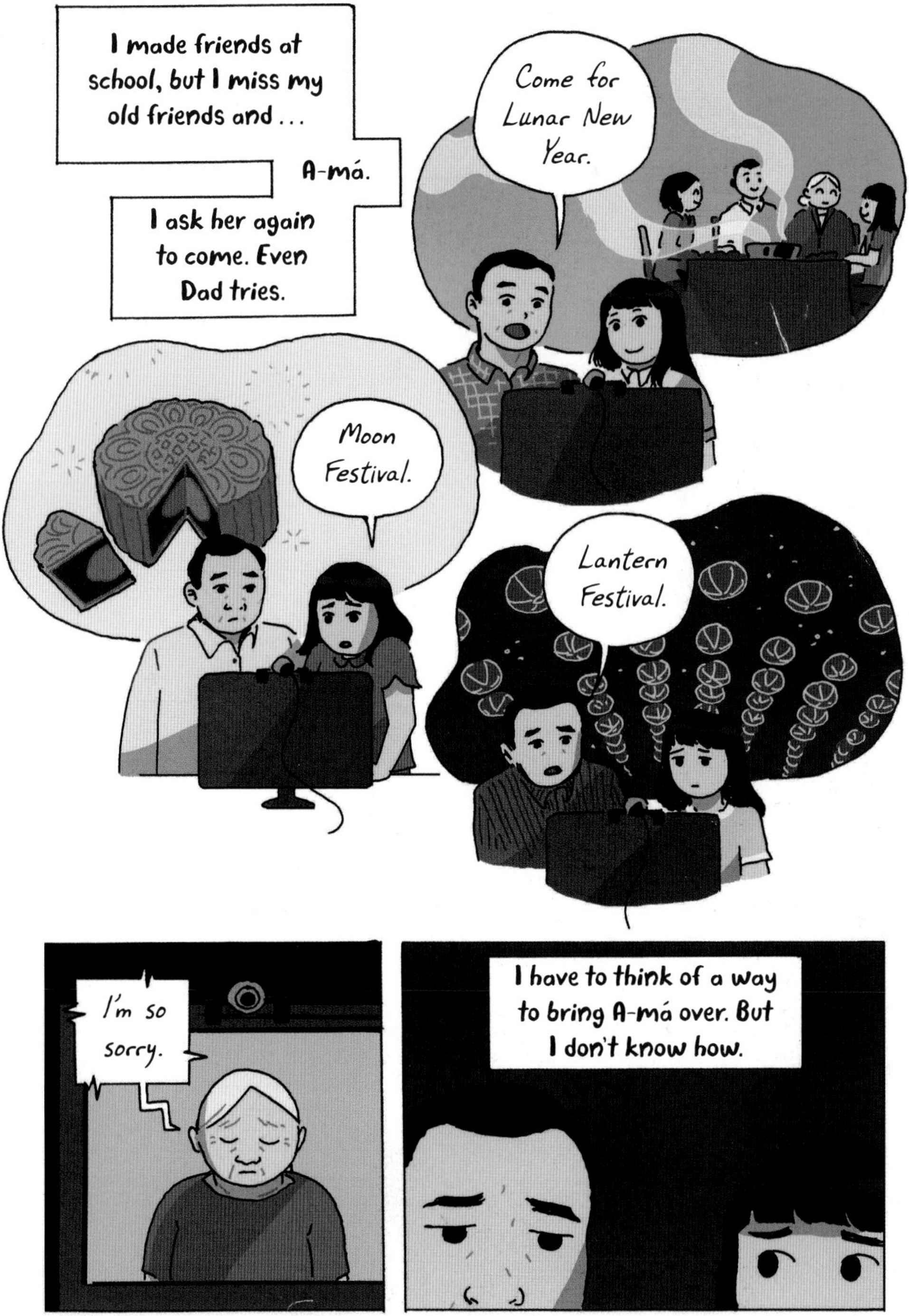
I made friends at school, but I miss my old friends and . . .
A-má.
I ask her again to come. Even Dad tries.
Come for Lunar New Year.
Moon Festival.
Lantern Festival.
I'm so sorry.
I have to think of a way to bring A-má over. But I don't know how.

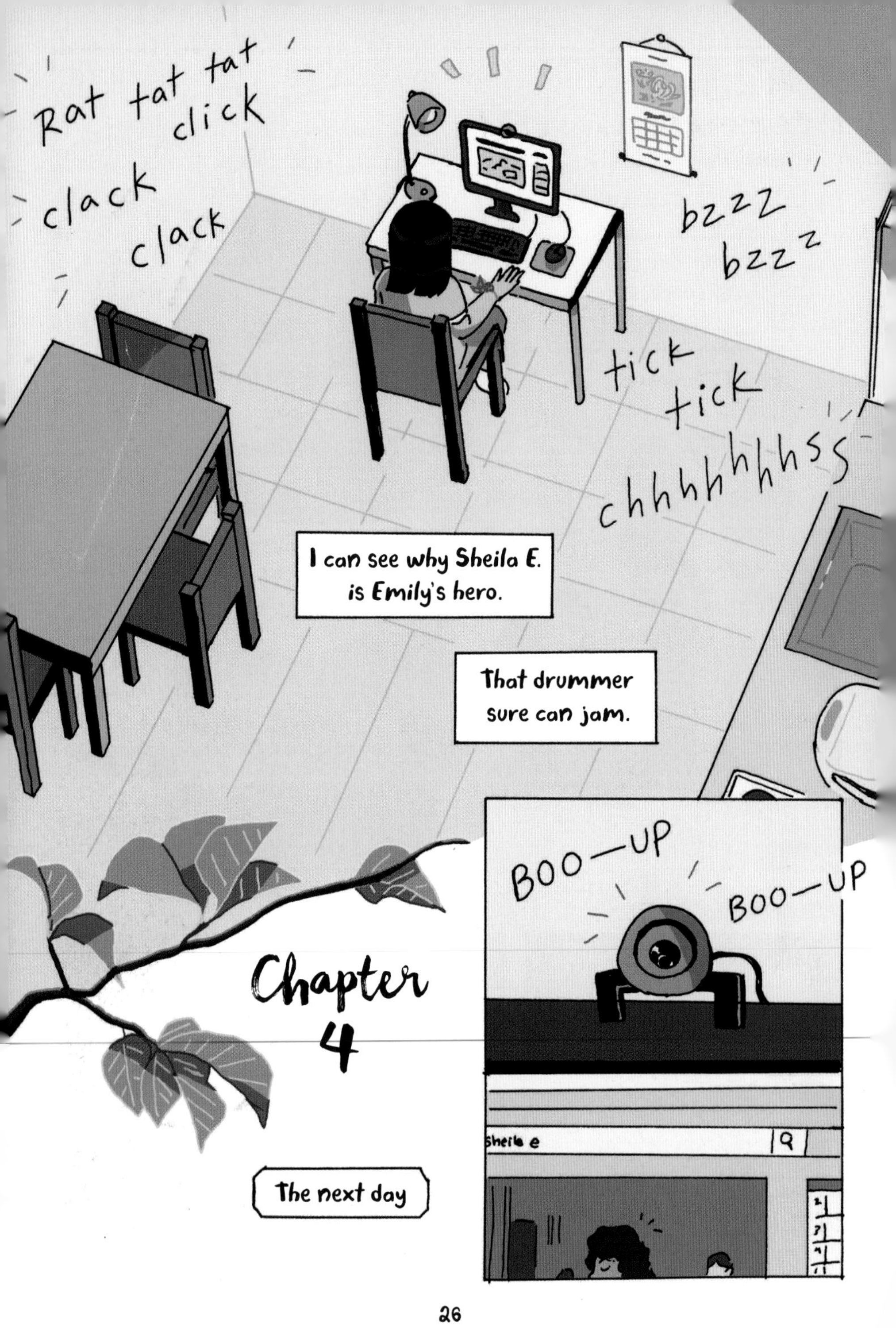
Rat tat tat
click
clack
clack
bzzz
bzzz
tick
tick
chhhhhhss
I can see why Sheila E. is Emily's hero.
That drummer sure can jam.
Chapter 4
The next day
BOO—UP
BOO—UP
sheila e

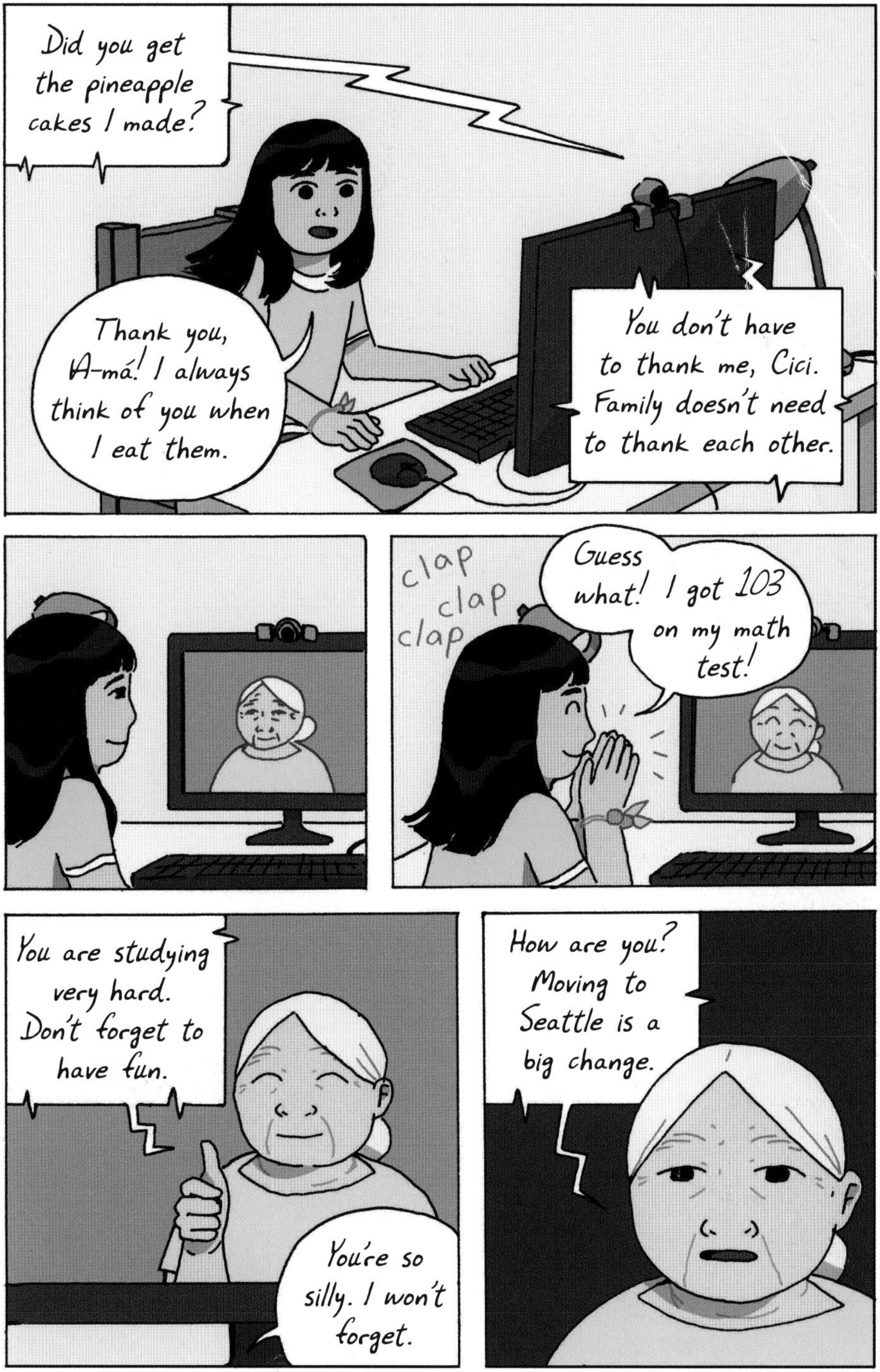
Did you get the pineapple cakes I made?
Thank you, A-má! I always think of you when I eat them.
You don't have to thank me, Cici. Family doesn't need to thank each other.
clap clap clap
Guess what! I got 103 on my math test!
You are studying very hard. Don't forget to have fun.
You're so silly. I won't forget.
How are you? Moving to Seattle is a big change.

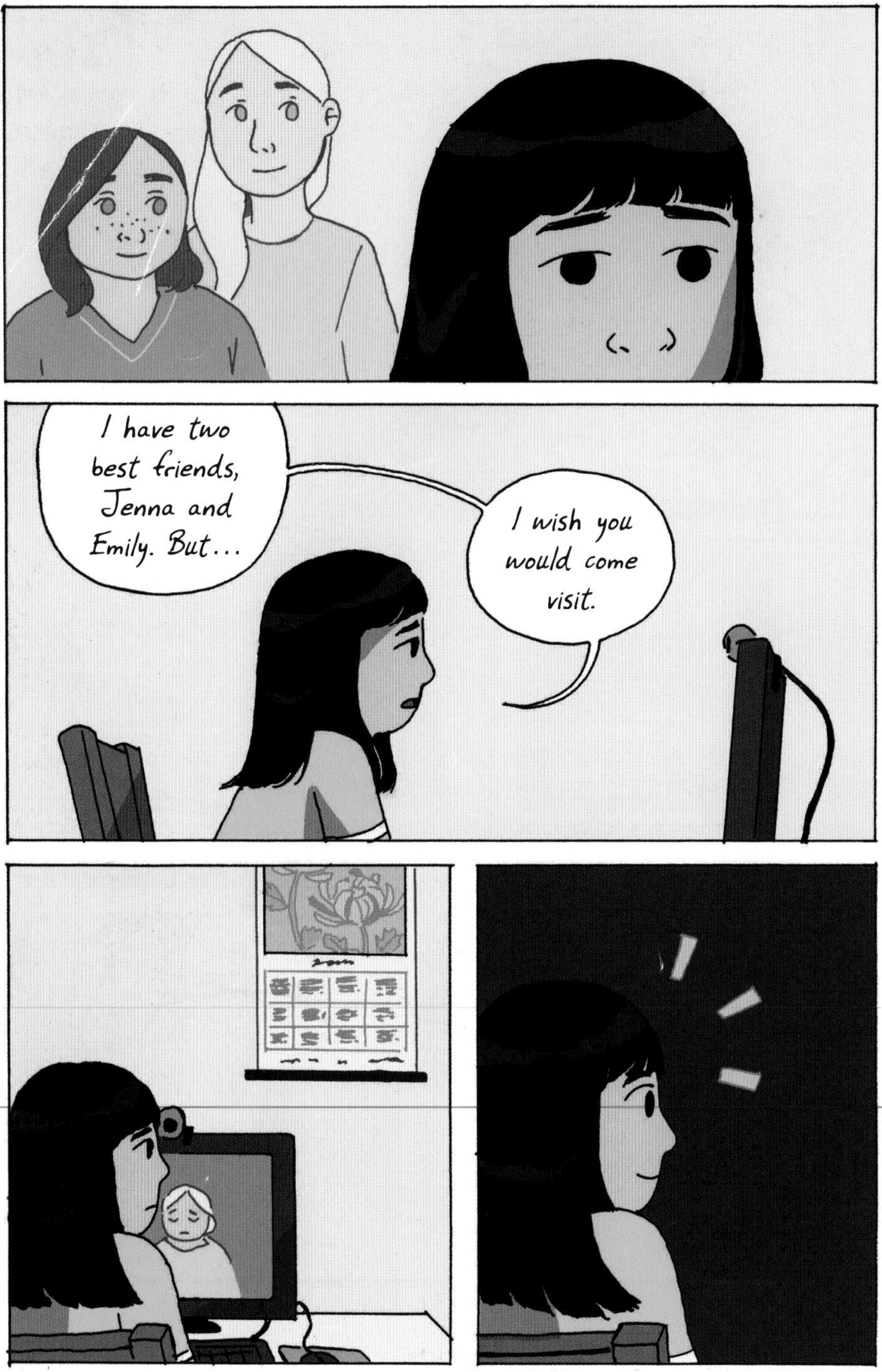
I have two best friends, Jenna and Emily. But...
I wish you would come visit.

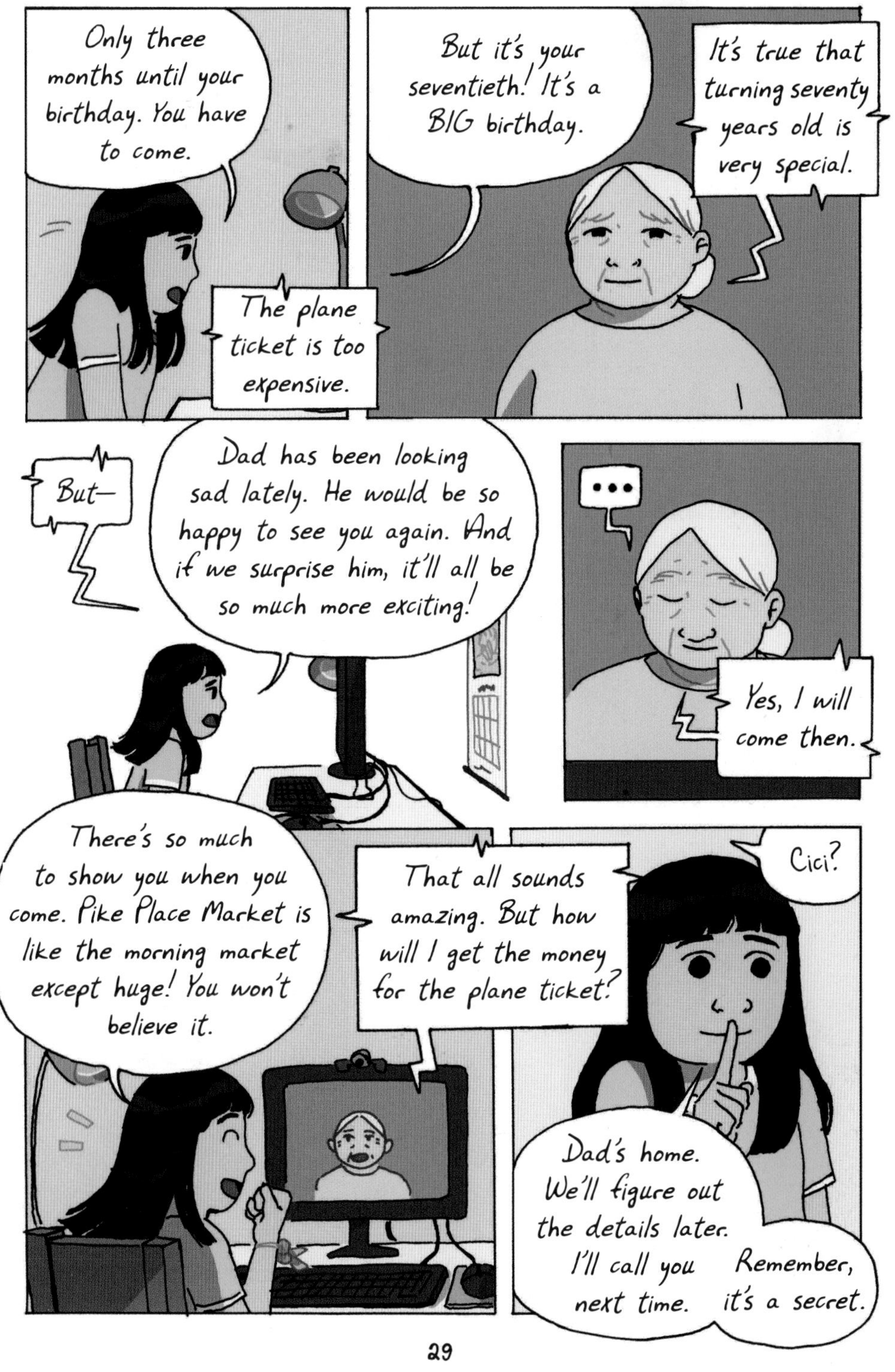
Only three months until your birthday. You have to come.
The plane ticket is too expensive.
But it's your seventieth! It's a BIG birthday.
It's true that turning seventy years old is very special.
But—
Dad has been looking sad lately. He would be so happy to see you again. And if we surprise him, it'll all be so much more exciting!
...
Yes, I will come then.
There's so much to show you when you come. Pike Place Market is like the morning market except huge! You won't believe it.
That all sounds amazing. But how will I get the money for the plane ticket?
Cici?
Dad's home. We'll figure out the details later. I'll call you next time.
Remember, it's a secret.

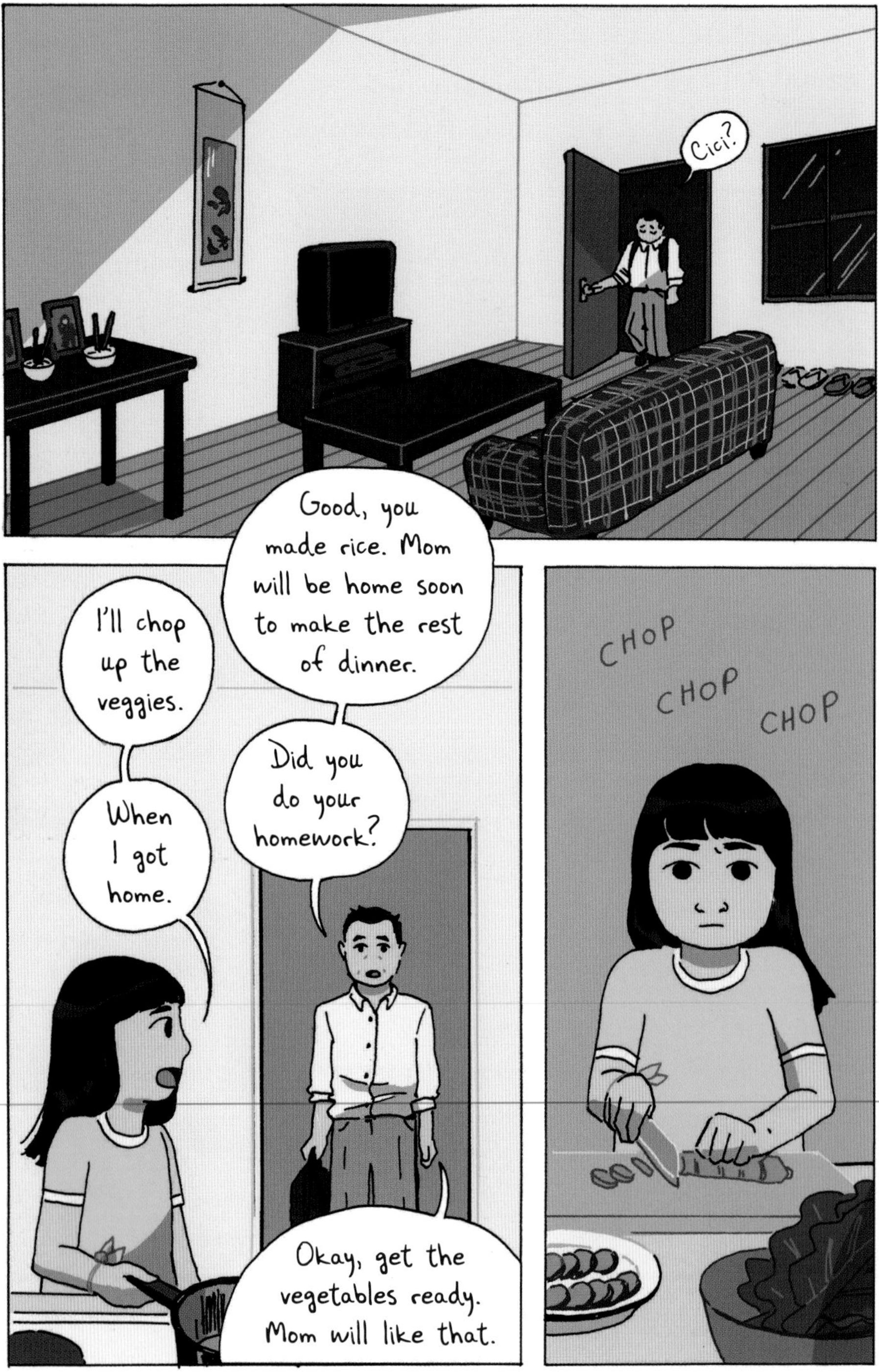
Cici?
Good, you made rice. Mom will be home soon to make the rest of dinner.
I'll chop up the veggies.
Did you do your homework?
When I got home.
Okay, get the vegetables ready. Mom will like that.
CHOP
CHOP
CHOP

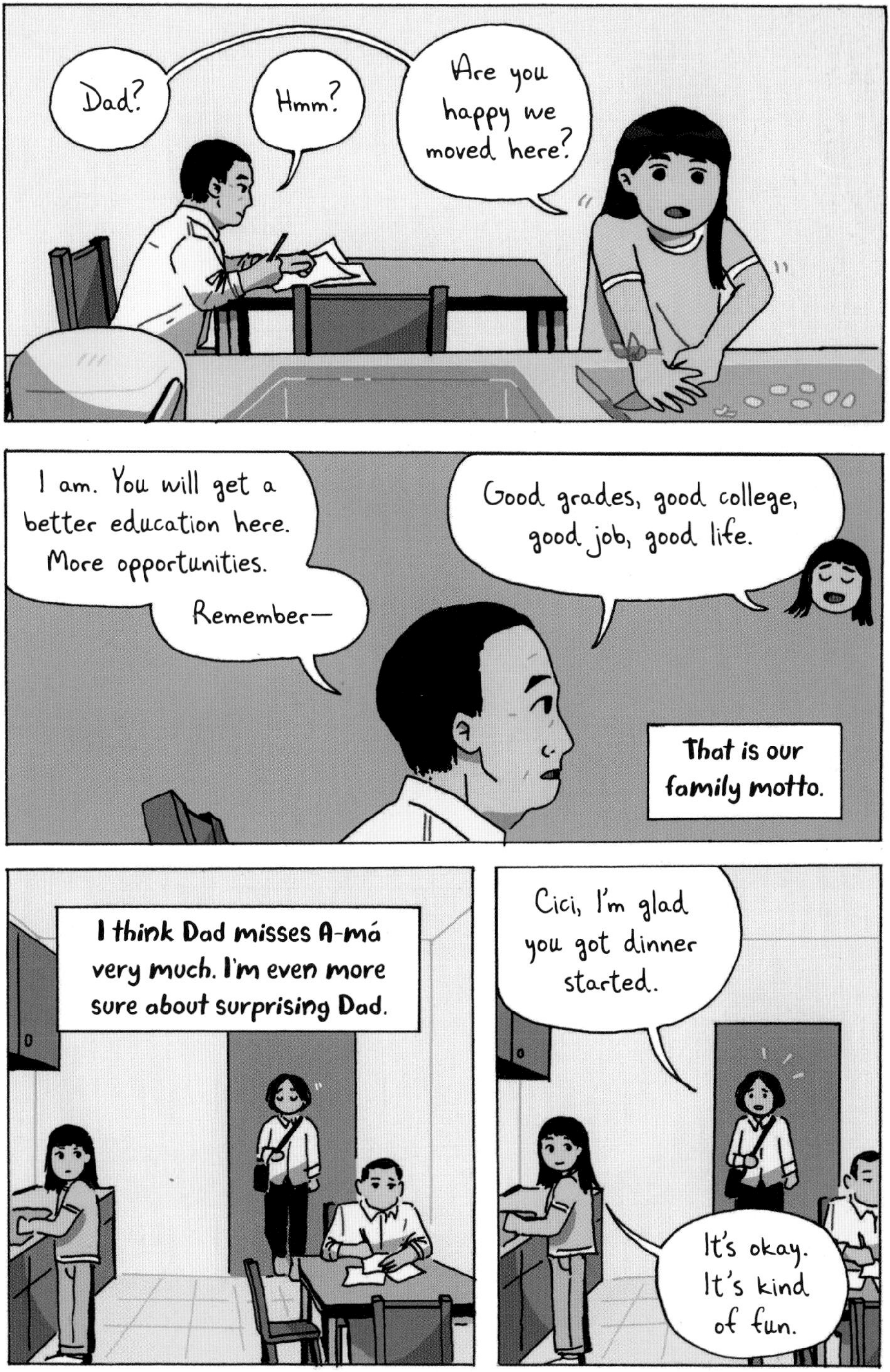

Dad?
Hmm?
Are you happy we moved here?
I am. You will get a better education here. More opportunities.
Remember—
Good grades, good college, good job, good life.
That is our family motto.
I think Dad misses A-má very much. I'm even more sure about surprising Dad.
Cici, I'm glad you got dinner started.
It's okay. It's kind of fun.

Chapter 5

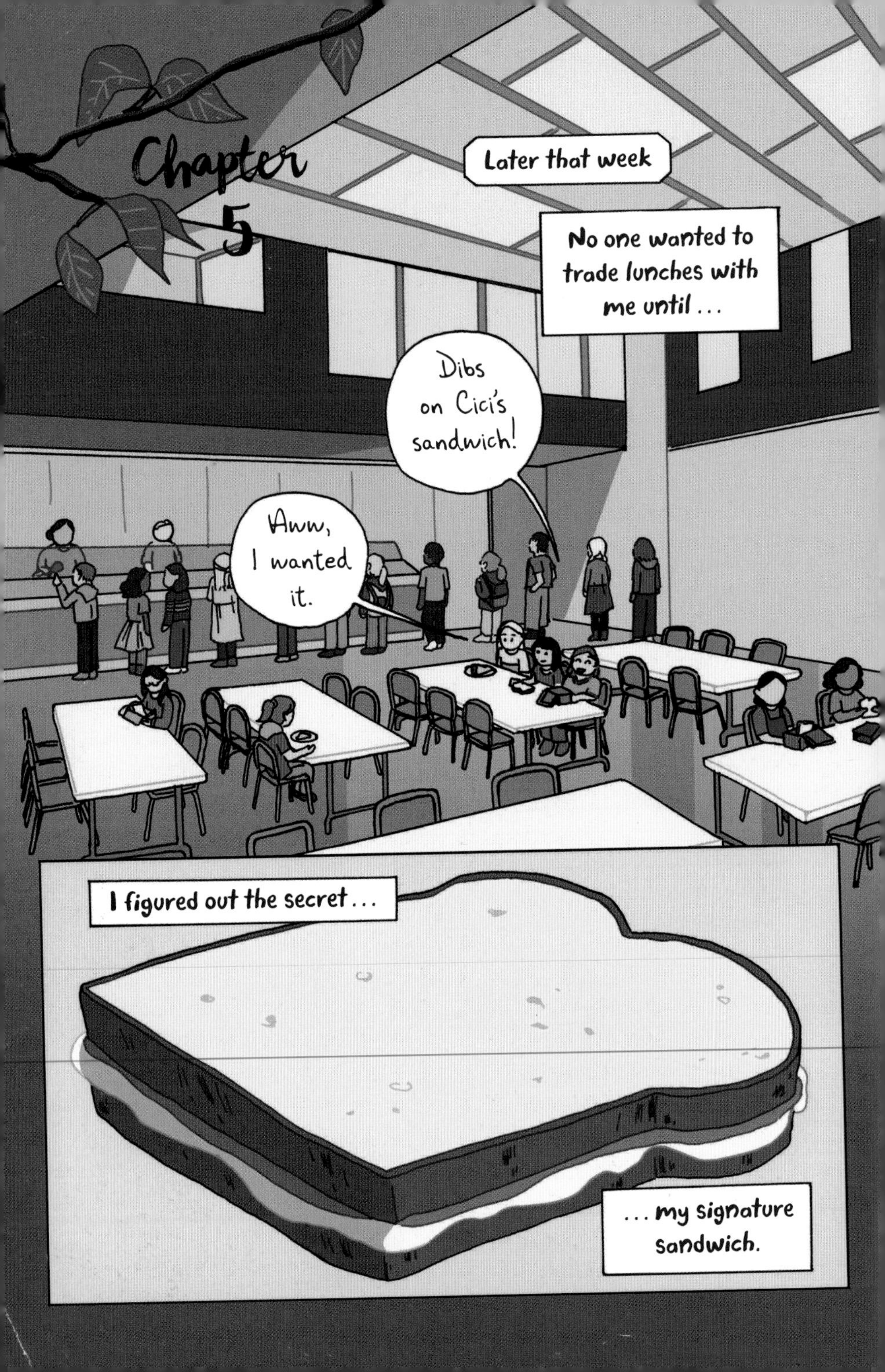
Later that week
No one wanted to trade lunches with me until . . .
Dibs on Cici's sandwich!
Aww, I wanted it.
I figured out the secret . . .
. . . my signature sandwich.

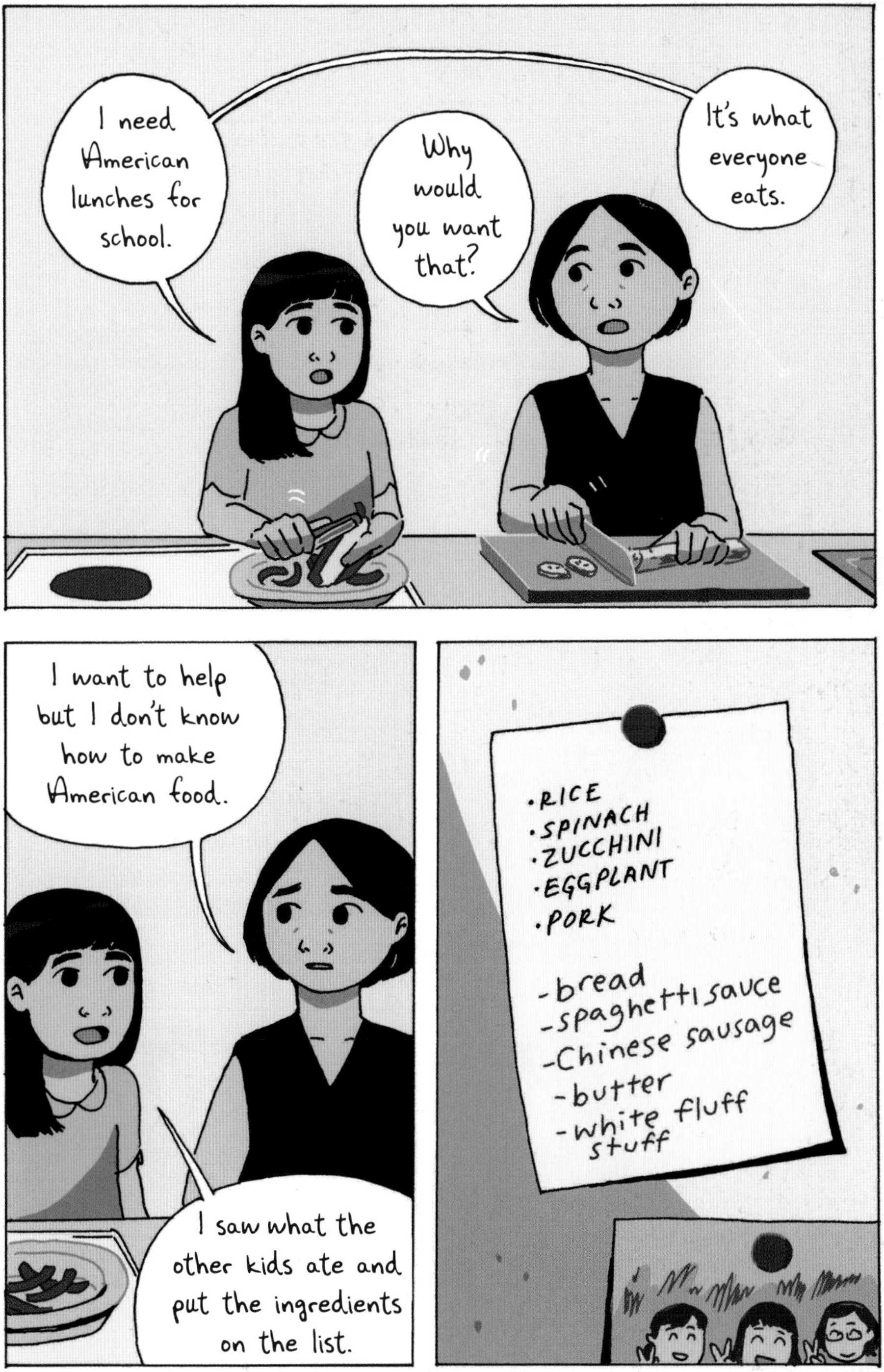
I need American lunches for school.
Why would you want that?
It's what everyone eats.
I want to help but I don't know how to make American food.
I saw what the other kids ate and put the ingredients on the list.
•RICE
•SPINACH
•ZUCCHINI
•EGGPLANT
•PORK
-bread
-spaghetti sauce
-Chinese sausage
-butter
-white fluff stuff

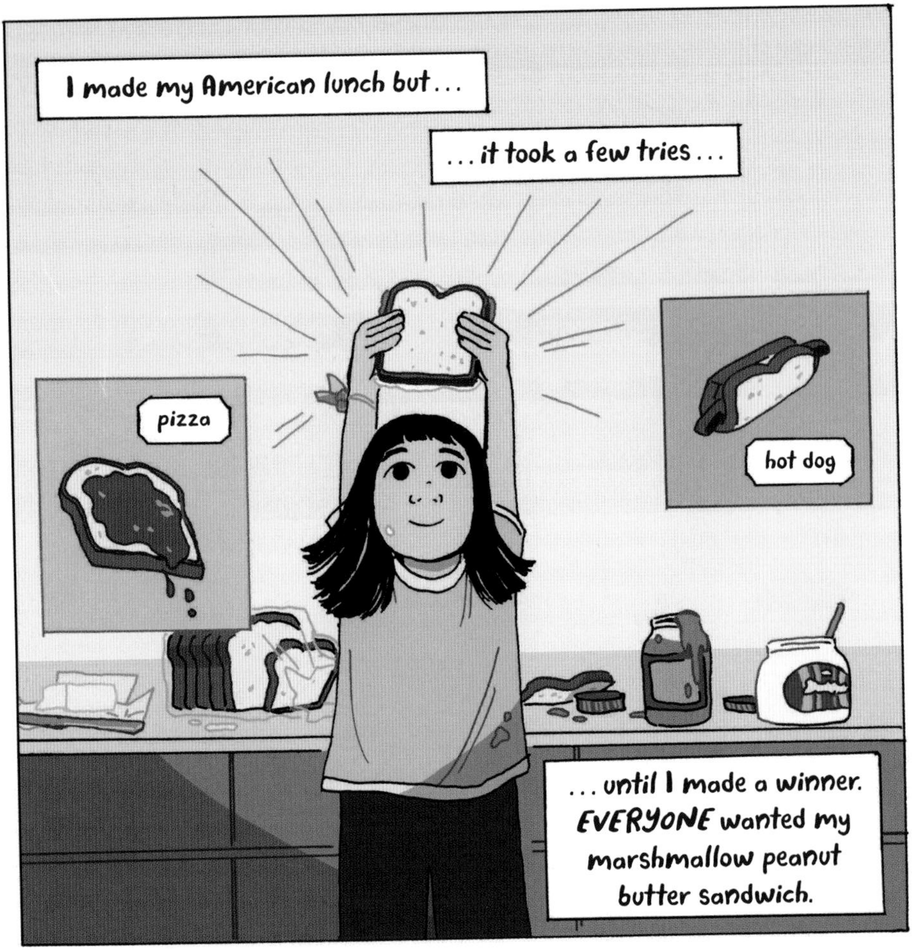
I made my American lunch but...
...it took a few tries...
pizza
hot dog
...until I made a winner. EVERYONE wanted my marshmallow peanut butter sandwich.

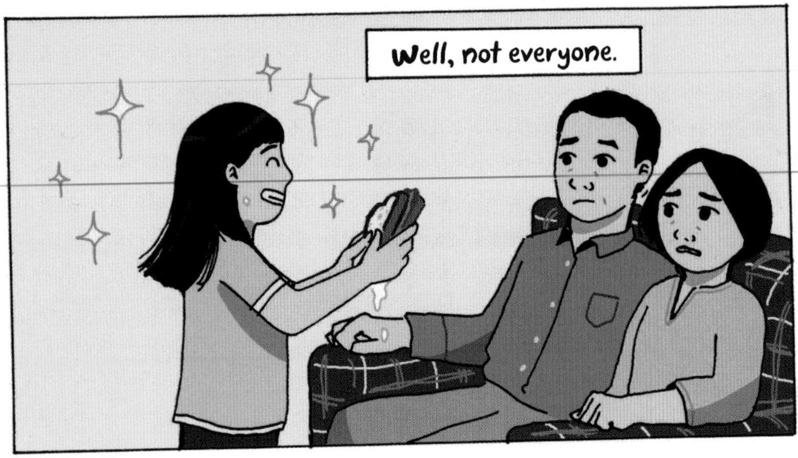
Well, not everyone.

Chapter 6

Back to the present

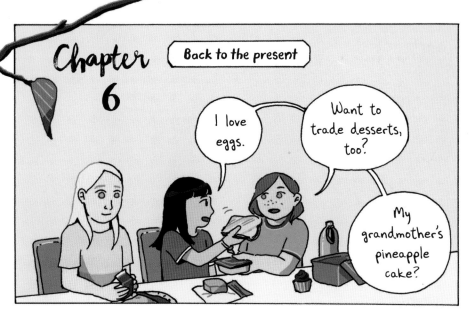

I love eggs.

Want to trade desserts, too?

My grandmother's pineapple cake?

A-má's pineapple cake makes me think of her. And that reminds me that I need money for the plane ticket.

Okay, I can't say no to that look.

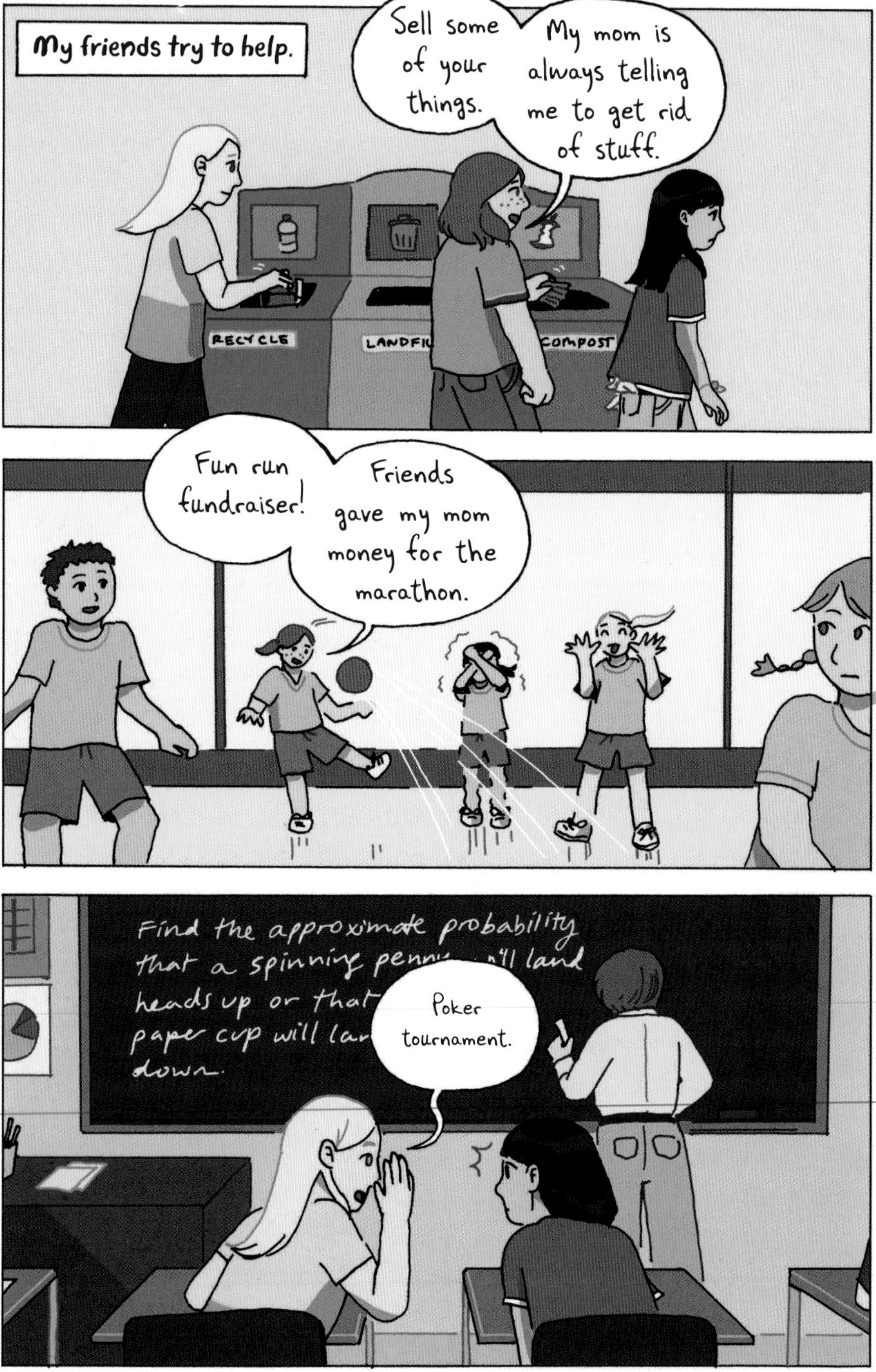
My friends try to help.
Sell some of your things.
My mom is always telling me to get rid of stuff.
RECYCLE
LANDFI
COMPOST
Fun run fundraiser!
Friends gave my mom money for the marathon.
Find the approximate probability
that a spinning penn ill land
heads up or that
paper cup will la
down.
Poker tournament.

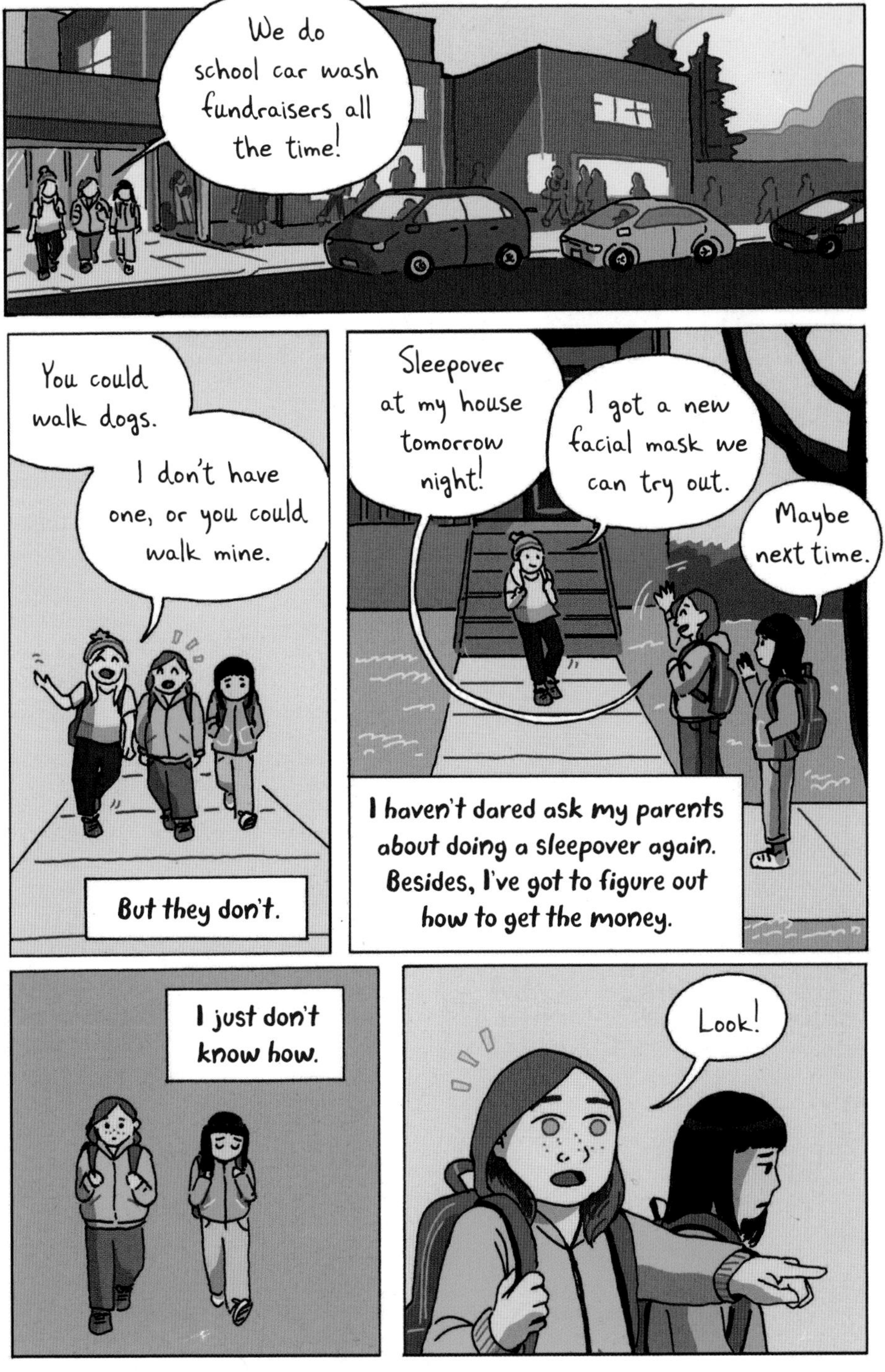
We do school car wash fundraisers all the time!
You could walk dogs.
I don't have one, or you could walk mine.
But they don't.
Sleepover at my house tomorrow night!
I got a new facial mask we can try out.
Maybe next time.
I haven't dared ask my parents about doing a sleepover again. Besides, I've got to figure out how to get the money.
I just don't know how.
Look!

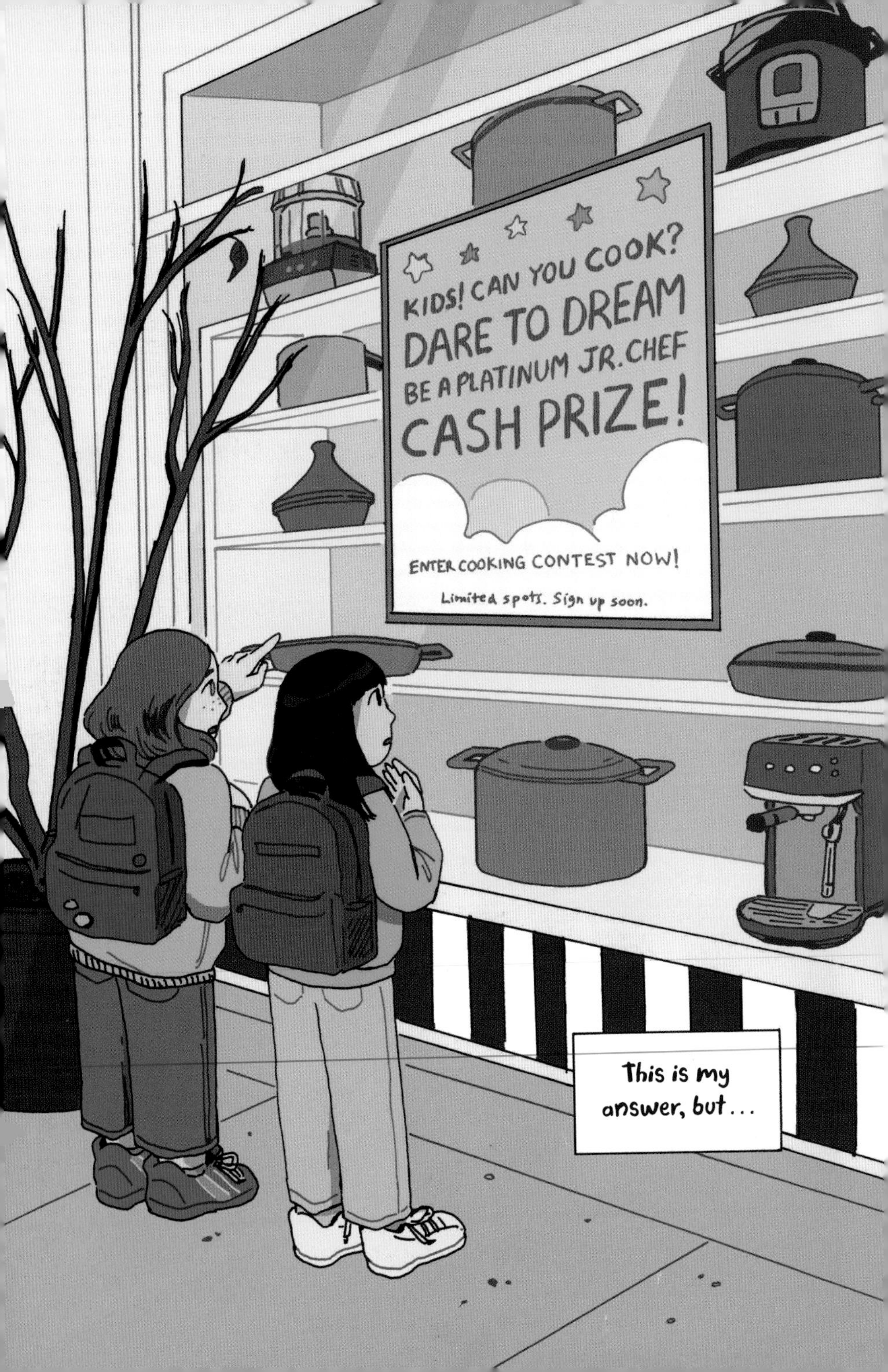
KIDS! CAN YOU COOK?
DARE TO DREAM
BE A PLATINUM JR. CHEF
CASH PRIZE!
ENTER COOKING CONTEST NOW!
Limited spots. Sign up soon.
This is my answer, but...

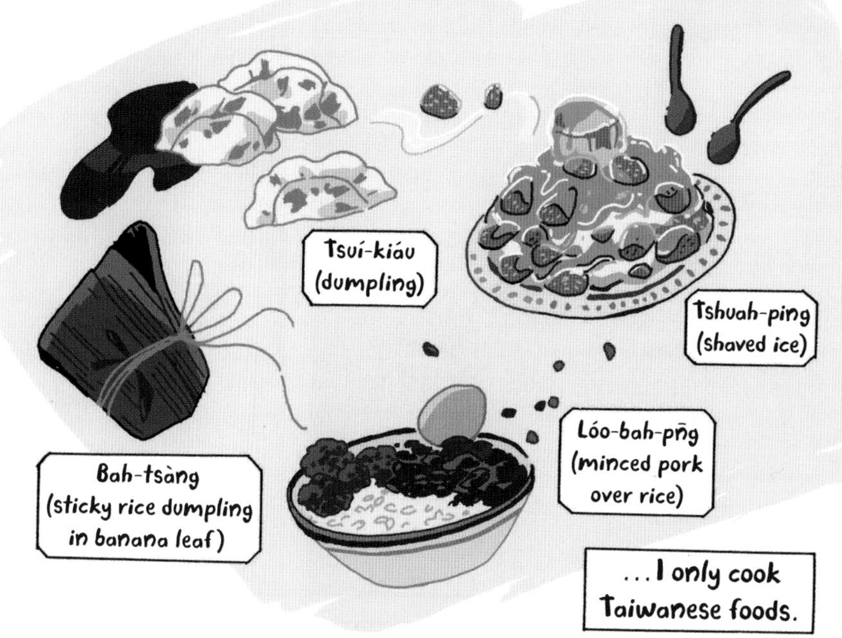
Tsuí-kiáu
(dumpling)
Tshuah-ping
(shaved ice)
Bah-tsàng
(sticky rice dumpling
in banana leaf)
Lóo-bah-pn̄g
(minced pork
over rice)
...I only cook
Taiwanese foods.

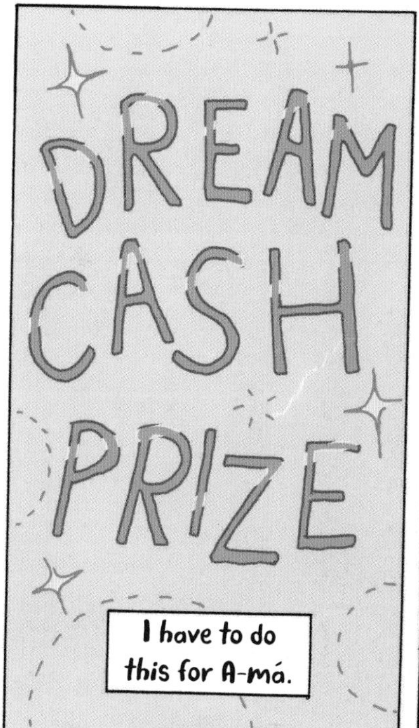
DREAM
CASH
PRIZE
I have to do
this for A-má.

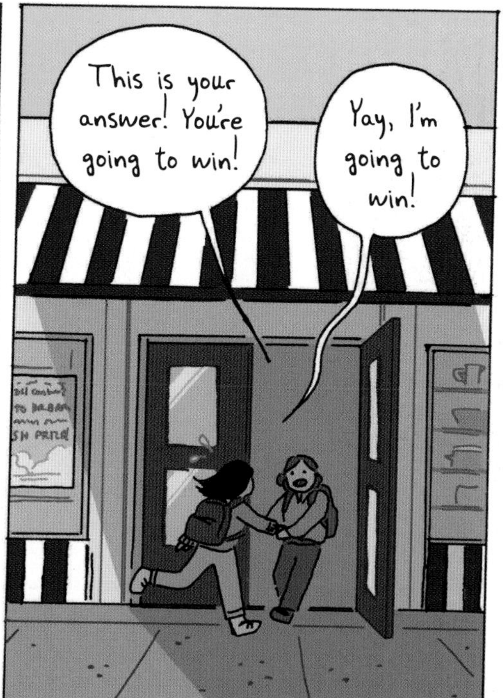
This is your
answer! You're
going to win!
Yay, I'm
going to
win!

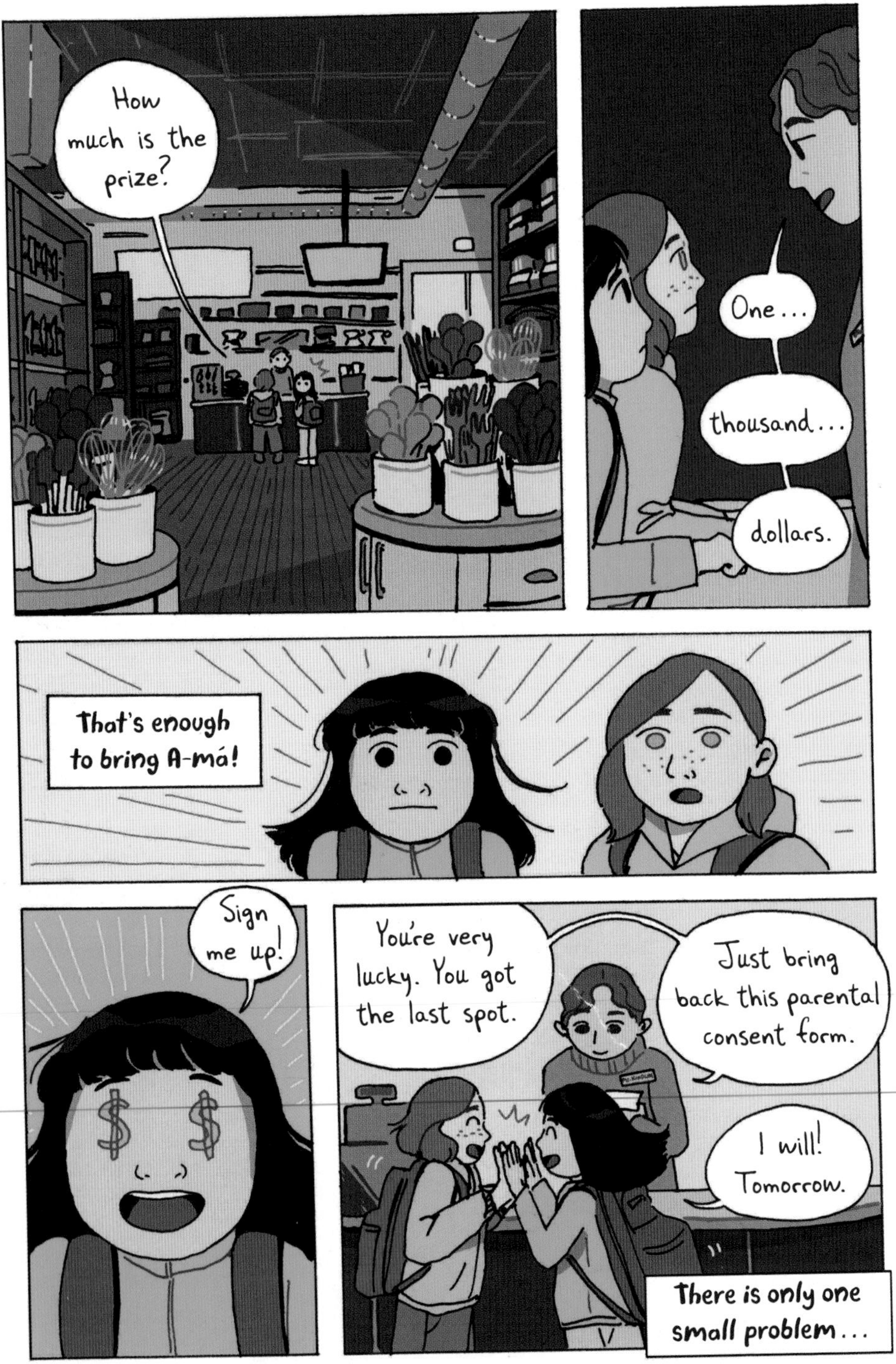
How much is the prize?
One...
thousand...
dollars.
That's enough to bring A-má!
Sign me up!
You're very lucky. You got the last spot.
Just bring back this parental consent form.
I will! Tomorrow.
There is only one small problem...

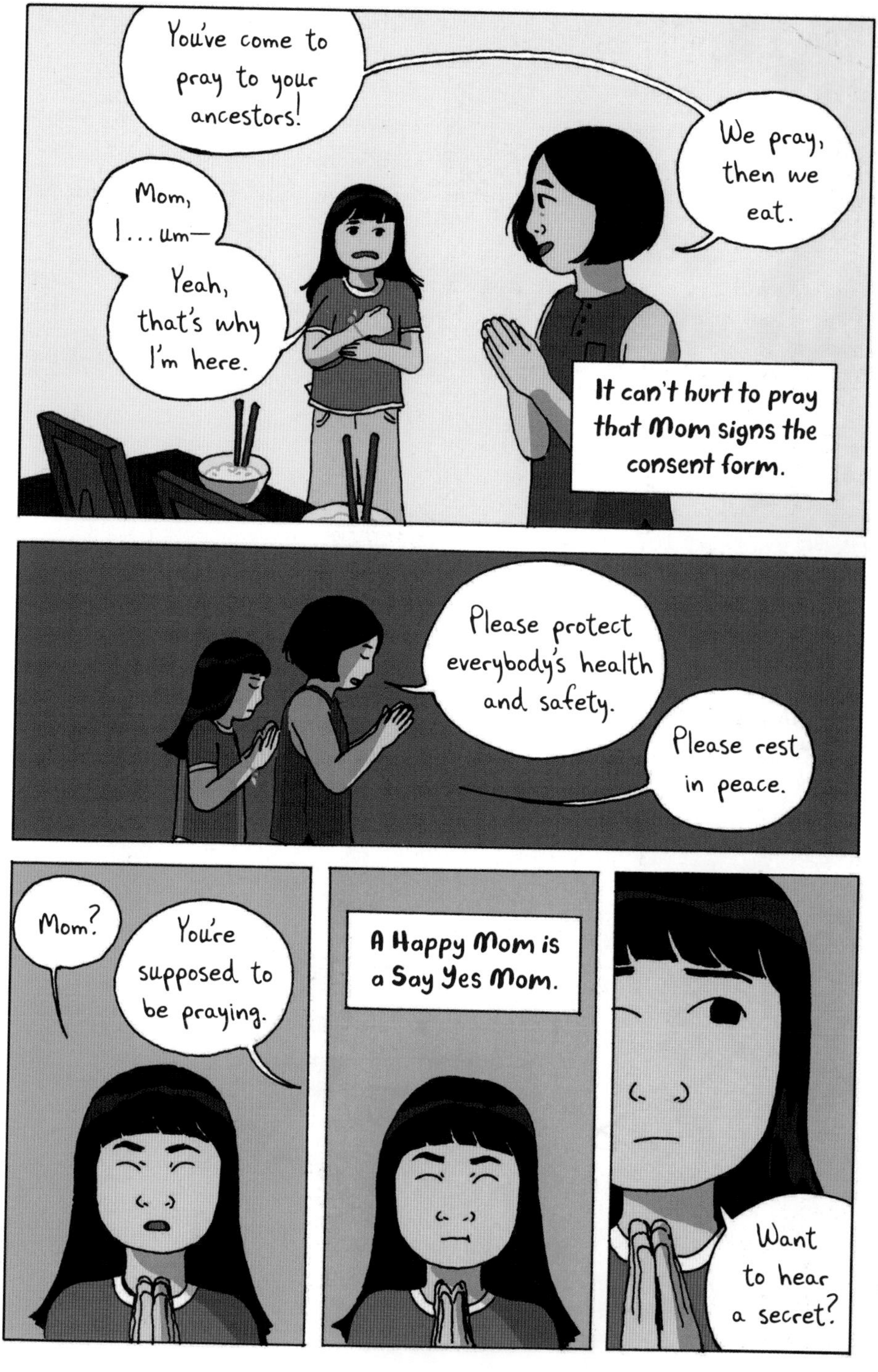
You've come to pray to your ancestors!
We pray, then we eat.
Mom, I... um—
Yeah, that's why I'm here.
It can't hurt to pray that Mom signs the consent form.
Please protect everybody's health and safety.
Please rest in peace.
Mom?
You're supposed to be praying.
A Happy Mom is a Say Yes Mom.
Want to hear a secret?

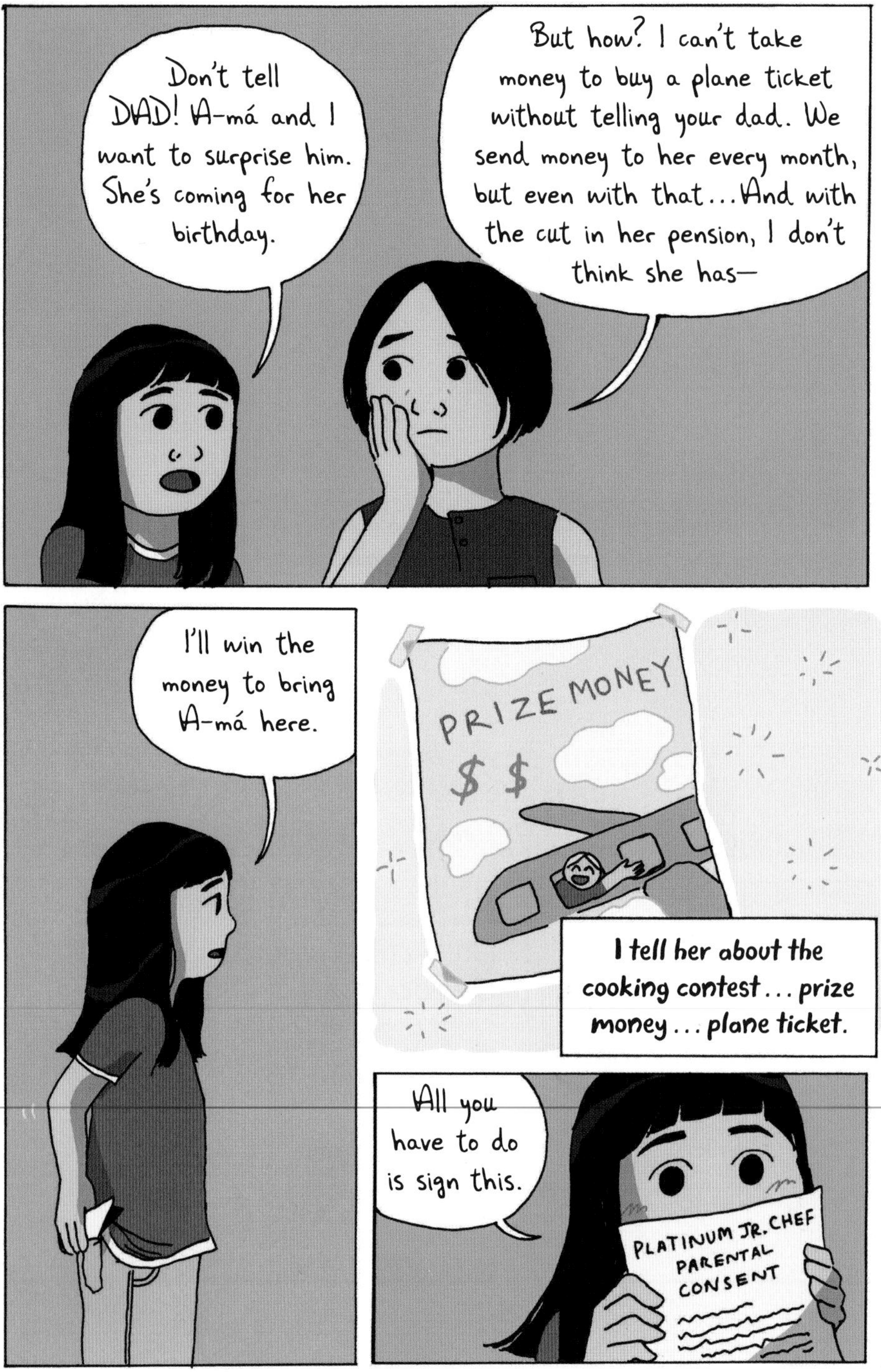
Don't tell DAD! A-má and I want to surprise him. She's coming for her birthday.
But how? I can't take money to buy a plane ticket without telling your dad. We send money to her every month, but even with that...And with the cut in her pension, I don't think she has—
I'll win the money to bring A-má here.
PRIZE MONEY
$ $
I tell her about the cooking contest... prize money... plane ticket.
All you have to do is sign this.
PLATINUM JR. CHEF PARENTAL CONSENT

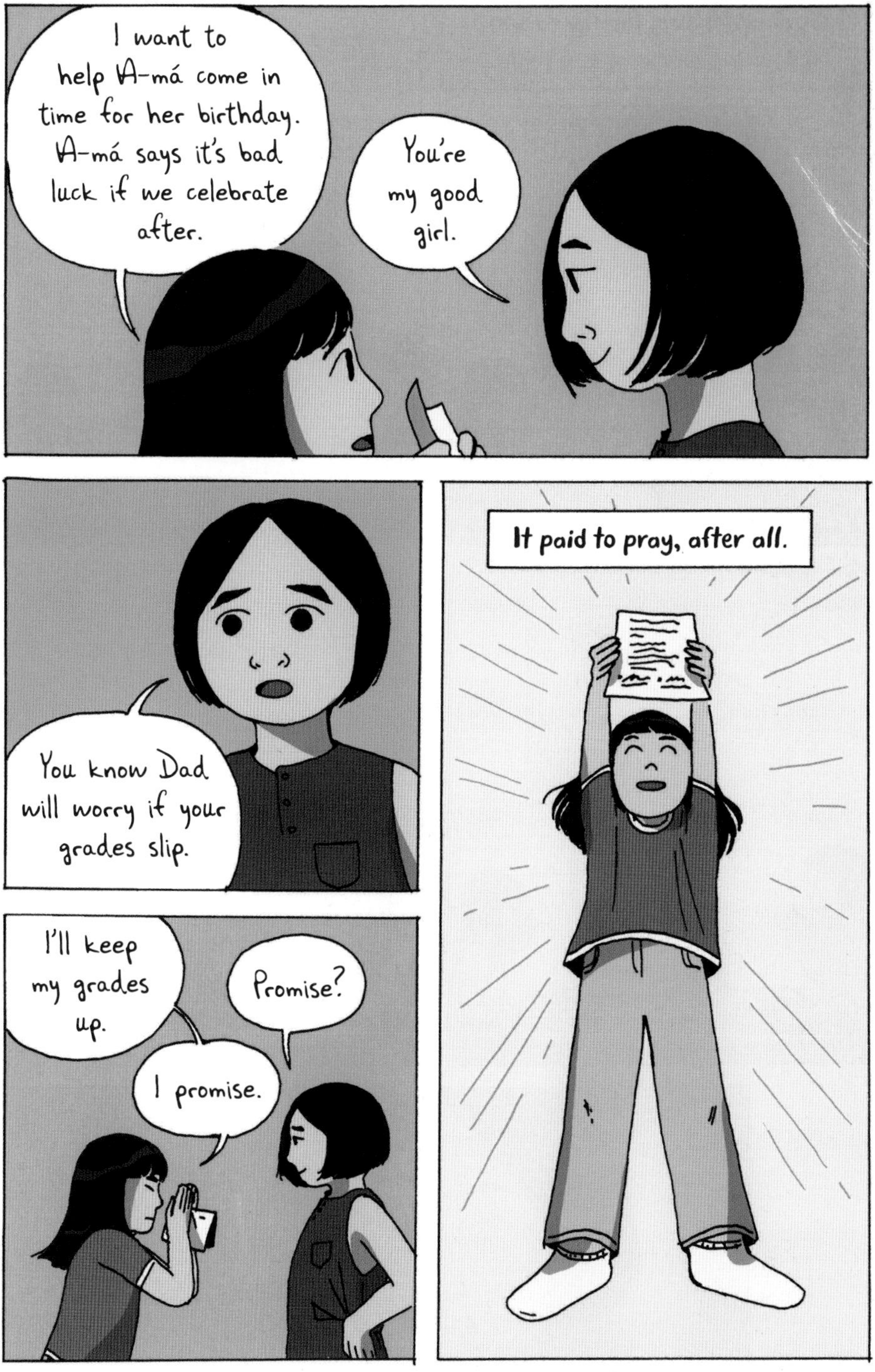
I want to help A-má come in time for her birthday. A-má says it's bad luck if we celebrate after.
You're my good girl.
You know Dad will worry if your grades slip.
I'll keep my grades up.
Promise?
I promise.
It paid to pray, after all.

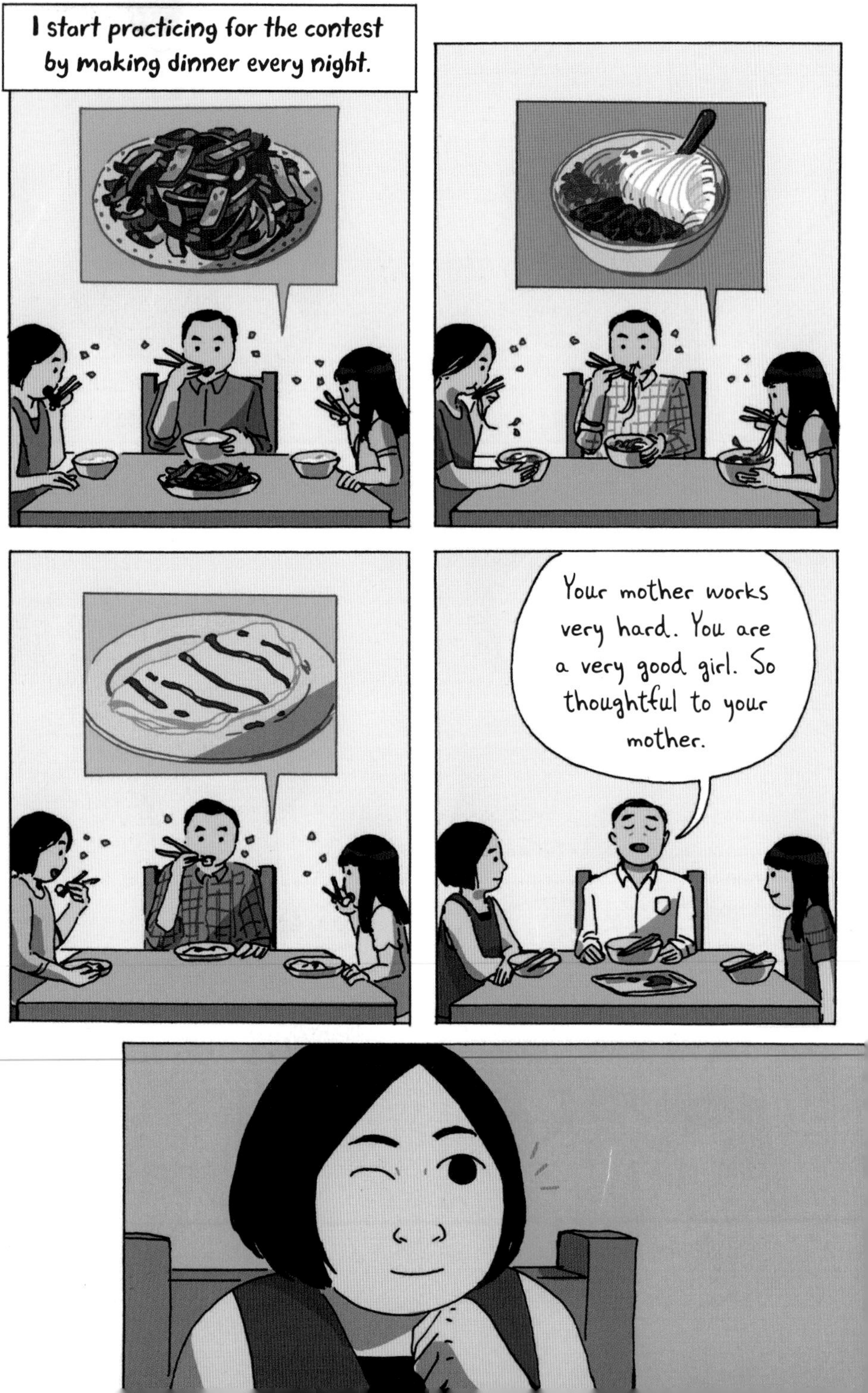
I start practicing for the contest by making dinner every night.
Your mother works very hard. You are a very good girl. So thoughtful to your mother.

Chapter 7

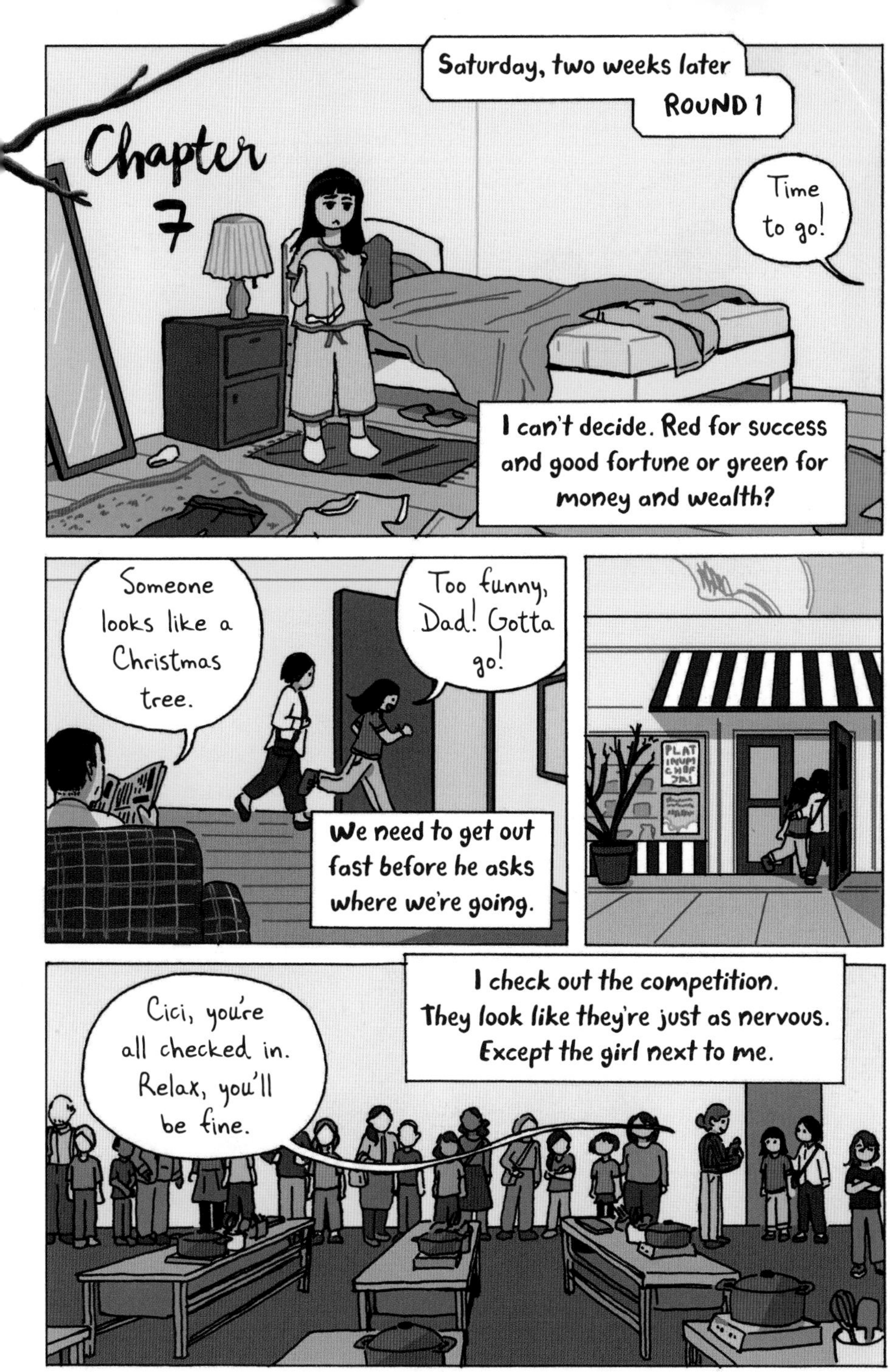

Saturday, two weeks later
ROUND 1
Time to go!
I can't decide. Red for success and good fortune or green for money and wealth?
Someone looks like a Christmas tree.
Too funny, Dad! Gotta go!
We need to get out fast before he asks where we're going.
I check out the competition. They look like they're just as nervous. Except the girl next to me.
Cici, you're all checked in. Relax, you'll be fine.

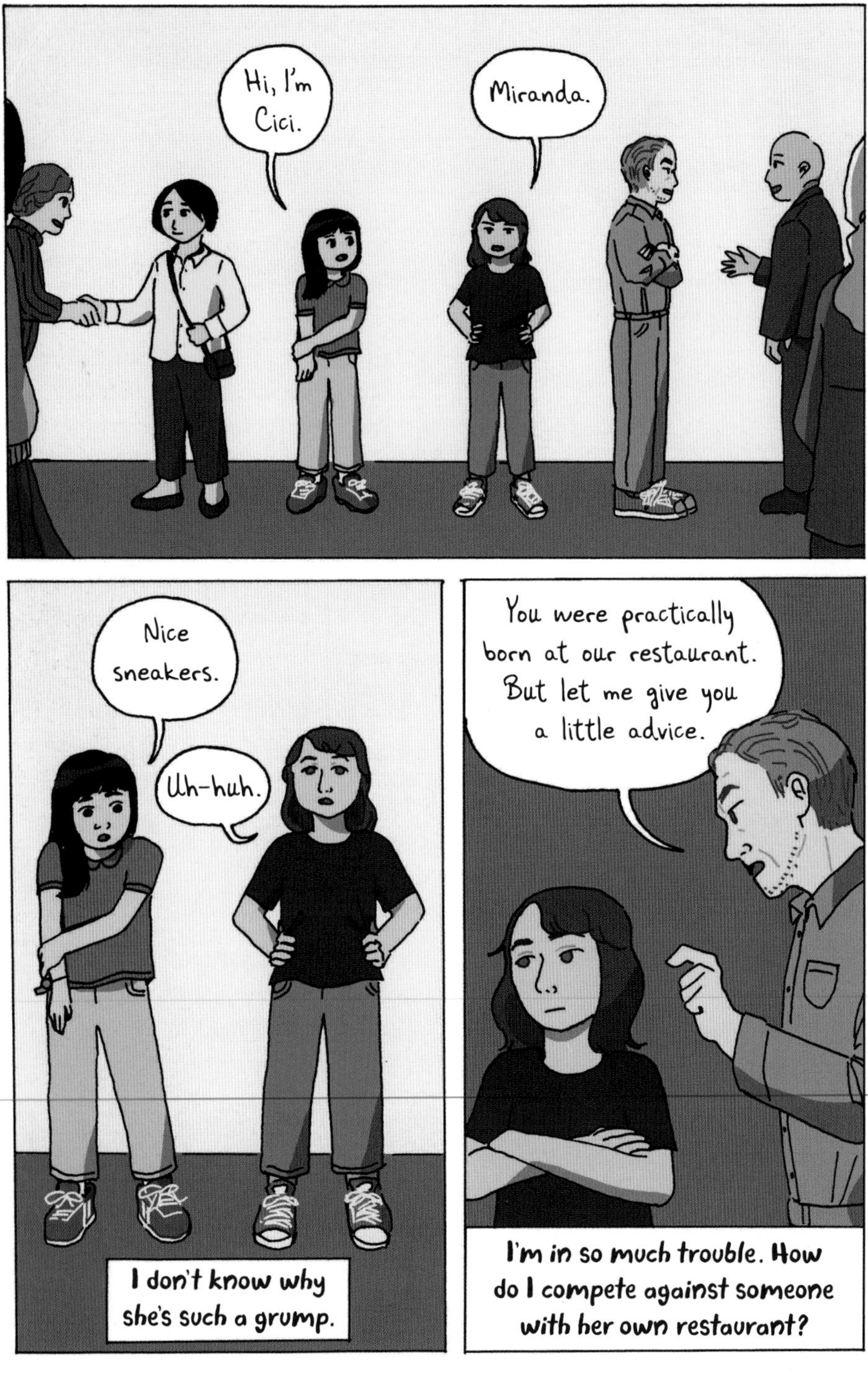
Hi, I'm Cici.
Miranda.
Nice sneakers.
Uh-huh.
I don't know why she's such a grump.
You were practically born at our restaurant. But let me give you a little advice.
I'm in so much trouble. How do I compete against someone with her own restaurant?

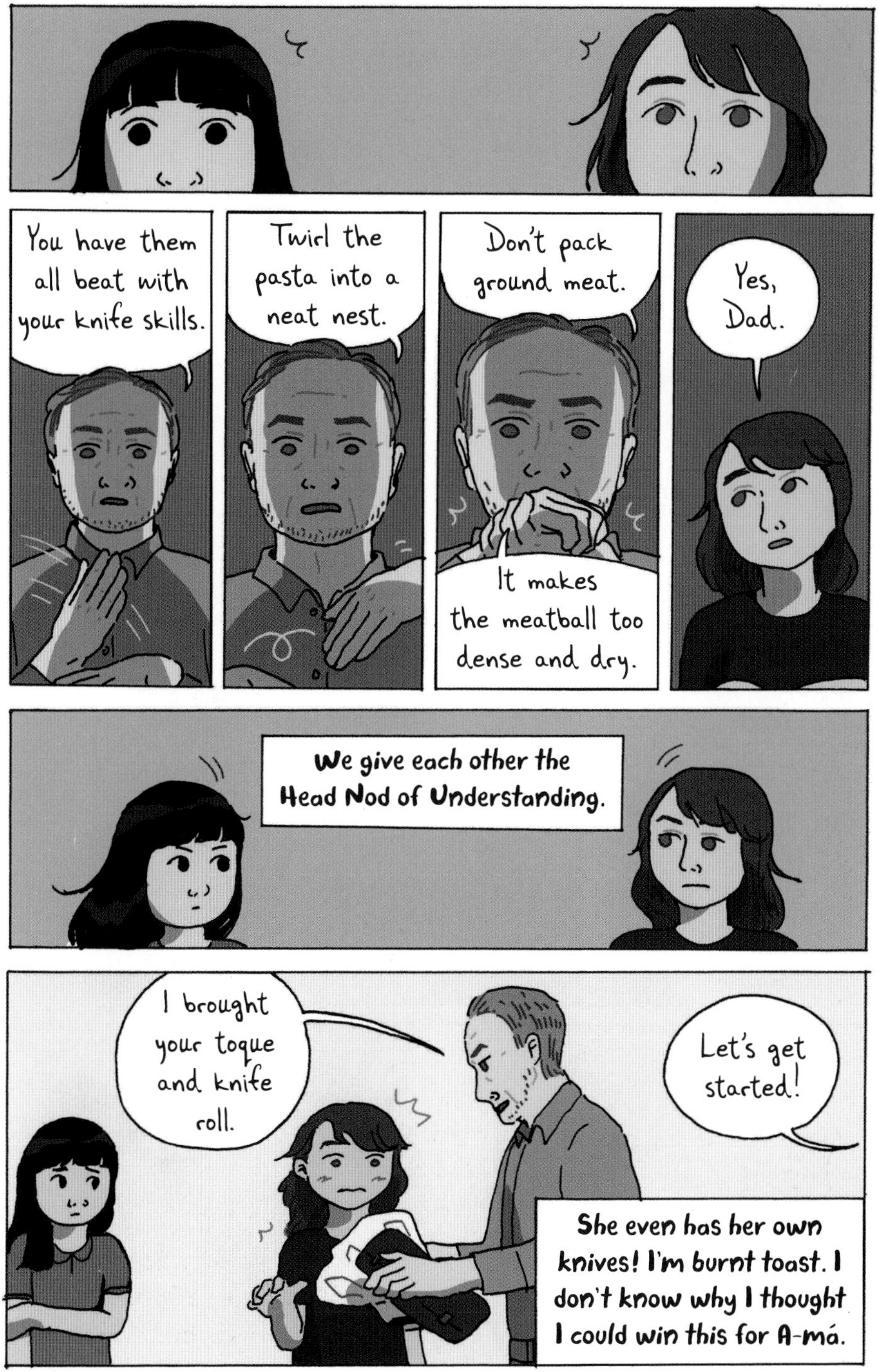
You have them all beat with your knife skills.
Twirl the pasta into a neat nest.
Don't pack ground meat.
It makes the meatball too dense and dry.
Yes, Dad.
We give each other the Head Nod of Understanding.
I brought your toque and knife roll.
Let's get started!
She even has her own knives! I'm burnt toast. I don't know why I thought I could win this for A-má.

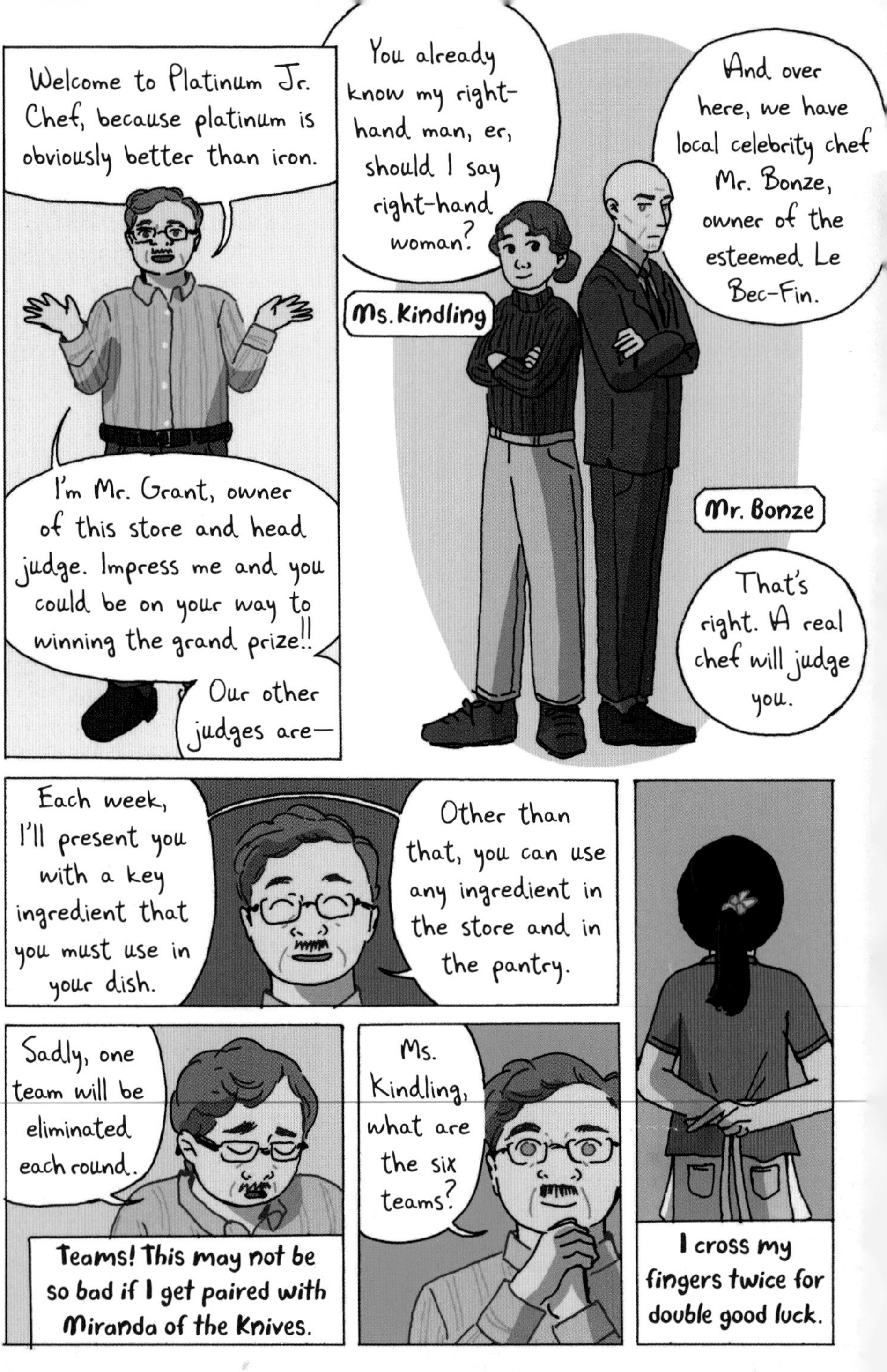
Welcome to Platinum Jr. Chef, because platinum is obviously better than iron.
I'm Mr. Grant, owner of this store and head judge. Impress me and you could be on your way to winning the grand prize!!
Our other judges are—
You already know my right-hand man, er, should I say right-hand woman?
Ms. Kindling
And over here, we have local celebrity chef Mr. Bonze, owner of the esteemed Le Bec-Fin.
Mr. Bonze
That's right. A real chef will judge you.
Each week, I'll present you with a key ingredient that you must use in your dish.
Other than that, you can use any ingredient in the store and in the pantry.
Sadly, one team will be eliminated each round.
Teams! This may not be so bad if I get paired with Miranda of the Knives.
Ms. Kindling, what are the six teams?
I cross my fingers twice for double good luck.

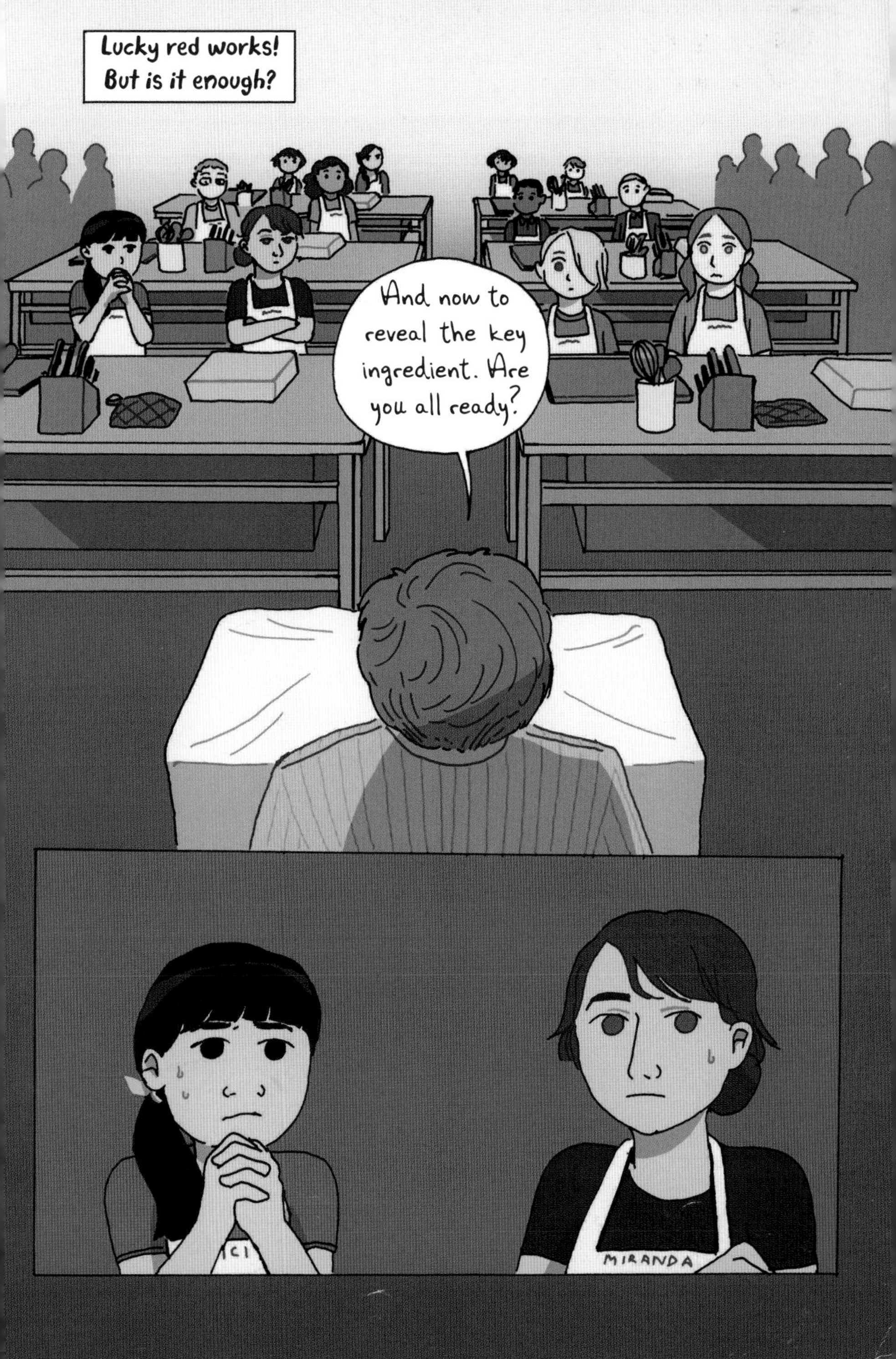
Lucky red works! But is it enough?
And now to reveal the key ingredient. Are you all ready?
MIRANDA

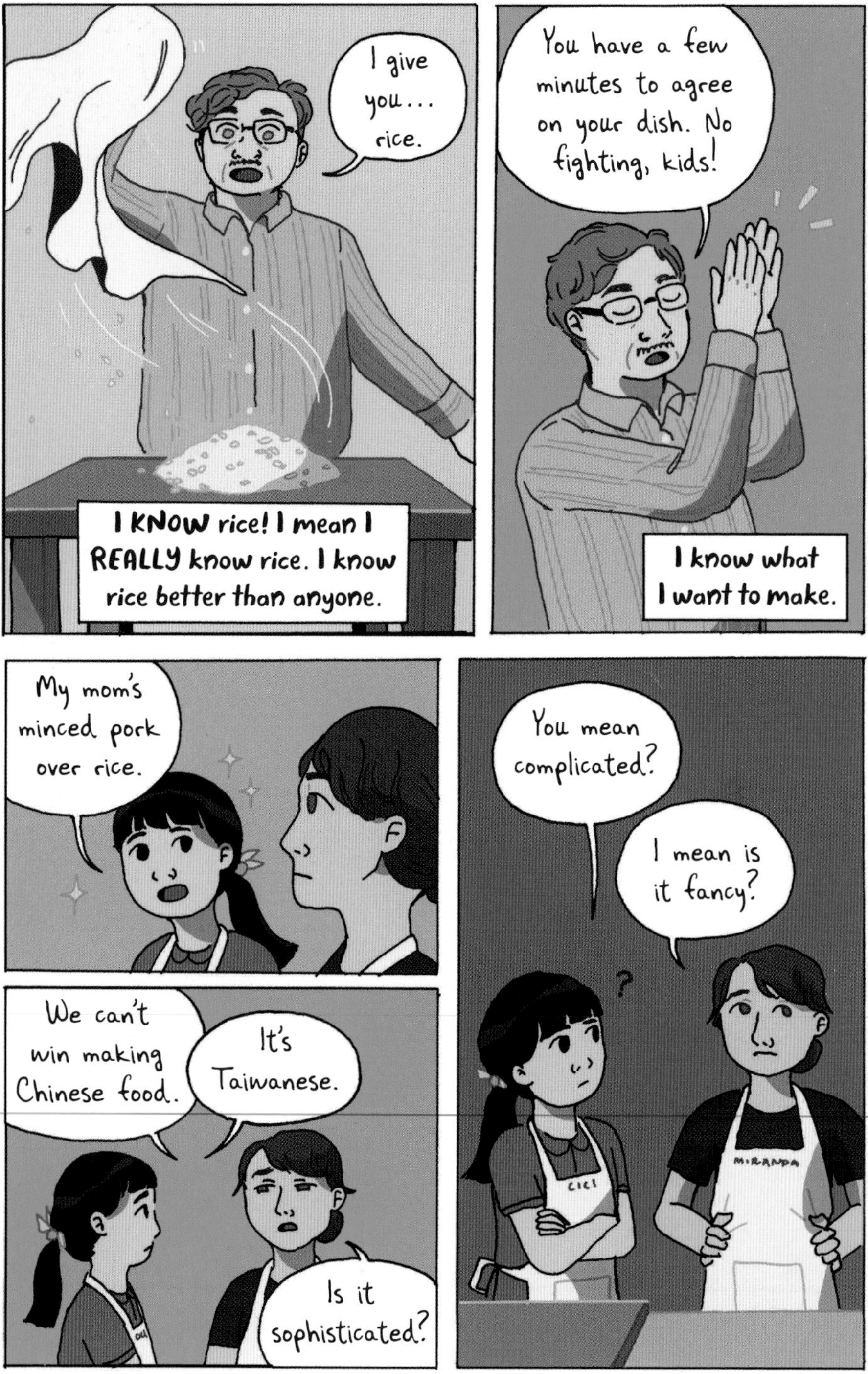
I give you... rice.
I KNOW rice! I mean I REALLY know rice. I know rice better than anyone.
You have a few minutes to agree on your dish. No fighting, kids!
I know what I want to make.
My mom's minced pork over rice.
You mean complicated?
I mean is it fancy?
?
We can't win making Chinese food.
It's Taiwanese.
Is it sophisticated?
CICI
MIRANDA

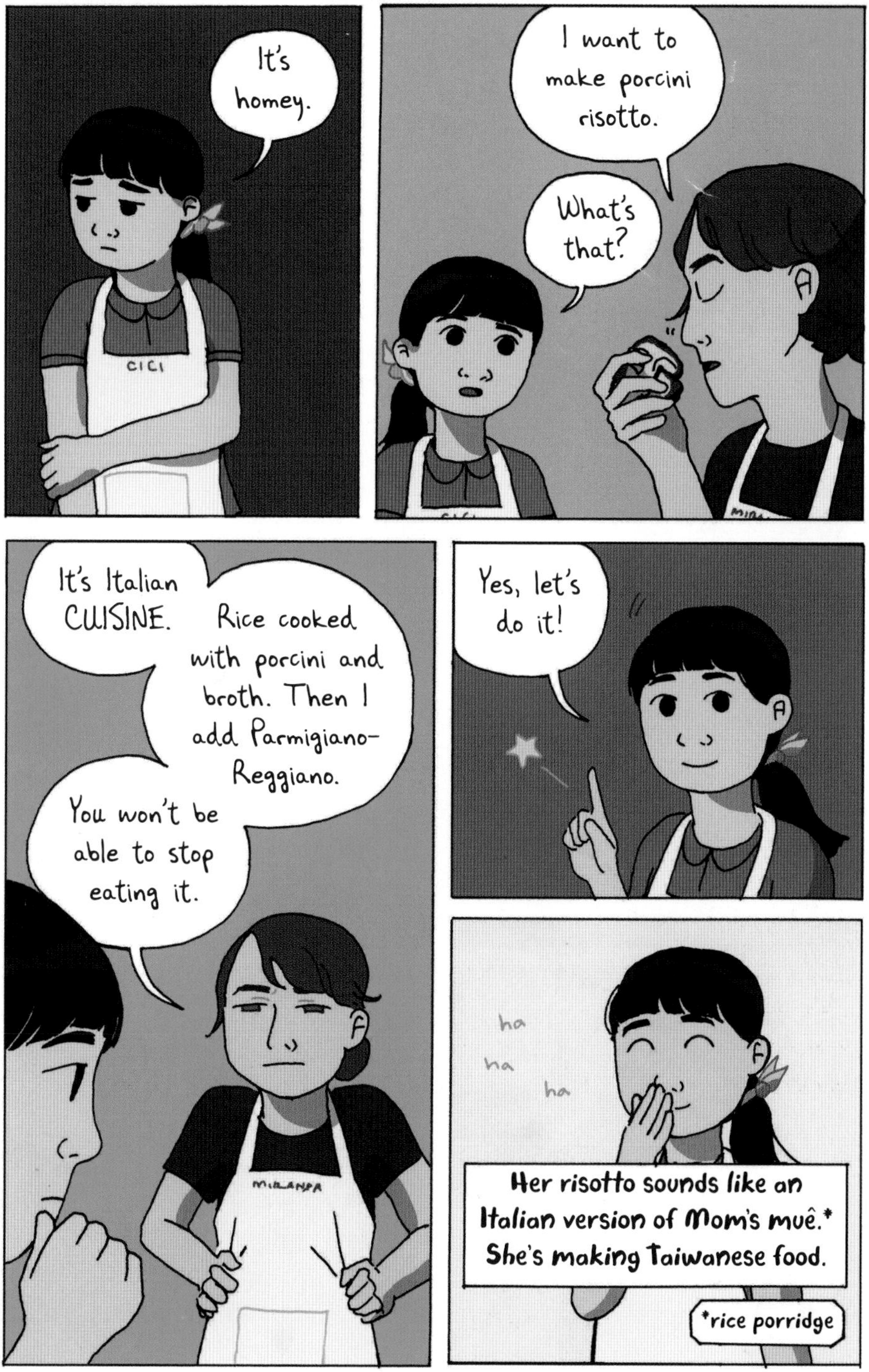
It's homey.
CICI
I want to make porcini risotto.
What's that?
It's Italian CUISINE.
Rice cooked with porcini and broth. Then I add Parmigiano-Reggiano.
You won't be able to stop eating it.
MIRANDA
Yes, let's do it!
ha ha ha
Her risotto sounds like an Italian version of Mom's muê.* She's making Taiwanese food.
*rice porridge

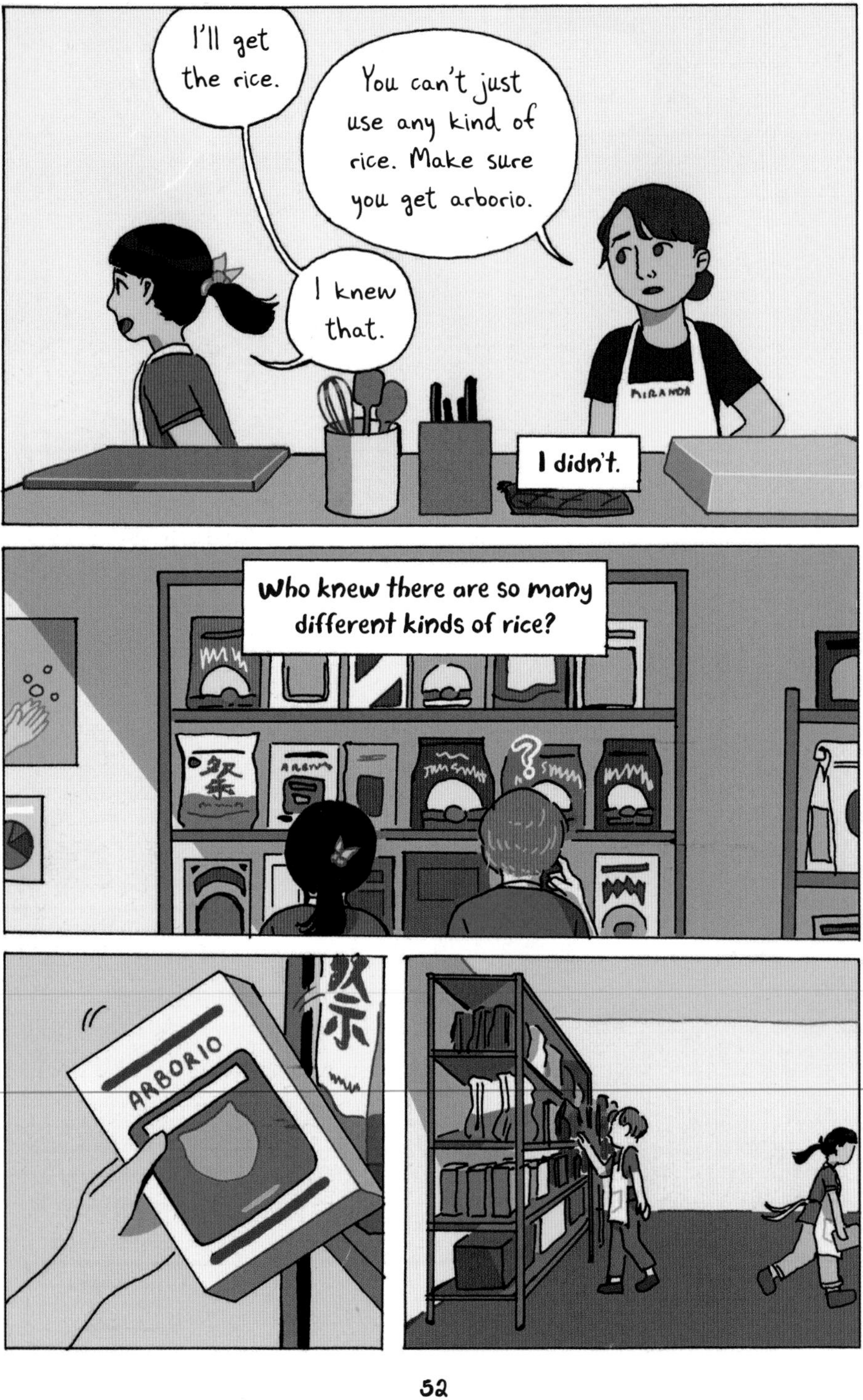
I'll get the rice.
You can't just use any kind of rice. Make sure you get arborio.
I knew that.
I didn't.
MIRANDA
Who knew there are so many different kinds of rice?
ARBORIO

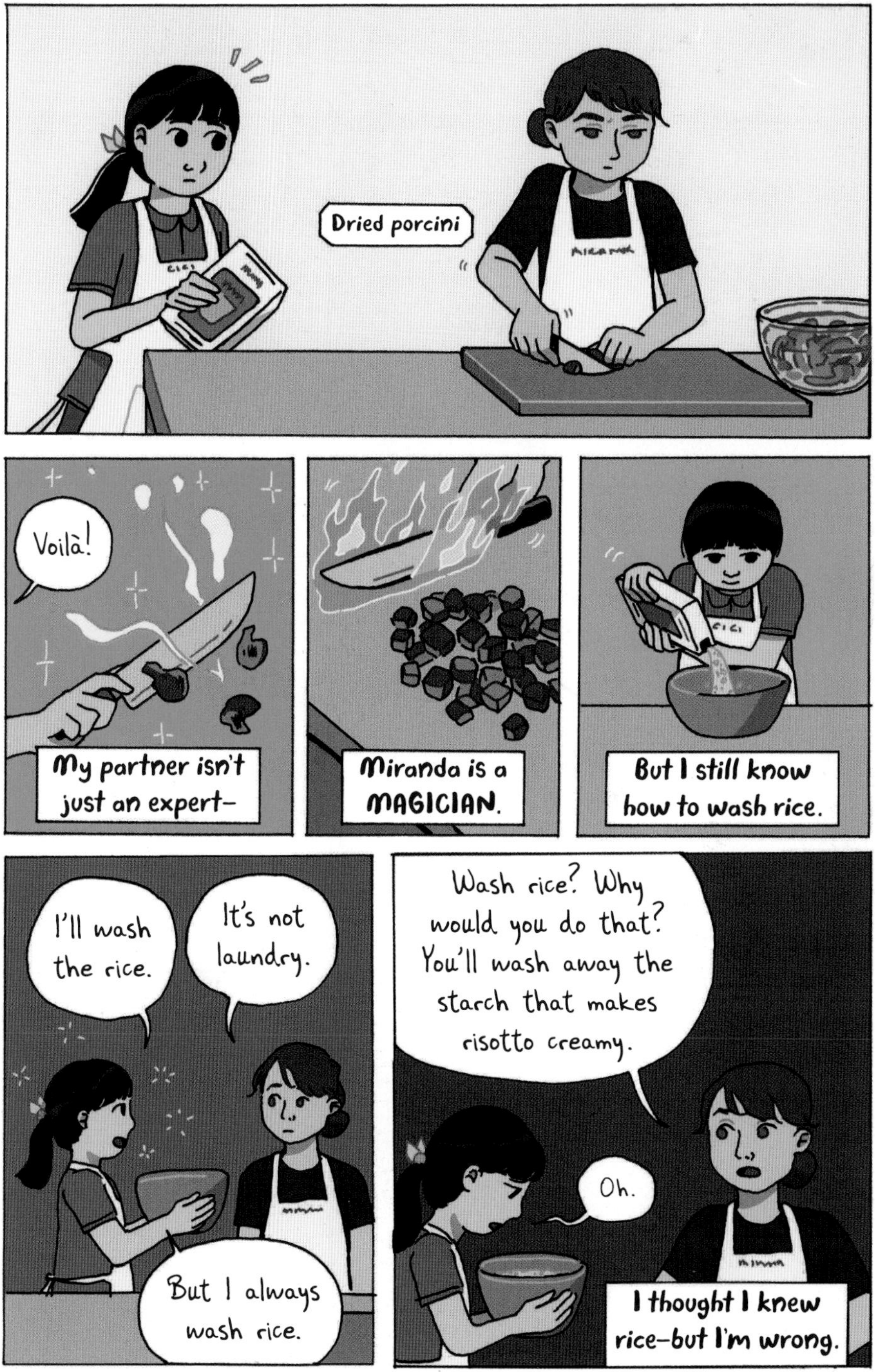

Dried porcini
Voilà!
My partner isn't just an expert-
Miranda is a MAGICIAN.
But I still know how to wash rice.
I'll wash the rice.
It's not laundry.
But I always wash rice.
Wash rice? Why would you do that? You'll wash away the starch that makes risotto creamy.
Oh.
I thought I knew rice-but I'm wrong.

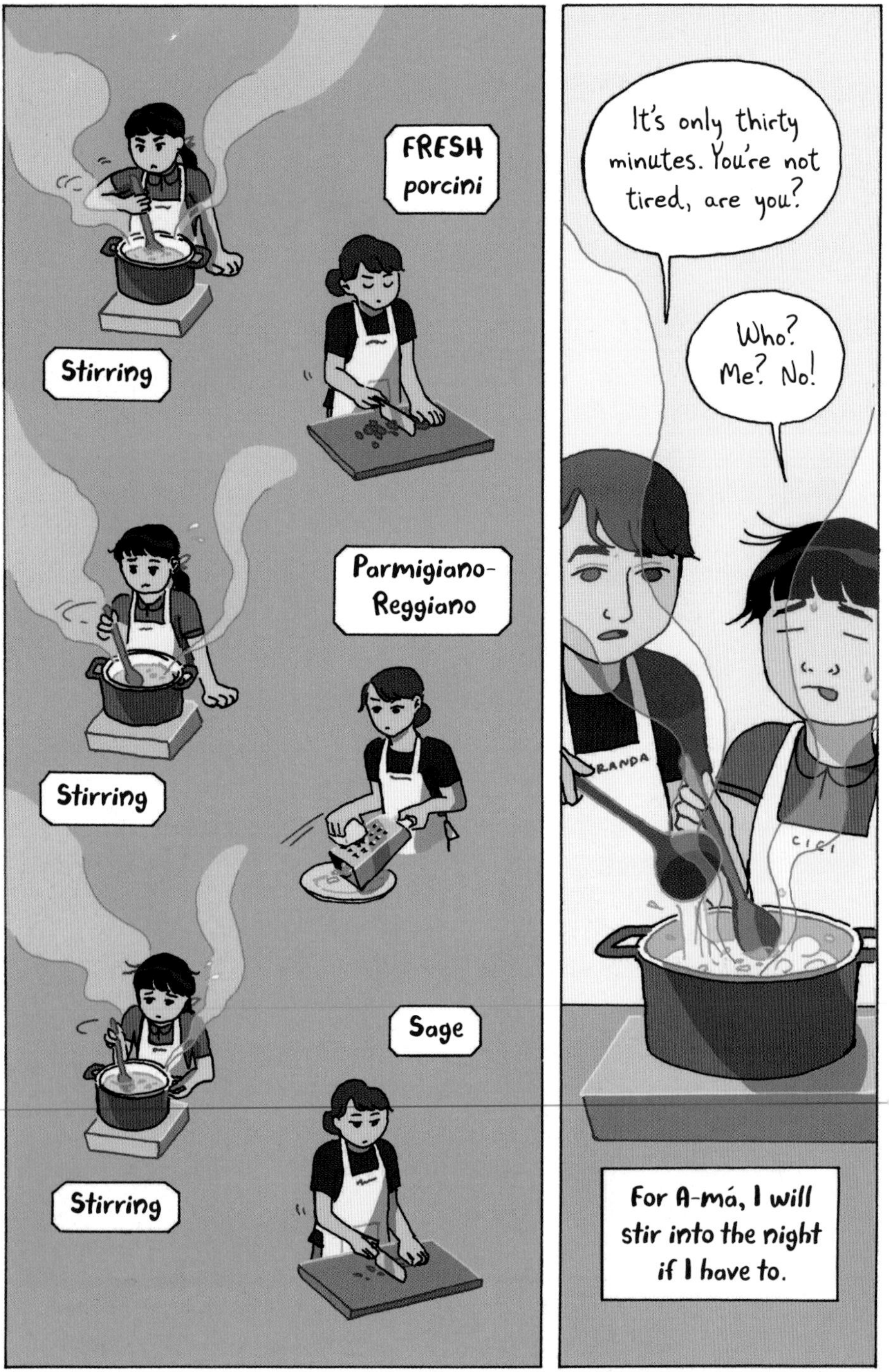
Stirring
FRESH porcini
Stirring
Parmigiano-Reggiano
Stirring
Sage
It's only thirty minutes. You're not tired, are you?
Who? Me? No!
For A-má, I will stir into the night if I have to.

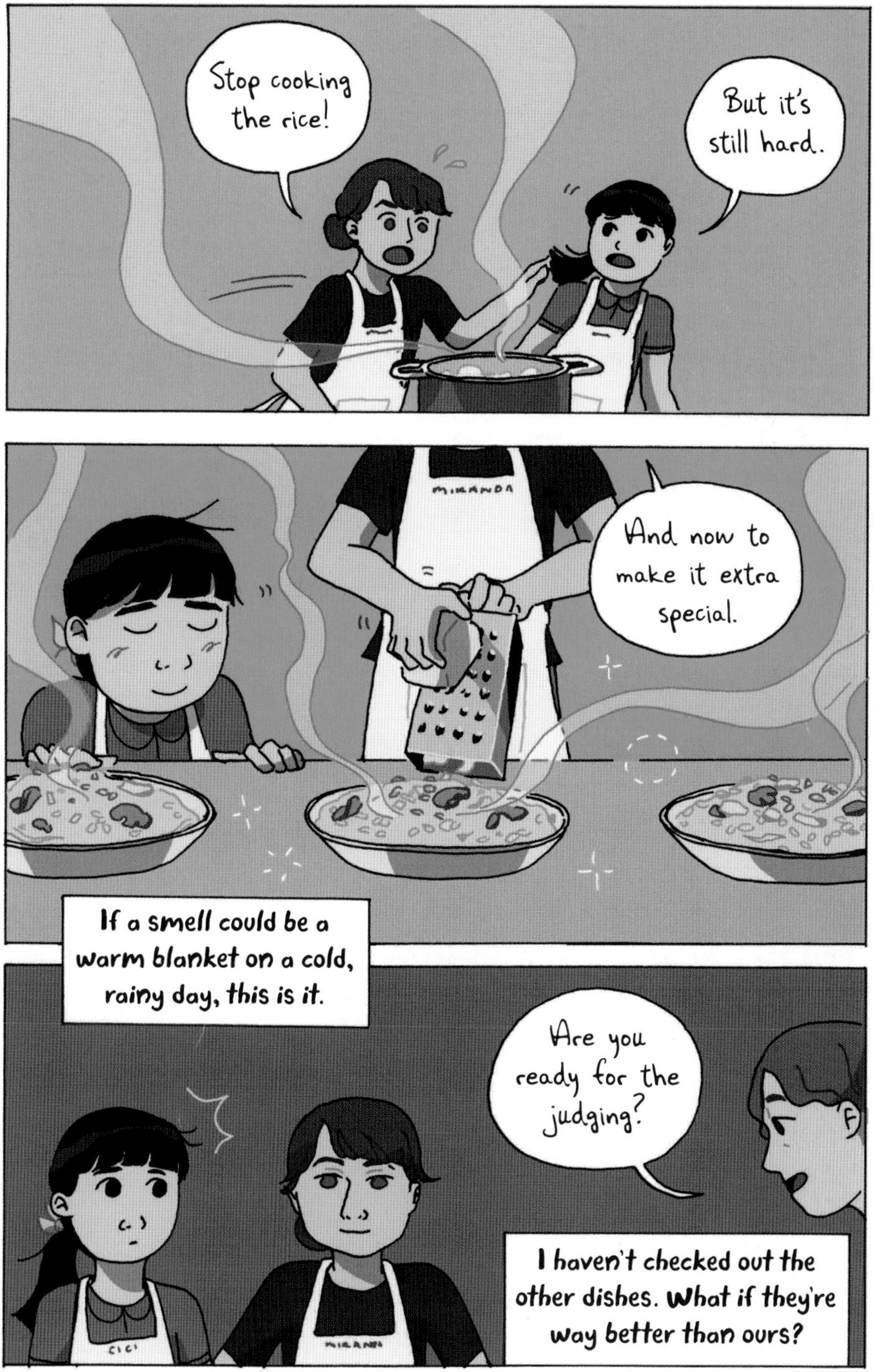
Stop cooking the rice!
But it's still hard.
And now to make it extra special.
If a smell could be a warm blanket on a cold, rainy day, this is it.
Are you ready for the judging?
I haven't checked out the other dishes. What if they're way better than ours?

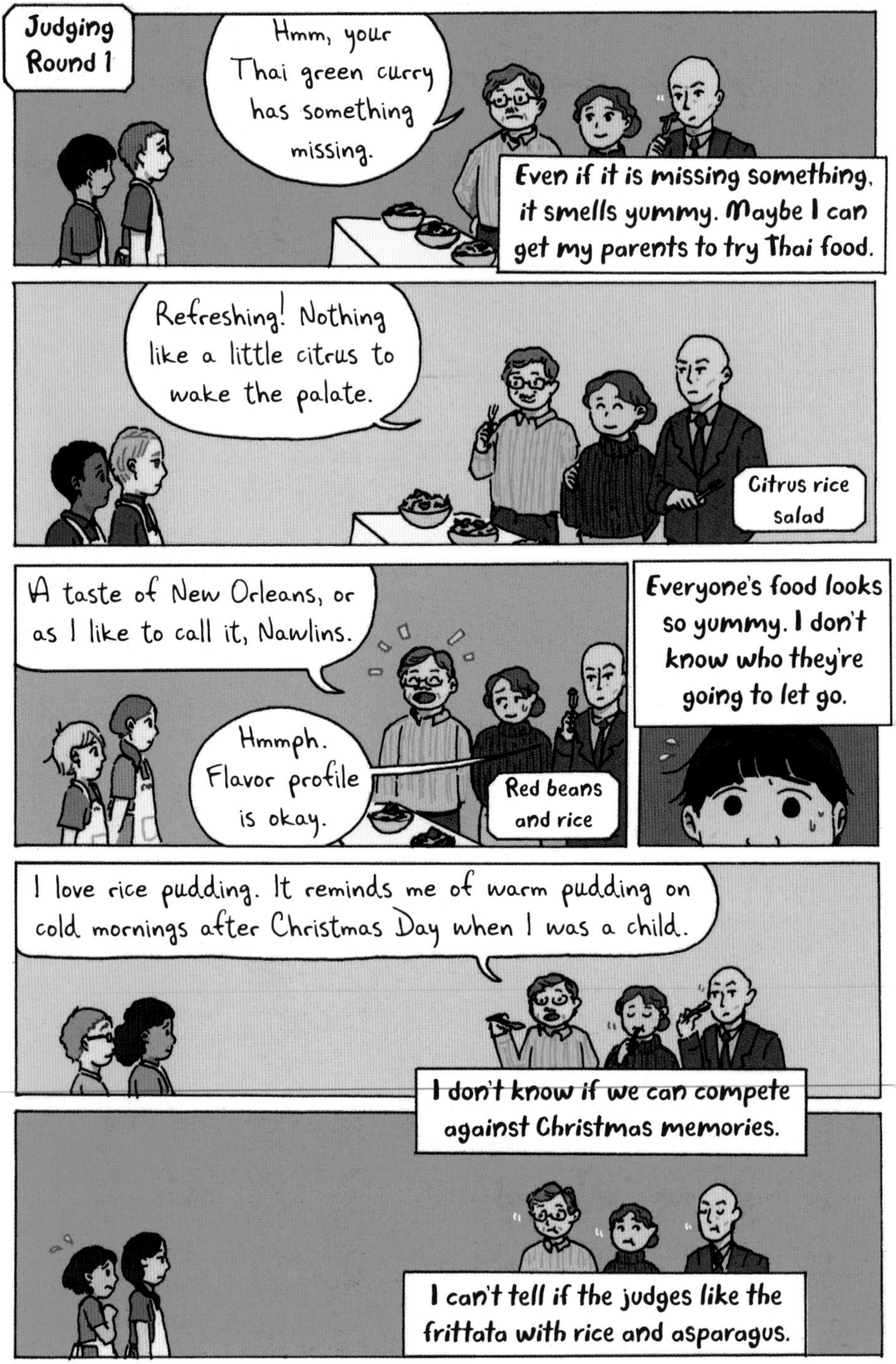
Judging Round 1
Hmm, your Thai green curry has something missing.
Even if it is missing something, it smells yummy. Maybe I can get my parents to try Thai food.
Refreshing! Nothing like a little citrus to wake the palate.
Citrus rice salad
A taste of New Orleans, or as I like to call it, Nawlins.
Hmmph. Flavor profile is okay.
Red beans and rice
Everyone's food looks so yummy. I don't know who they're going to let go.
I love rice pudding. It reminds me of warm pudding on cold mornings after Christmas Day when I was a child.
I don't know if we can compete against Christmas memories.
I can't tell if the judges like the frittata with rice and asparagus.

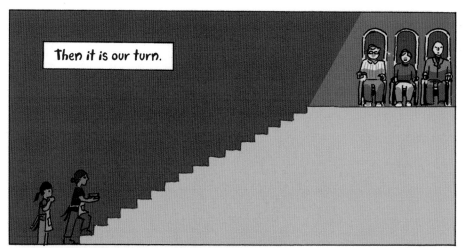

Then it is our turn.

Somehow the walk to the judges takes forever.

And then in a split second, ready or not, we're there.

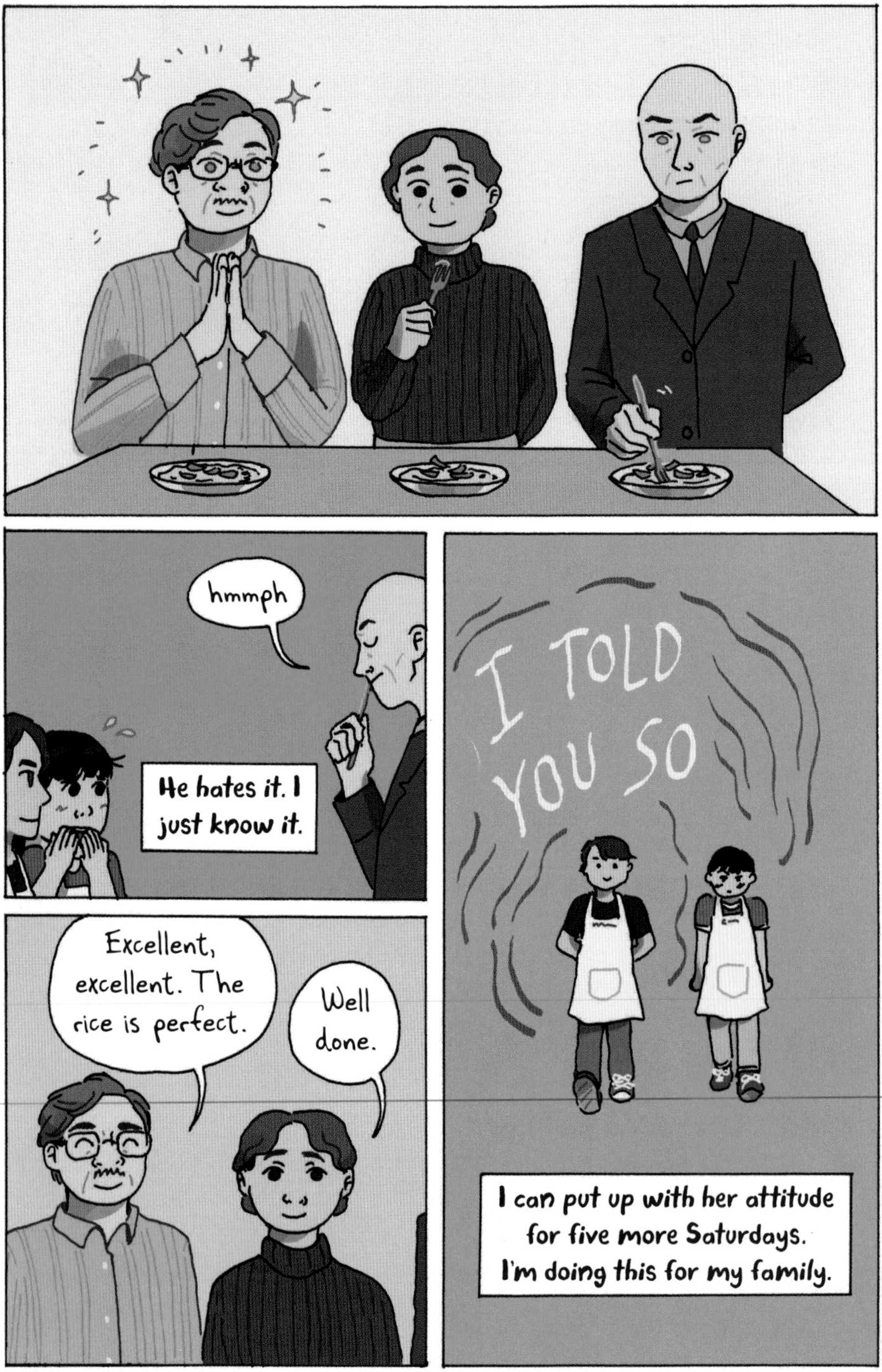
hmmph
He hates it. I just know it.
Excellent, excellent. The rice is perfect.
Well done.
I TOLD YOU SO
I can put up with her attitude for five more Saturdays. I'm doing this for my family.

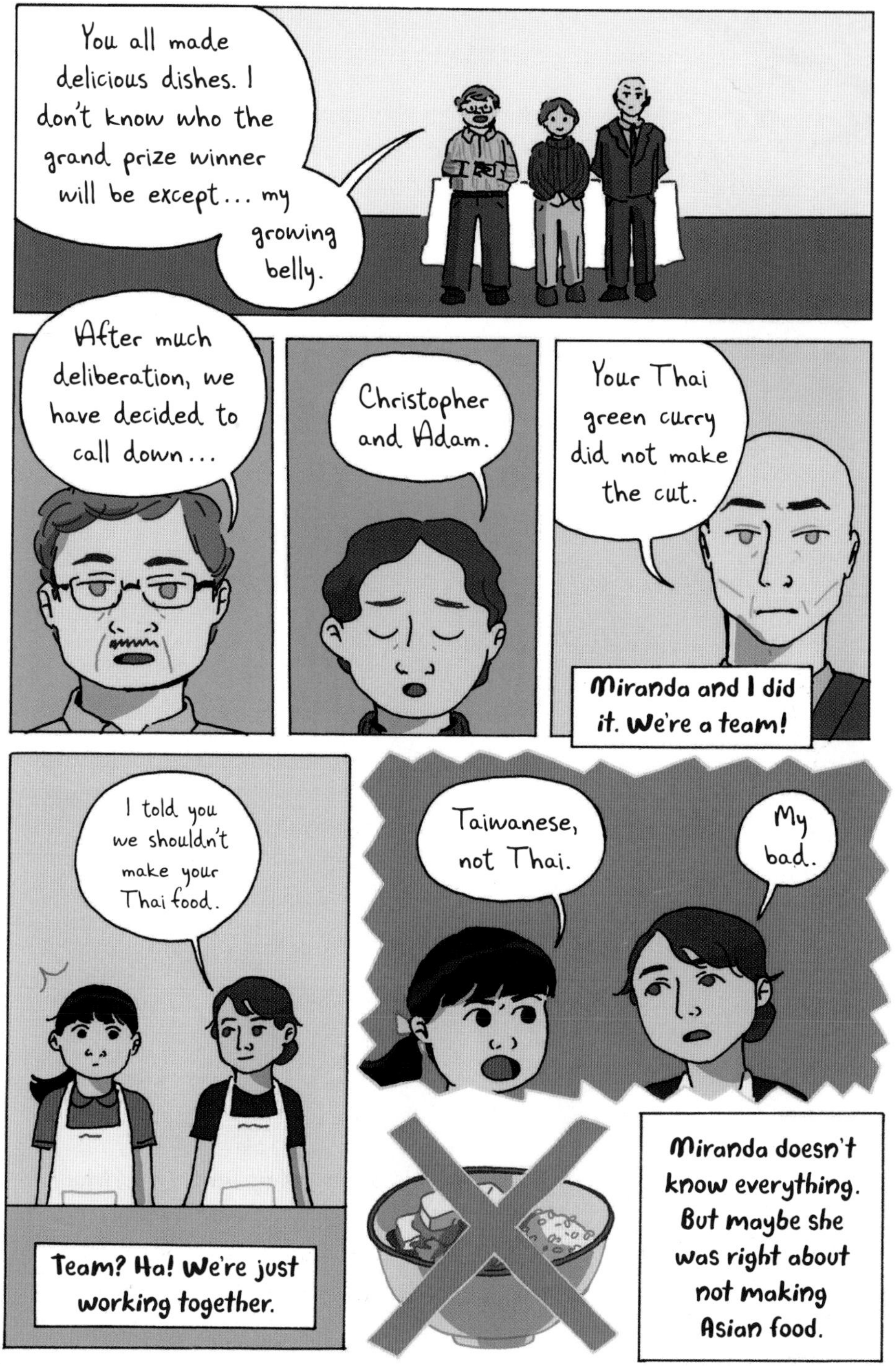
You all made delicious dishes. I don't know who the grand prize winner will be except... my growing belly.
After much deliberation, we have decided to call down...
Christopher and Adam.
Your Thai green curry did not make the cut.
Miranda and I did it. We're a team!
I told you we shouldn't make your Thai food.
Team? Ha! We're just working together.
Taiwanese, not Thai.
My bad.
Miranda doesn't know everything. But maybe she was right about not making Asian food.

Chapter 8

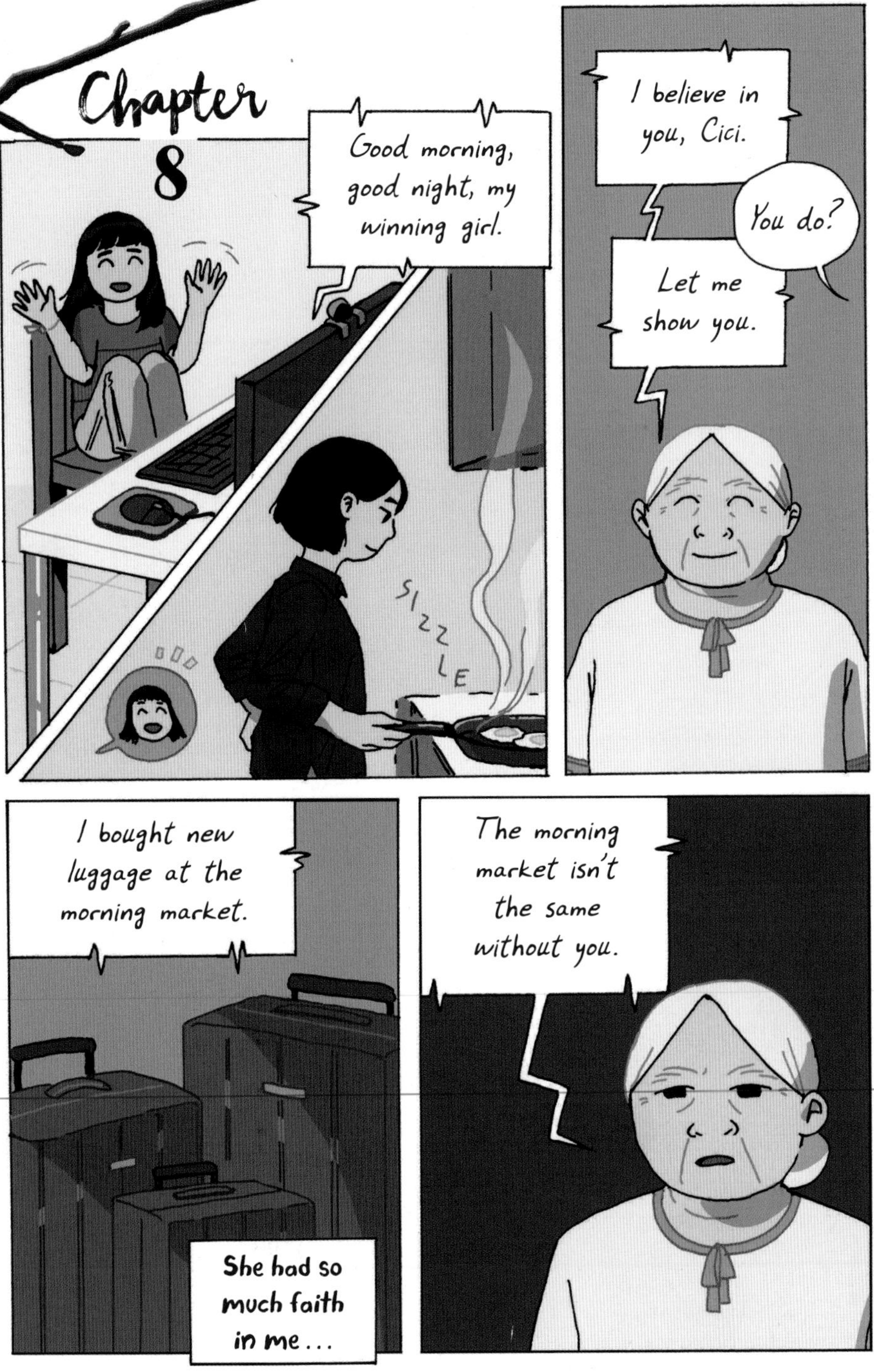
Good morning, good night, my winning girl.
SIZZLE
I believe in you, Cici.
You do?
Let me show you.
I bought new luggage at the morning market.
She had so much faith in me...
The morning market isn't the same without you.

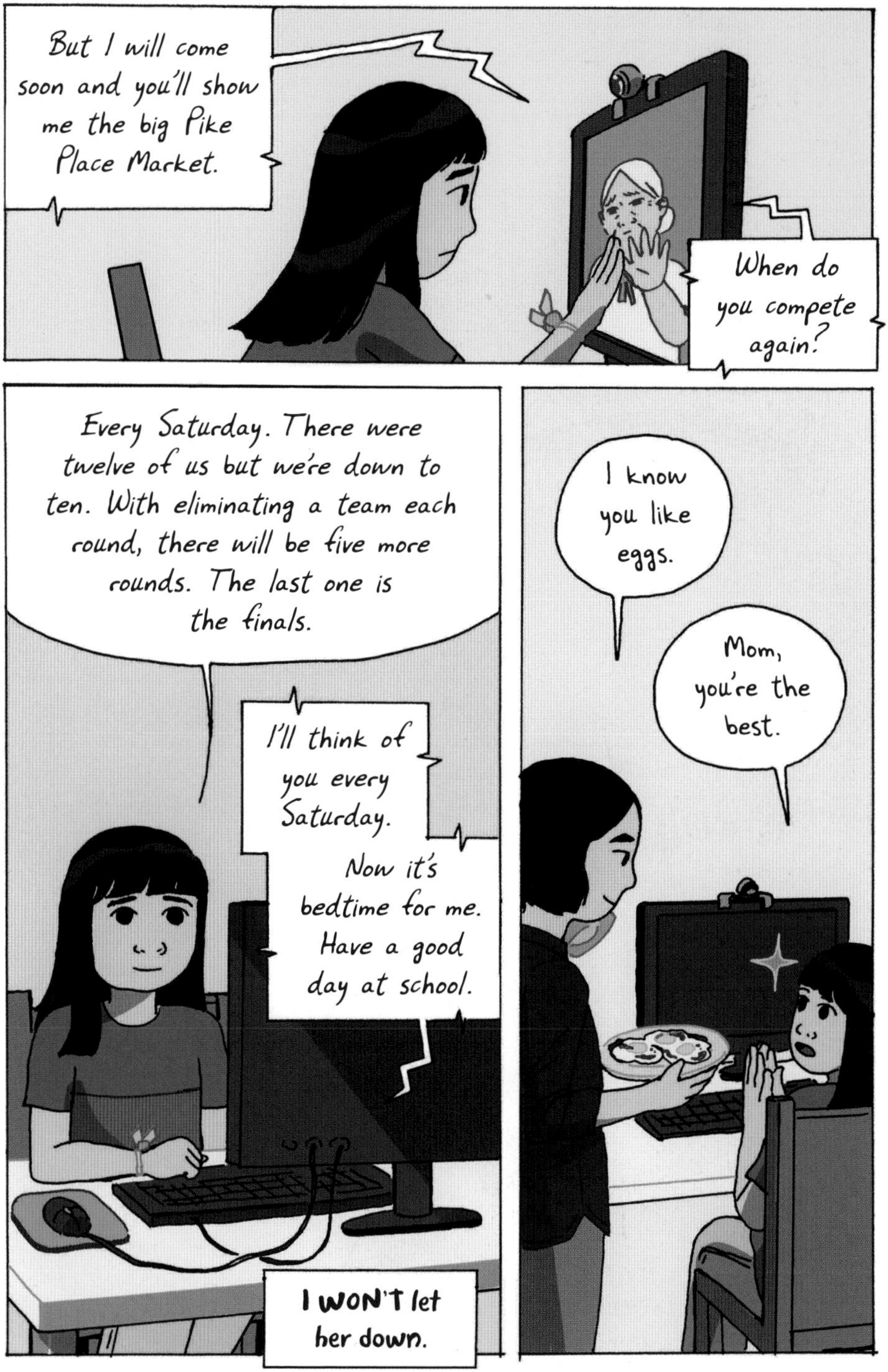
But I will come soon and you'll show me the big Pike Place Market.
When do you compete again?
Every Saturday. There were twelve of us but we're down to ten. With eliminating a team each round, there will be five more rounds. The last one is the finals.
I'll think of you every Saturday.
Now it's bedtime for me. Have a good day at school.
I WON'T let her down.
I know you like eggs.
Mom, you're the best.

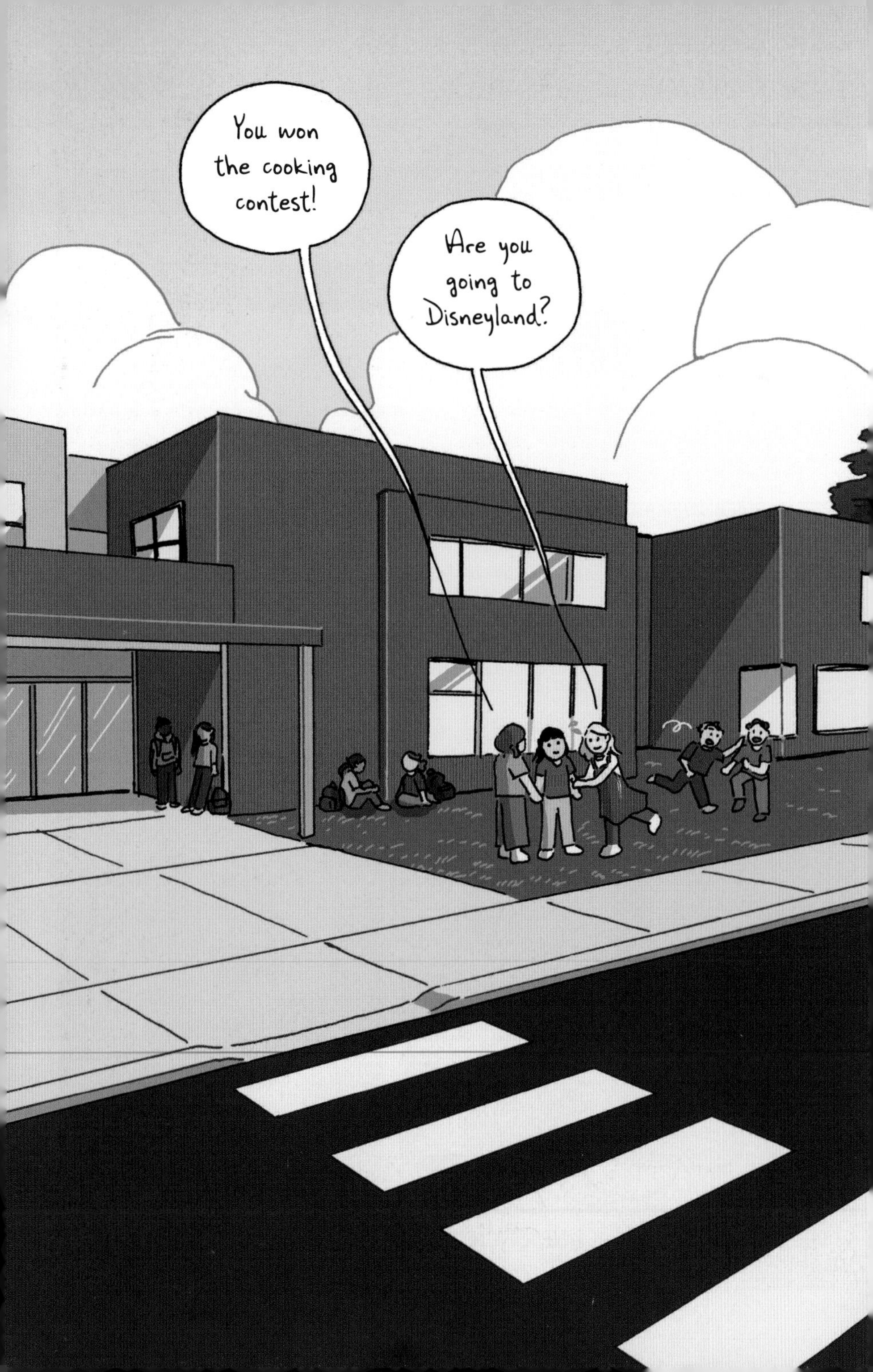
You won the cooking contest!
Are you going to Disneyland?

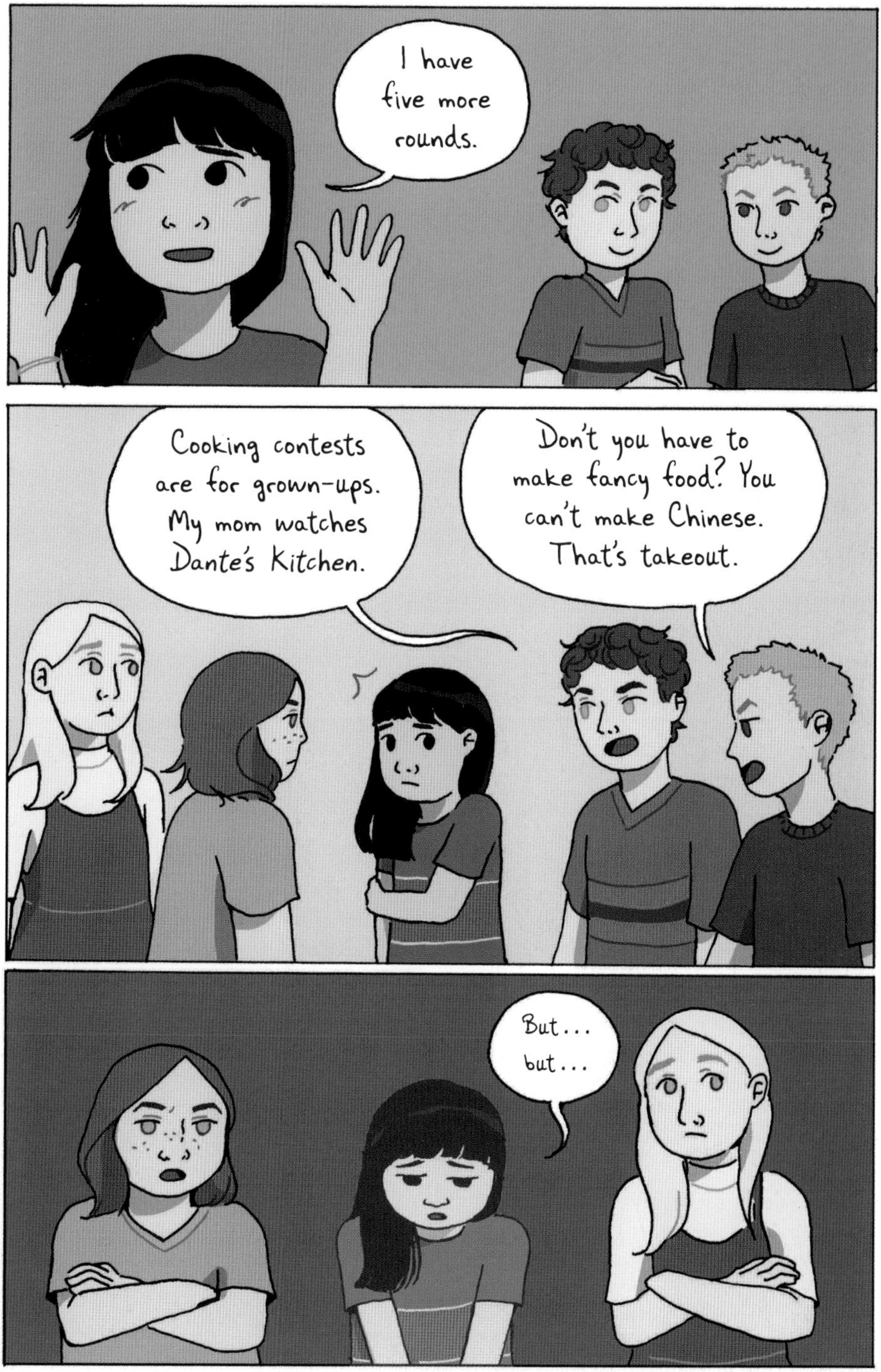
I have five more rounds.
Cooking contests are for grown-ups. My mom watches Dante's Kitchen.
Don't you have to make fancy food? You can't make Chinese. That's takeout.
But... but...

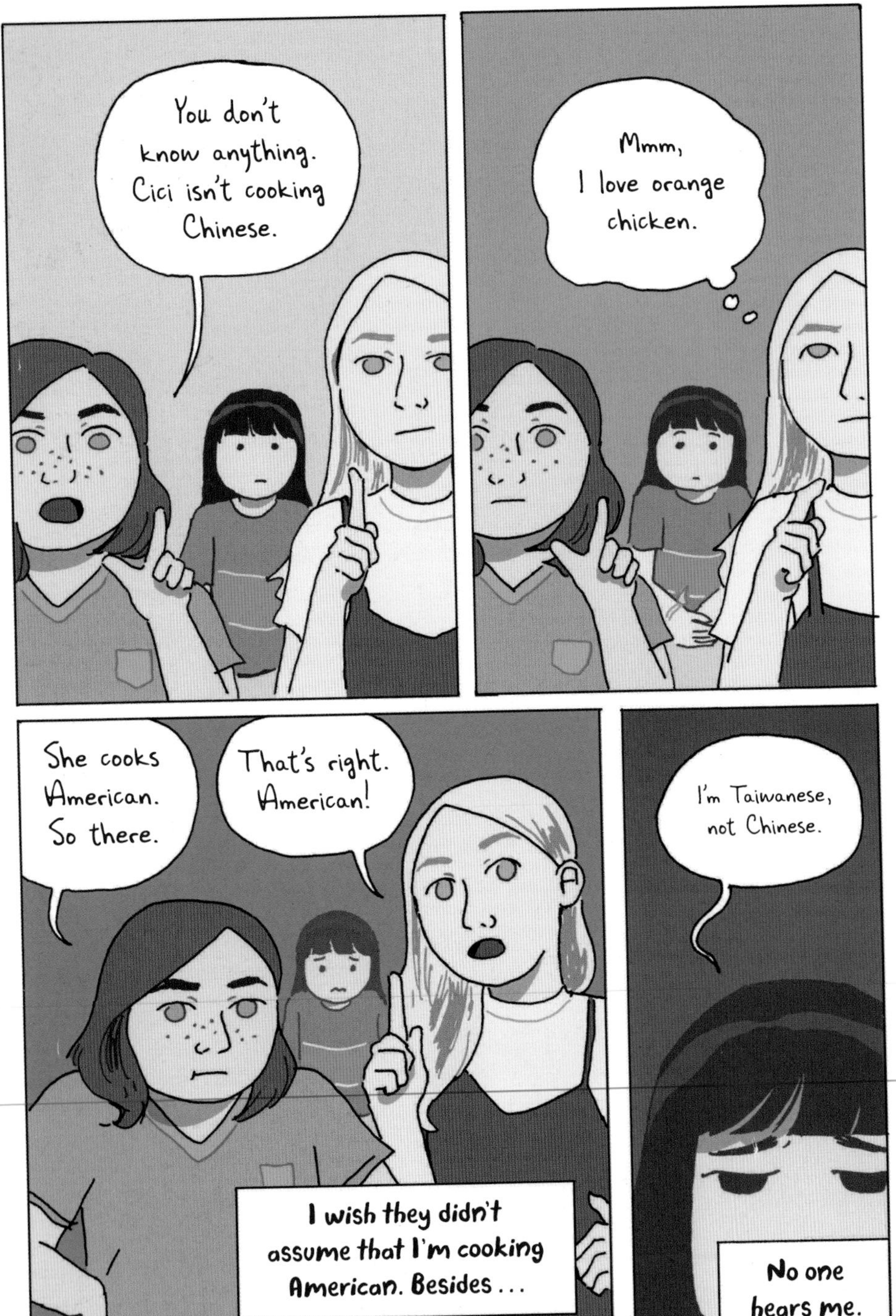

You don't know anything. Cici isn't cooking Chinese.
Mmm, I love orange chicken.
She cooks American. So there.
That's right. American!
I wish they didn't assume that I'm cooking American. Besides . . .
I'm Taiwanese, not Chinese.
No one hears me.

Chapter 9

ROUND 2

I've got Miranda, but is she enough?

We're going to win this.

Um, I hope we got this.

My dad always says hope is—

MIRANDA

CICI

snap

a dull blade.

I think her family motto just took mine to the mat.

GRADES COLLEGE JOB LIFE

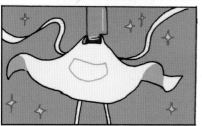

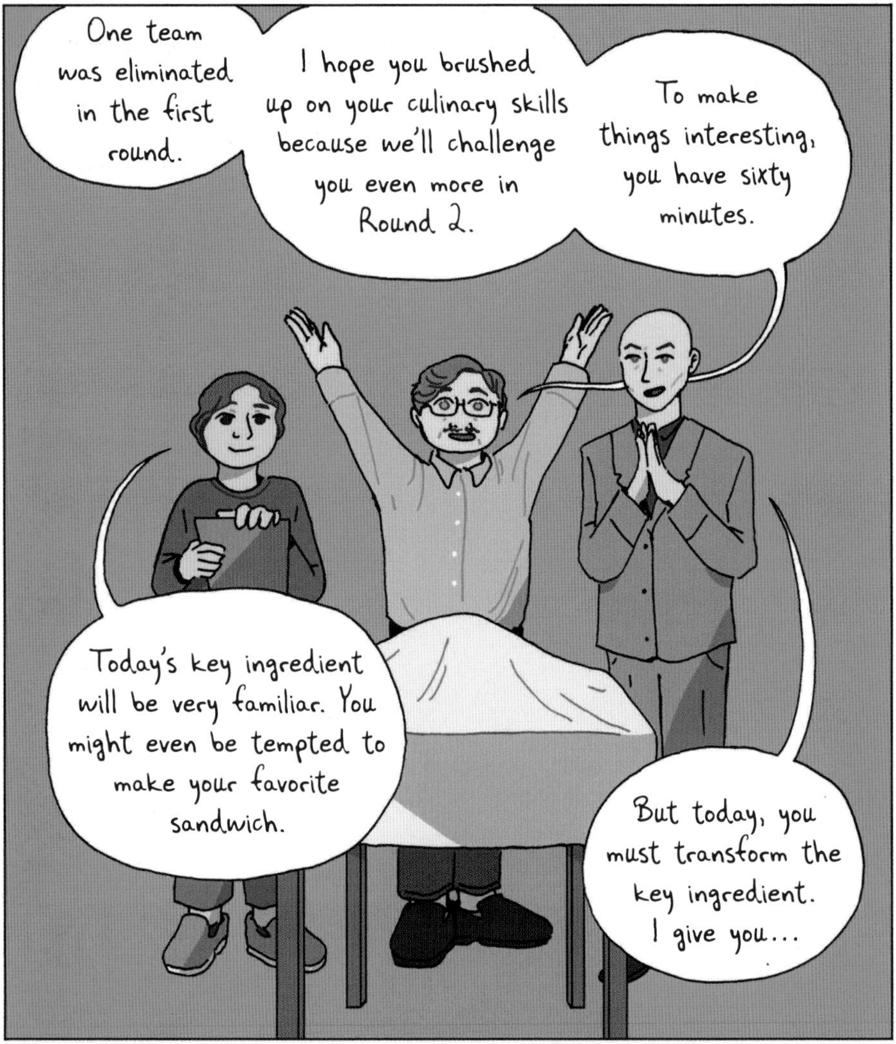
One team was eliminated in the first round.
I hope you brushed up on your culinary skills because we'll challenge you even more in Round 2.
To make things interesting, you have sixty minutes.
Today's key ingredient will be very familiar. You might even be tempted to make your favorite sandwich.
But today, you must transform the key ingredient. I give you...

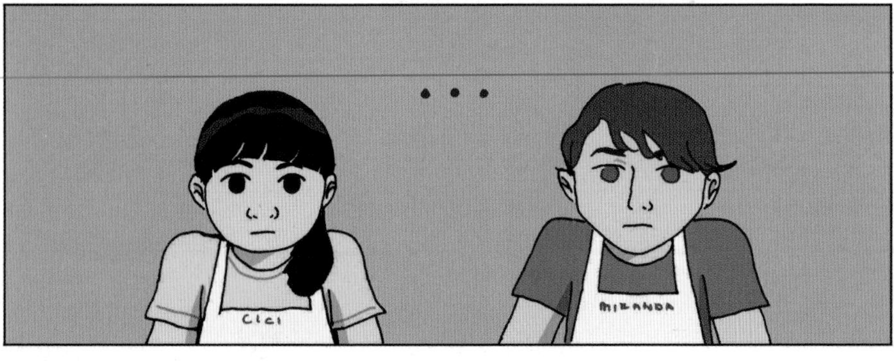
...
CICI
MIRANDA

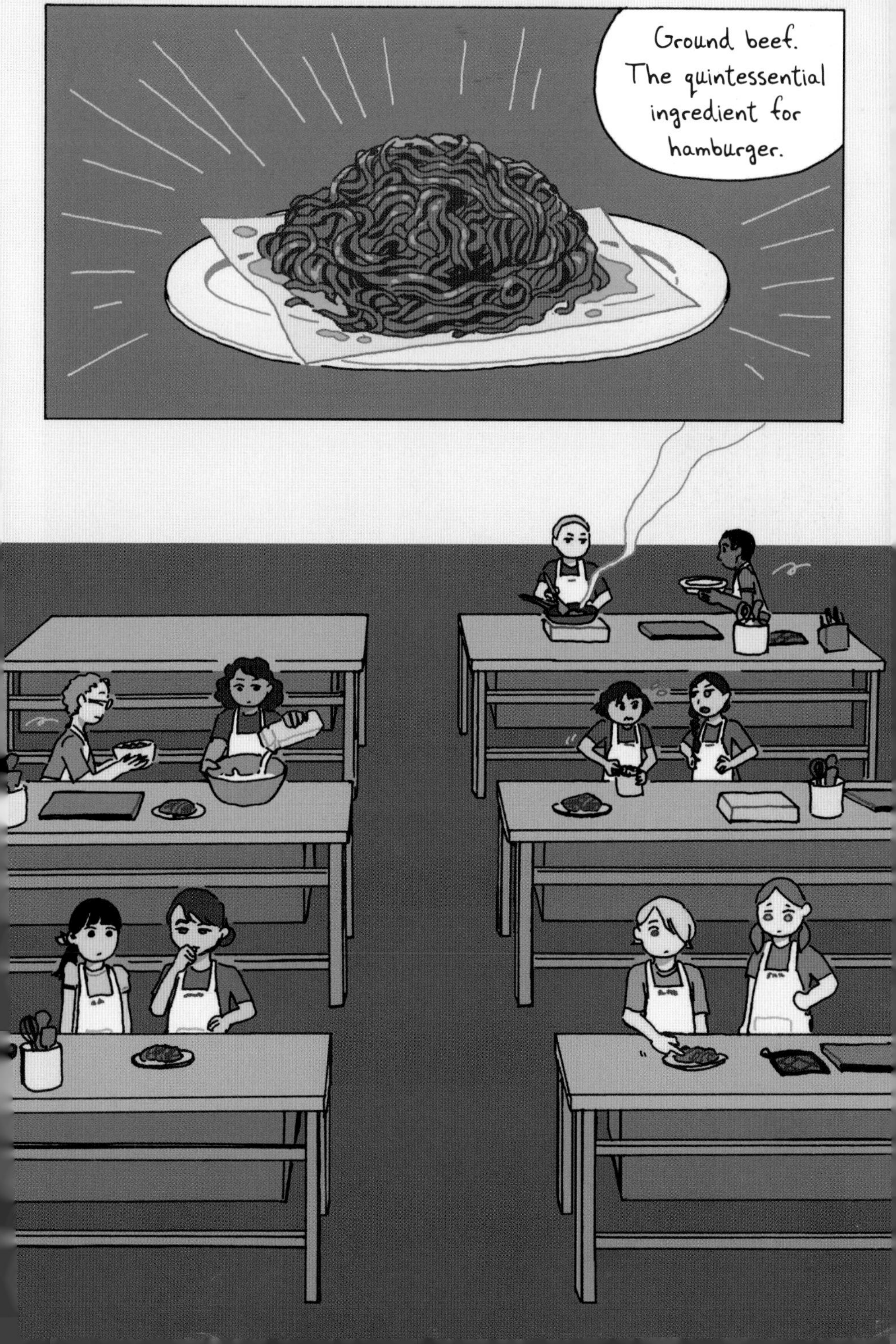
Ground beef. The quintessential ingredient for hamburger.

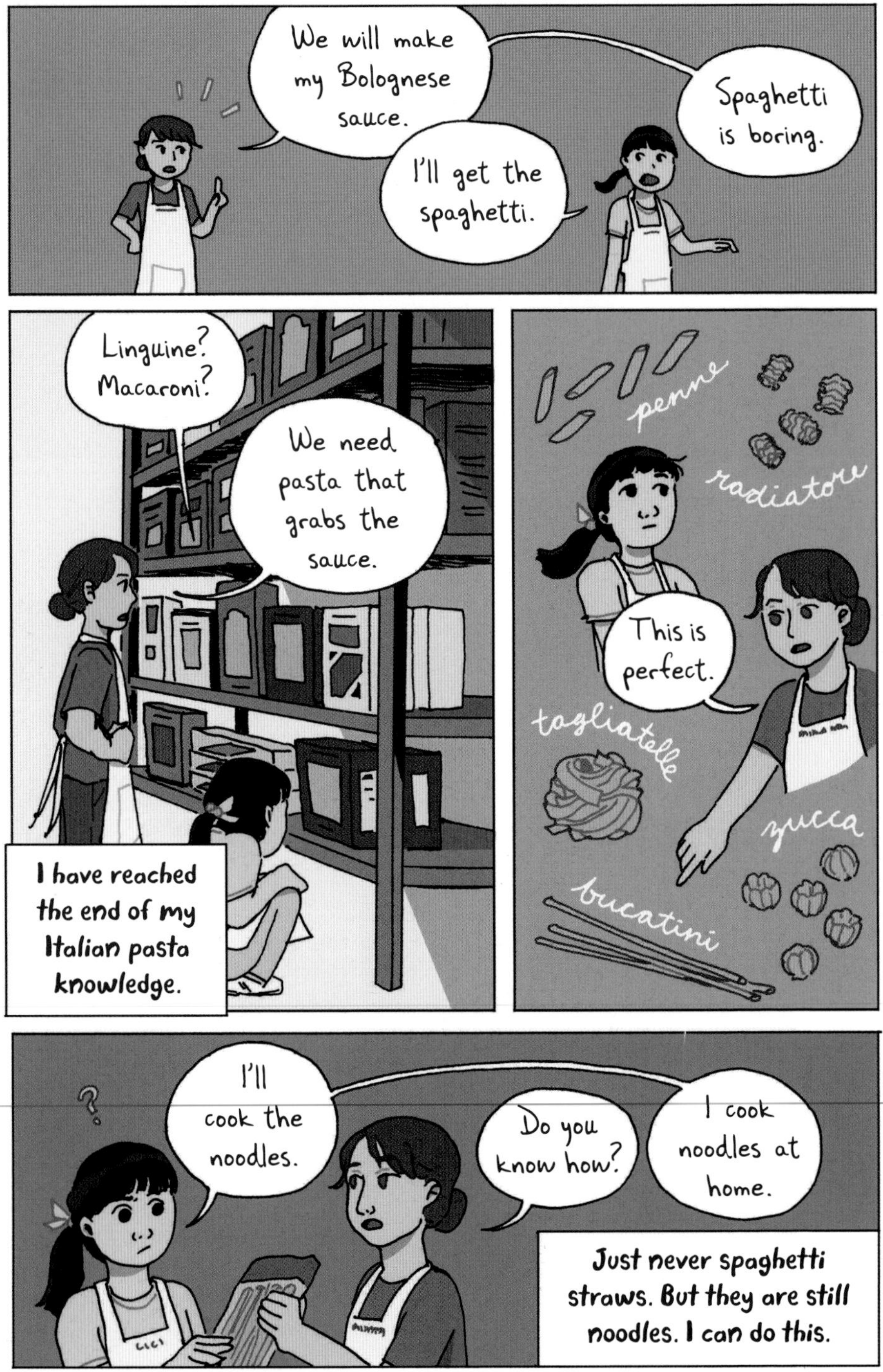

We will make my Bolognese sauce.
Spaghetti is boring.
I'll get the spaghetti.
Linguine? Macaroni?
We need pasta that grabs the sauce.
I have reached the end of my Italian pasta knowledge.
penne
radiatore
This is perfect.
tagliatelle
zucca
bucatini
I'll cook the noodles.
Do you know how?
I cook noodles at home.
Just never spaghetti straws. But they are still noodles. I can do this.

I help Miranda gather the rest of the ingredients.

My heart thumps in nervous time.

I'll chop onions and you brown the meat.

You're like a samurai.

With a lot of practice, I could work the knife like her.

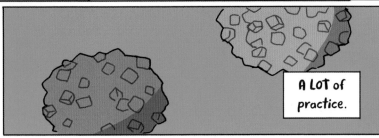

A LOT of practice.

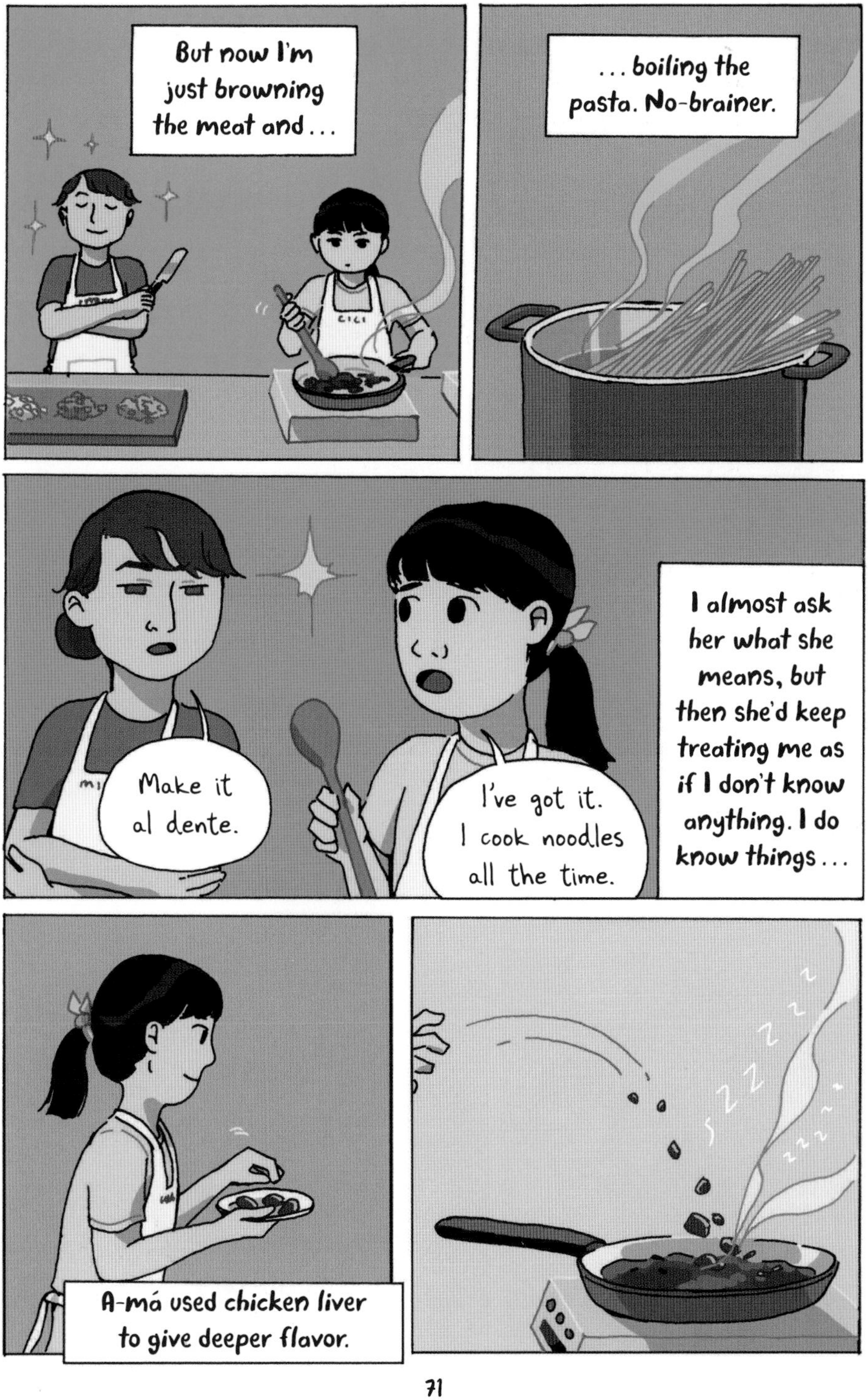
But now I'm just browning the meat and . . .
. . . boiling the pasta. No-brainer.
Make it al dente.
I've got it. I cook noodles all the time.
I almost ask her what she means, but then she'd keep treating me as if I don't know anything. I do know things . . .
A-má used chicken liver to give deeper flavor.

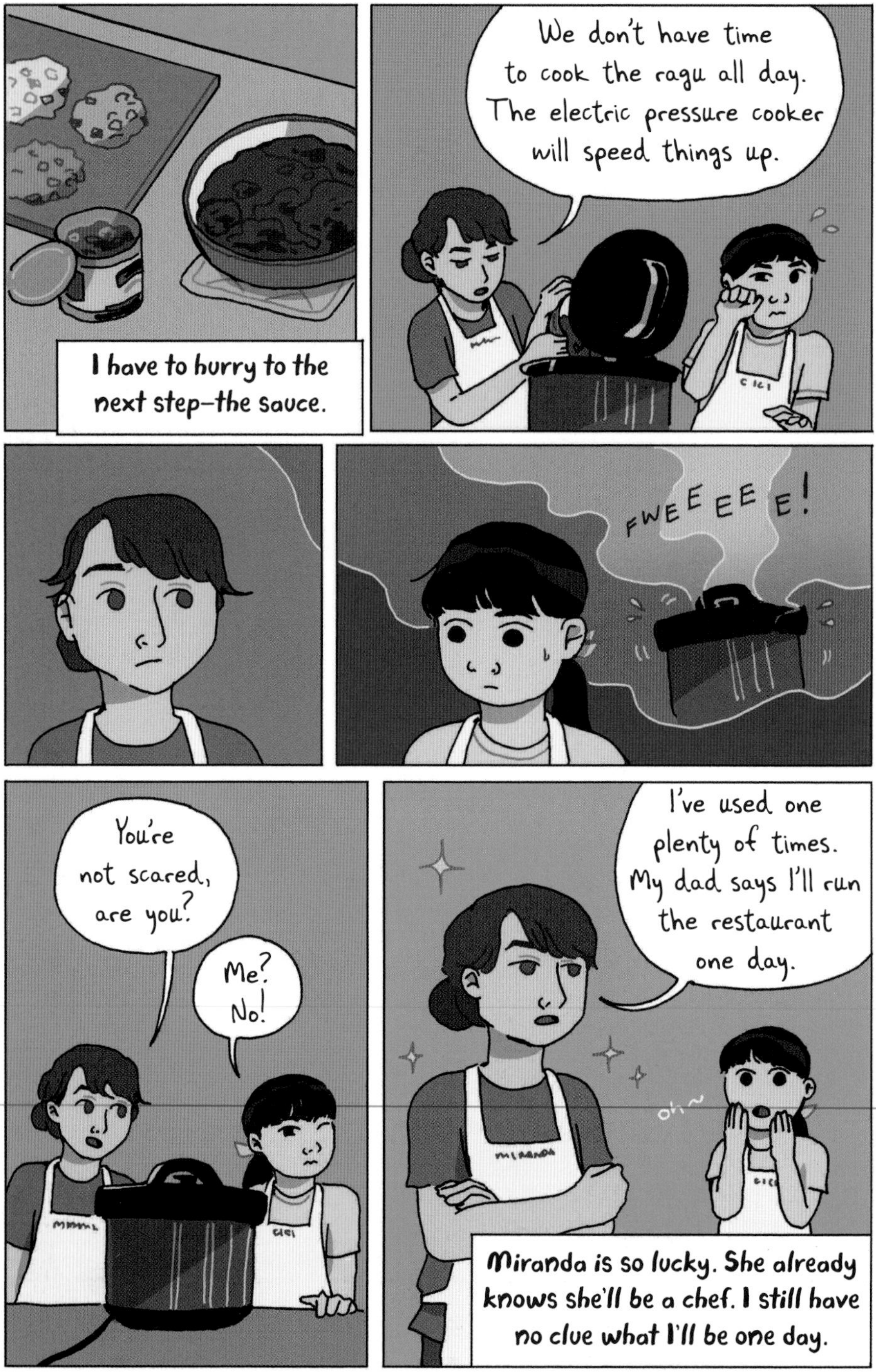
I have to hurry to the next step–the sauce.
We don't have time to cook the ragu all day. The electric pressure cooker will speed things up.
FWEEEEEE!
You're not scared, are you?
Me? No!
I've used one plenty of times. My dad says I'll run the restaurant one day.
Miranda is so lucky. She already knows she'll be a chef. I still have no clue what I'll be one day.

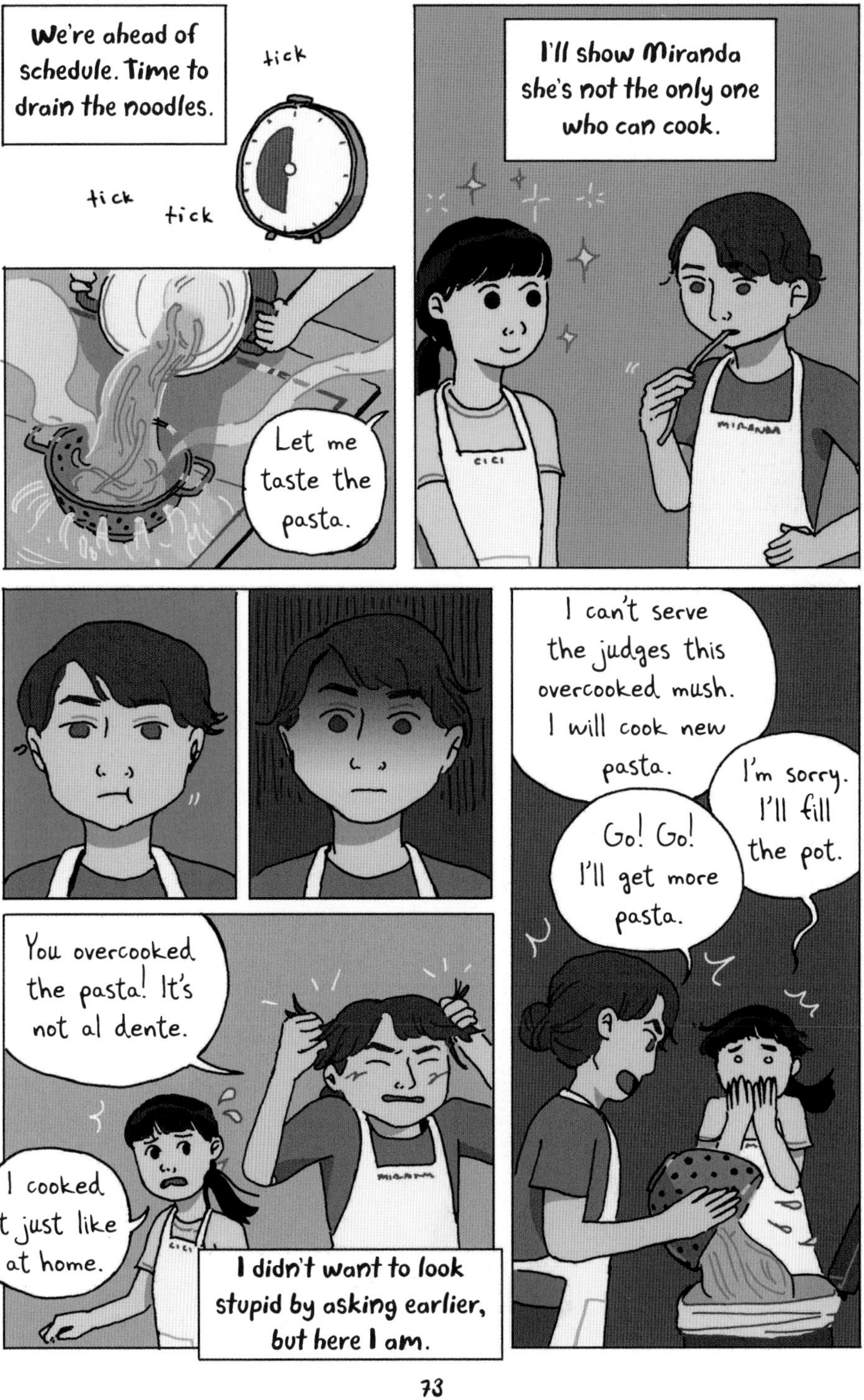

We're ahead of schedule. Time to drain the noodles.
tick
tick
tick
Let me taste the pasta.
I'll show Miranda she's not the only one who can cook.
CICI
MIRANDA
You overcooked the pasta! It's not al dente.
I cooked it just like at home.
I didn't want to look stupid by asking earlier, but here I am.
I can't serve the judges this overcooked mush. I will cook new pasta.
I'm sorry. I'll fill the pot.
Go! Go! I'll get more pasta.

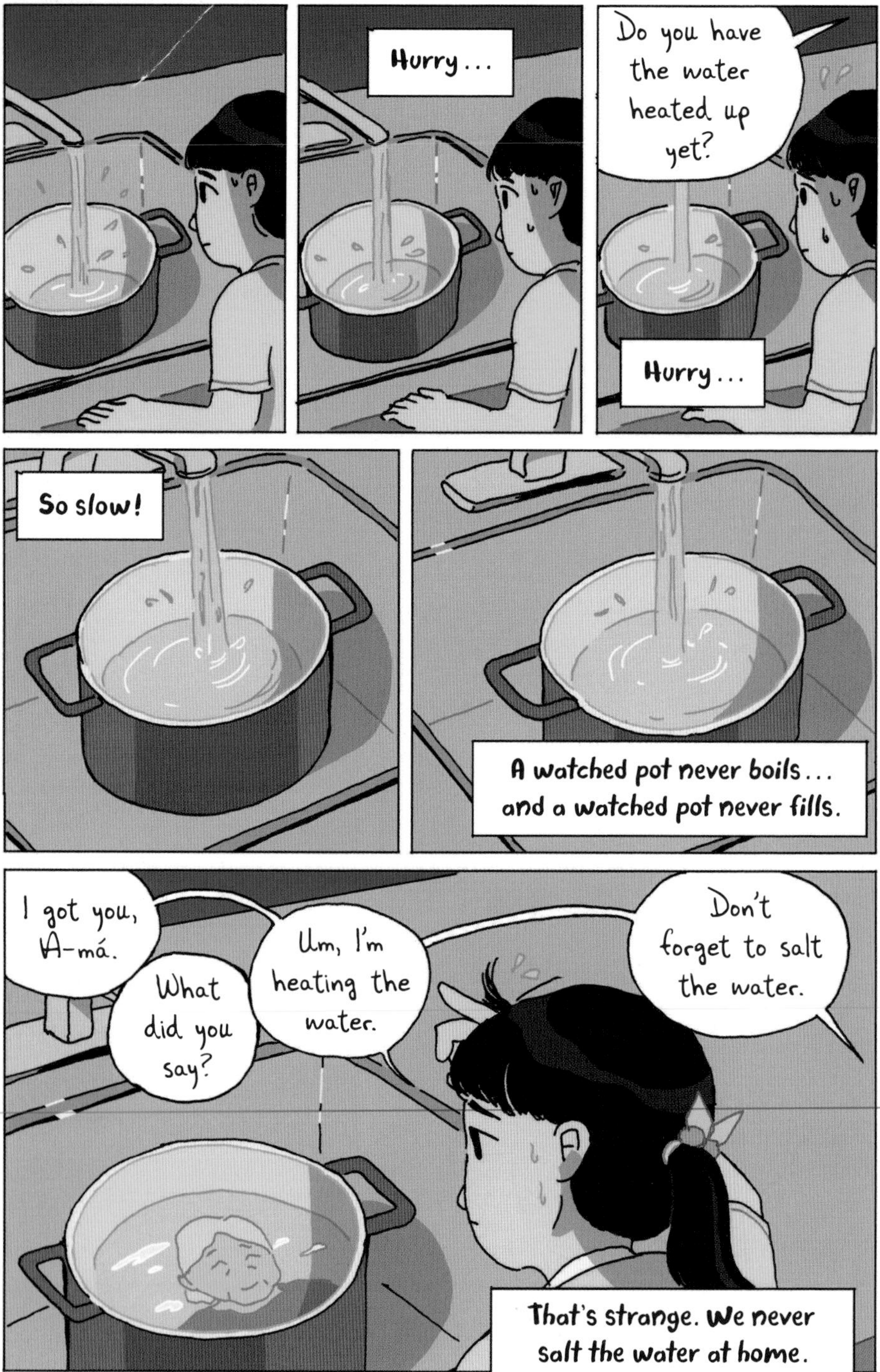
Hurry...
Do you have the water heated up yet?
Hurry...
So slow!
A watched pot never boils... and a watched pot never fills.
I got you, A-má.
What did you say?
Um, I'm heating the water.
Don't forget to salt the water.
That's strange. We never salt the water at home.

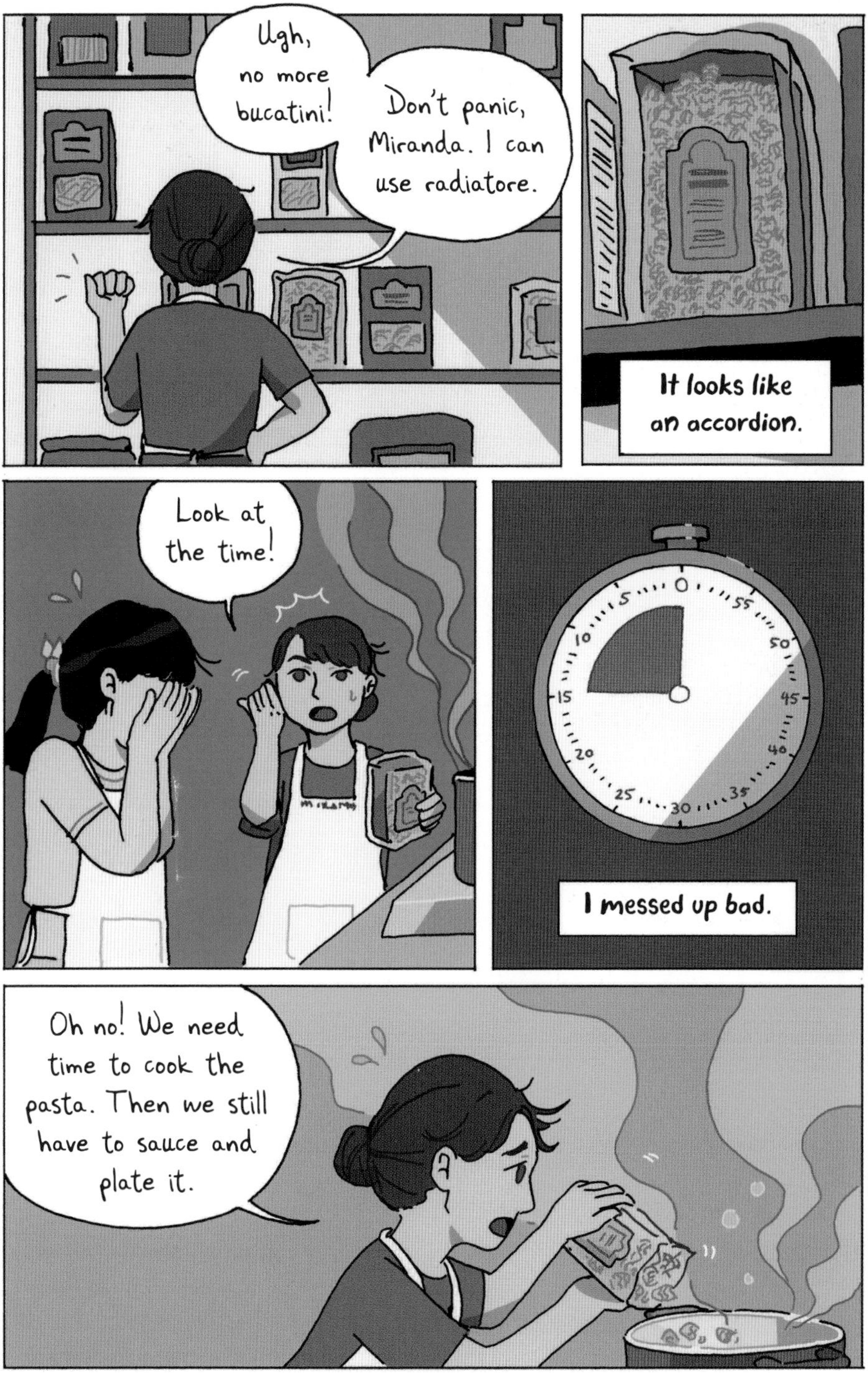
Ugh, no more bucatini!
Don't panic, Miranda. I can use radiatore.
It looks like an accordion.
Look at the time!
I messed up bad.
Oh no! We need time to cook the pasta. Then we still have to sauce and plate it.

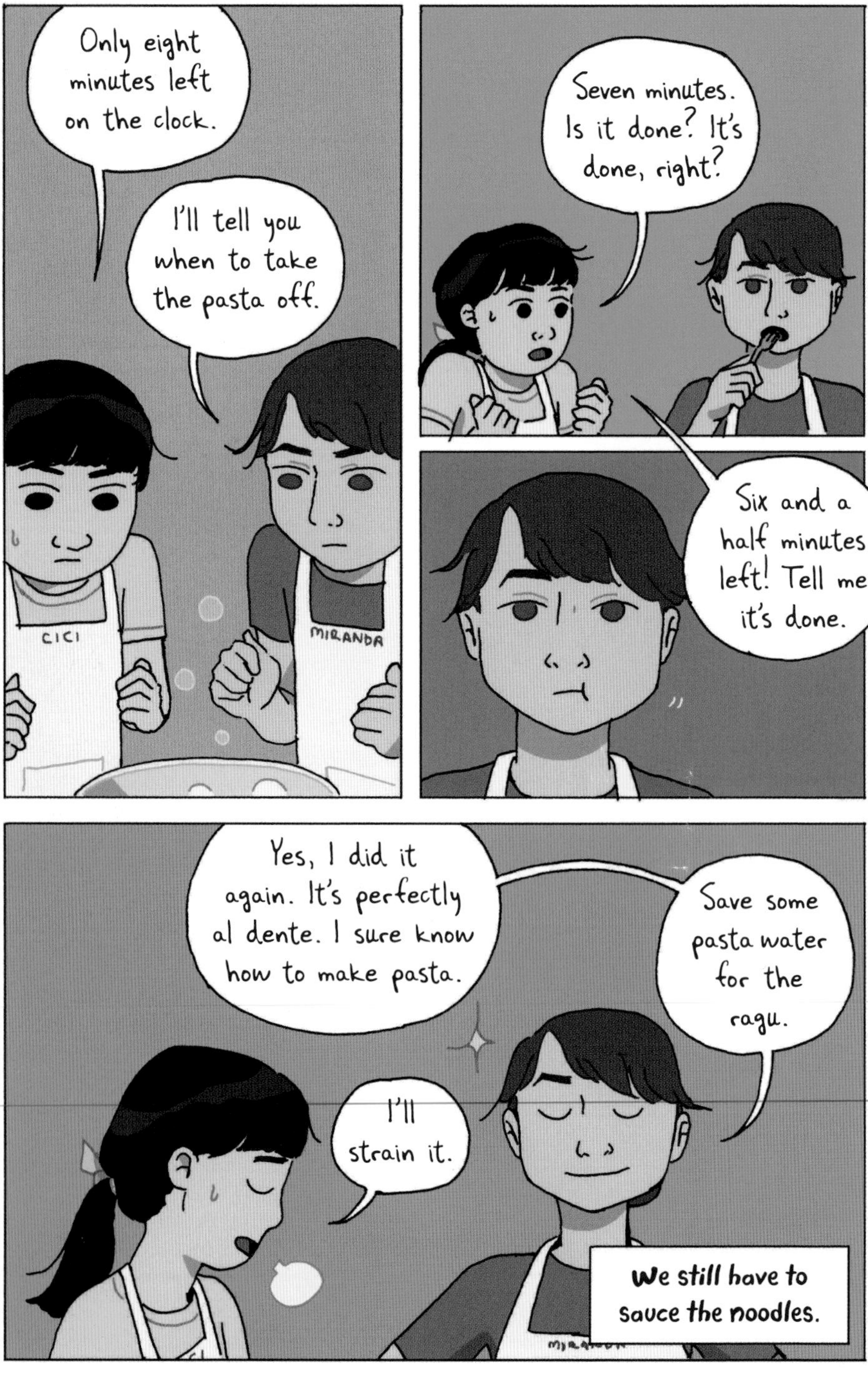
Only eight minutes left on the clock.
I'll tell you when to take the pasta off.
CICI
MIRANDA
Seven minutes. Is it done? It's done, right?
Six and a half minutes left! Tell me it's done.
Yes, I did it again. It's perfectly al dente. I sure know how to make pasta.
Save some pasta water for the ragu.
I'll strain it.
We still have to sauce the noodles.

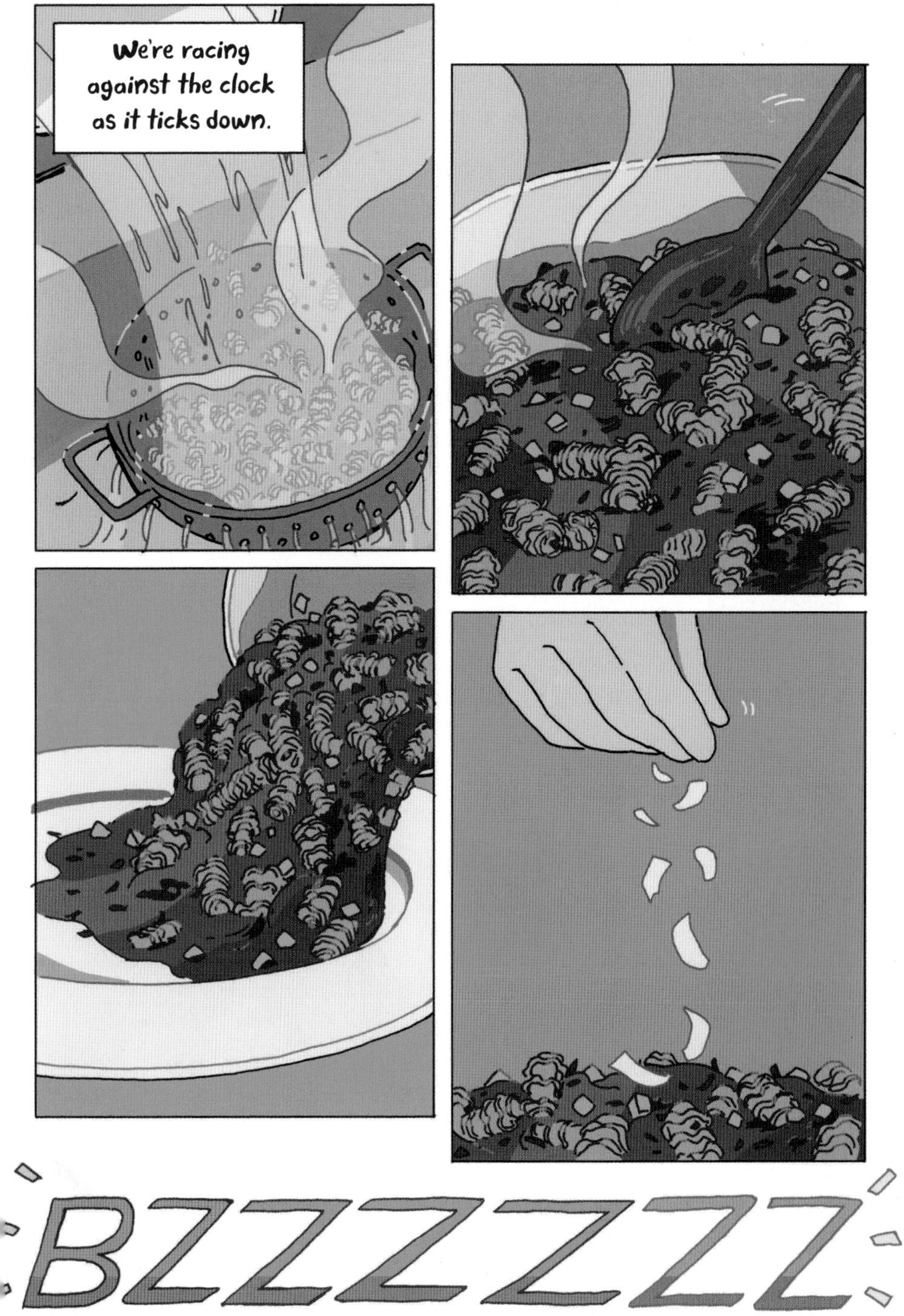
We're racing against the clock as it ticks down.
BZZZZZZ

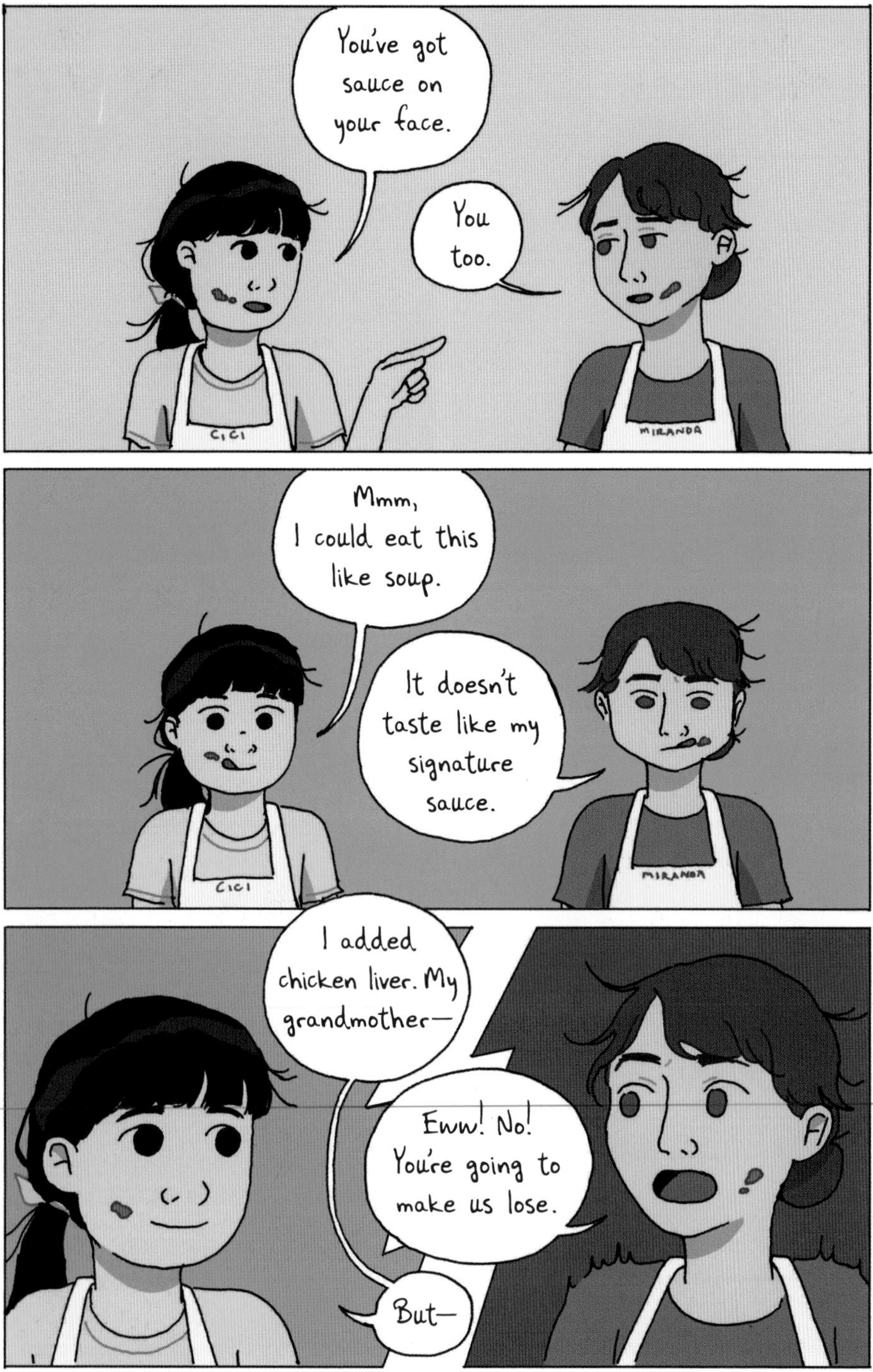
CICI
MIRANDA
You've got sauce on your face.
You too.
Mmm, I could eat this like soup.
It doesn't taste like my signature sauce.
CICI
MIRANDA
I added chicken liver. My grandmother—
Eww! No! You're going to make us lose.
But—

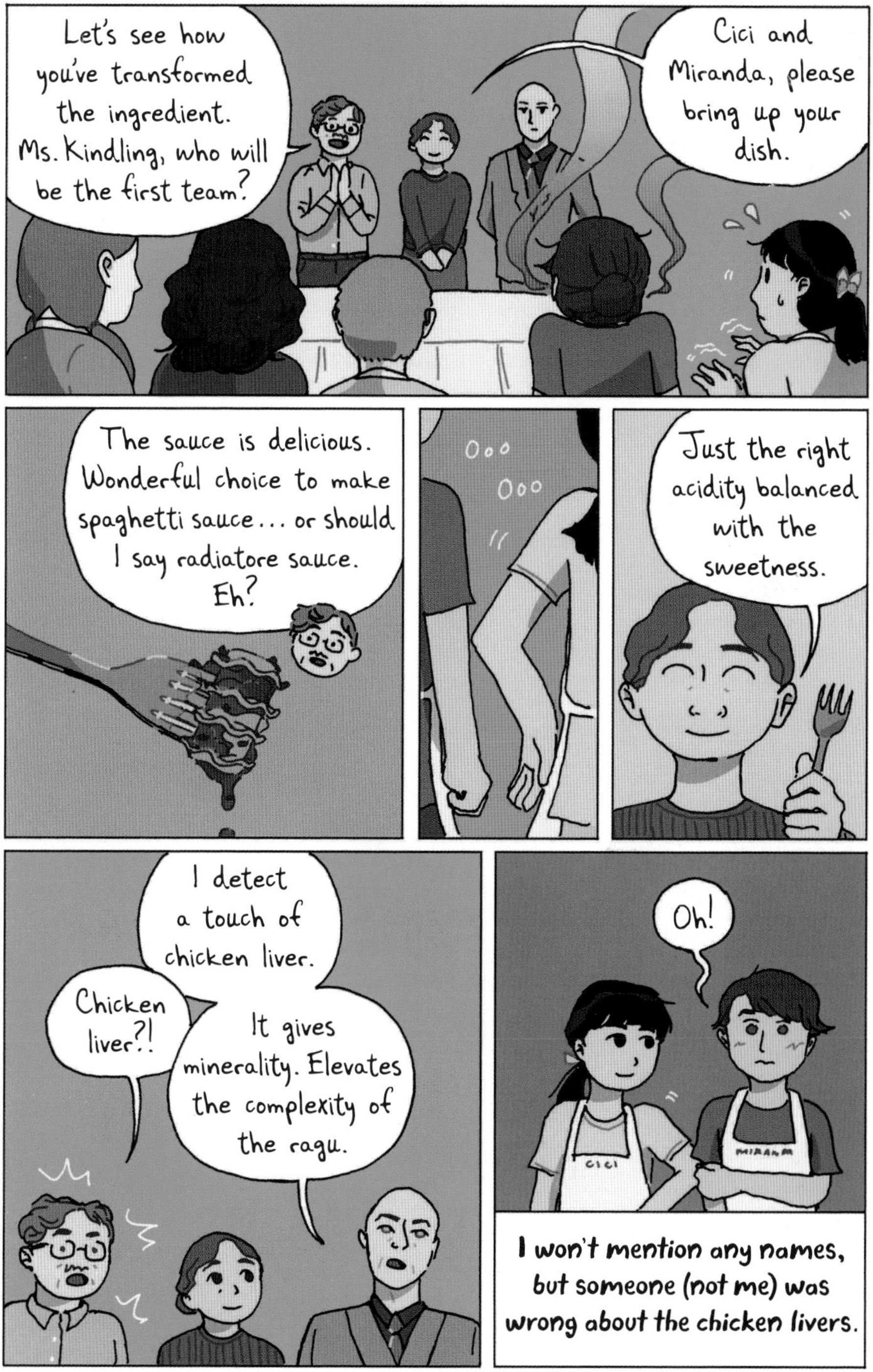
Let's see how you've transformed the ingredient. Ms. Kindling, who will be the first team?
Cici and Miranda, please bring up your dish.
The sauce is delicious. Wonderful choice to make spaghetti sauce... or should I say radiatore sauce. Eh?
Ooo
Ooo
Just the right acidity balanced with the sweetness.
I detect a touch of chicken liver.
Chicken liver?!
It gives minerality. Elevates the complexity of the ragu.
Oh!
CICI
MIRANDA
I won't mention any names, but someone (not me) was wrong about the chicken livers.

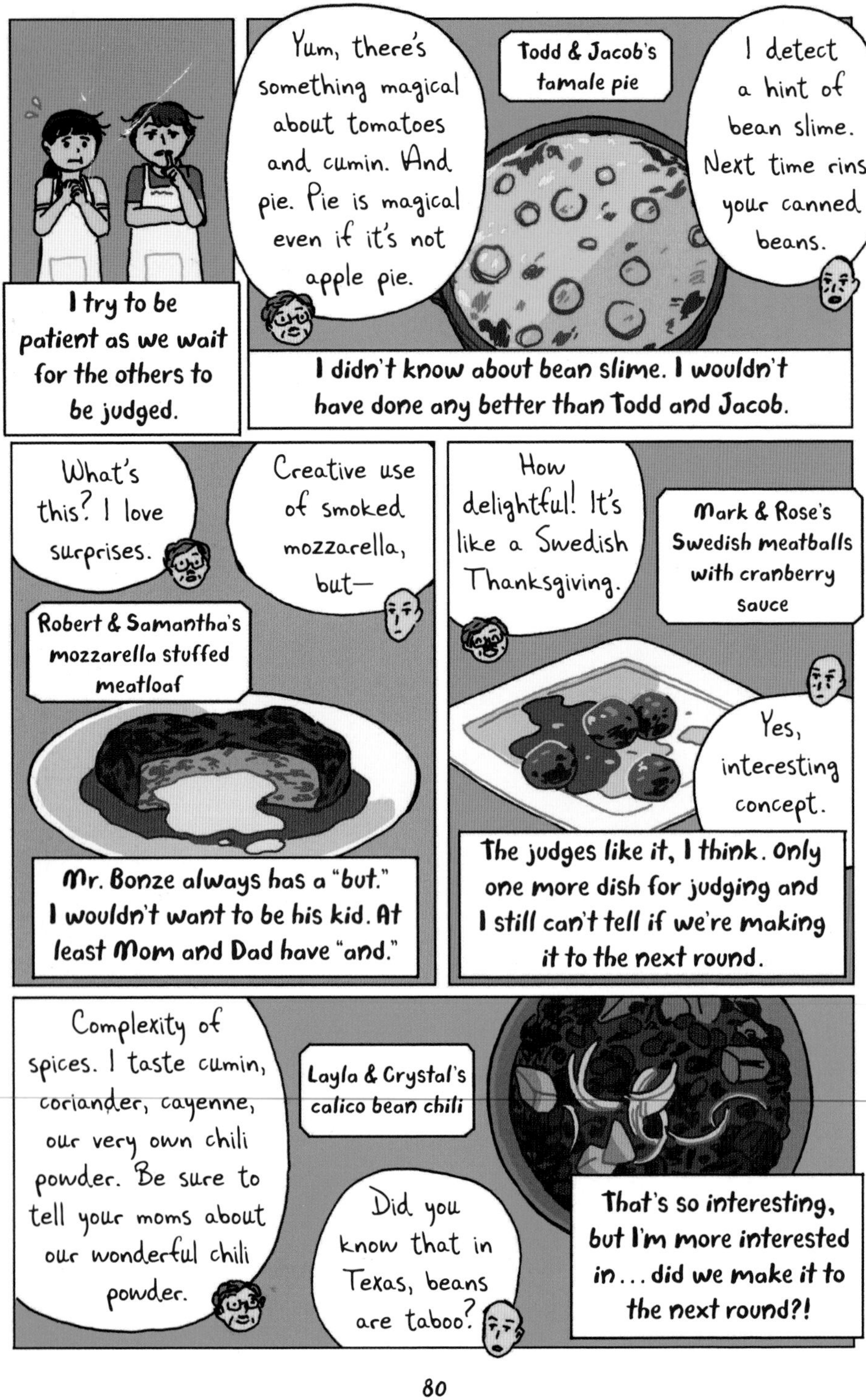
I try to be patient as we wait for the others to be judged.
Yum, there's something magical about tomatoes and cumin. And pie. Pie is magical even if it's not apple pie.
Todd & Jacob's tamale pie
I detect a hint of bean slime. Next time rinse your canned beans.
I didn't know about bean slime. I wouldn't have done any better than Todd and Jacob.
What's this? I love surprises.
Creative use of smoked mozzarella, but—
Robert & Samantha's mozzarella stuffed meatloaf
Mr. Bonze always has a "but." I wouldn't want to be his kid. At least Mom and Dad have "and."
How delightful! It's like a Swedish Thanksgiving.
Mark & Rose's Swedish meatballs with cranberry sauce
Yes, interesting concept.
The judges like it, I think. Only one more dish for judging and I still can't tell if we're making it to the next round.
Complexity of spices. I taste cumin, coriander, cayenne, our very own chili powder. Be sure to tell your moms about our wonderful chili powder.
Layla & Crystal's calico bean chili
Did you know that in Texas, beans are taboo?
That's so interesting, but I'm more interested in... did we make it to the next round?!

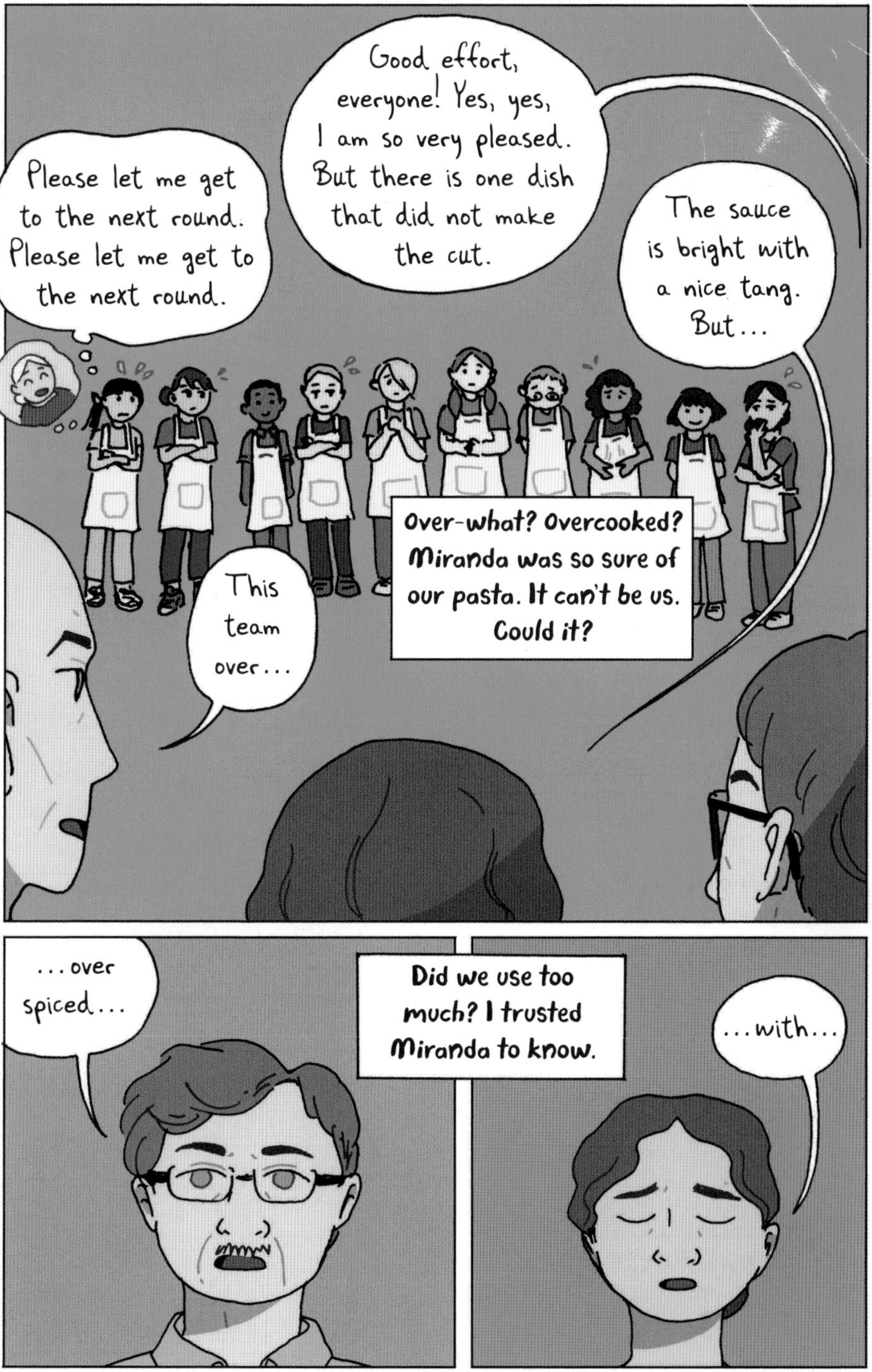
Please let me get to the next round. Please let me get to the next round.
Good effort, everyone! Yes, yes, I am so very pleased. But there is one dish that did not make the cut.
The sauce is bright with a nice tang. But...
This team over...
Over-what? Overcooked? Miranda was so sure of our pasta. It can't be us. Could it?
...over spiced...
Did we use too much? I trusted Miranda to know.
...with...

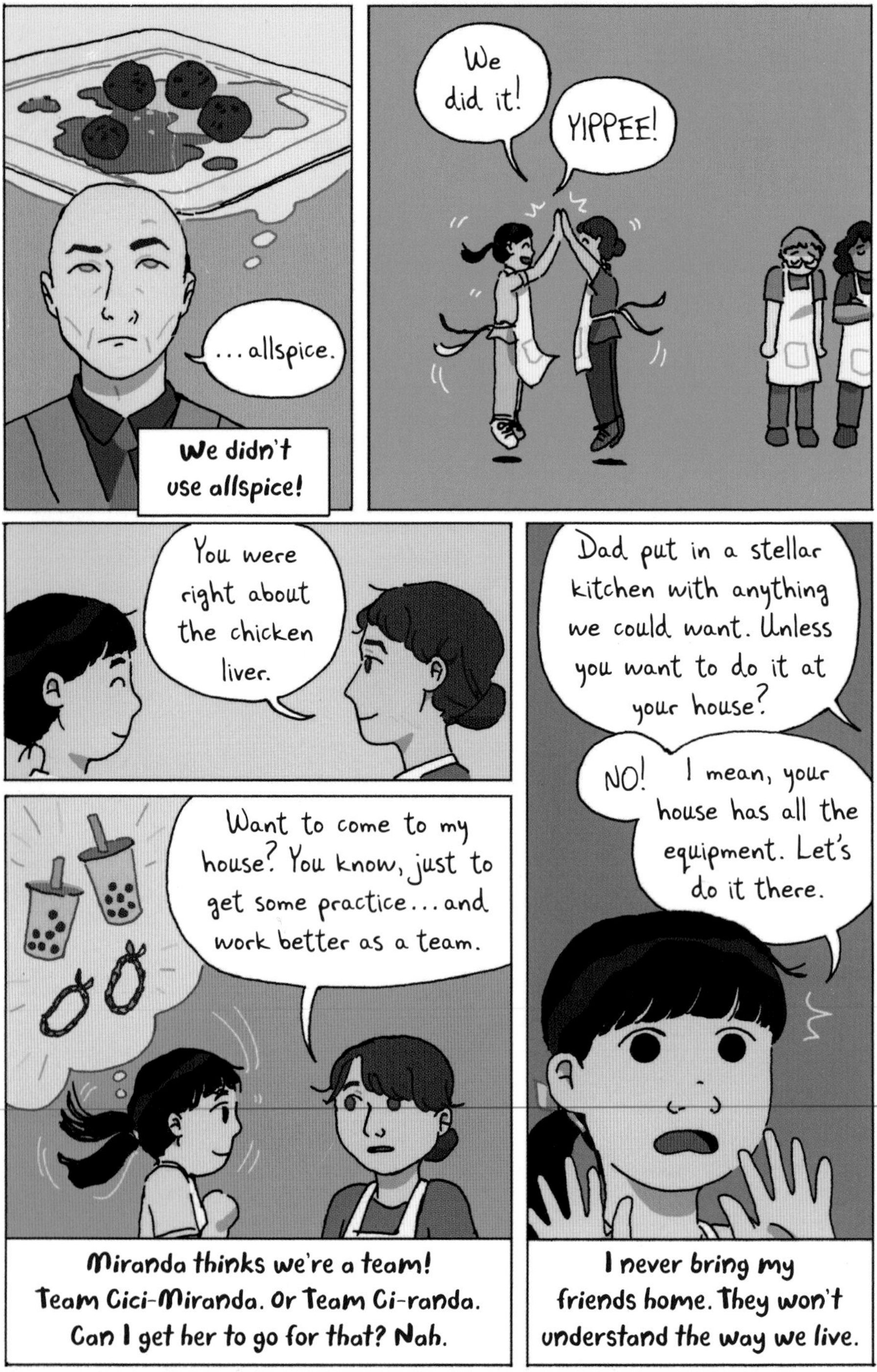

...allspice.
We didn't use allspice!
We did it!
YIPPEE!
You were right about the chicken liver.
Dad put in a stellar kitchen with anything we could want. Unless you want to do it at your house?
NO! I mean, your house has all the equipment. Let's do it there.
Want to come to my house? You know, just to get some practice... and work better as a team.
Miranda thinks we're a team! Team Cici-Miranda. Or Team Ci-randa. Can I get her to go for that? Nah.
I never bring my friends home. They won't understand the way we live.

Chapter 10

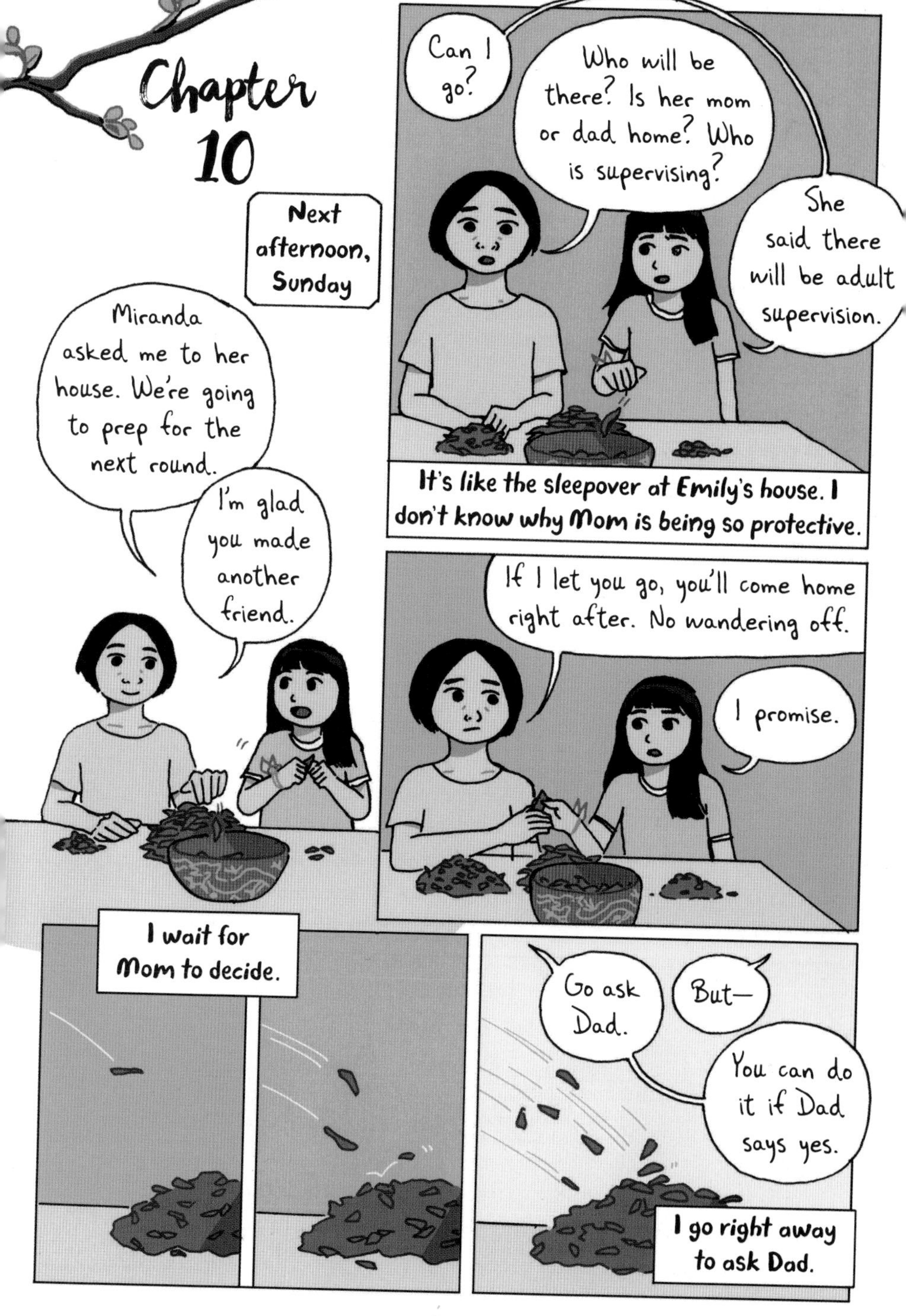
Next afternoon, Sunday
Miranda asked me to her house. We're going to prep for the next round.
I'm glad you made another friend.
Can I go?
Who will be there? Is her mom or dad home? Who is supervising?
She said there will be adult supervision.
It's like the sleepover at Emily's house. I don't know why Mom is being so protective.
If I let you go, you'll come home right after. No wandering off.
I promise.
I wait for Mom to decide.
Go ask Dad.
But—
You can do it if Dad says yes.
I go right away to ask Dad.

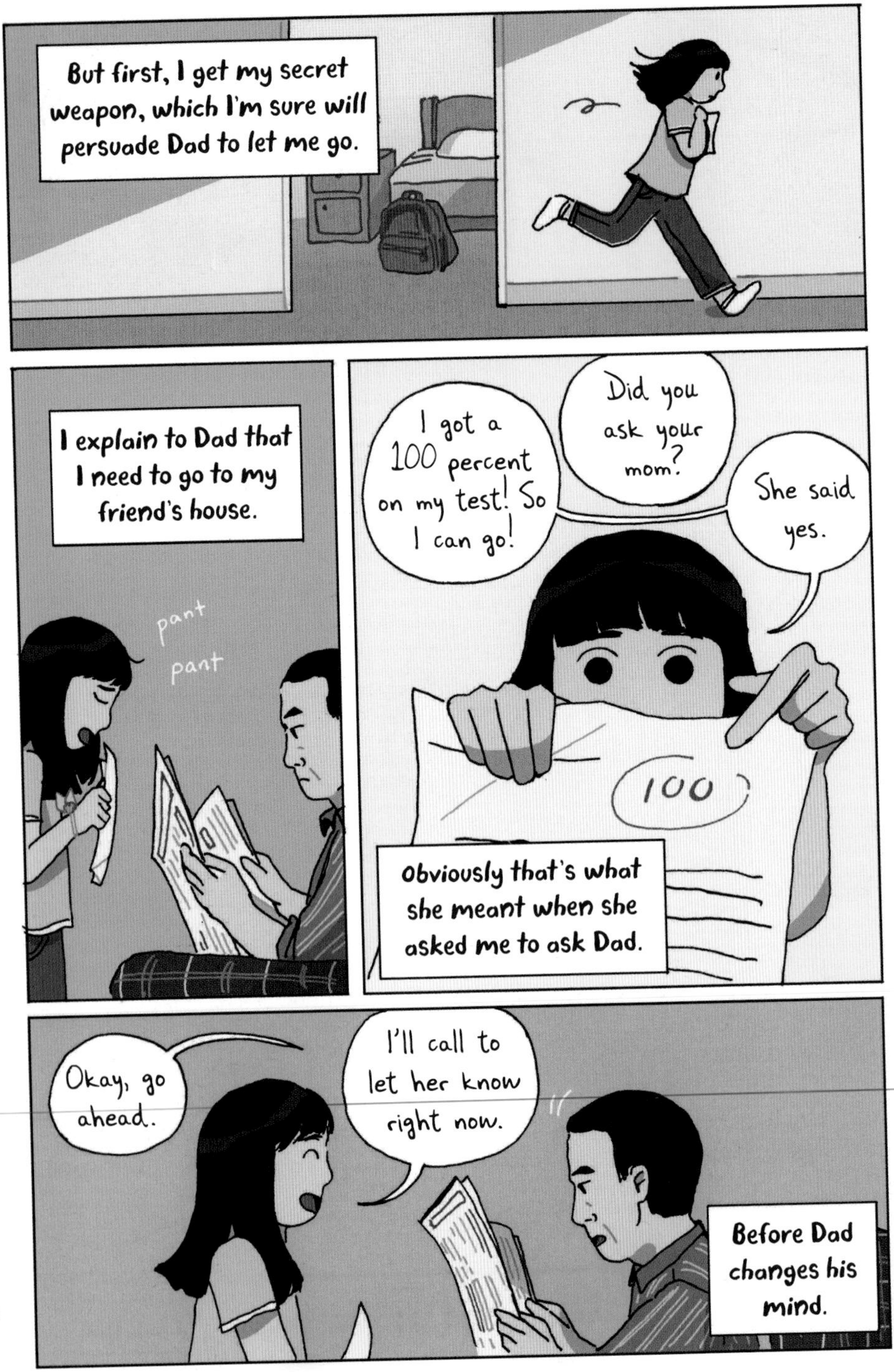

But first, I get my secret weapon, which I'm sure will persuade Dad to let me go.
I explain to Dad that I need to go to my friend's house.
pant
pant
I got a 100 percent on my test! So I can go!
Did you ask your mom?
She said yes.
100
Obviously that's what she meant when she asked me to ask Dad.
Okay, go ahead.
I'll call to let her know right now.
Before Dad changes his mind.

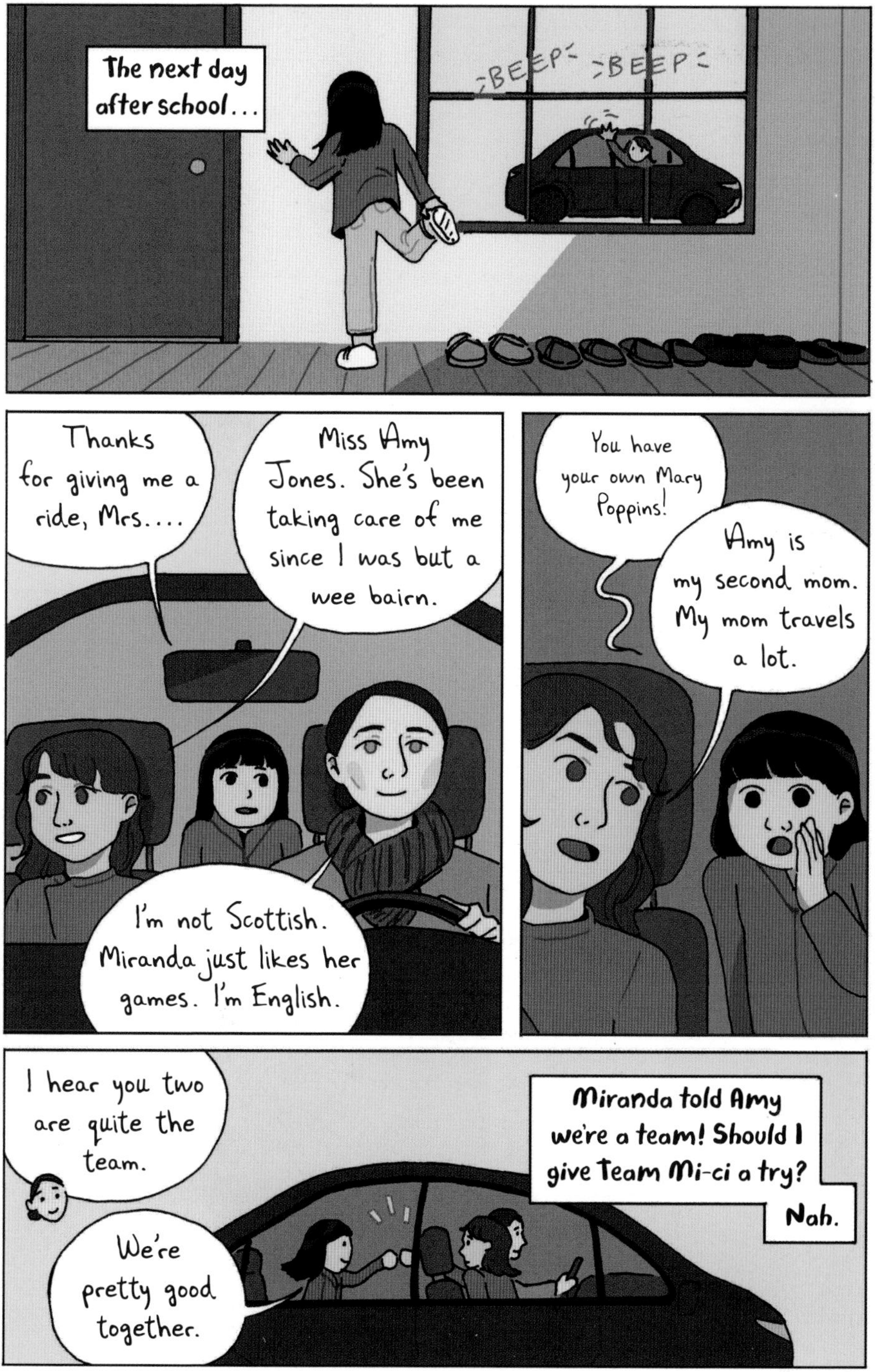
The next day after school...
>BEEP< >BEEP<
Thanks for giving me a ride, Mrs....
Miss Amy Jones. She's been taking care of me since I was but a wee bairn.
I'm not Scottish. Miranda just likes her games. I'm English.
You have your own Mary Poppins!
Amy is my second mom. My mom travels a lot.
I hear you two are quite the team.
We're pretty good together.
Miranda told Amy we're a team! Should I give Team Mi-ci a try?
Nah.

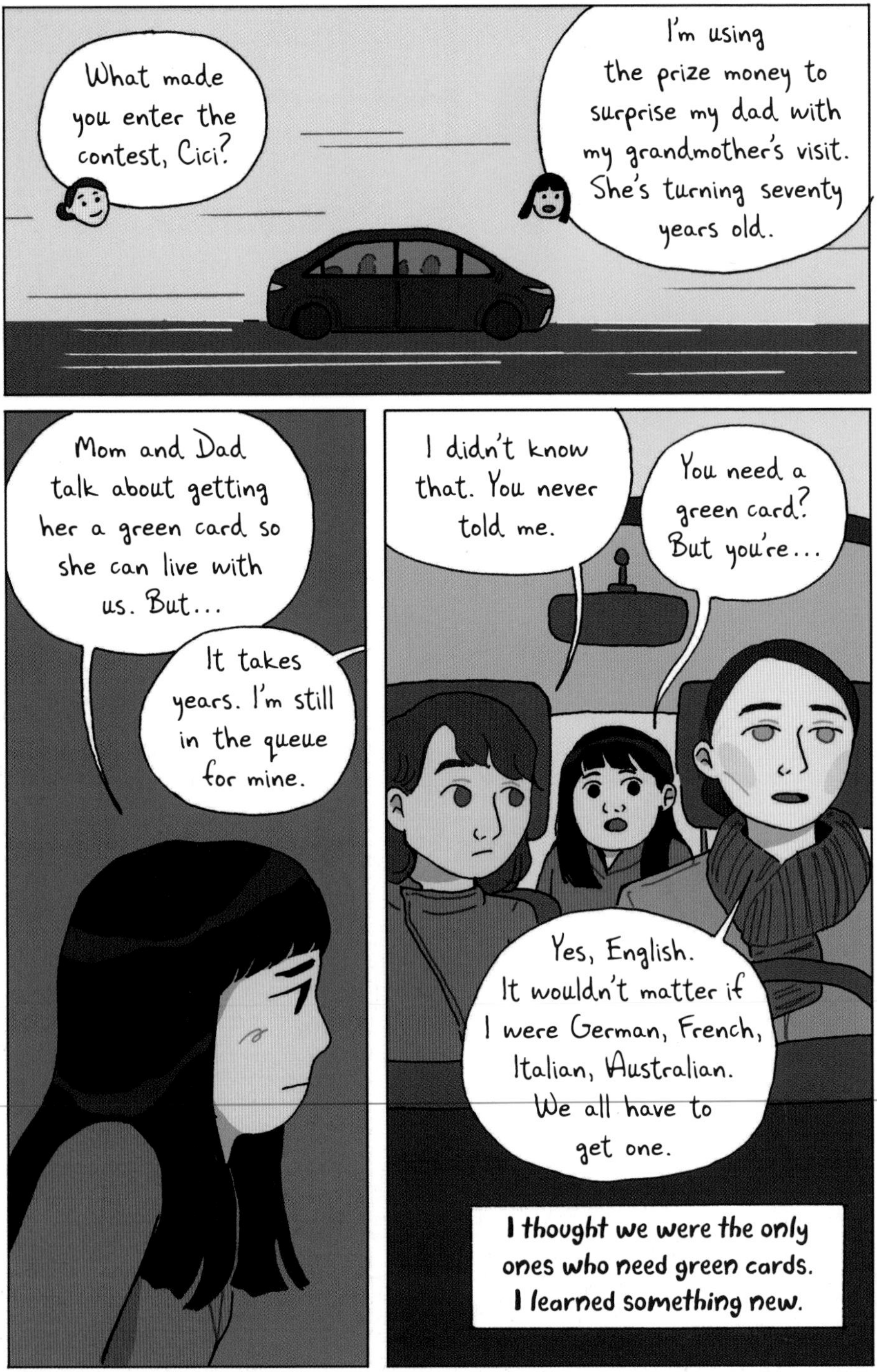
What made you enter the contest, Cici?
I'm using the prize money to surprise my dad with my grandmother's visit. She's turning seventy years old.
Mom and Dad talk about getting her a green card so she can live with us. But...
It takes years. I'm still in the queue for mine.
I didn't know that. You never told me.
You need a green card? But you're...
Yes, English. It wouldn't matter if I were German, French, Italian, Australian. We all have to get one.
I thought we were the only ones who need green cards. I learned something new.

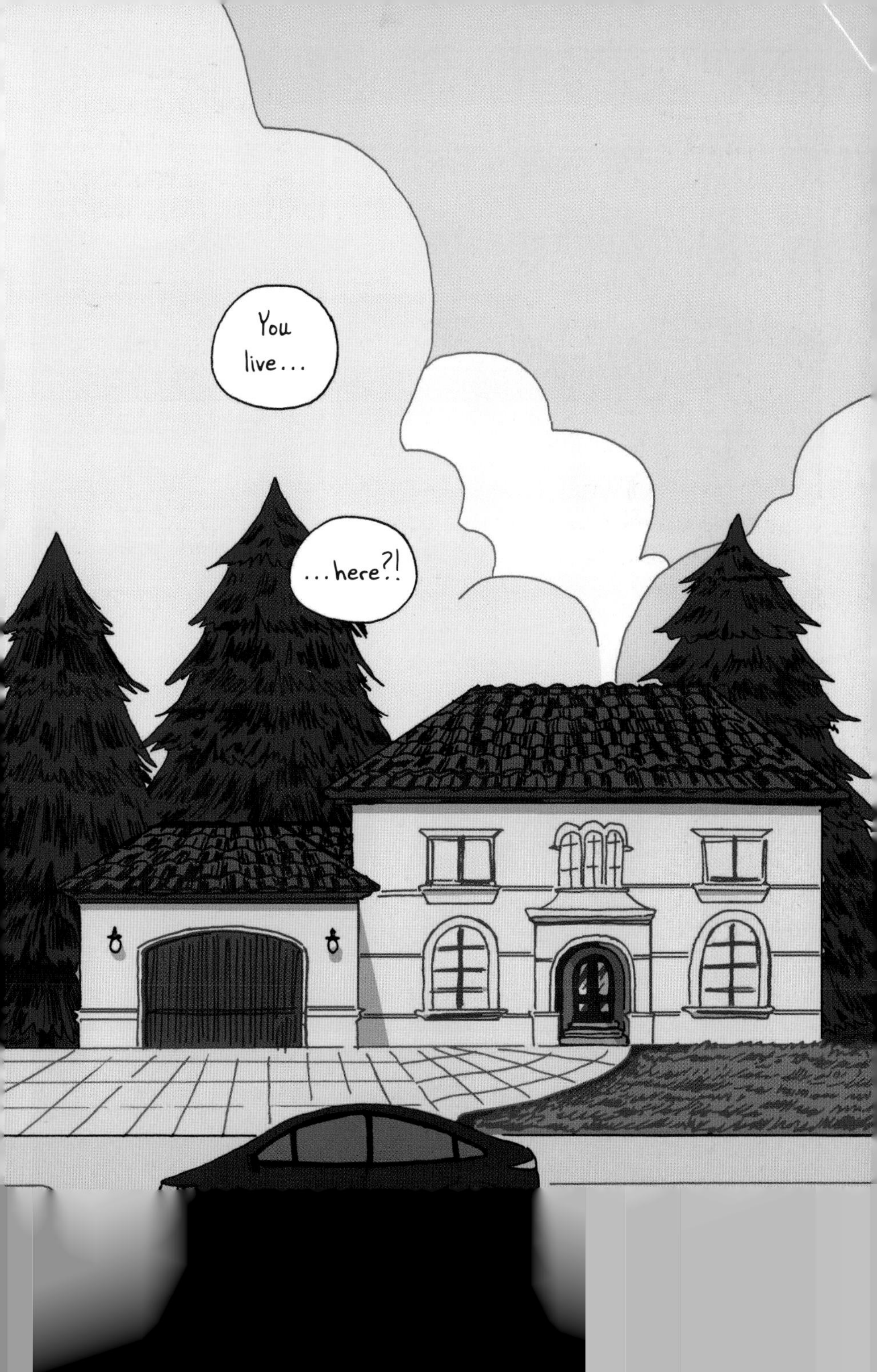
You live...
...here?!

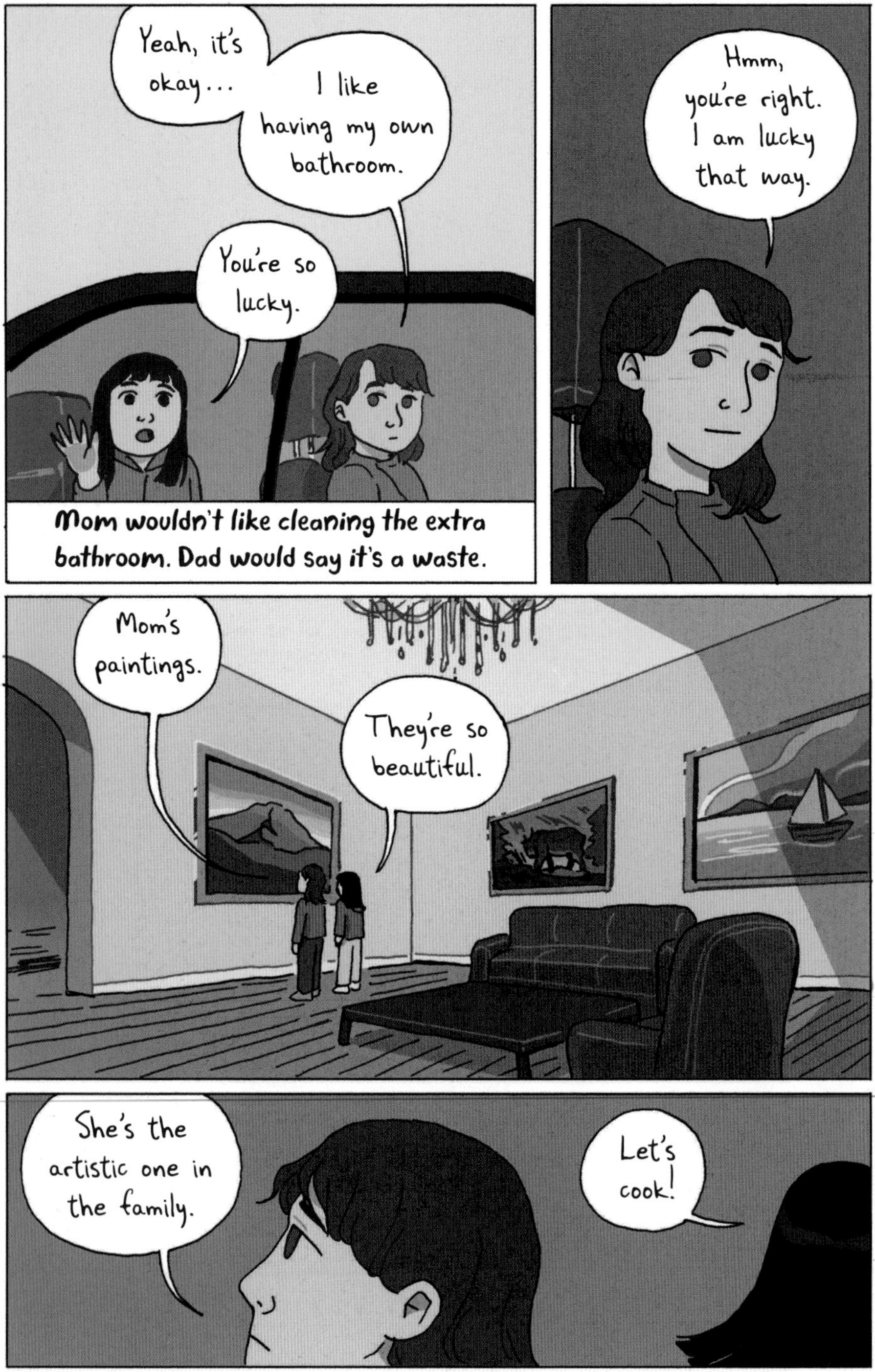
Yeah, it's okay...
I like having my own bathroom.
You're so lucky.
Mom wouldn't like cleaning the extra bathroom. Dad would say it's a waste.
Hmm, you're right. I am lucky that way.
Mom's paintings.
They're so beautiful.
She's the artistic one in the family.
Let's cook!

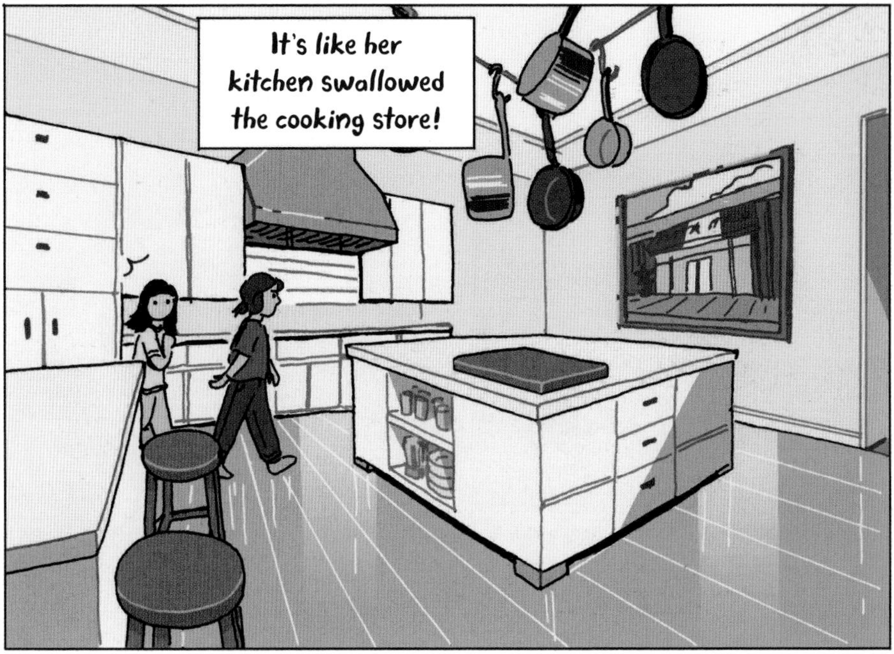
It's like her kitchen swallowed the cooking store!

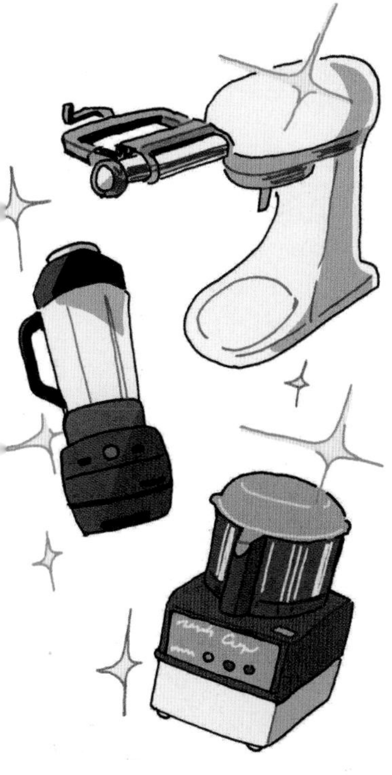

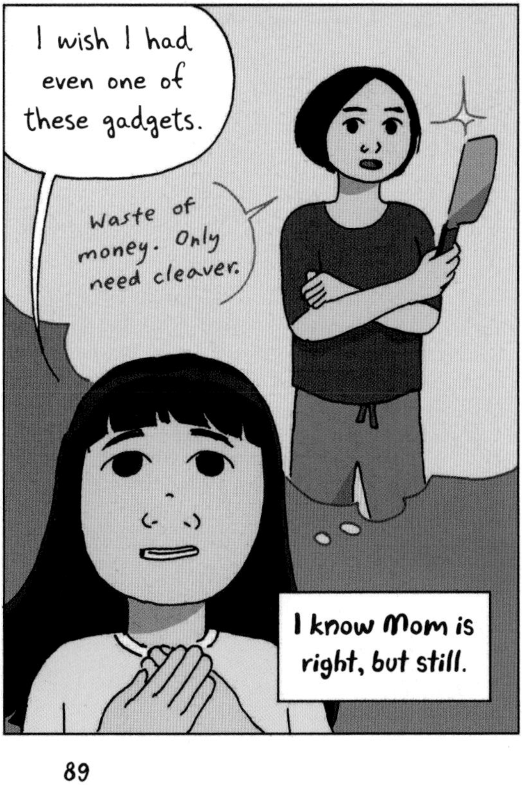
I wish I had even one of these gadgets.
Waste of money. Only need cleaver.
I know Mom is right, but still.

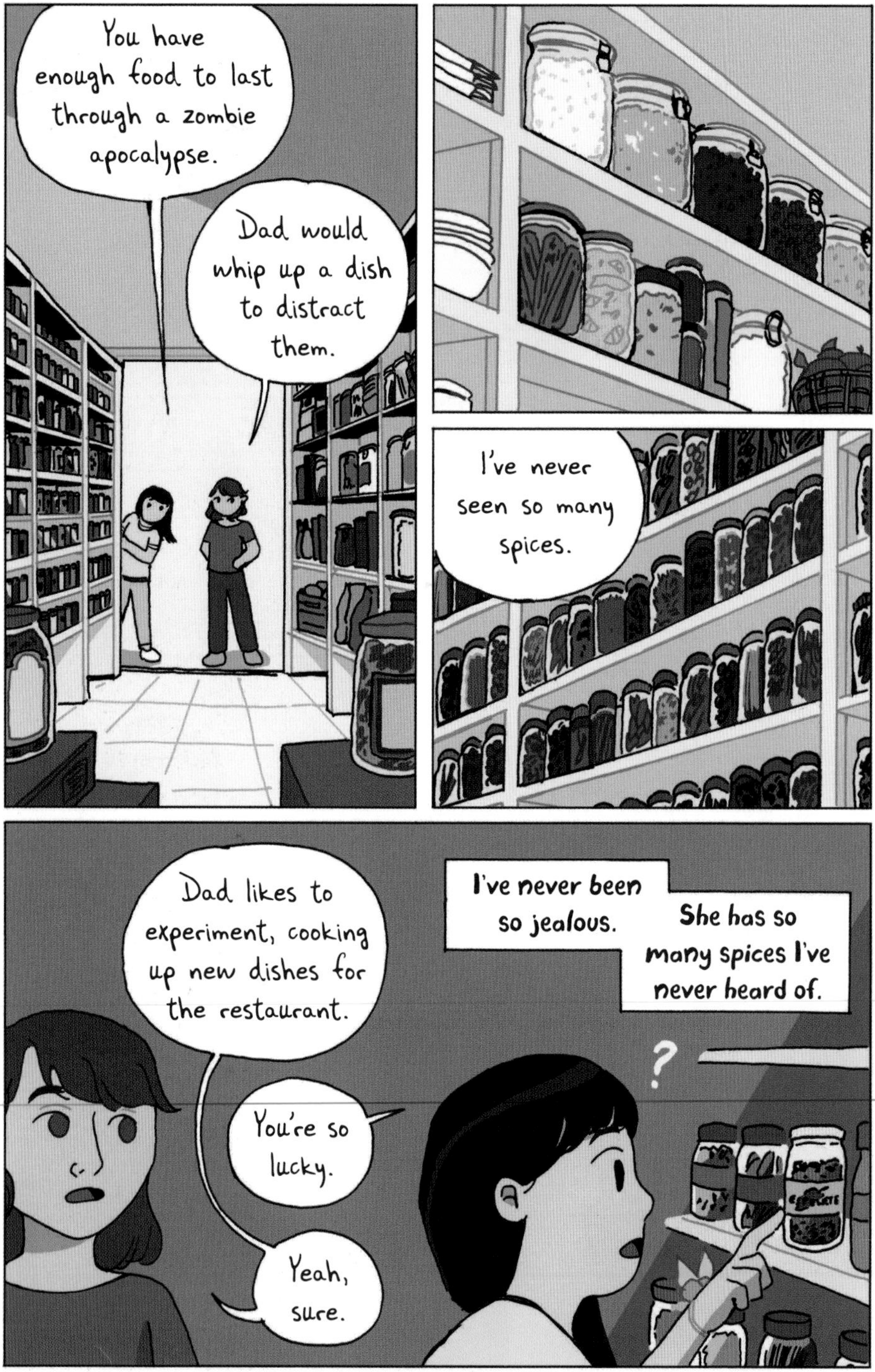
You have enough food to last through a zombie apocalypse.
Dad would whip up a dish to distract them.
I've never seen so many spices.
Dad likes to experiment, cooking up new dishes for the restaurant.
I've never been so jealous.
She has so many spices I've never heard of.
?
You're so lucky.
Yeah, sure.

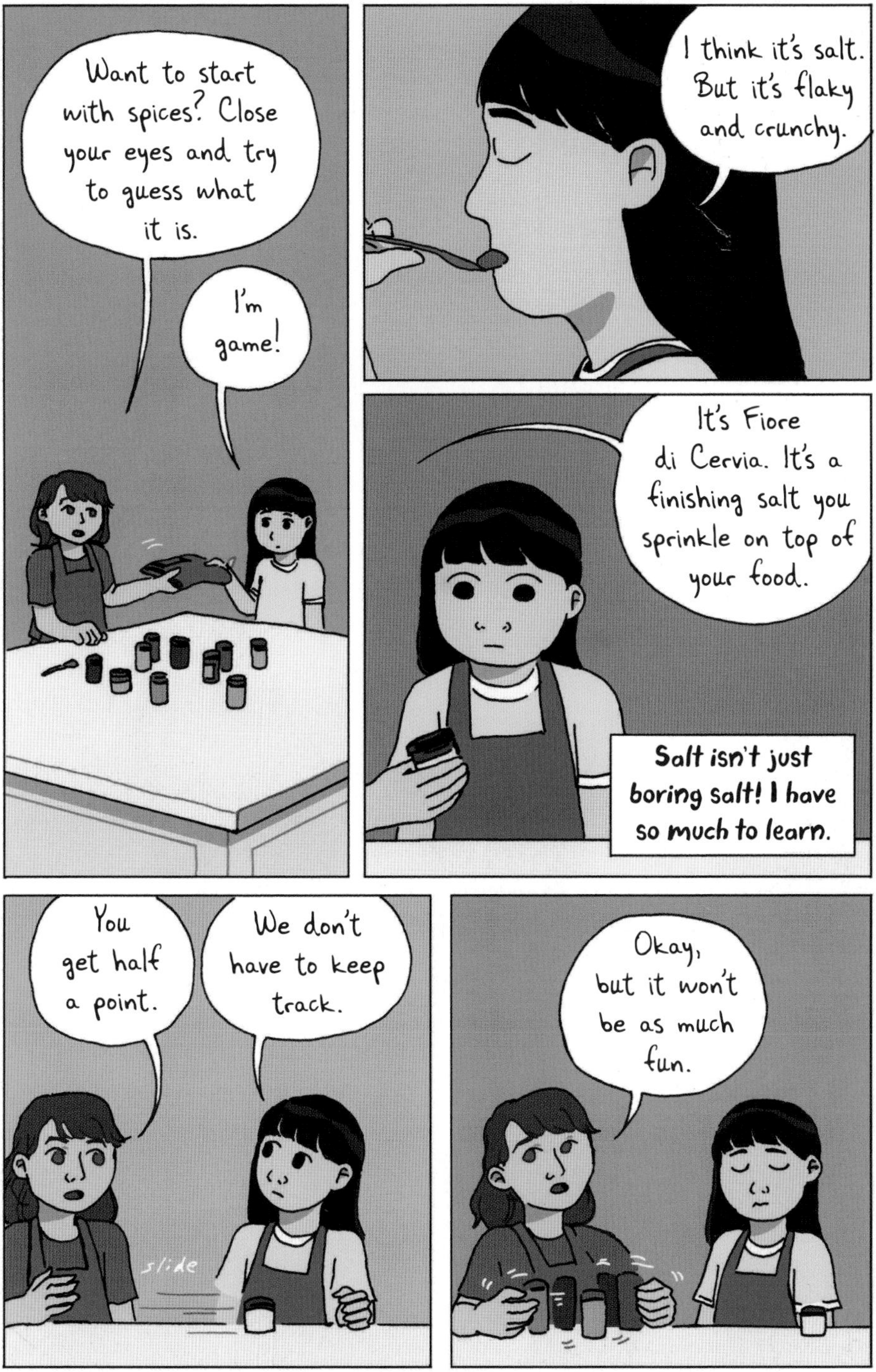
Want to start with spices? Close your eyes and try to guess what it is.
I'm game!
I think it's salt. But it's flaky and crunchy.
It's Fiore di Cervia. It's a finishing salt you sprinkle on top of your food.
Salt isn't just boring salt! I have so much to learn.
You get half a point.
We don't have to keep track.
slide
Okay, but it won't be as much fun.

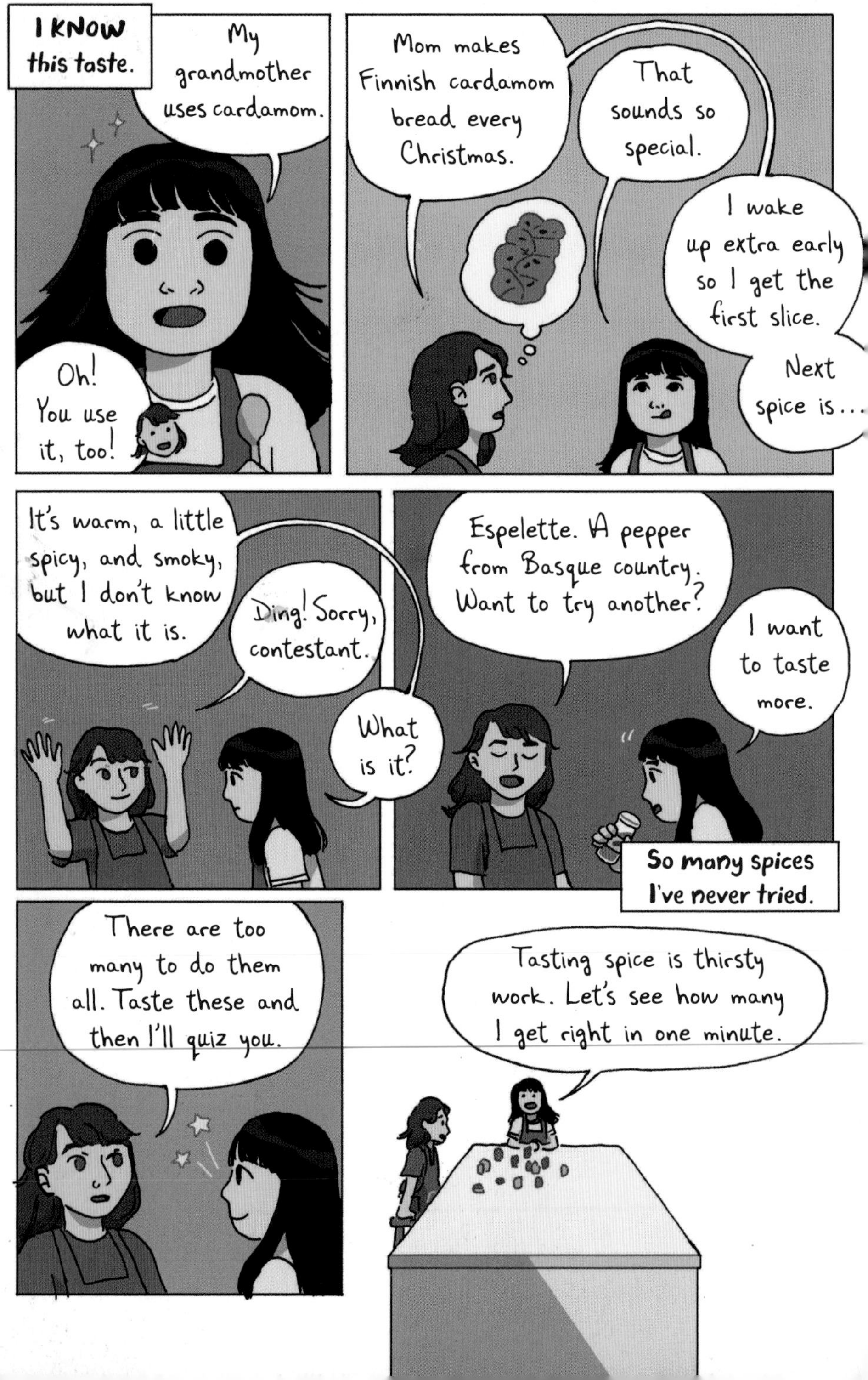
I KNOW this taste.
My grandmother uses cardamom.
Oh! You use it, too!
Mom makes Finnish cardamom bread every Christmas.
That sounds so special.
I wake up extra early so I get the first slice.
Next spice is...
It's warm, a little spicy, and smoky, but I don't know what it is.
Ding! Sorry, contestant.
What is it?
Espelette. A pepper from Basque country. Want to try another?
I want to taste more.
So many spices I've never tried.
There are too many to do them all. Taste these and then I'll quiz you.
Tasting spice is thirsty work. Let's see how many I get right in one minute.

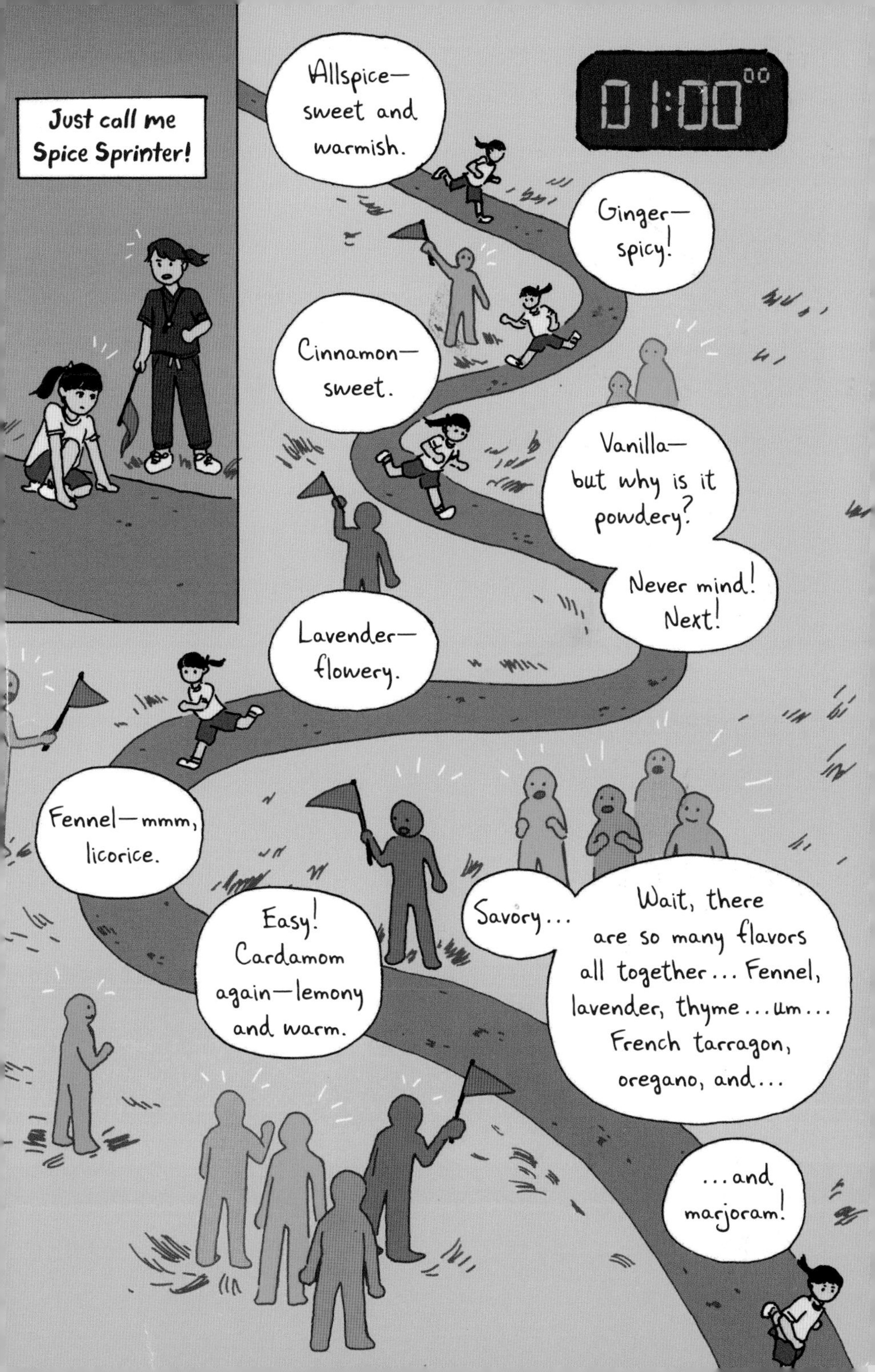
Just call me Spice Sprinter!
01:00 00
Allspice—sweet and warmish.
Ginger—spicy!
Cinnamon—sweet.
Vanilla—but why is it powdery?
Never mind! Next!
Lavender—flowery.
Fennel—mmm, licorice.
Easy! Cardamom again—lemony and warm.
Savory...
Wait, there are so many flavors all together... Fennel, lavender, thyme...um... French tarragon, oregano, and...
...and marjoram!

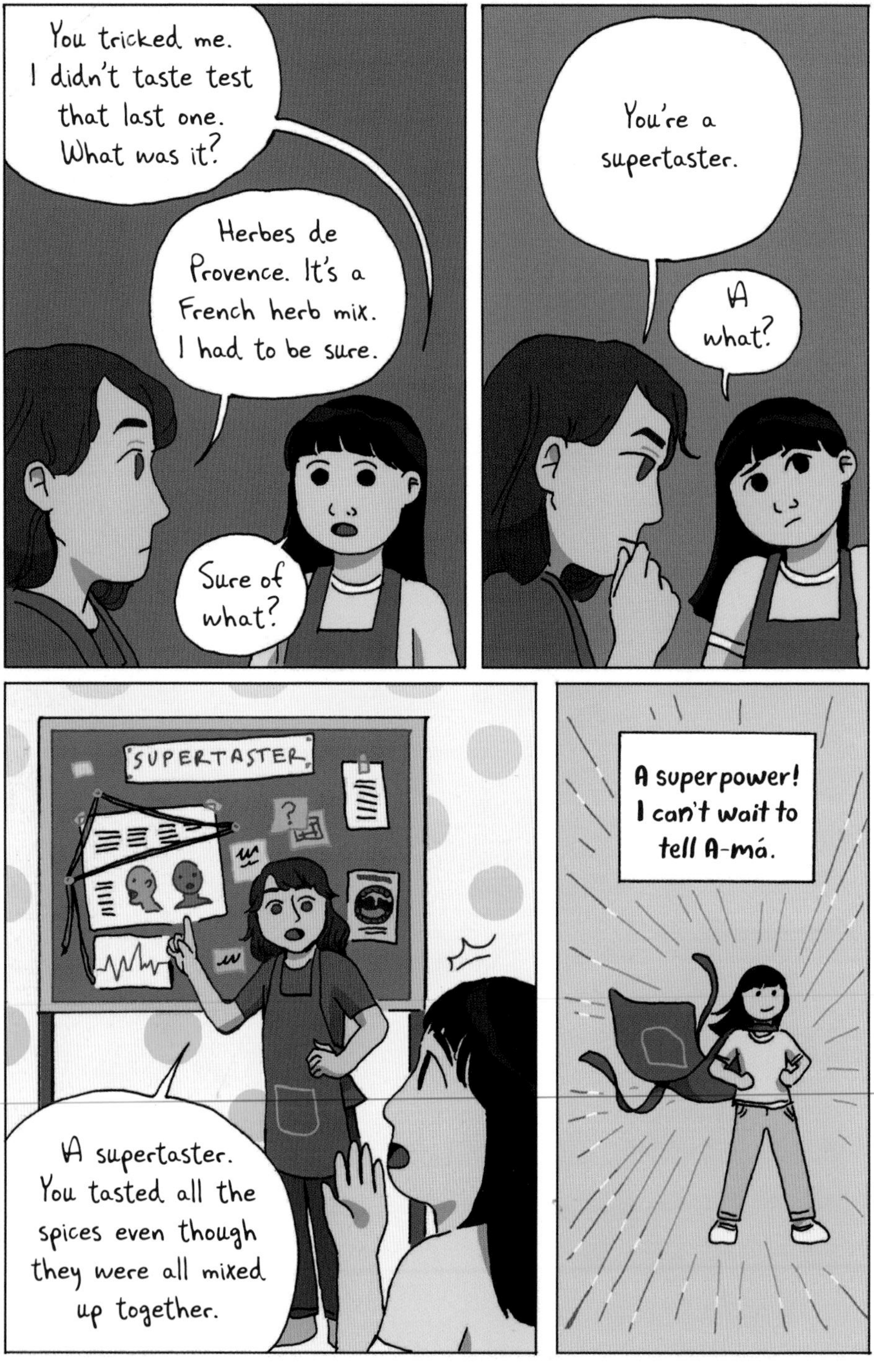
You tricked me. I didn't taste test that last one. What was it?
Herbes de Provence. It's a French herb mix. I had to be sure.
Sure of what?
You're a supertaster.
A what?
SUPERTASTER
A supertaster. You tasted all the spices even though they were all mixed up together.
A superpower! I can't wait to tell A-má.

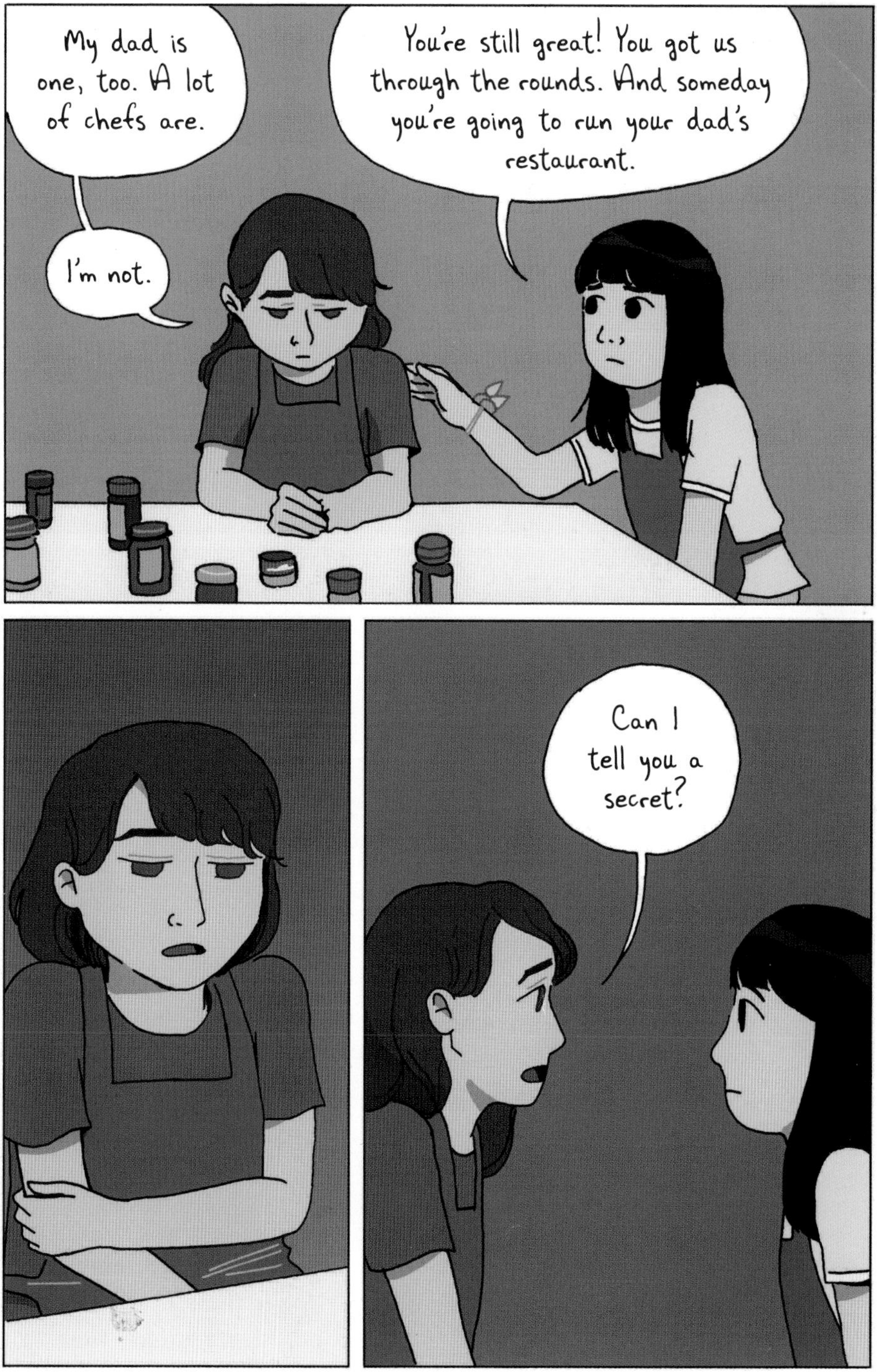
My dad is one, too. A lot of chefs are.
I'm not.
You're still great! You got us through the rounds. And someday you're going to run your dad's restaurant.
Can I tell you a secret?

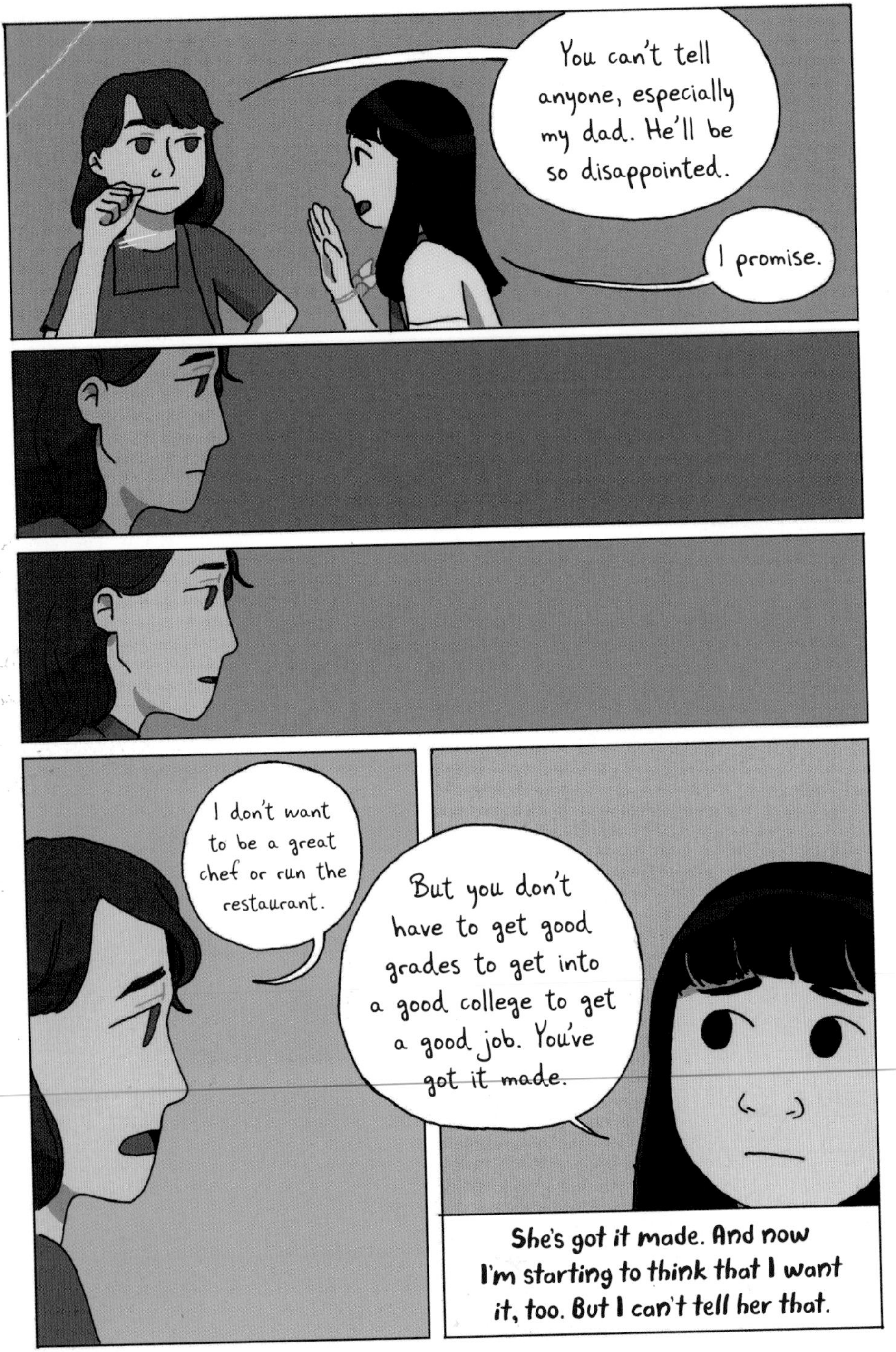
You can't tell anyone, especially my dad. He'll be so disappointed.
I promise.
I don't want to be a great chef or run the restaurant.
But you don't have to get good grades to get into a good college to get a good job. You've got it made.
She's got it made. And now I'm starting to think that I want it, too. But I can't tell her that.

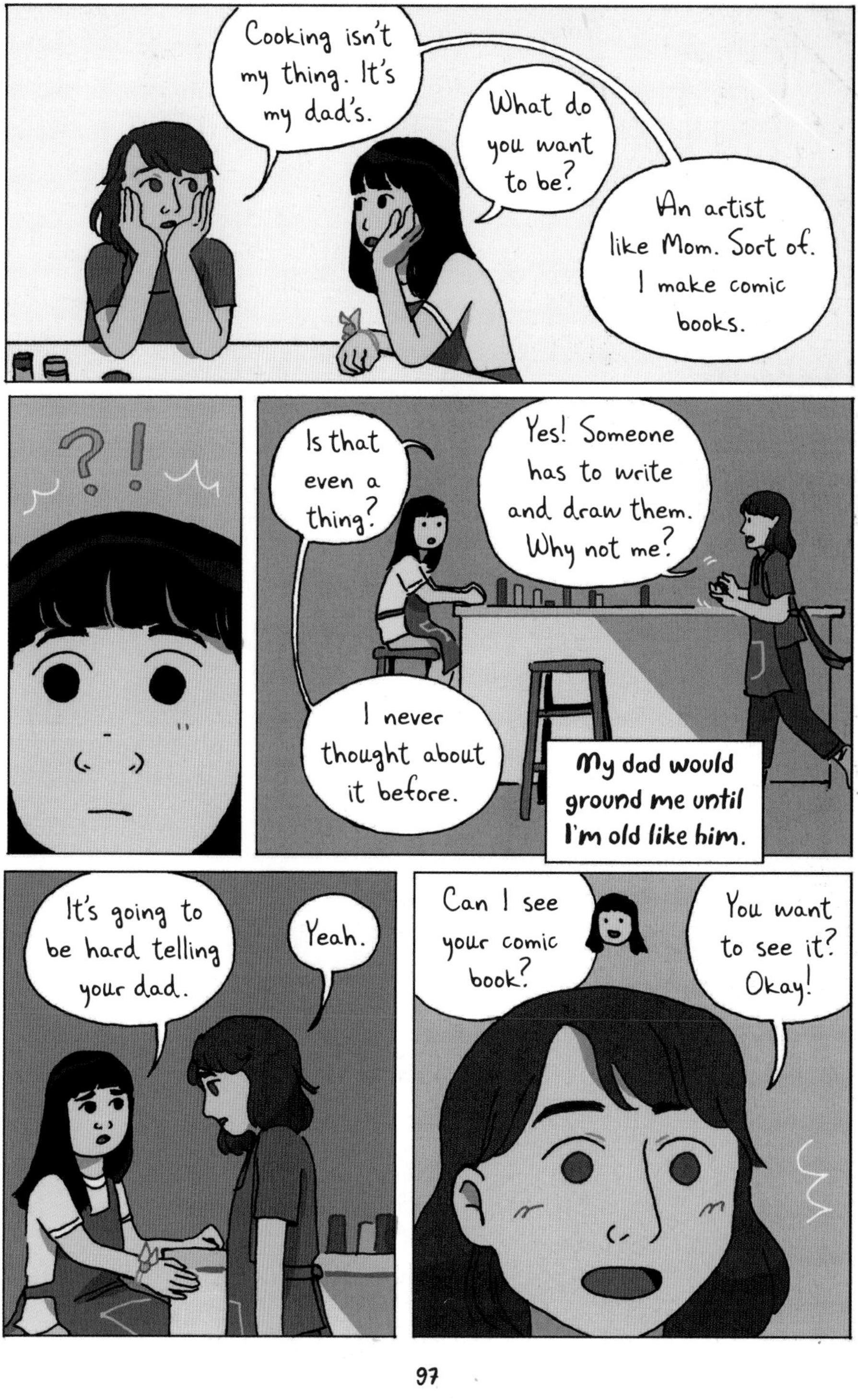
Cooking isn't my thing. It's my dad's.
What do you want to be?
An artist like Mom. Sort of. I make comic books.
?!
Is that even a thing?
Yes! Someone has to write and draw them. Why not me?
I never thought about it before.
My dad would ground me until I'm old like him.
It's going to be hard telling your dad.
Yeah.
Can I see your comic book?
You want to see it? Okay!

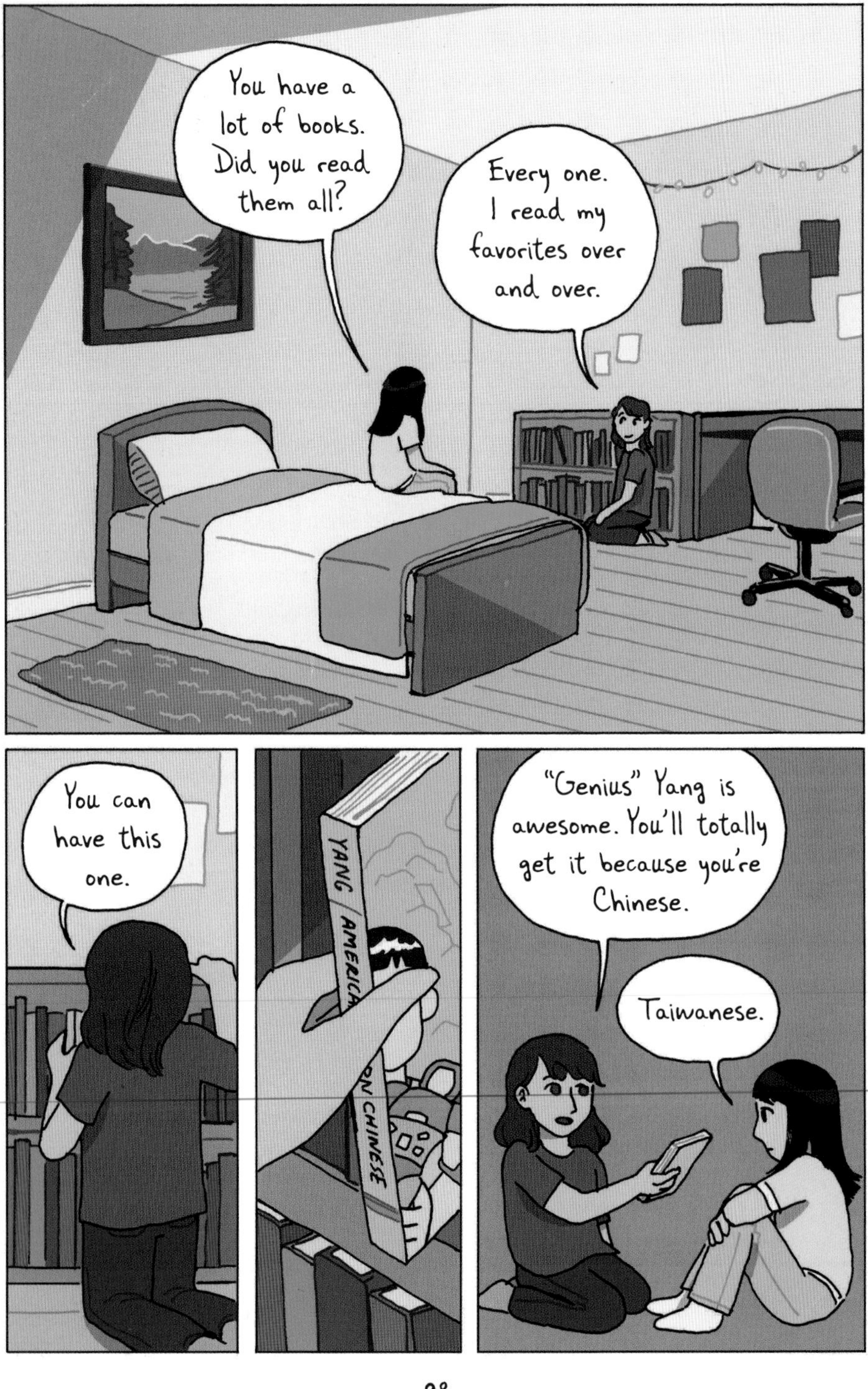
You have a lot of books. Did you read them all?
Every one. I read my favorites over and over.
You can have this one.
YANG AMERICAN CHINESE
"Genius" Yang is awesome. You'll totally get it because you're Chinese.
Taiwanese.

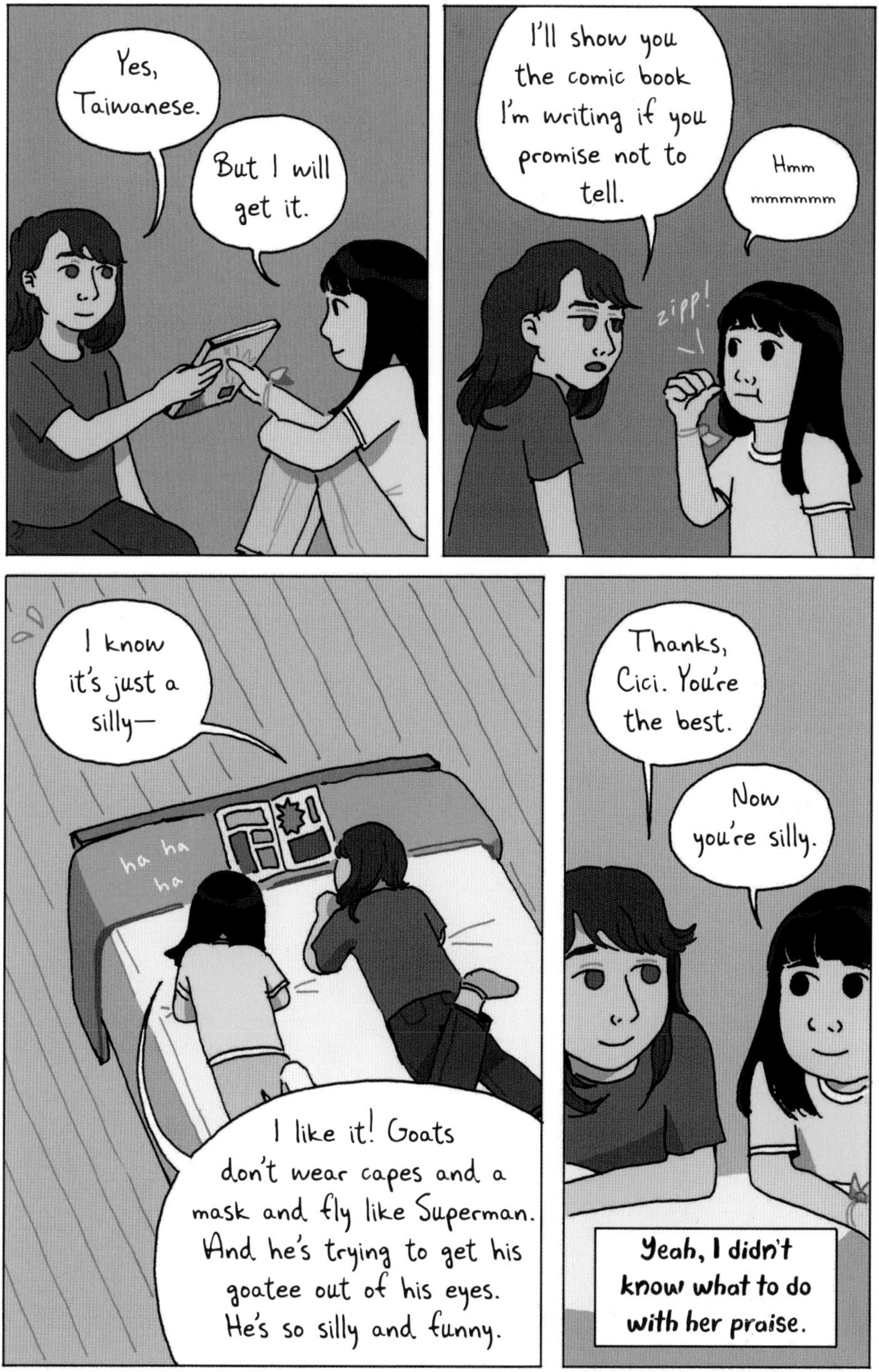
Yes, Taiwanese.
But I will get it.
I'll show you the comic book I'm writing if you promise not to tell.
Hmm mmmmmm
zipp!
I know it's just a silly—
ha ha ha
I like it! Goats don't wear capes and a mask and fly like Superman. And he's trying to get his goatee out of his eyes. He's so silly and funny.
Thanks, Cici. You're the best.
Now you're silly.
Yeah, I didn't know what to do with her praise.

Chapter 11

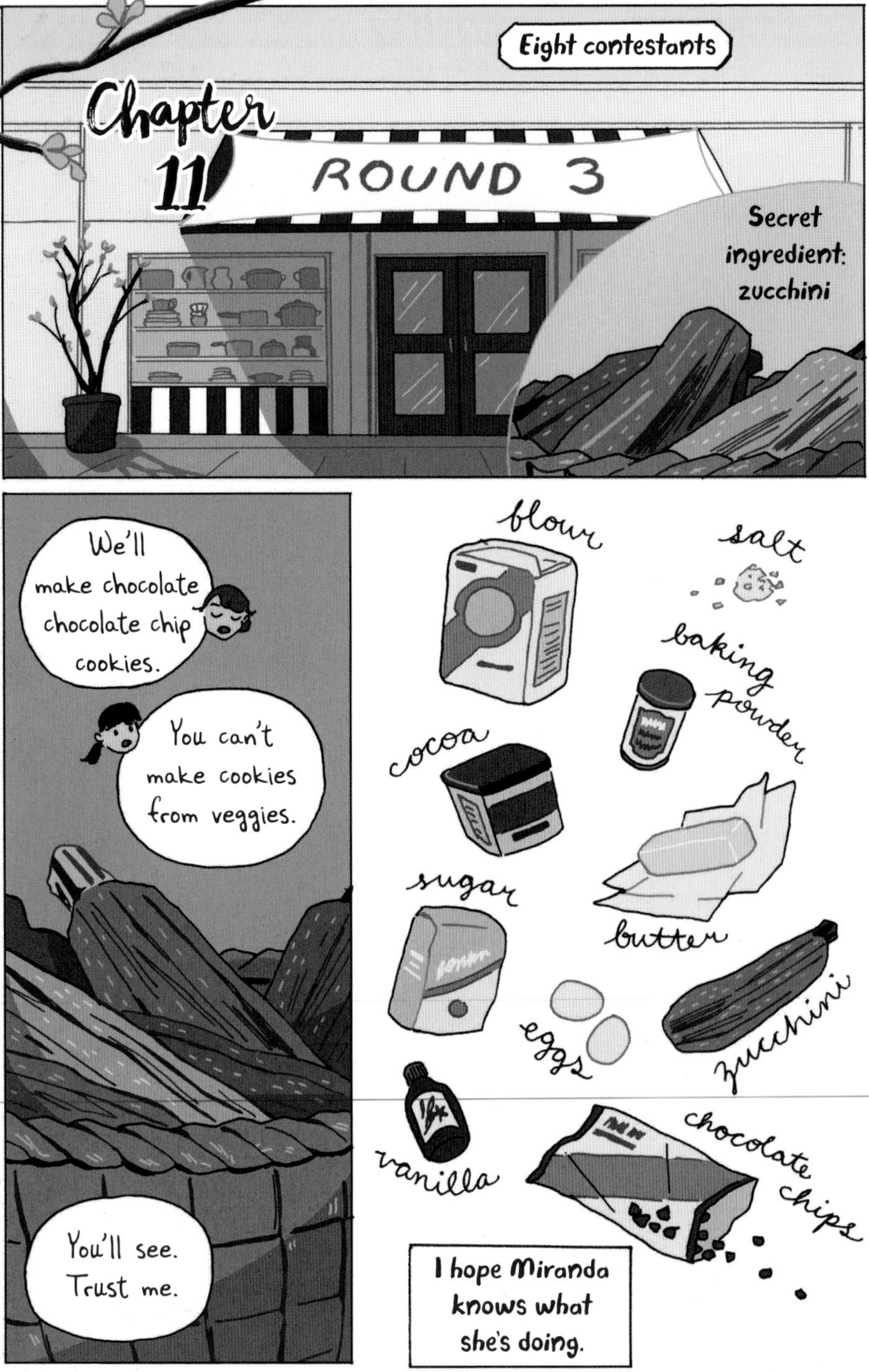

Eight contestants
ROUND 3
Secret ingredient: zucchini
We'll make chocolate chocolate chip cookies.
You can't make cookies from veggies.
You'll see. Trust me.
flour
salt
baking powder
cocoa
butter
sugar
eggs
zucchini
vanilla
chocolate chips
I hope Miranda knows what she's doing.

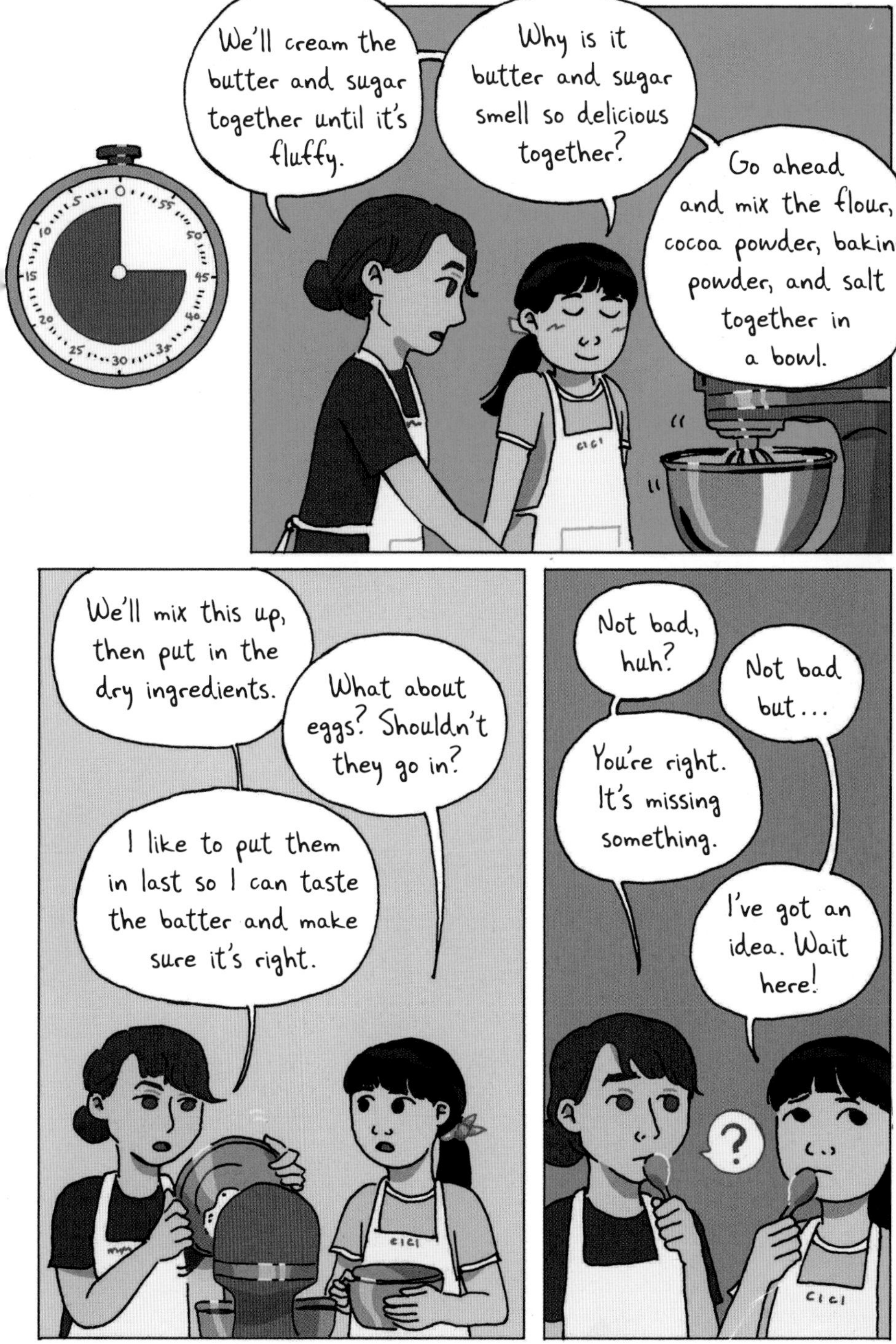
We'll cream the butter and sugar together until it's fluffy.
Why is it butter and sugar smell so delicious together?
Go ahead and mix the flour, cocoa powder, baking powder, and salt together in a bowl.
We'll mix this up, then put in the dry ingredients.
What about eggs? Shouldn't they go in?
I like to put them in last so I can taste the batter and make sure it's right.
Not bad, huh?
Not bad but...
You're right. It's missing something.
I've got an idea. Wait here!

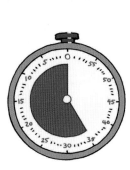

Bay leaf, bouquet garni, caraway... and then I find it.

I know exactly what we need to add.

We can sprinkle it on top of the cookies.

SMOKED SEA SALT

Maybe. I'll bake up a couple of samples.

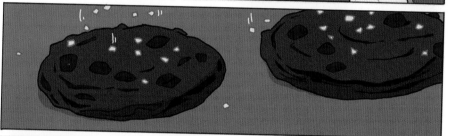

You WERE right! I can't stop eating these.

CICI

I know I shouldn't be so happy that she approves.

I am the supertaster, after all. But still it feels good.

Layla and Crystal. You brought home the bacon on the zucchini fries.

Your dish is a kid pleaser. Kudos on that.

But a bit uninspired.

I feel bad for Layla and Crystal. I bet the kids in school would gobble them up.

Todd and Jacob, your zucchini cake is moist, and the addition of walnuts adds a nice crunch.

The cream cheese frosting gives it a nice tang to contrast with the sweetness of the cake.

Tsk, tsk. I see you ran out of time to bake your cake. The middle is inedible.

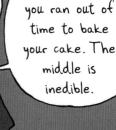

Robert and Samantha, your scrambled eggs with grated zucchini is a nice variation on regular scrambles. Nicely done.

I really liked the lightness of the eggs.

Hmm, a bit runny. Next time you should squeeze more moisture out of the zucchini. I hope the last team does better.

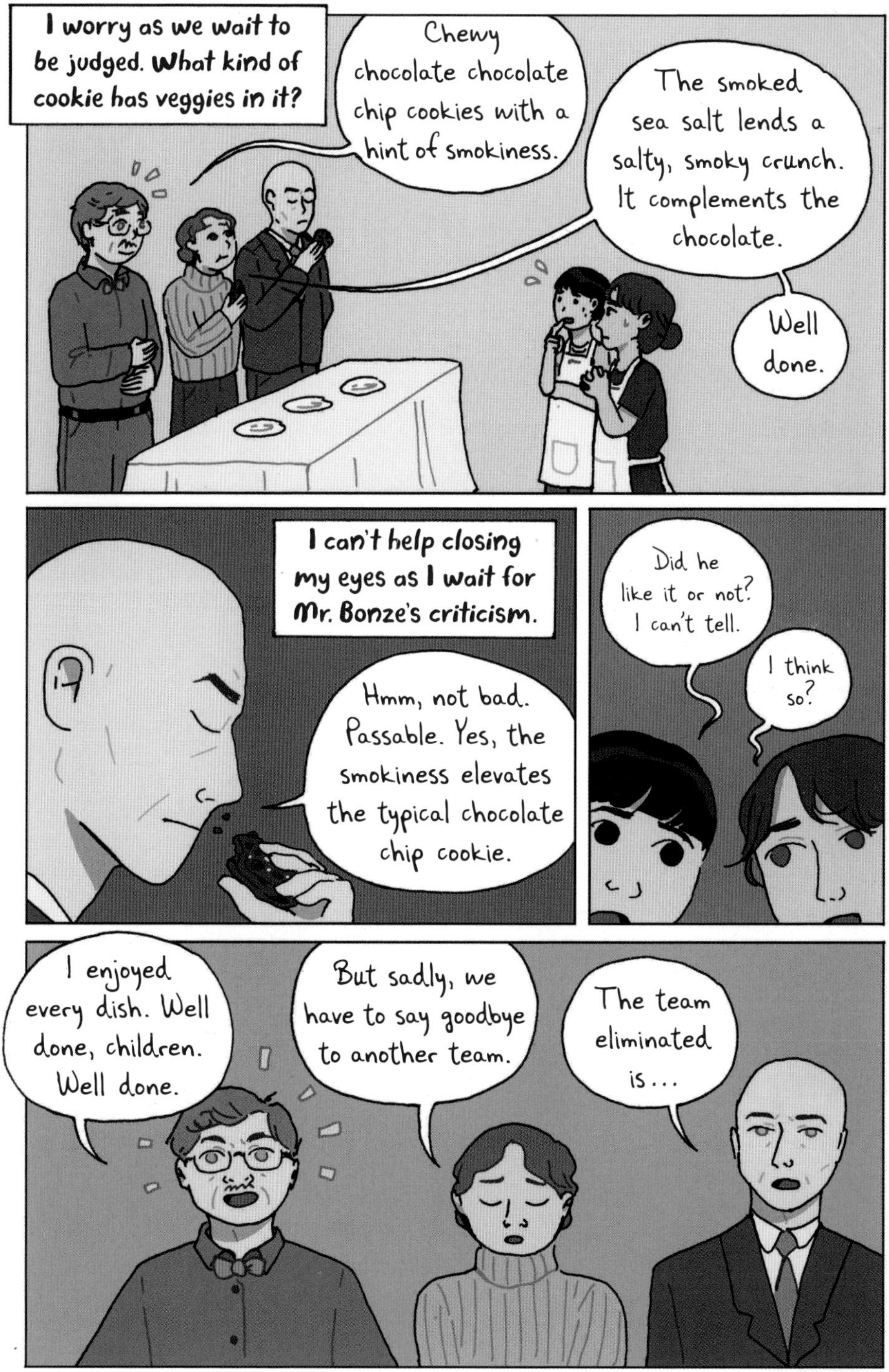
I worry as we wait to be judged. What kind of cookie has veggies in it?
Chewy chocolate chocolate chip cookies with a hint of smokiness.
The smoked sea salt lends a salty, smoky crunch. It complements the chocolate.
Well done.
I can't help closing my eyes as I wait for Mr. Bonze's criticism.
Hmm, not bad. Passable. Yes, the smokiness elevates the typical chocolate chip cookie.
Did he like it or not? I can't tell.
I think so?
I enjoyed every dish. Well done, children. Well done.
But sadly, we have to say goodbye to another team.
The team eliminated is...

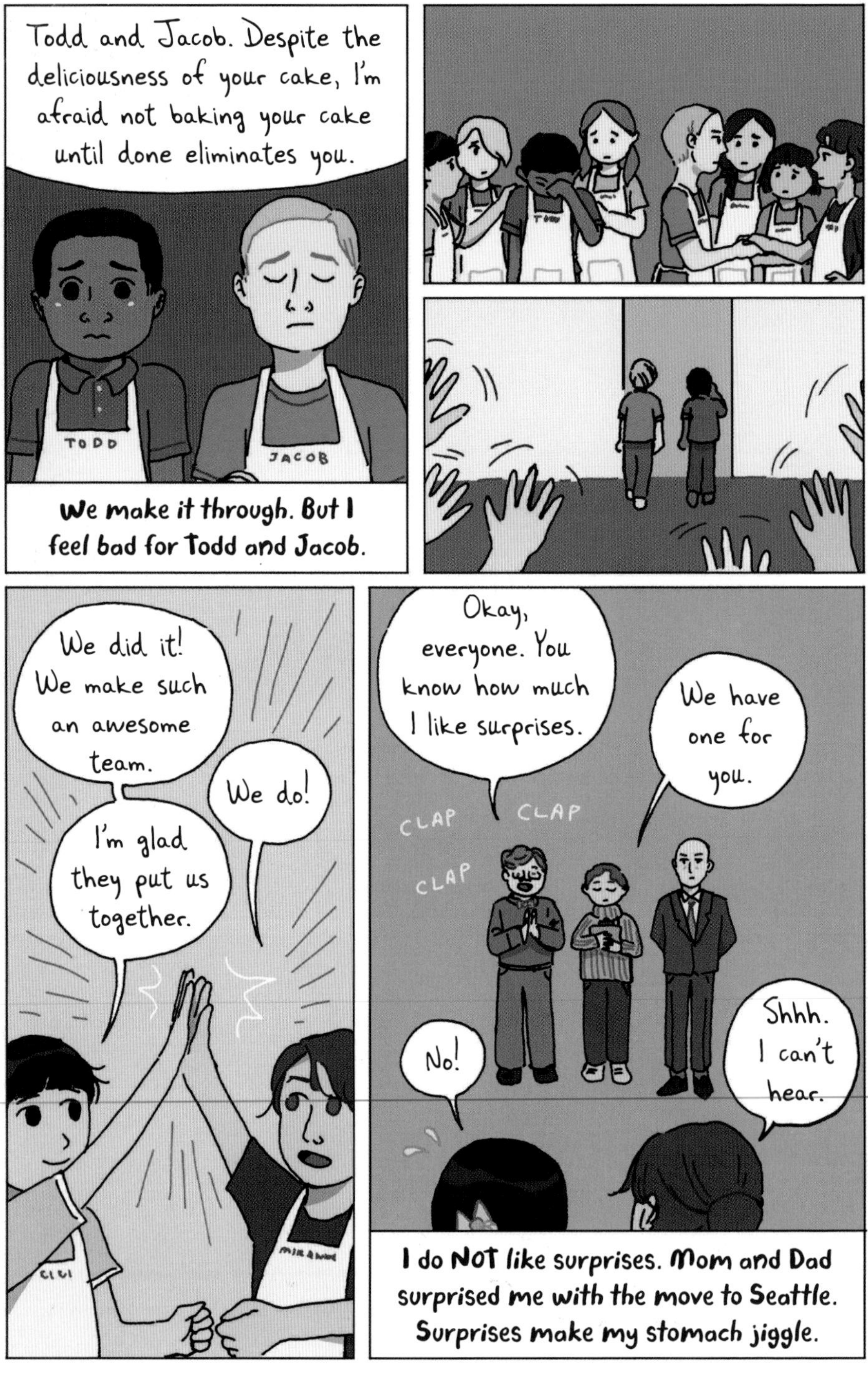
Todd and Jacob. Despite the deliciousness of your cake, I'm afraid not baking your cake until done eliminates you.
TODD
JACOB
We make it through. But I feel bad for Todd and Jacob.
TODD
We did it! We make such an awesome team.
I'm glad they put us together.
We do!
Okay, everyone. You know how much I like surprises.
We have one for you.
CLAP
CLAP
CLAP
No!
Shhh. I can't hear.
I do NOT like surprises. Mom and Dad surprised me with the move to Seattle. Surprises make my stomach jiggle.

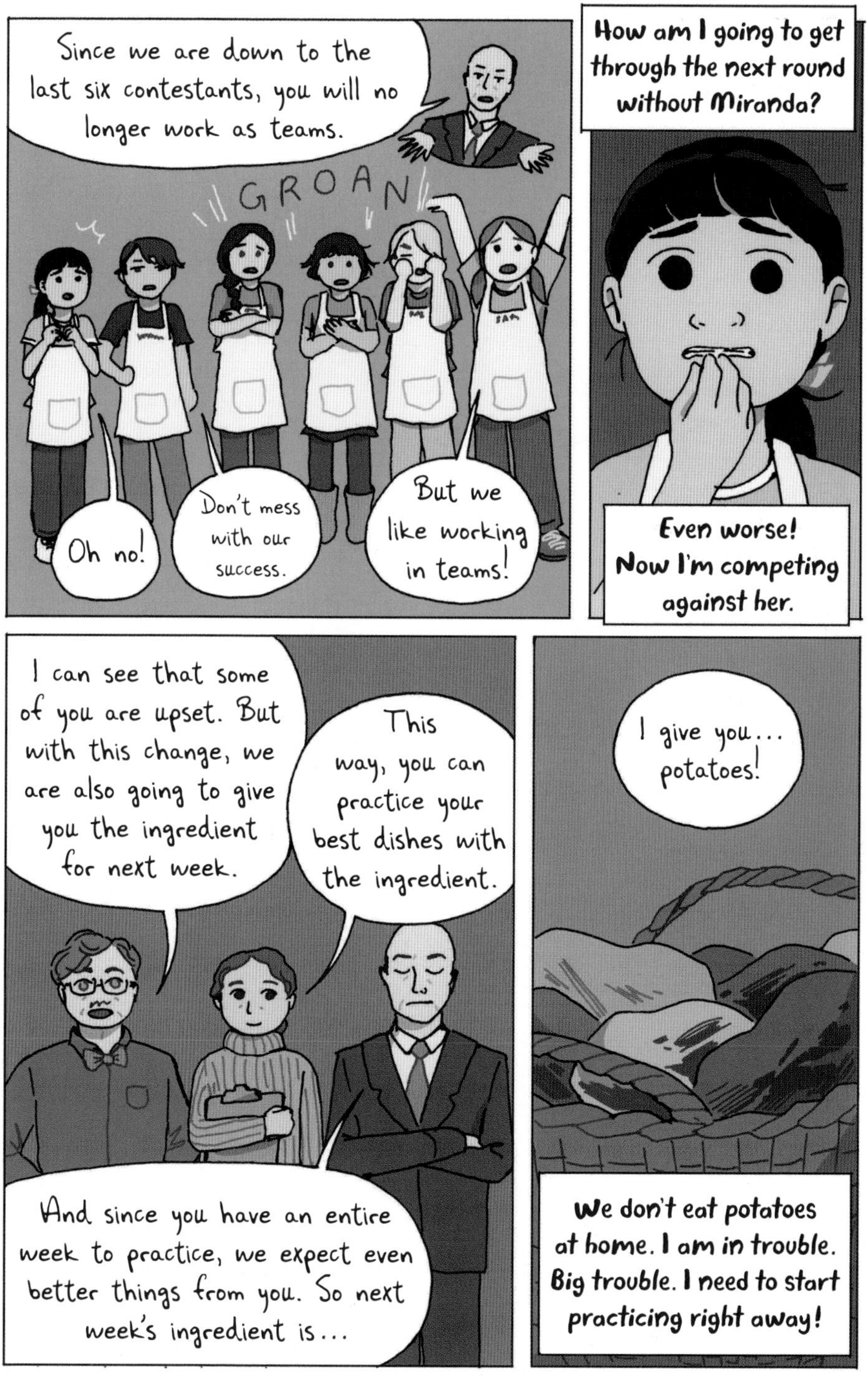
Since we are down to the last six contestants, you will no longer work as teams.
GROAN
Oh no!
Don't mess with our success.
But we like working in teams!
How am I going to get through the next round without Miranda?
Even worse! Now I'm competing against her.
I can see that some of you are upset. But with this change, we are also going to give you the ingredient for next week.
This way, you can practice your best dishes with the ingredient.
And since you have an entire week to practice, we expect even better things from you. So next week's ingredient is...
I give you... potatoes!
We don't eat potatoes at home. I am in trouble. Big trouble. I need to start practicing right away!

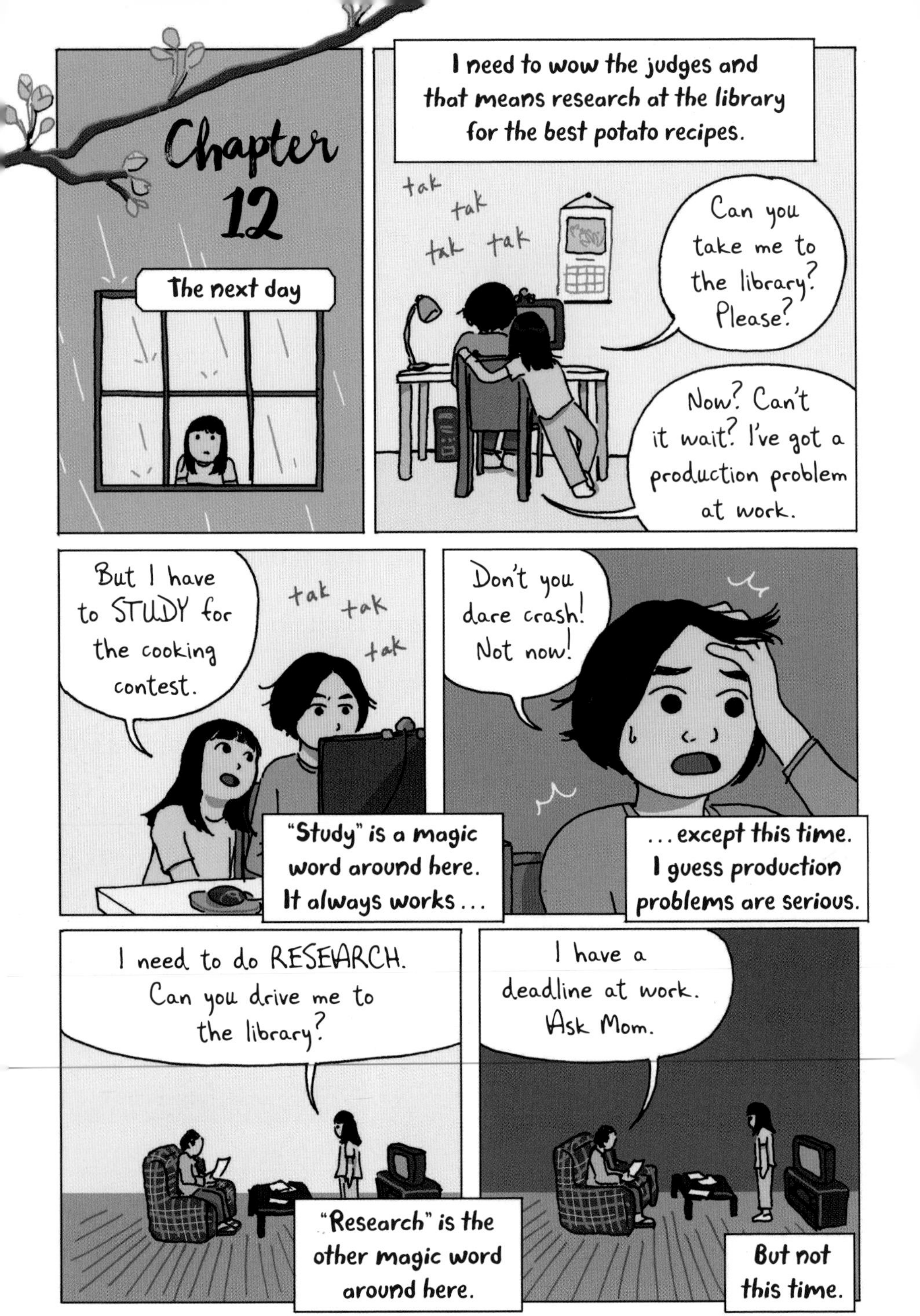
Chapter 12
The next day
I need to wow the judges and that means research at the library for the best potato recipes.
tak tak tak tak
Can you take me to the library? Please?
Now? Can't it wait? I've got a production problem at work.
But I have to STUDY for the cooking contest.
tak tak tak
"Study" is a magic word around here. It always works . . .
Don't you dare crash! Not now!
. . . except this time. I guess production problems are serious.
I need to do RESEARCH. Can you drive me to the library?
"Research" is the other magic word around here.
I have a deadline at work. Ask Mom.
But not this time.

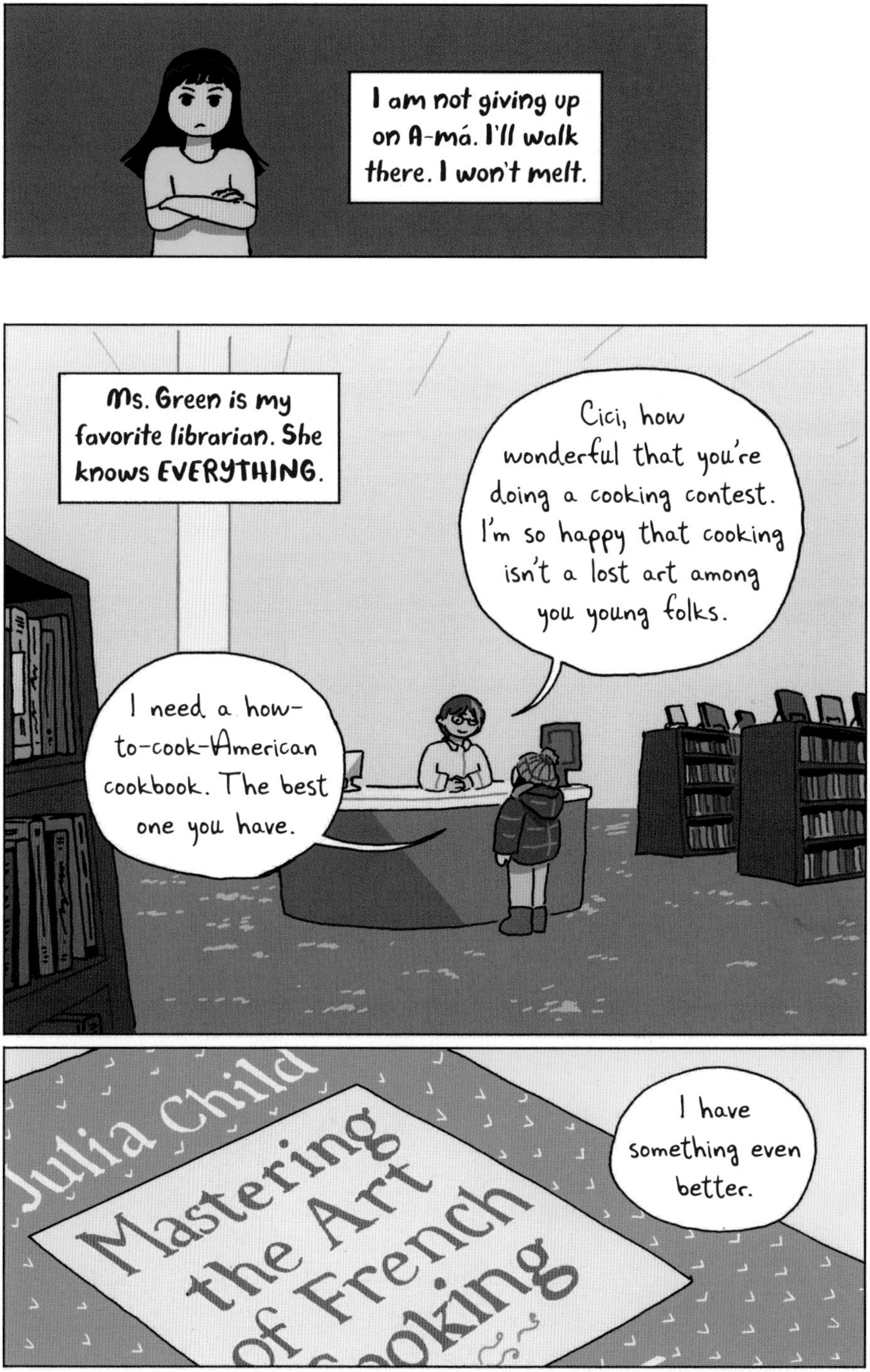
I am not giving up on A-má. I'll walk there. I won't melt.
Ms. Green is my favorite librarian. She knows EVERYTHING.
Cici, how wonderful that you're doing a cooking contest. I'm so happy that cooking isn't a lost art among you young folks.
I need a how-to-cook-American cookbook. The best one you have.
Julia Child
Mastering the Art of French Cooking
I have something even better.

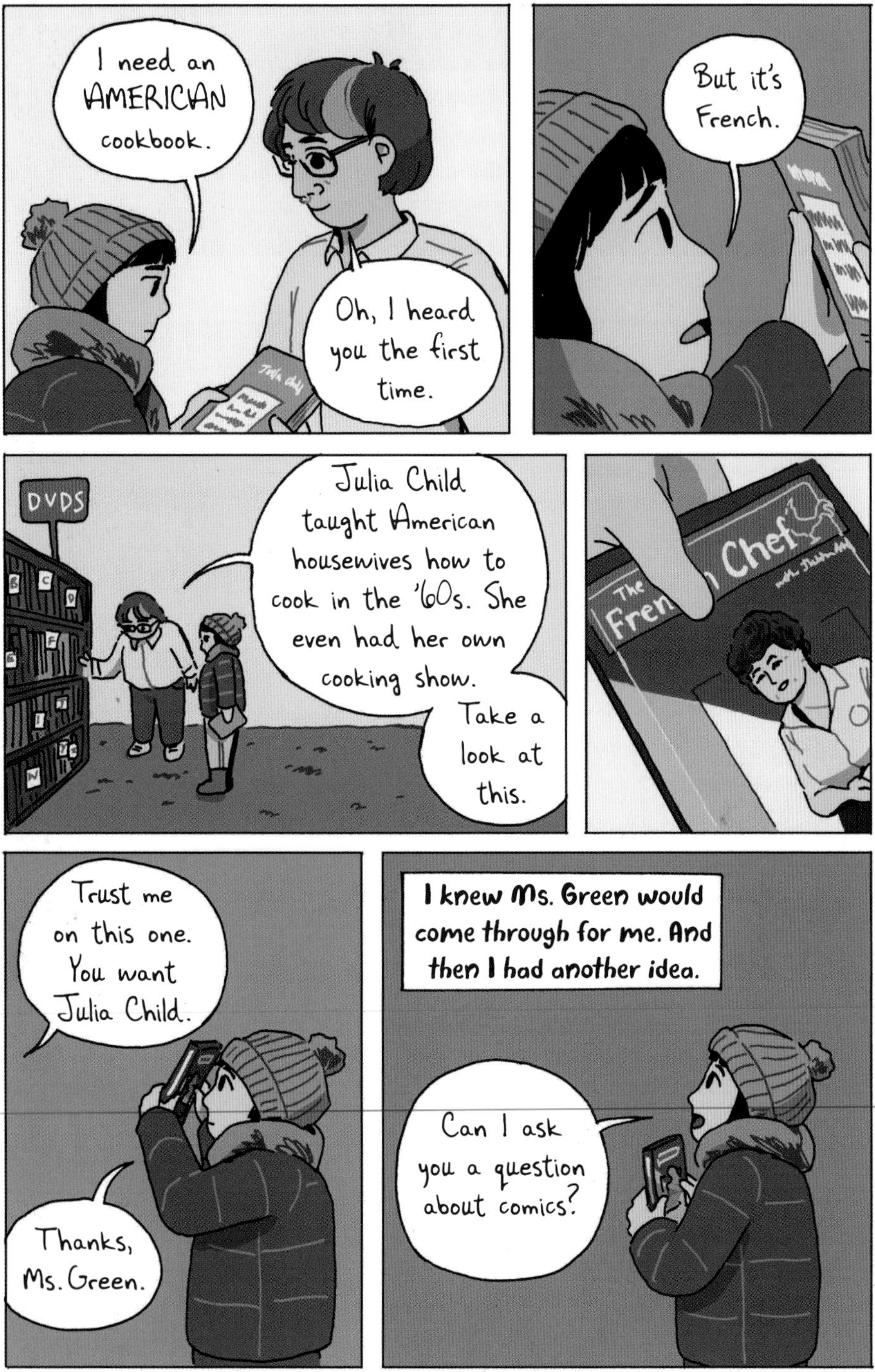
I need an AMERICAN cookbook.
Oh, I heard you the first time.
But it's French.
DVDS
Julia Child taught American housewives how to cook in the '60s. She even had her own cooking show.
Take a look at this.
The French Chef
Trust me on this one. You want Julia Child.
Thanks, Ms. Green.
I knew Ms. Green would come through for me. And then I had another idea.
Can I ask you a question about comics?

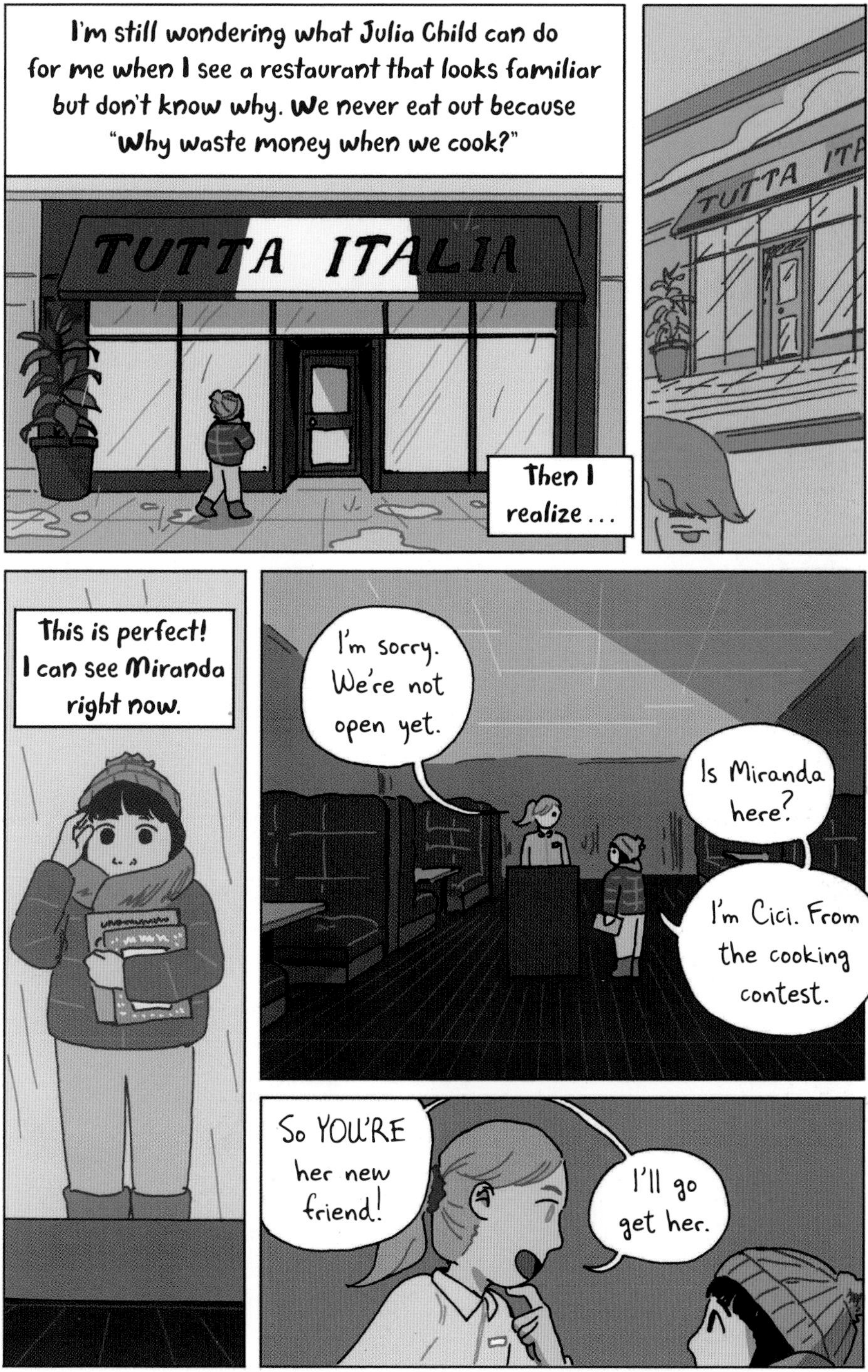

I'm still wondering what Julia Child can do for me when I see a restaurant that looks familiar but don't know why. We never eat out because "Why waste money when we cook?"
TUTTA ITALIA
Then I realize . . .
TUTTA ITA
This is perfect! I can see Miranda right now.
I'm sorry. We're not open yet.
Is Miranda here?
I'm Cici. From the cooking contest.
So YOU'RE her new friend!
I'll go get her.

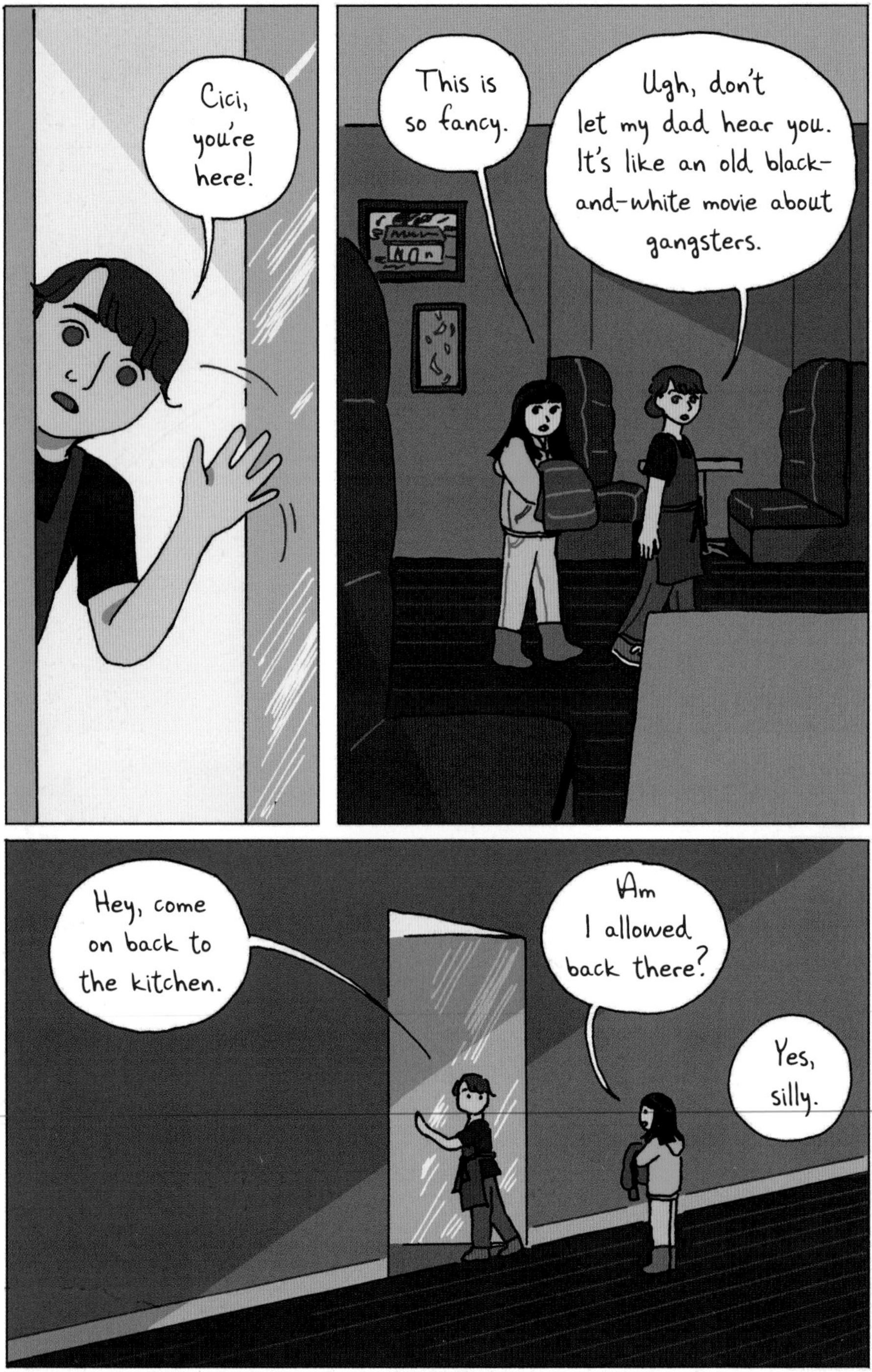
Cici, you're here!
This is so fancy.
Ugh, don't let my dad hear you. It's like an old black-and-white movie about gangsters.
Hey, come on back to the kitchen.
Am I allowed back there?
Yes, silly.

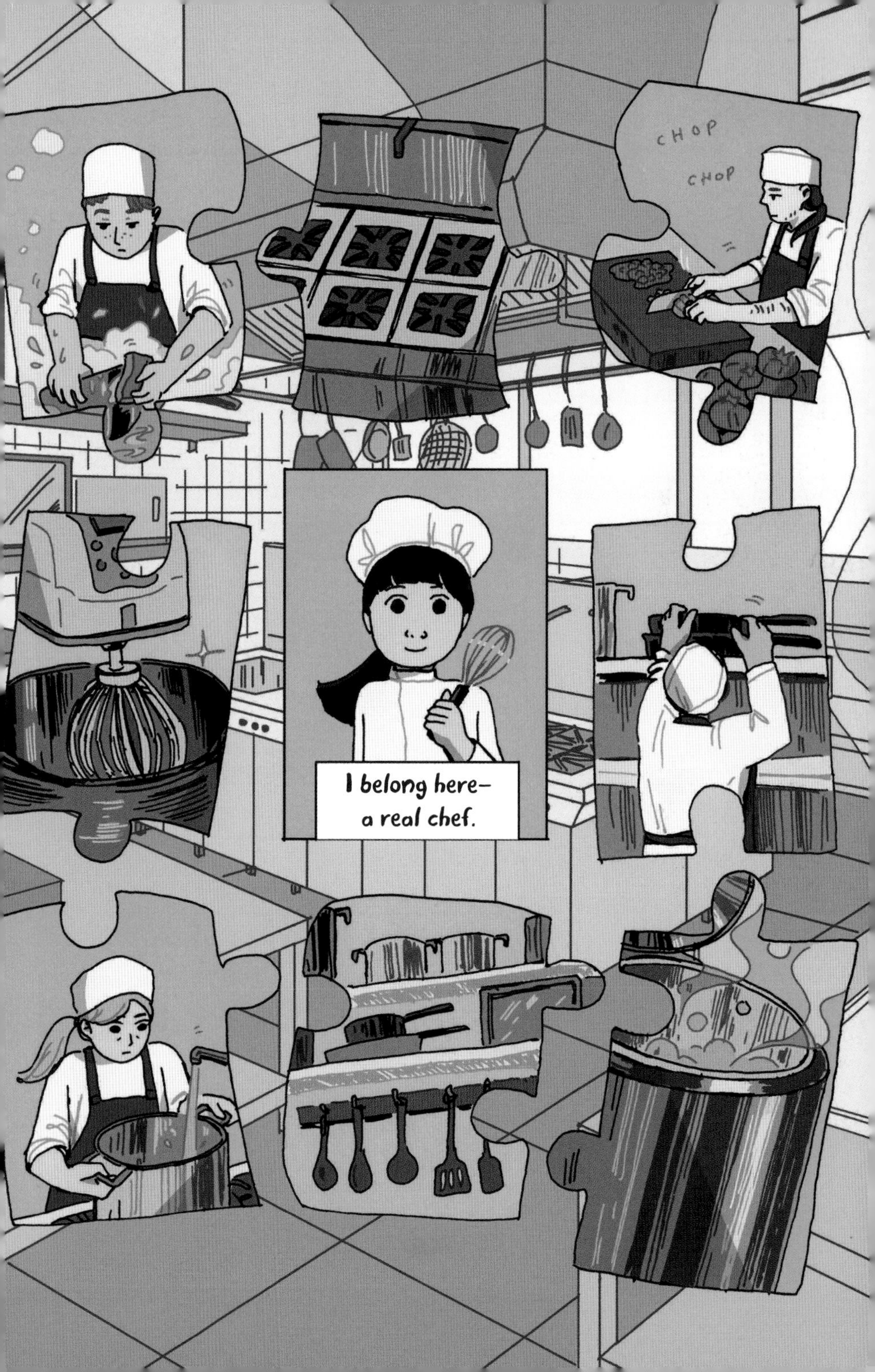
CHOP
CHOP
I belong here—
a real chef.

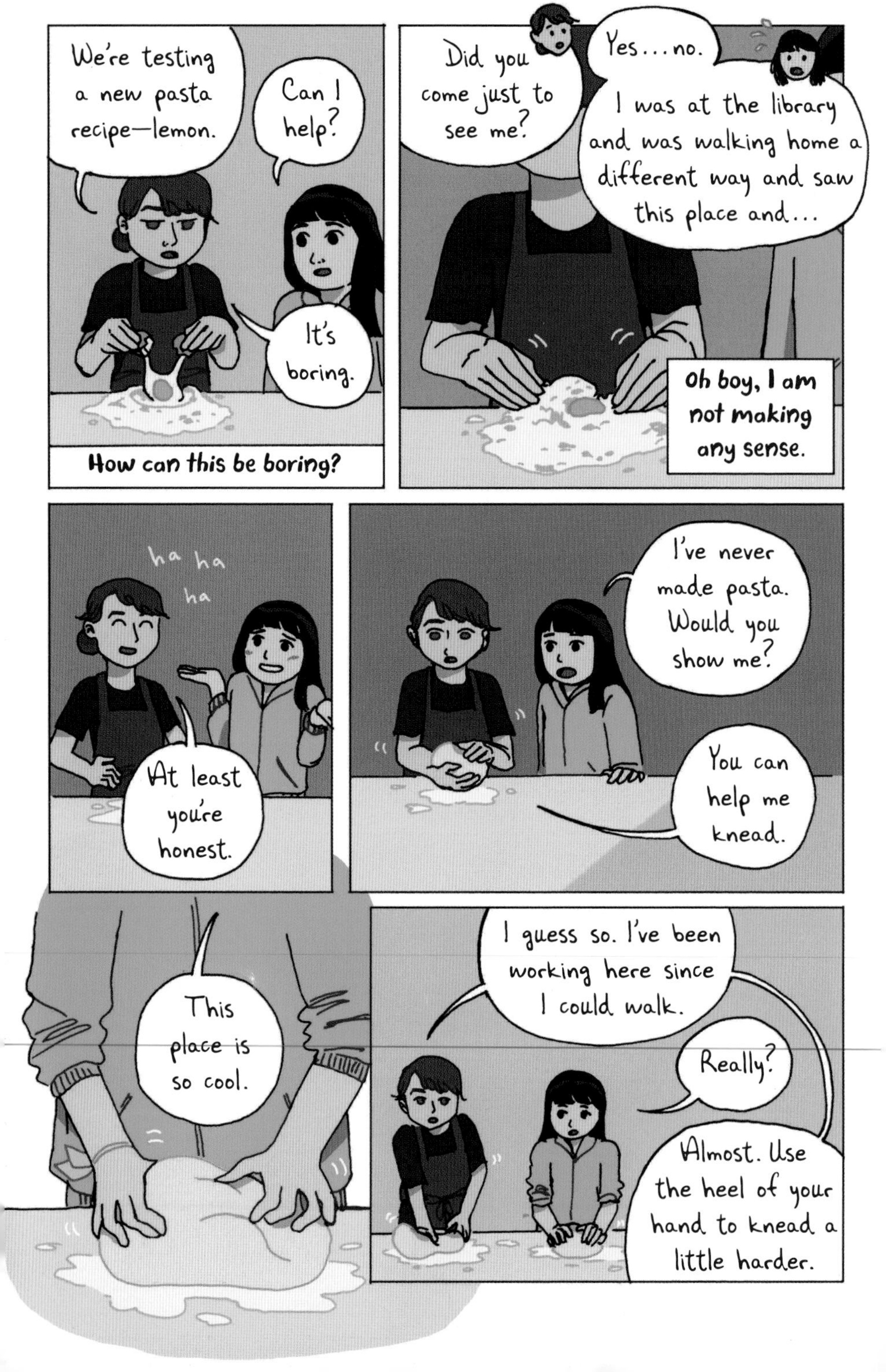
We're testing a new pasta recipe—lemon.
Can I help?
It's boring.
How can this be boring?
Did you come just to see me?
Yes...no.
I was at the library and was walking home a different way and saw this place and...
Oh boy, I am not making any sense.
ha ha ha
At least you're honest.
I've never made pasta. Would you show me?
You can help me knead.
This place is so cool.
I guess so. I've been working here since I could walk.
Really?
Almost. Use the heel of your hand to knead a little harder.

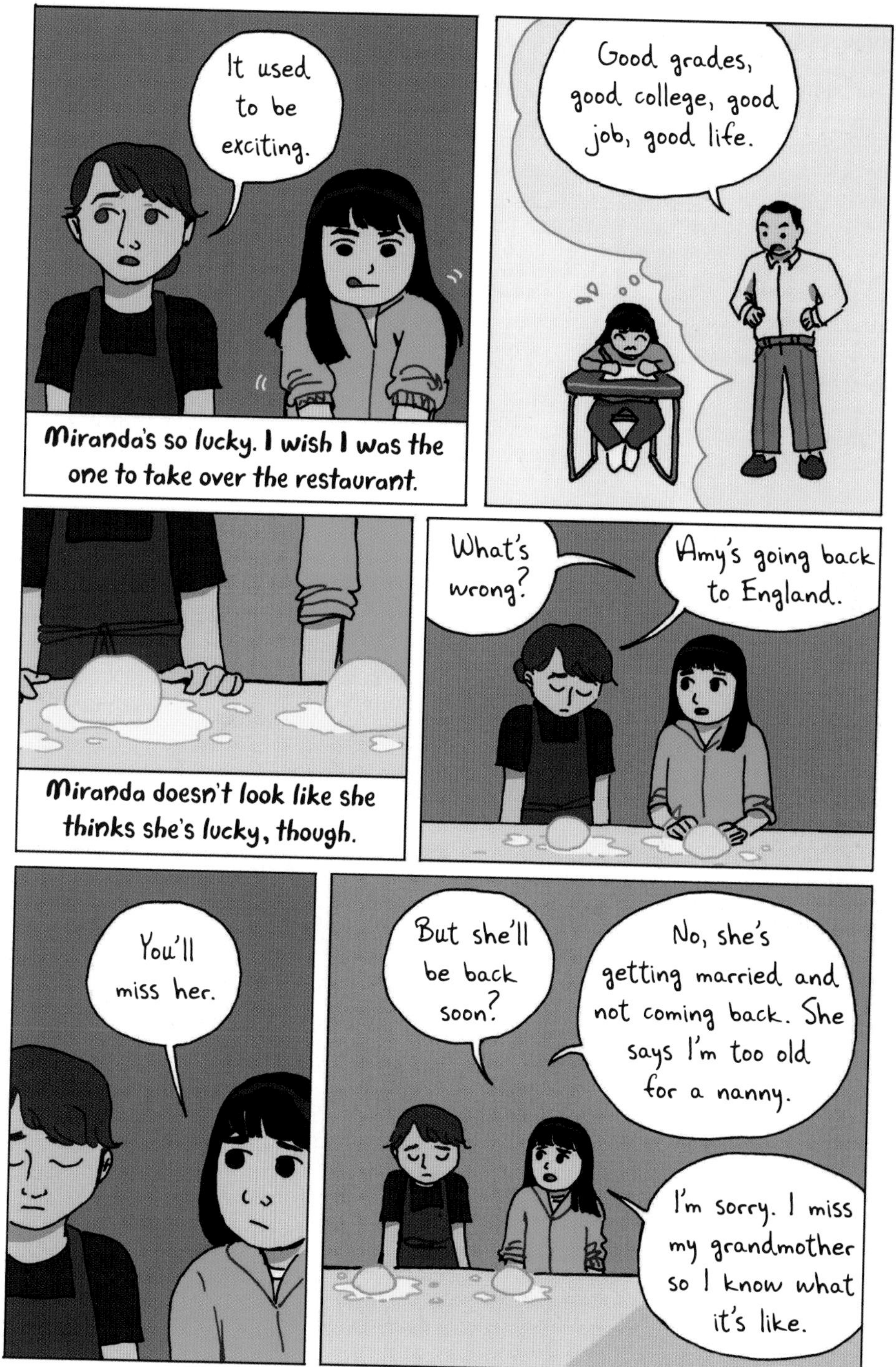
It used to be exciting.
Miranda's so lucky. I wish I was the one to take over the restaurant.
Good grades, good college, good job, good life.
Miranda doesn't look like she thinks she's lucky, though.
What's wrong?
Amy's going back to England.
You'll miss her.
But she'll be back soon?
No, she's getting married and not coming back. She says I'm too old for a nanny.
I'm sorry. I miss my grandmother so I know what it's like.

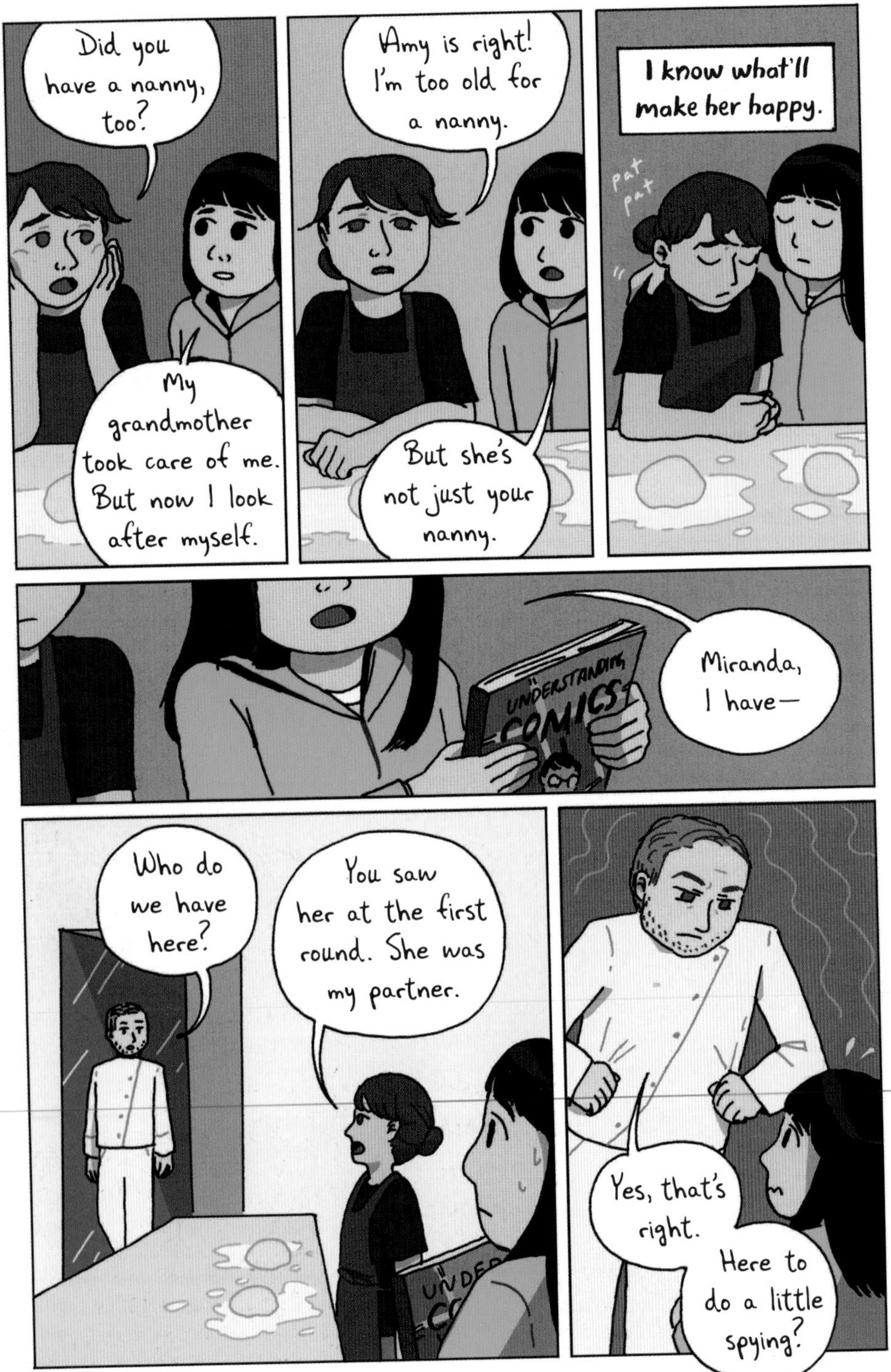
Did you have a nanny, too?
My grandmother took care of me. But now I look after myself.
Amy is right! I'm too old for a nanny.
But she's not just your nanny.
I know what'll make her happy.
pat pat
Miranda, I have—
UNDERSTANDING COMICS
Who do we have here?
You saw her at the first round. She was my partner.
Yes, that's right.
Here to do a little spying?

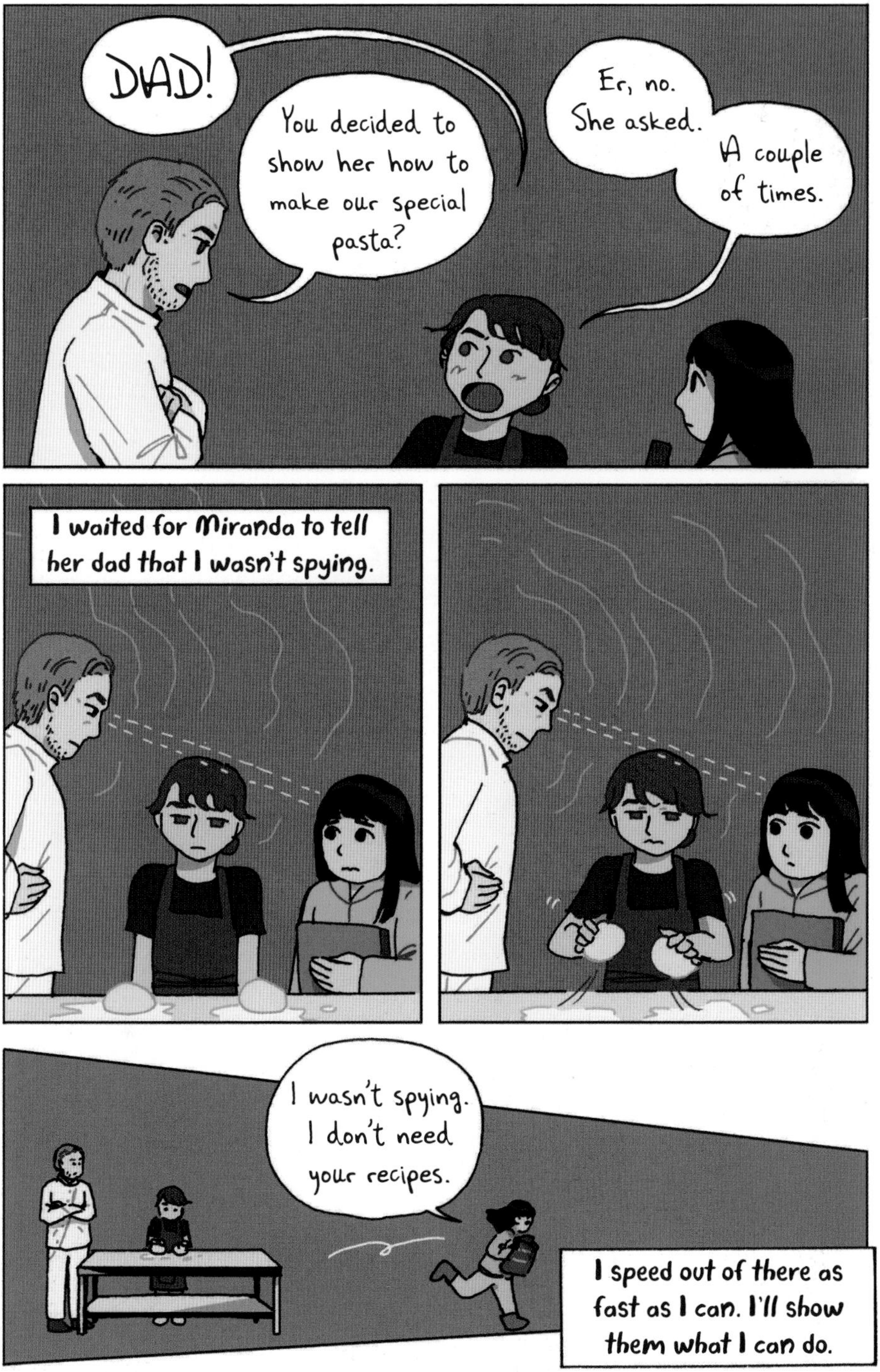
DAD!
You decided to show her how to make our special pasta?
Er, no. She asked.
A couple of times.
I waited for Miranda to tell her dad that I wasn't spying.
I wasn't spying. I don't need your recipes.
I speed out of there as fast as I can. I'll show them what I can do.

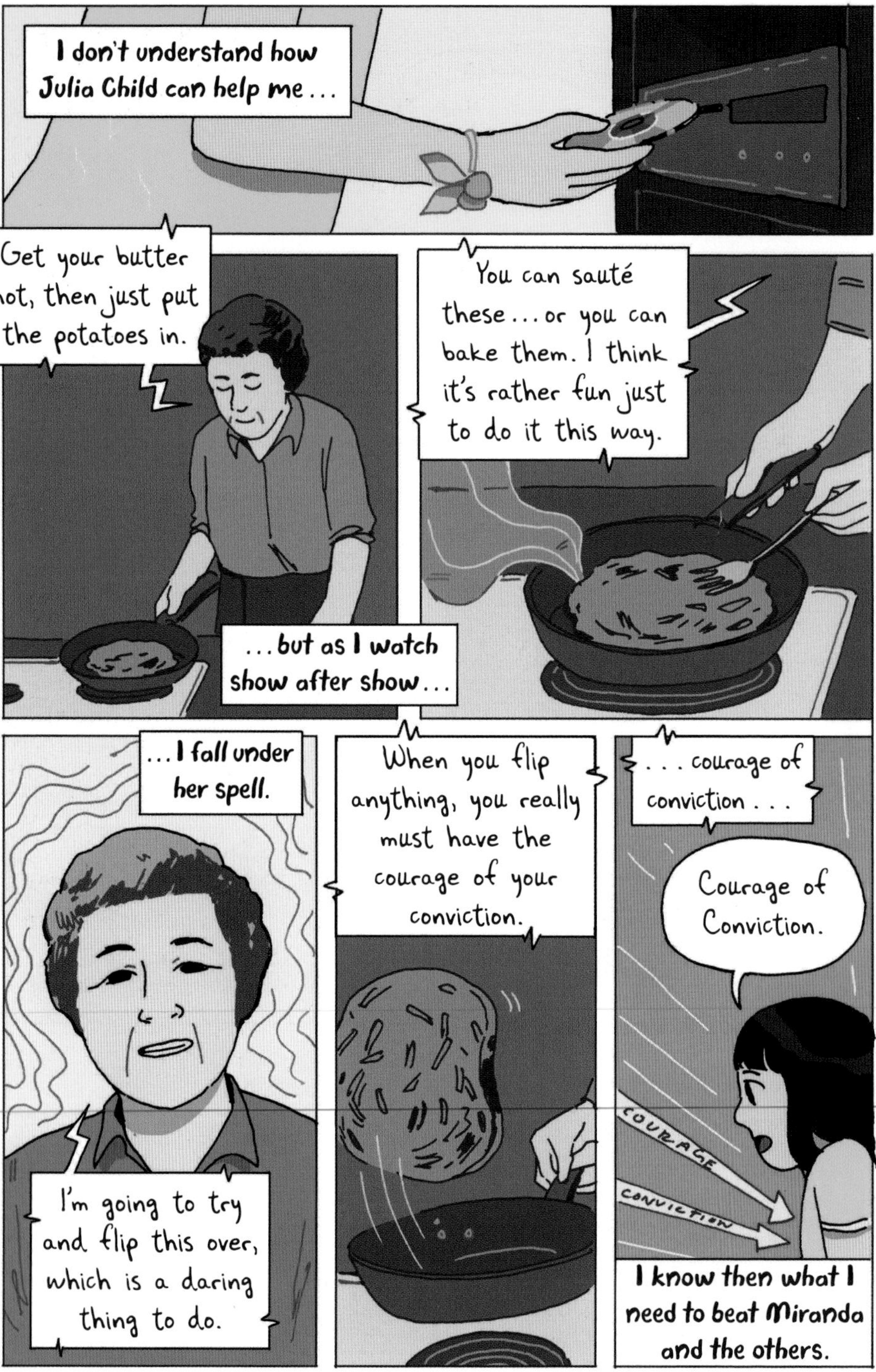
I don't understand how Julia Child can help me . . .
Get your butter hot, then just put the potatoes in.
You can sauté these . . . or you can bake them. I think it's rather fun just to do it this way.
. . . but as I watch show after show . . .
. . . I fall under her spell.
I'm going to try and flip this over, which is a daring thing to do.
When you flip anything, you really must have the courage of your conviction.
. . . courage of conviction . . .
Courage of Conviction.
COURAGE
CONVICTION
I know then what I need to beat Miranda and the others.

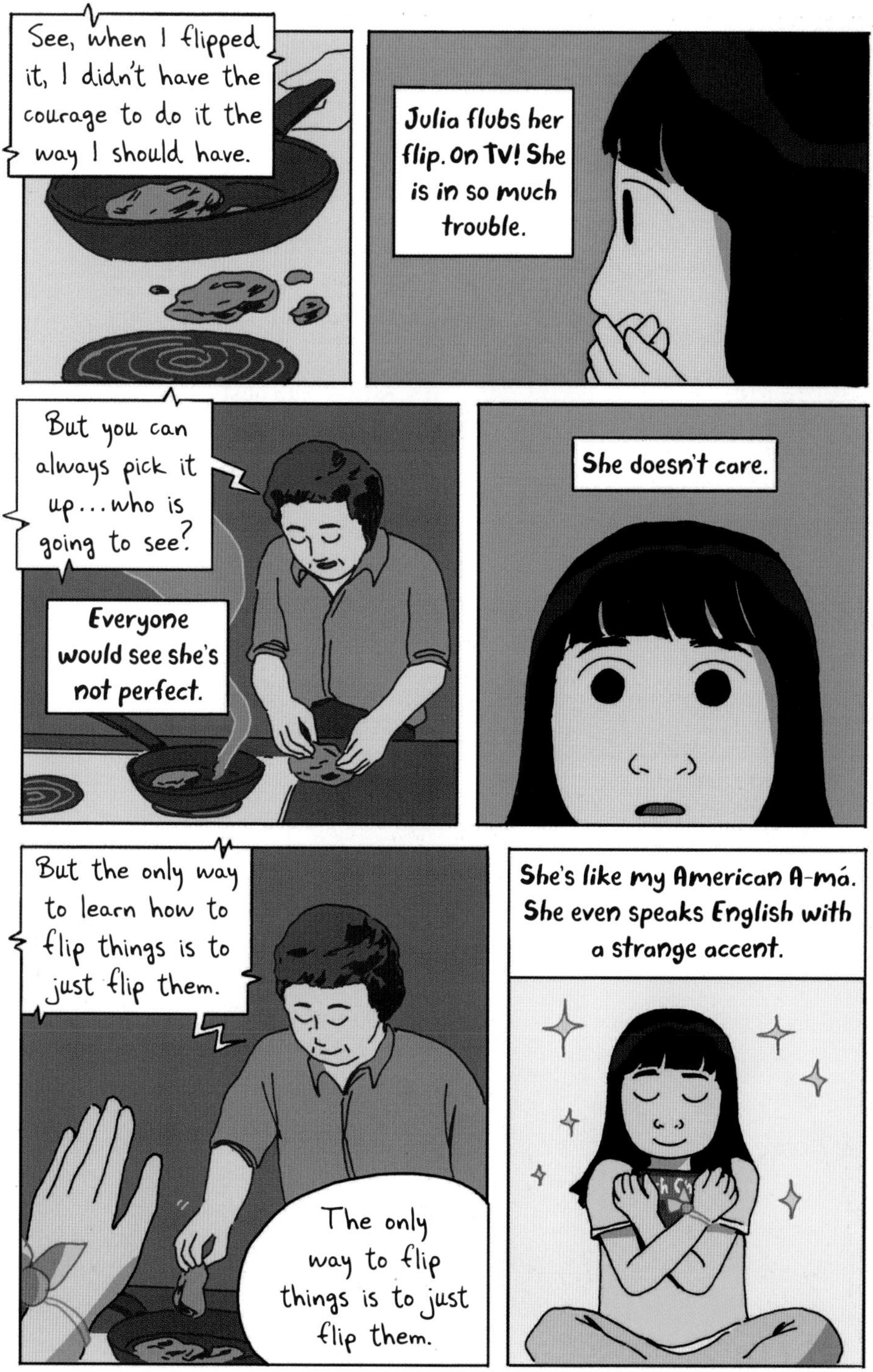
See, when I flipped it, I didn't have the courage to do it the way I should have.
Julia flubs her flip. On TV! She is in so much trouble.
But you can always pick it up...who is going to see?
Everyone would see she's not perfect.
She doesn't care.
But the only way to learn how to flip things is to just flip them.
The only way to flip things is to just flip them.
She's like my American A-má. She even speaks English with a strange accent.

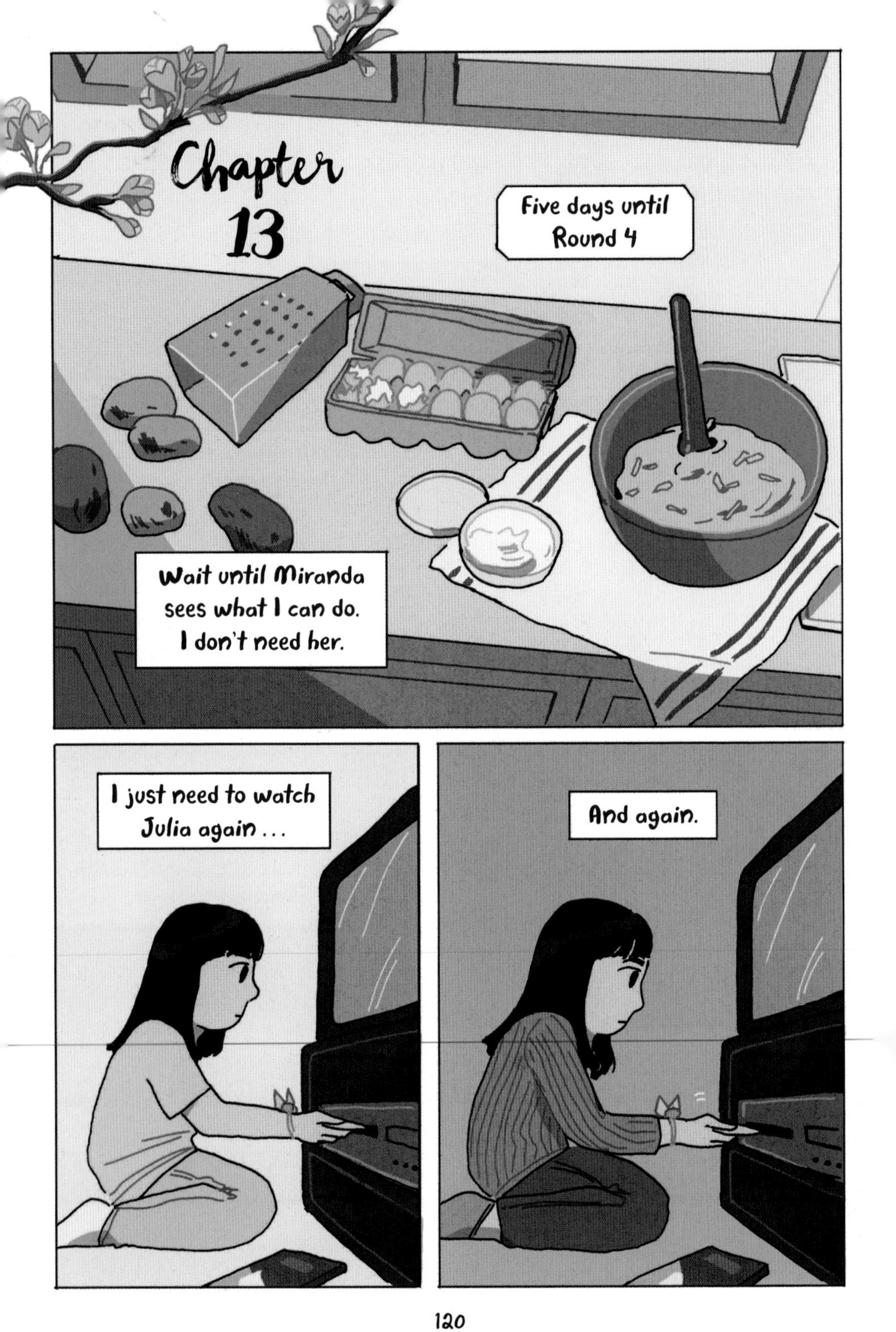
Chapter 13
Five days until Round 4
Wait until Miranda sees what I can do. I don't need her.
I just need to watch Julia again . . .
And again.

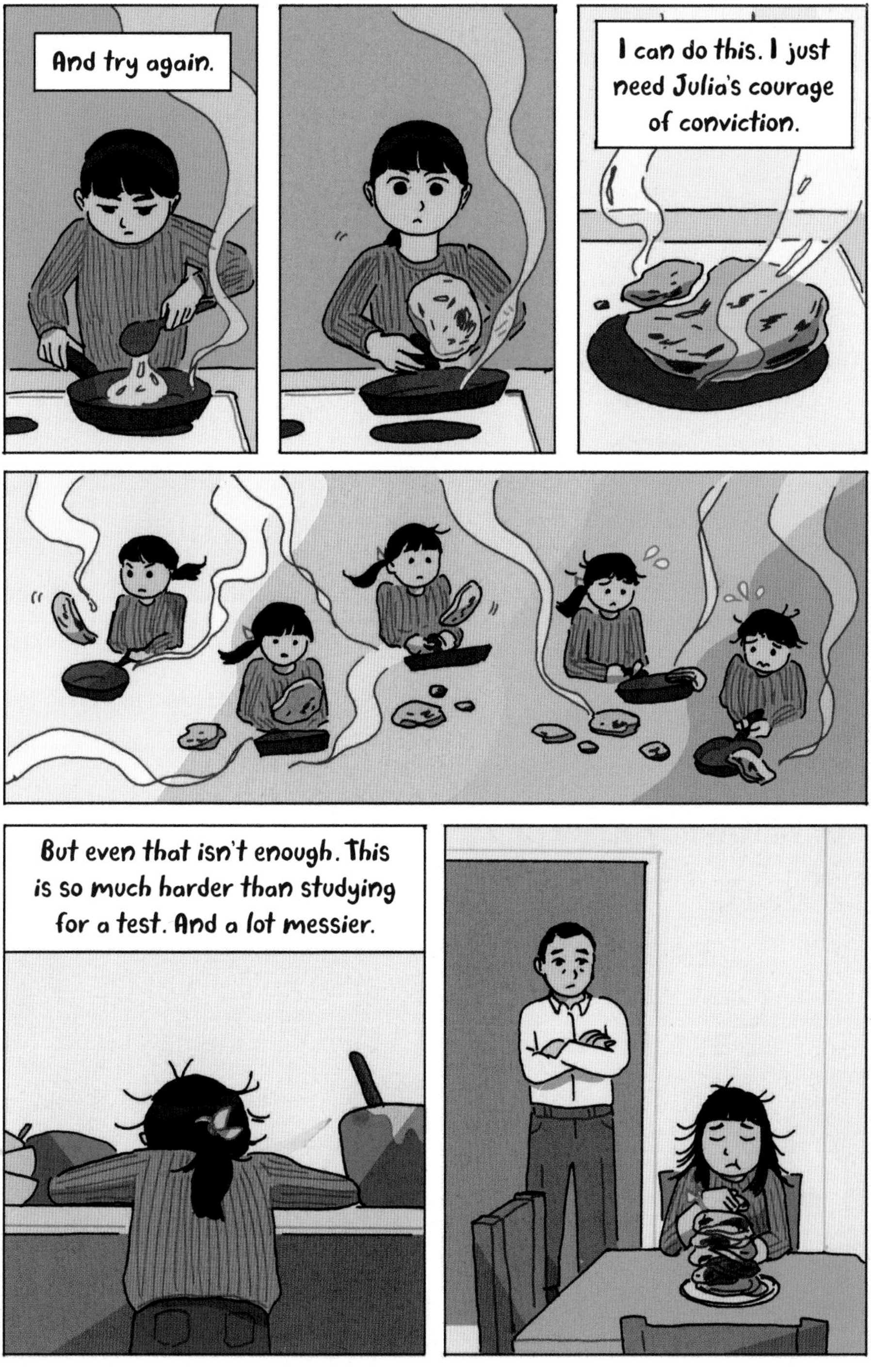
And try again.
I can do this. I just need Julia's courage of conviction.
But even that isn't enough. This is so much harder than studying for a test. And a lot messier.

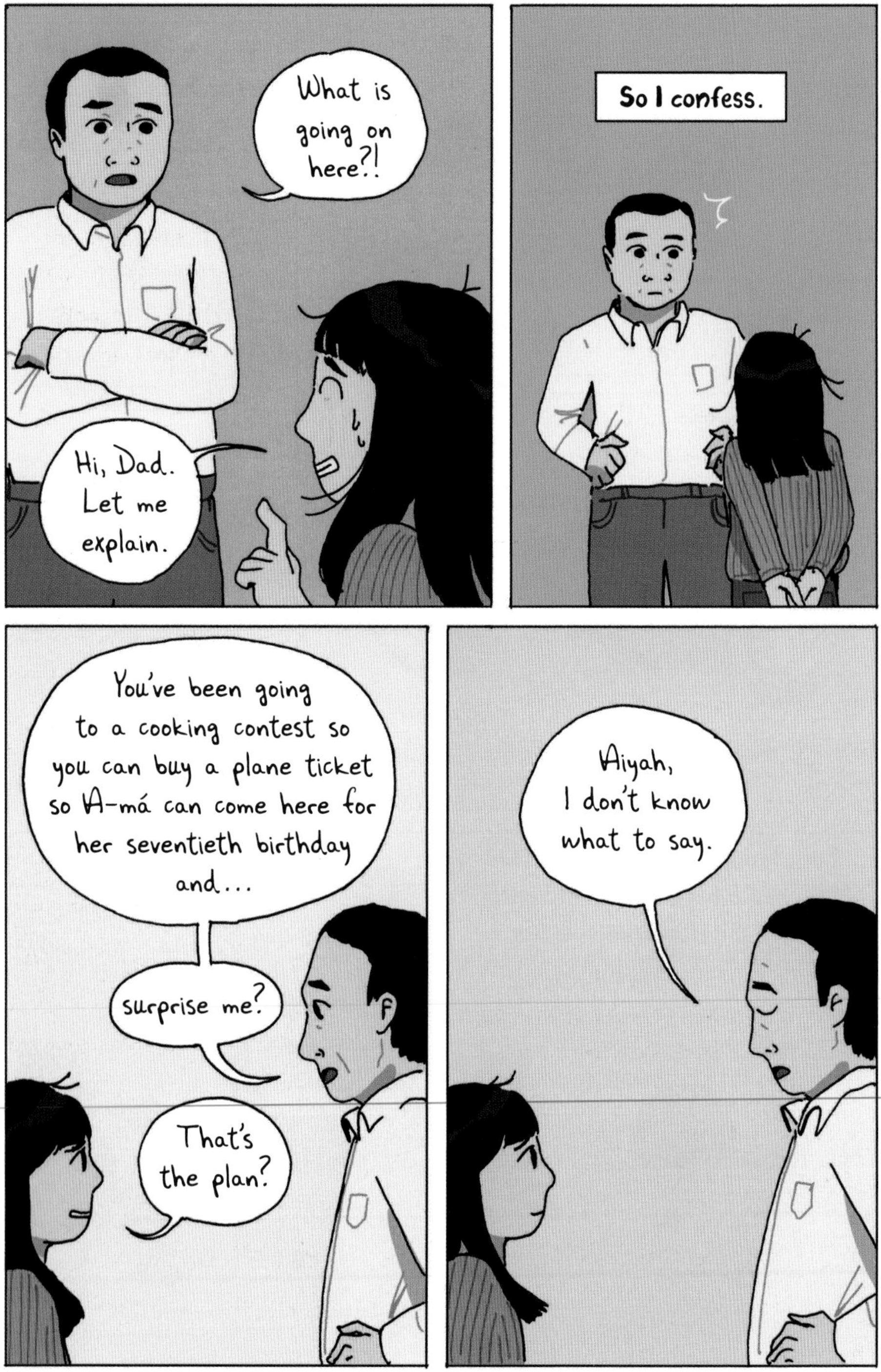
What is going on here?!
Hi, Dad. Let me explain.
So I confess.
You've been going to a cooking contest so you can buy a plane ticket so A-má can come here for her seventieth birthday and...
surprise me?
That's the plan?
Aiyah, I don't know what to say.

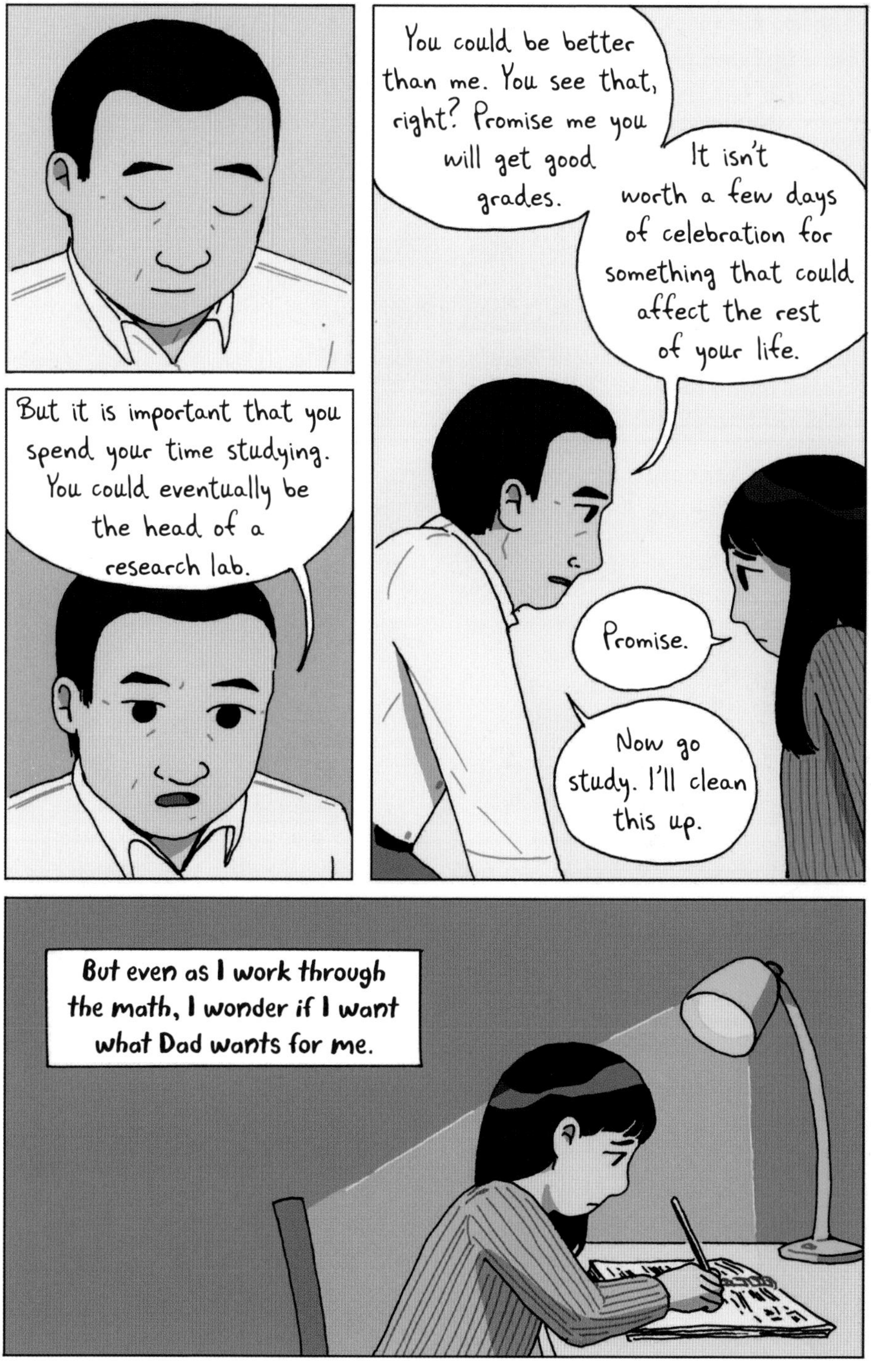
You could be better than me. You see that, right? Promise me you will get good grades.
It isn't worth a few days of celebration for something that could affect the rest of your life.
But it is important that you spend your time studying. You could eventually be the head of a research lab.
Promise.
Now go study. I'll clean this up.
But even as I work through the math, I wonder if I want what Dad wants for me.

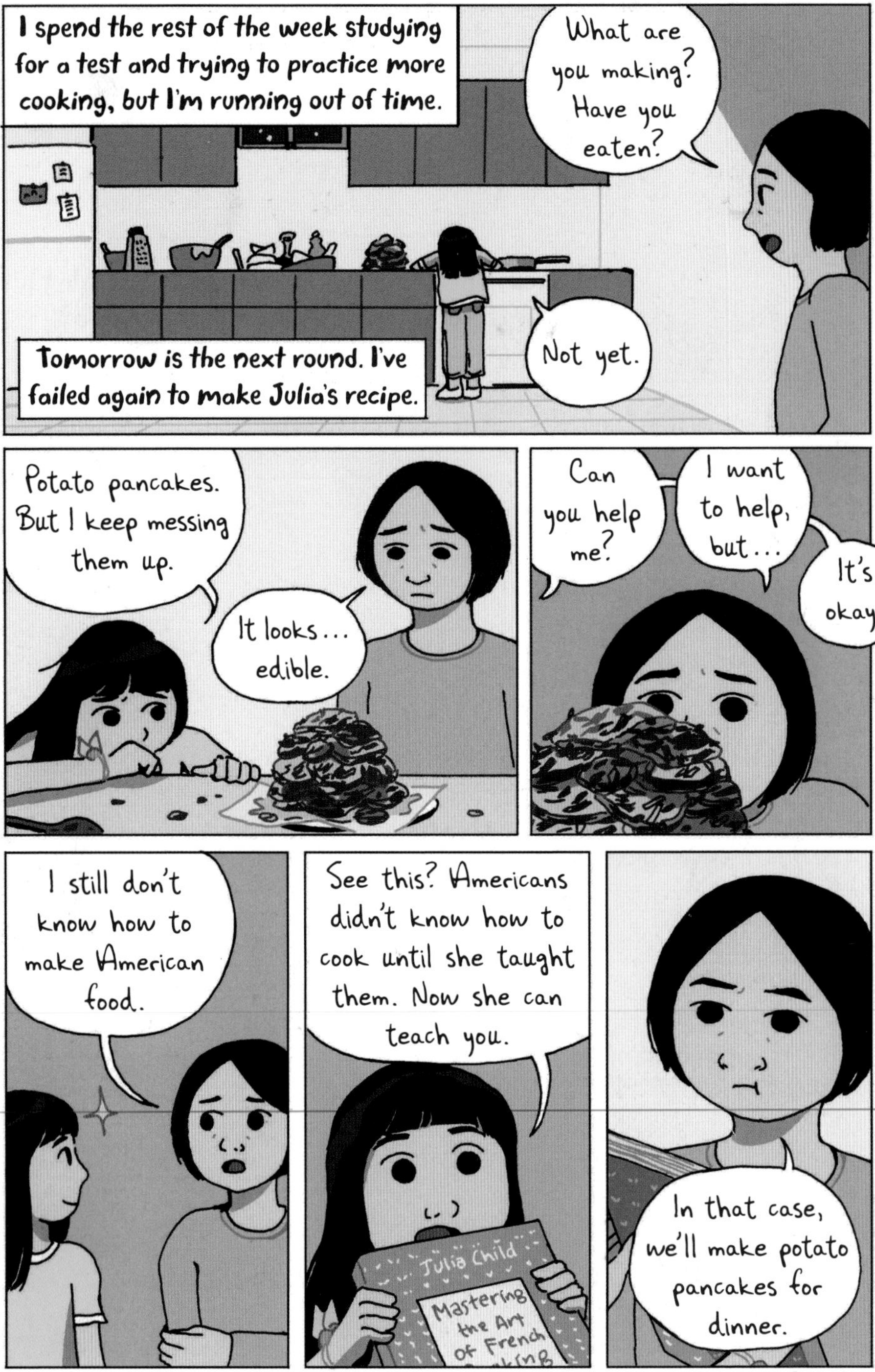

I spend the rest of the week studying for a test and trying to practice more cooking, but I'm running out of time.
What are you making? Have you eaten?
Not yet.
Tomorrow is the next round. I've failed again to make Julia's recipe.
Potato pancakes. But I keep messing them up.
It looks... edible.
Can you help me?
I want to help, but...
It's okay.
I still don't know how to make American food.
See this? Americans didn't know how to cook until she taught them. Now she can teach you.
Julia Child
Mastering the Art of French
In that case, we'll make potato pancakes for dinner.

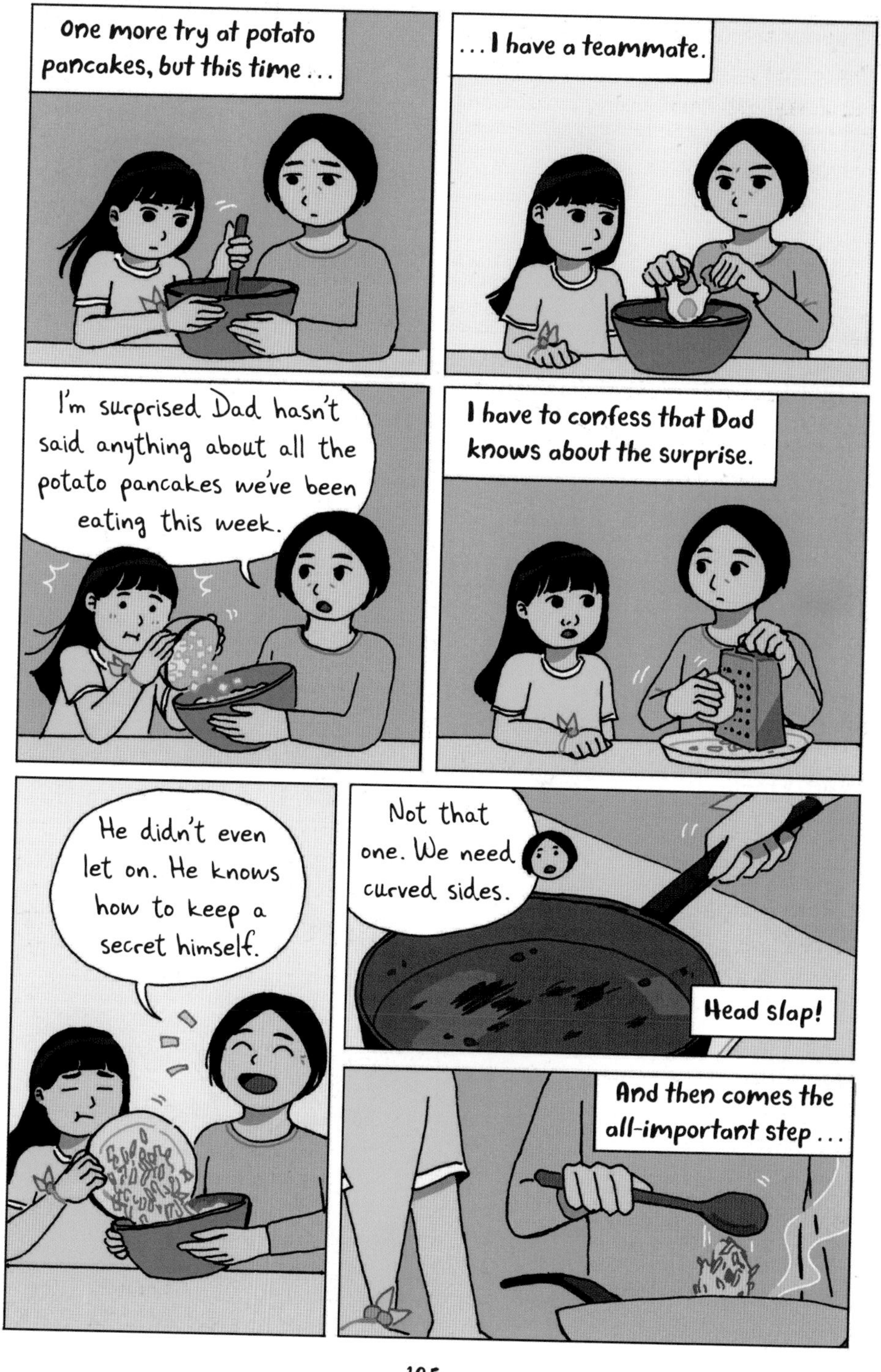
One more try at potato pancakes, but this time . . .
. . . I have a teammate.
I'm surprised Dad hasn't said anything about all the potato pancakes we've been eating this week.
I have to confess that Dad knows about the surprise.
He didn't even let on. He knows how to keep a secret himself.
Not that one. We need curved sides.
Head slap!
And then comes the all-important step . . .

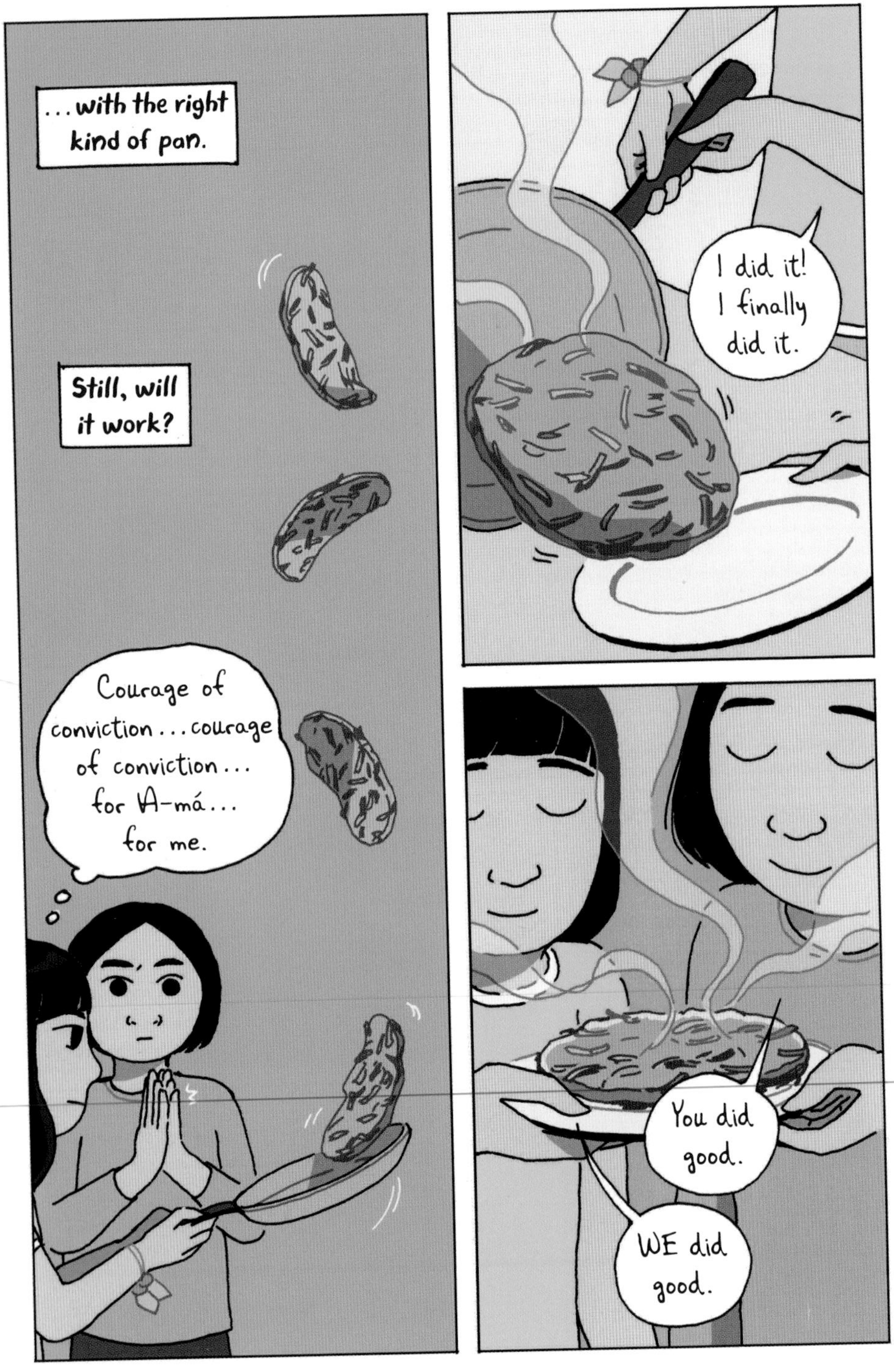
...with the right kind of pan.
Still, will it work?
Courage of conviction... courage of conviction... for A-má... for me.
I did it! I finally did it.
You did good.
WE did good.

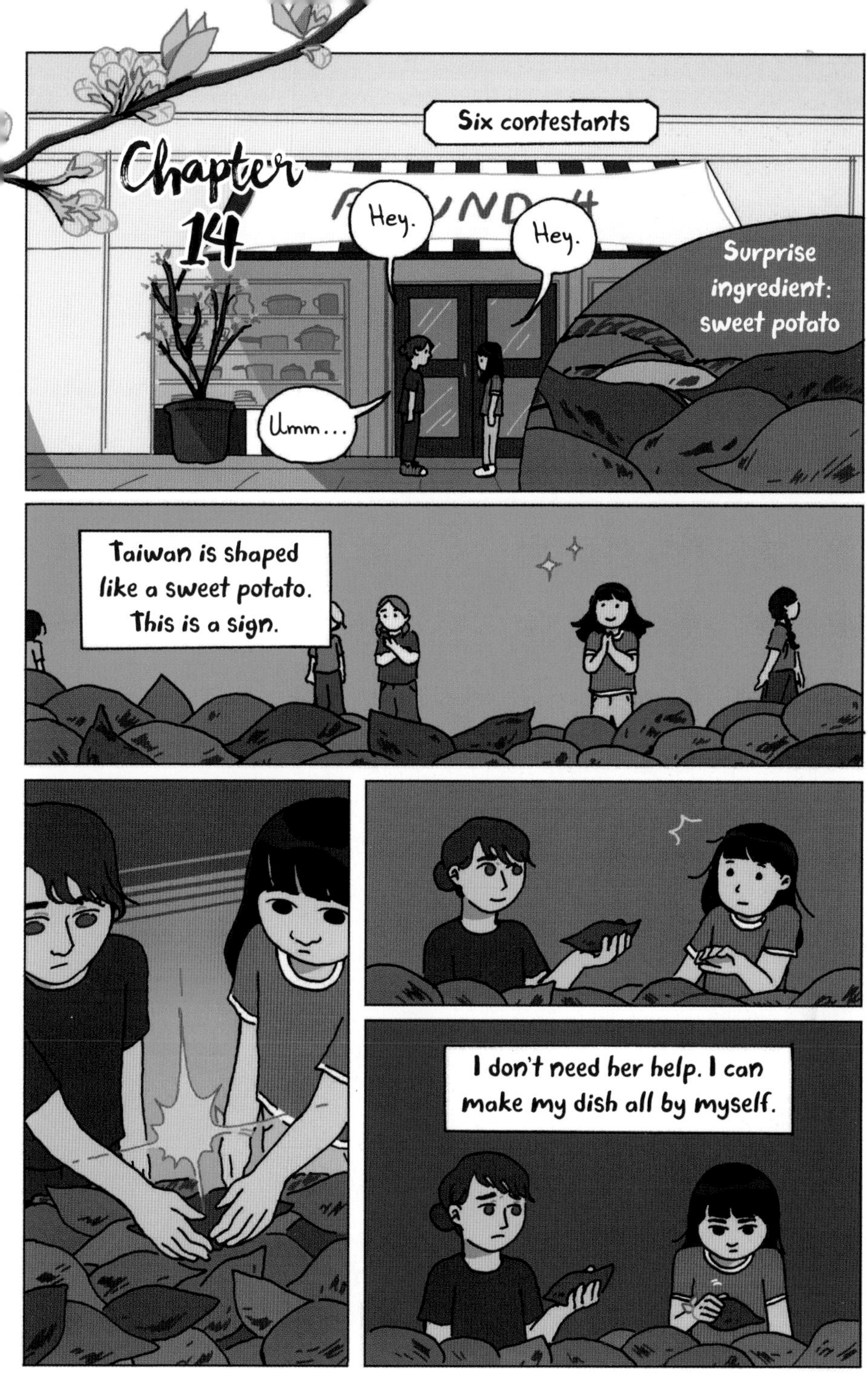
Chapter 14
Six contestants
ROUND 4
Hey.
Hey.
Umm...
Surprise ingredient: sweet potato
Taiwan is shaped like a sweet potato. This is a sign.
I don't need her help. I can make my dish all by myself.

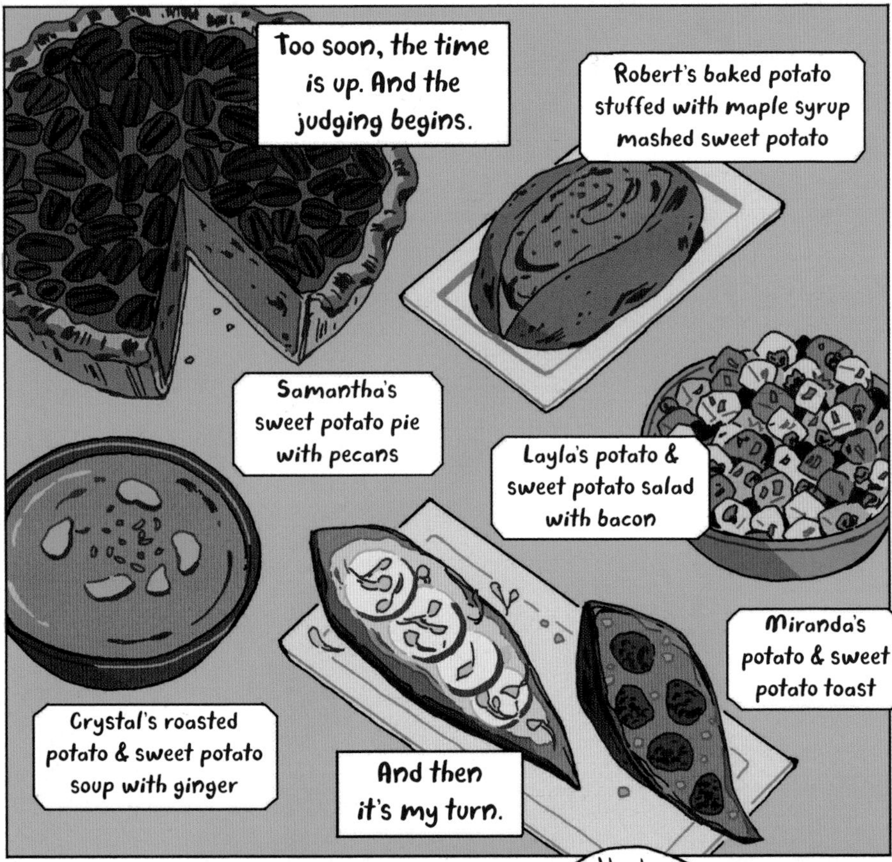
Too soon, the time is up. And the judging begins.
Robert's baked potato stuffed with maple syrup mashed sweet potato
Samantha's sweet potato pie with pecans
Layla's potato & sweet potato salad with bacon
Miranda's potato & sweet potato toast
Crystal's roasted potato & sweet potato soup with ginger
And then it's my turn.

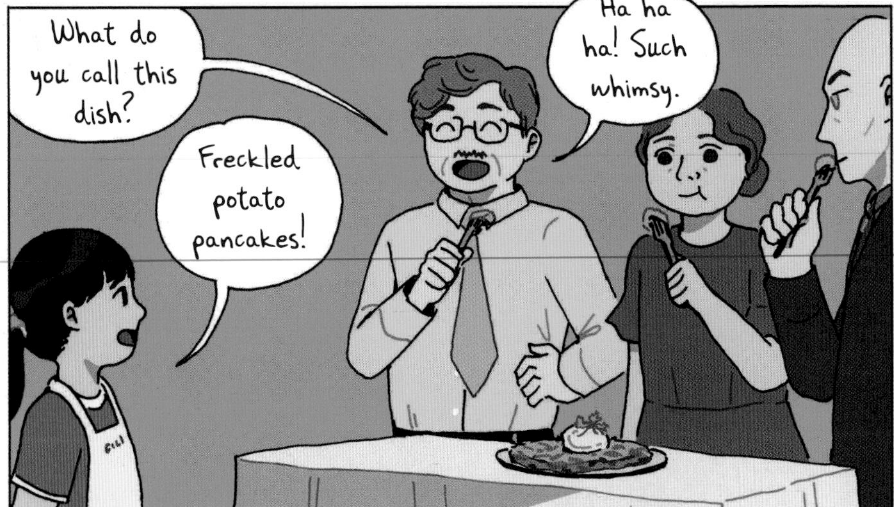
What do you call this dish?
Ha ha ha! Such whimsy.
Freckled potato pancakes!

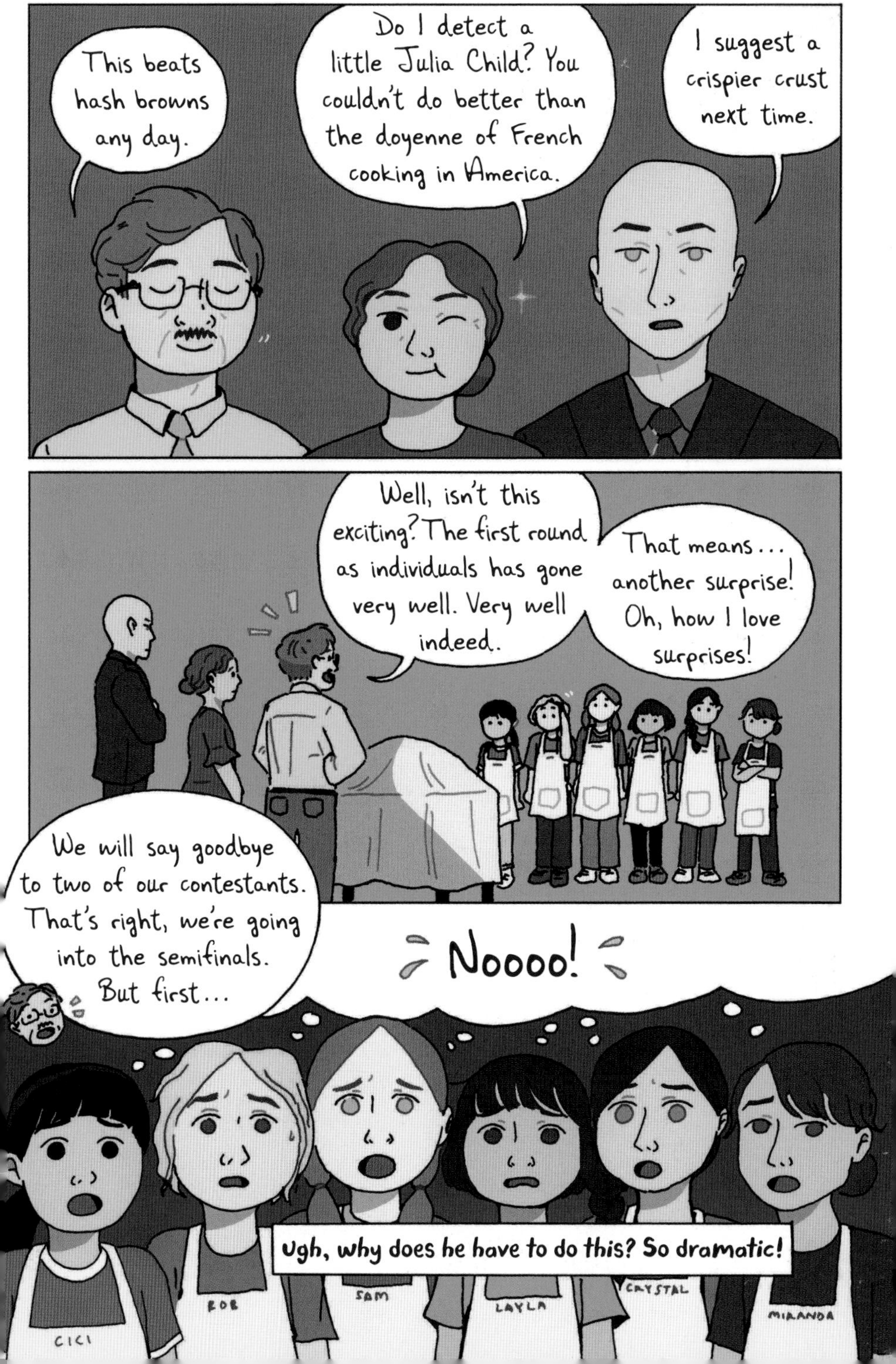
This beats hash browns any day.
Do I detect a little Julia Child? You couldn't do better than the doyenne of French cooking in America.
I suggest a crispier crust next time.
Well, isn't this exciting? The first round as individuals has gone very well. Very well indeed.
That means... another surprise! Oh, how I love surprises!
We will say goodbye to two of our contestants. That's right, we're going into the semifinals. But first...
Noooo!
Ugh, why does he have to do this? So dramatic!
CICI
ROB
SAM
LAYLA
CRYSTAL
MIRANDA

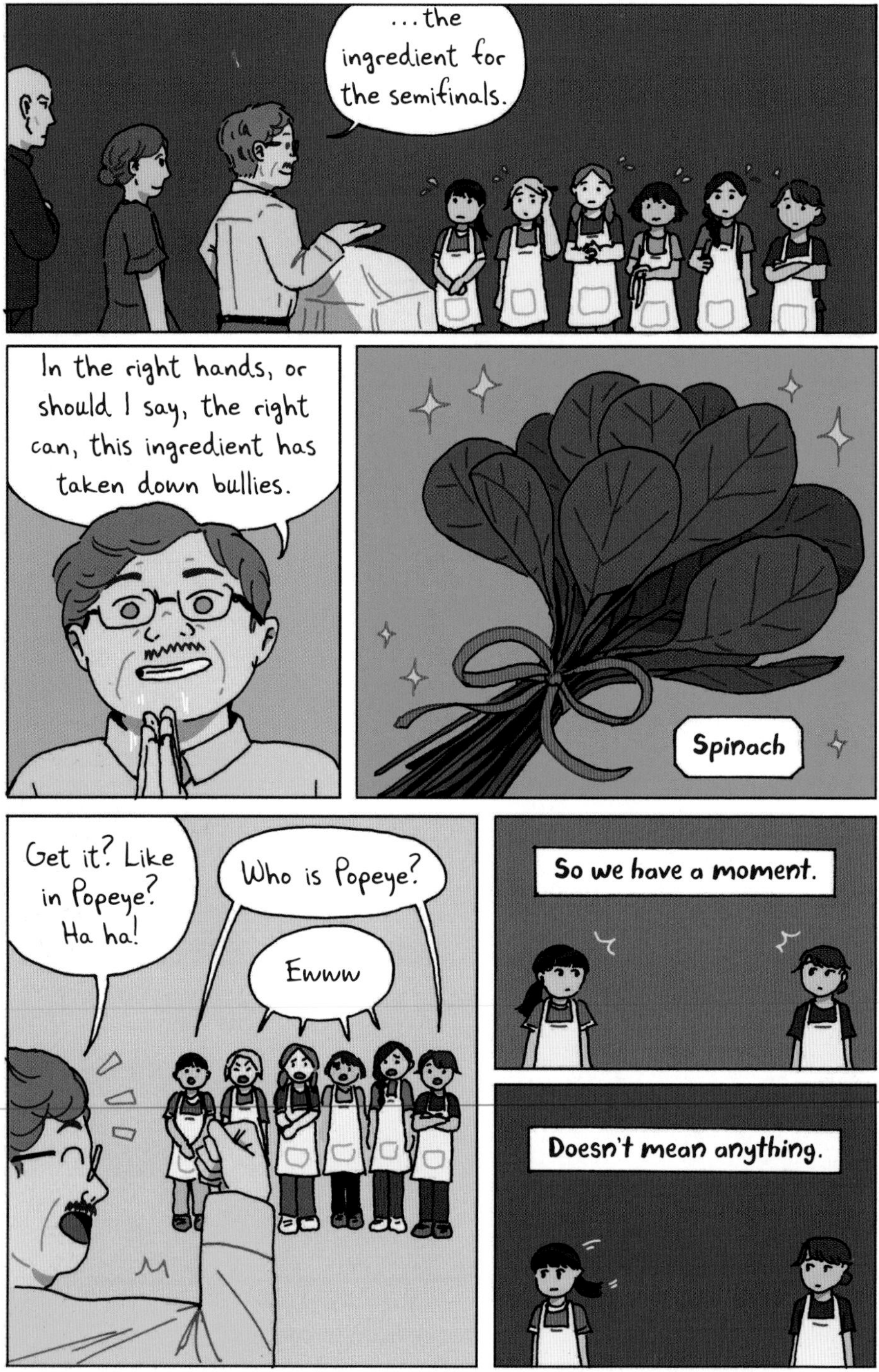
...the ingredient for the semifinals.
In the right hands, or should I say, the right can, this ingredient has taken down bullies.
Spinach
Get it? Like in Popeye? Ha ha!
Who is Popeye?
Ewww
So we have a moment.
Doesn't mean anything.

Chapter 15

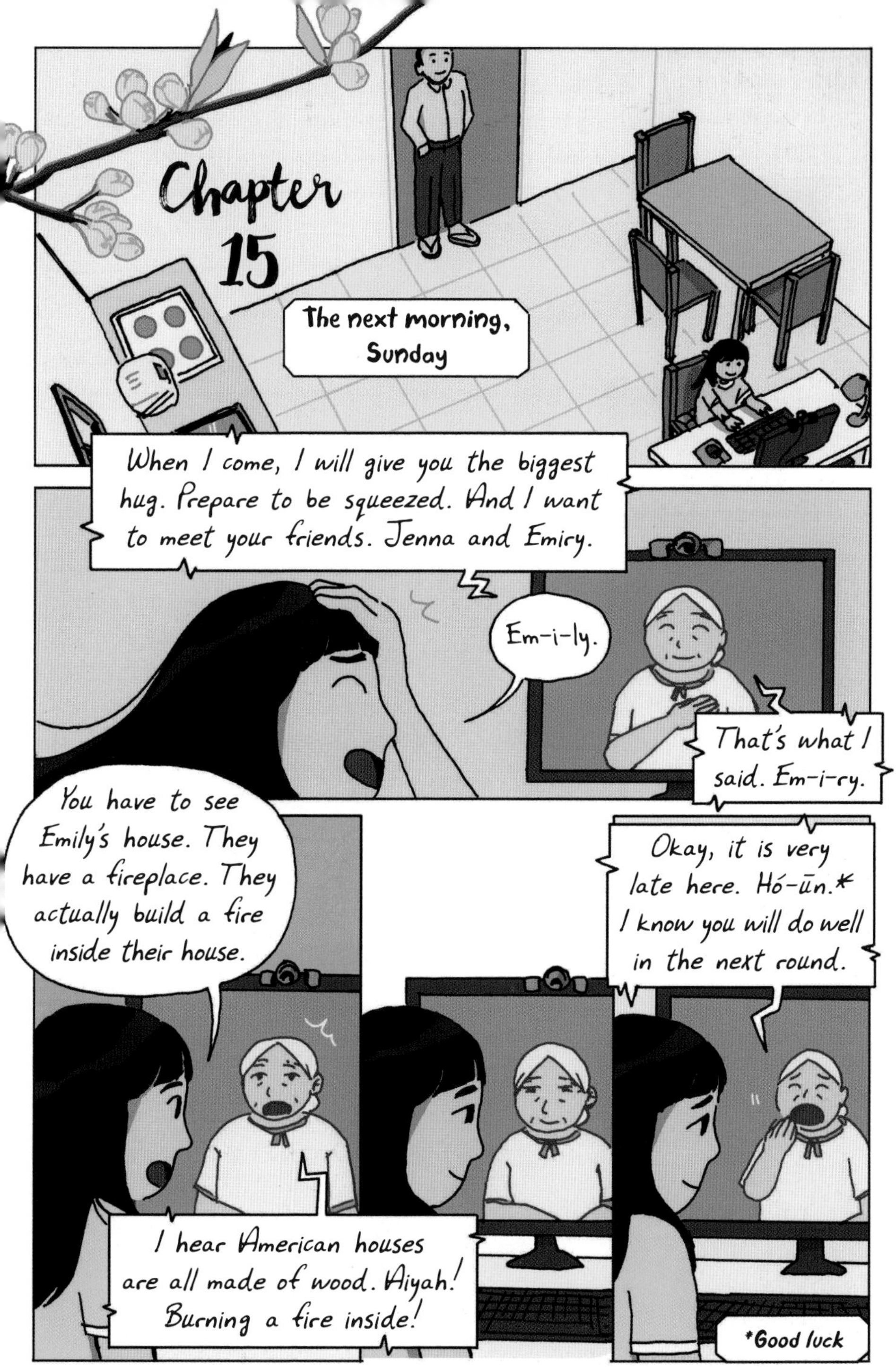
The next morning, Sunday
When I come, I will give you the biggest hug. Prepare to be squeezed. And I want to meet your friends. Jenna and Emiry.
Em-i-ly.
That's what I said. Em-i-ry.
You have to see Emily's house. They have a fireplace. They actually build a fire inside their house.
I hear American houses are all made of wood. Aiyah! Burning a fire inside!
Okay, it is very late here. Hó-ūn.* I know you will do well in the next round.
*Good luck

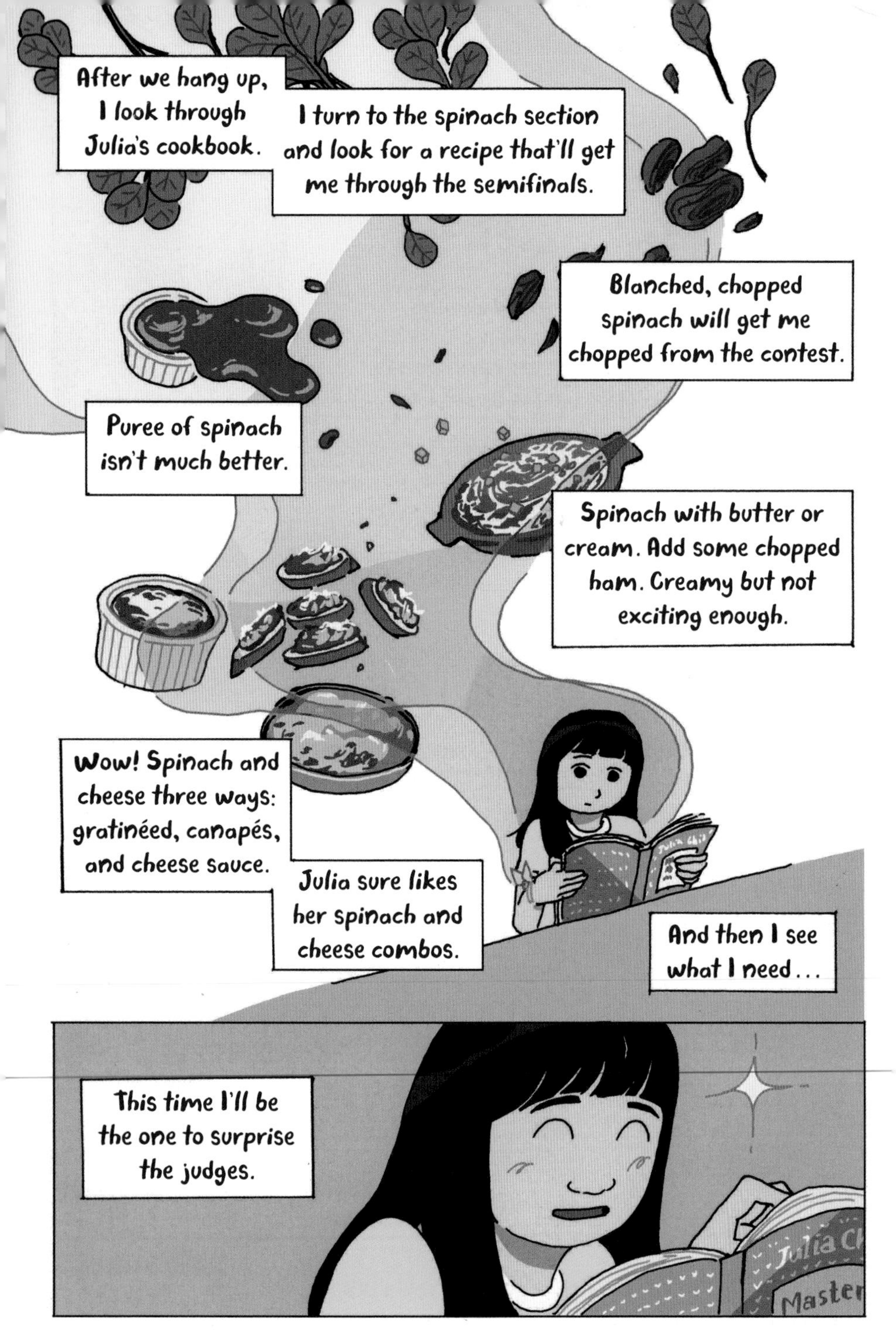
After we hang up, I look through Julia's cookbook.
I turn to the spinach section and look for a recipe that'll get me through the semifinals.
Blanched, chopped spinach will get me chopped from the contest.
Puree of spinach isn't much better.
Spinach with butter or cream. Add some chopped ham. Creamy but not exciting enough.
Wow! Spinach and cheese three ways: gratinéed, canapés, and cheese sauce.
Julia sure likes her spinach and cheese combos.
And then I see what I need...
This time I'll be the one to surprise the judges.
Julia Ch
Master

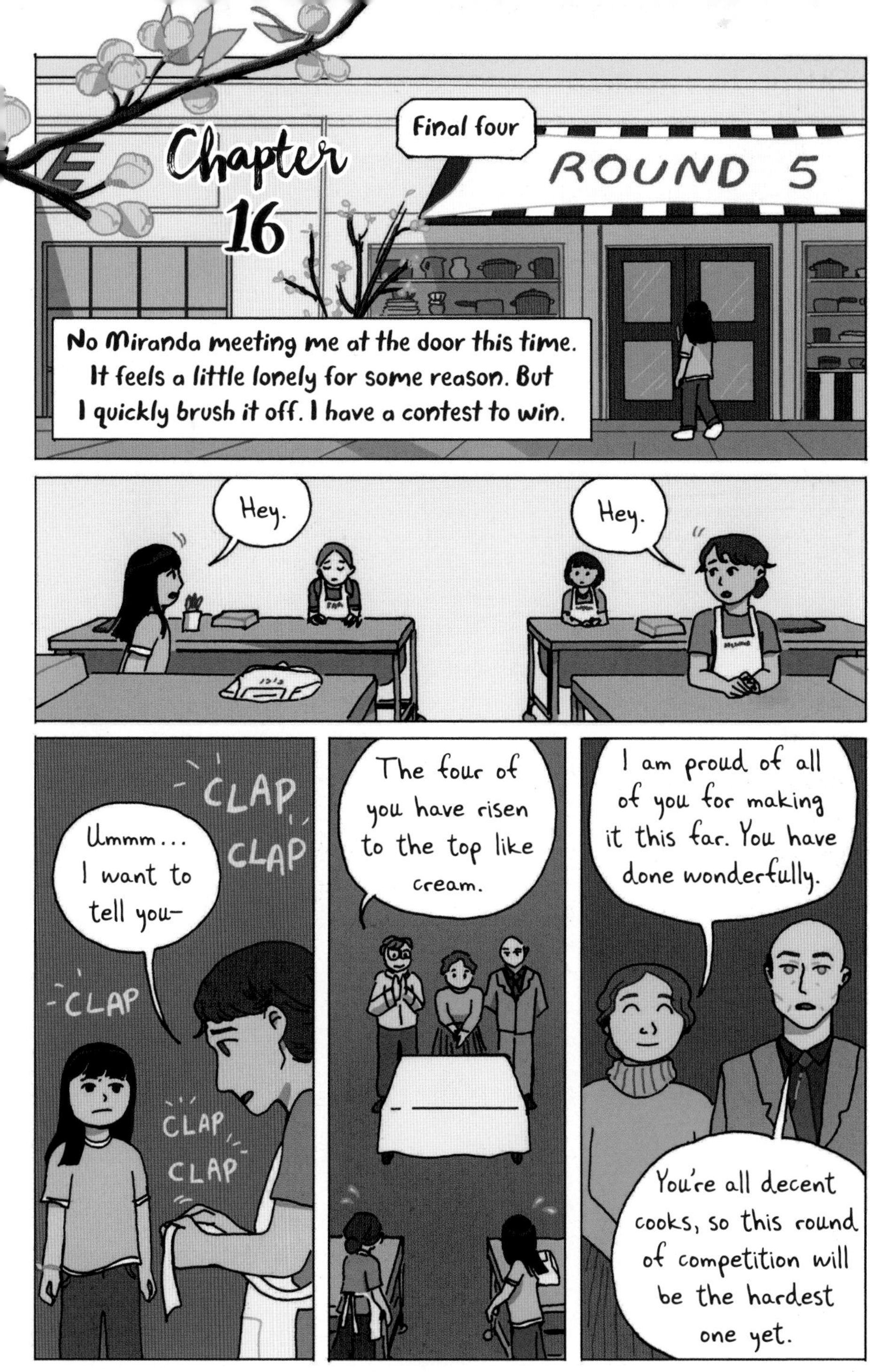
Chapter 16
Final four
ROUND 5
No Miranda meeting me at the door this time. It feels a little lonely for some reason. But I quickly brush it off. I have a contest to win.
Hey.
Hey.
CLAP
CLAP
Ummm... I want to tell you—
CLAP
CLAP
CLAP
The four of you have risen to the top like cream.
I am proud of all of you for making it this far. You have done wonderfully.
You're all decent cooks, so this round of competition will be the hardest one yet.

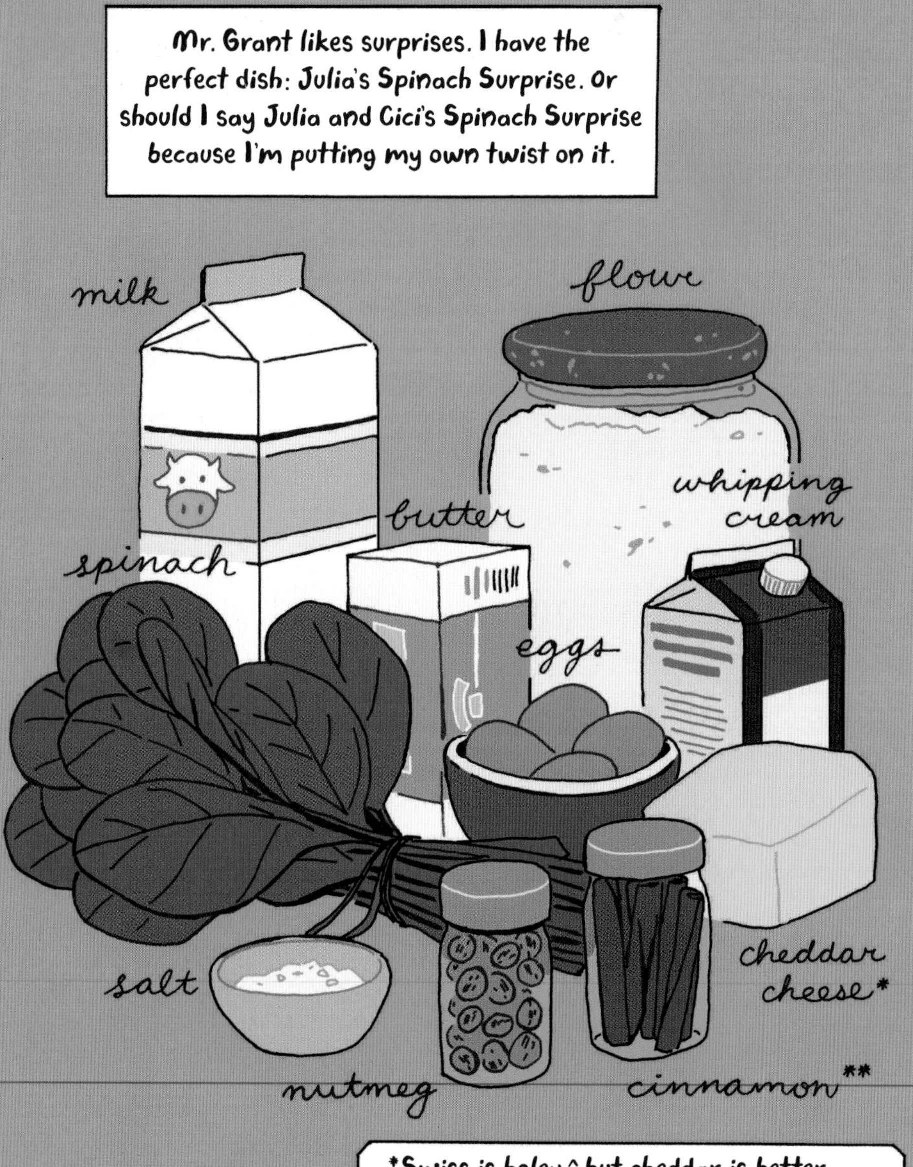
Mr. Grant likes surprises. I have the perfect dish: Julia's Spinach Surprise. Or should I say Julia and Cici's Spinach Surprise because I'm putting my own twist on it.
milk
flour
whipping cream
butter
spinach
eggs
cheddar cheese*
salt
nutmeg
cinnamon**
*Swiss is holey,^ but cheddar is better.
**I'm adding cinnamon since everything is better with it. But that's just my opinion.
^pun intended

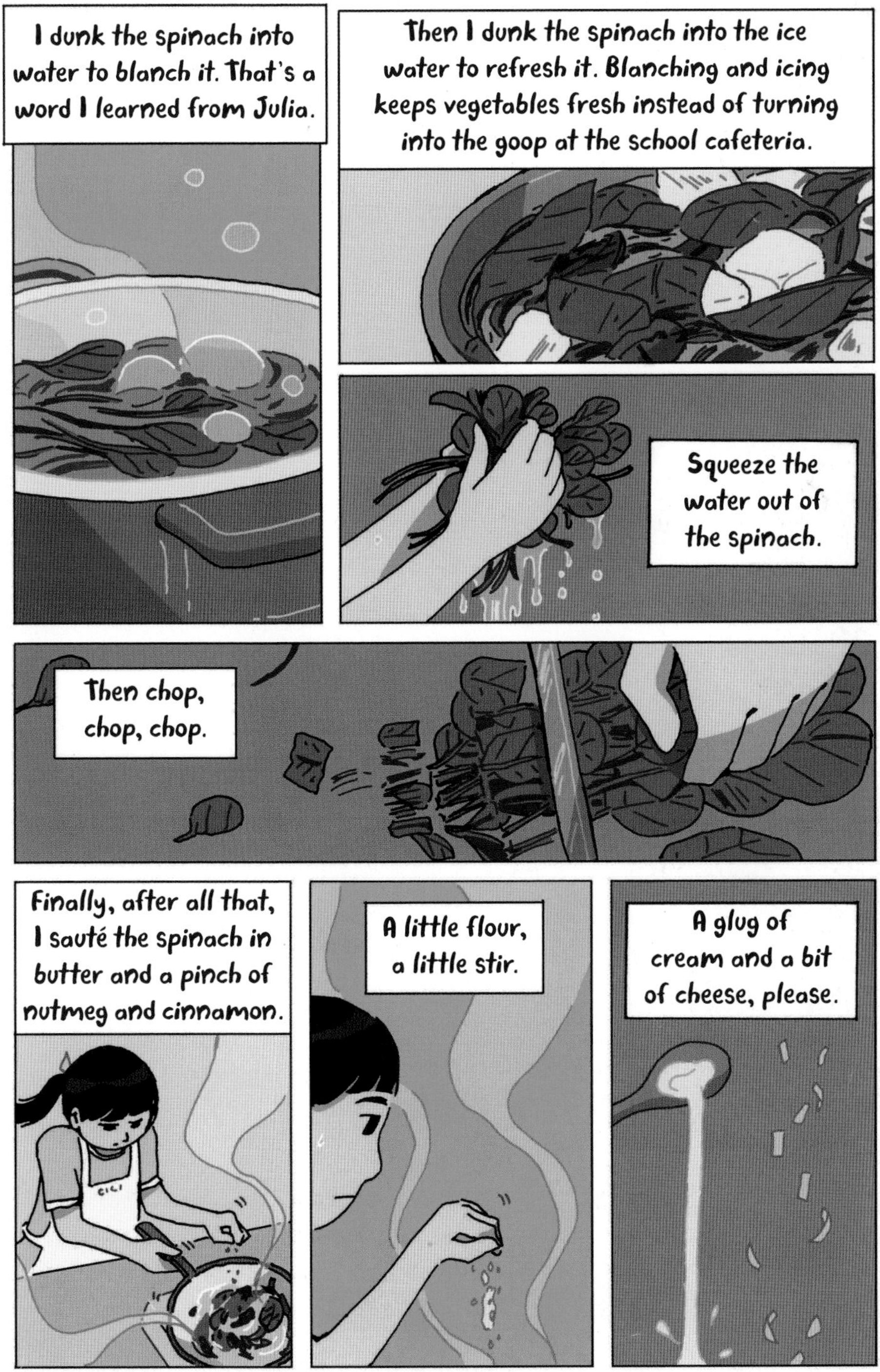
I dunk the spinach into water to blanch it. That's a word I learned from Julia.
Then I dunk the spinach into the ice water to refresh it. Blanching and icing keeps vegetables fresh instead of turning into the goop at the school cafeteria.
Squeeze the water out of the spinach.
Then chop, chop, chop.
Finally, after all that, I sauté the spinach in butter and a pinch of nutmeg and cinnamon.
CICI
A little flour, a little stir.
A glug of cream and a bit of cheese, please.

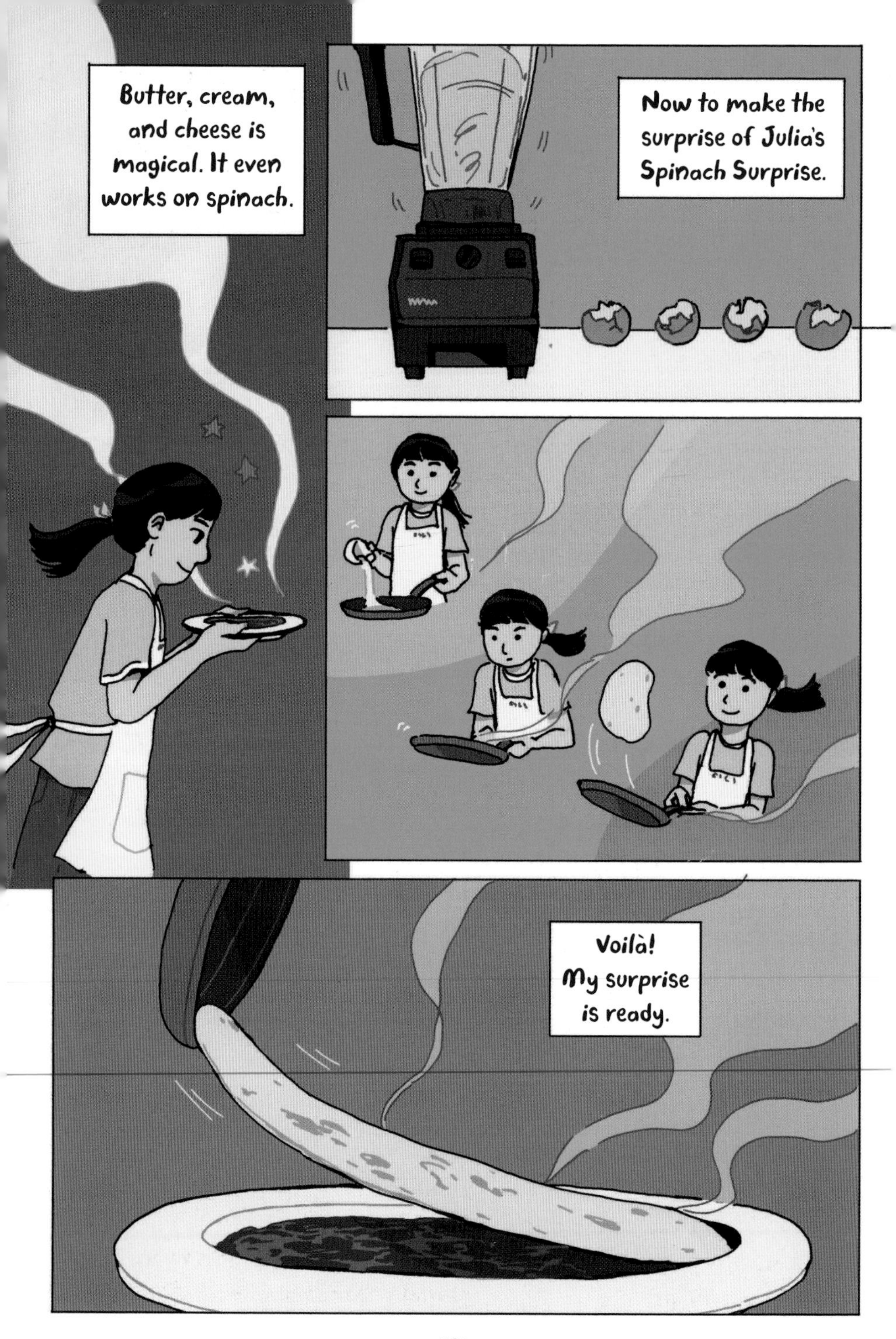
Butter, cream, and cheese is magical. It even works on spinach.
Now to make the surprise of Julia's Spinach Surprise.
Voilà! My surprise is ready.

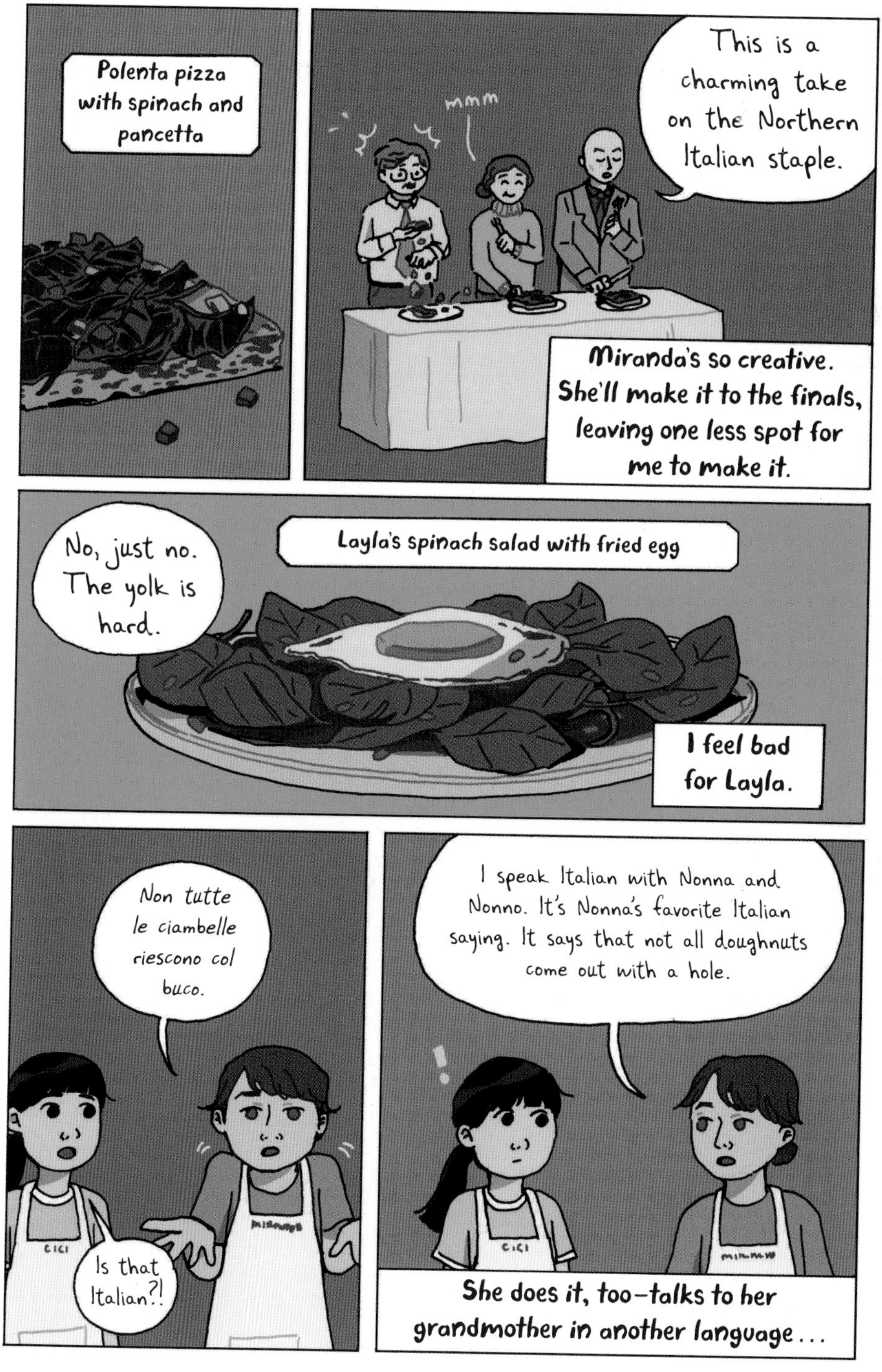
Polenta pizza with spinach and pancetta
mmm
This is a charming take on the Northern Italian staple.
Miranda's so creative. She'll make it to the finals, leaving one less spot for me to make it.
Layla's spinach salad with fried egg
No, just no. The yolk is hard.
I feel bad for Layla.
Non tutte le ciambelle riescono col buco.
Is that Italian?!
I speak Italian with Nonna and Nonno. It's Nonna's favorite Italian saying. It says that not all doughnuts come out with a hole.
!
She does it, too—talks to her grandmother in another language...

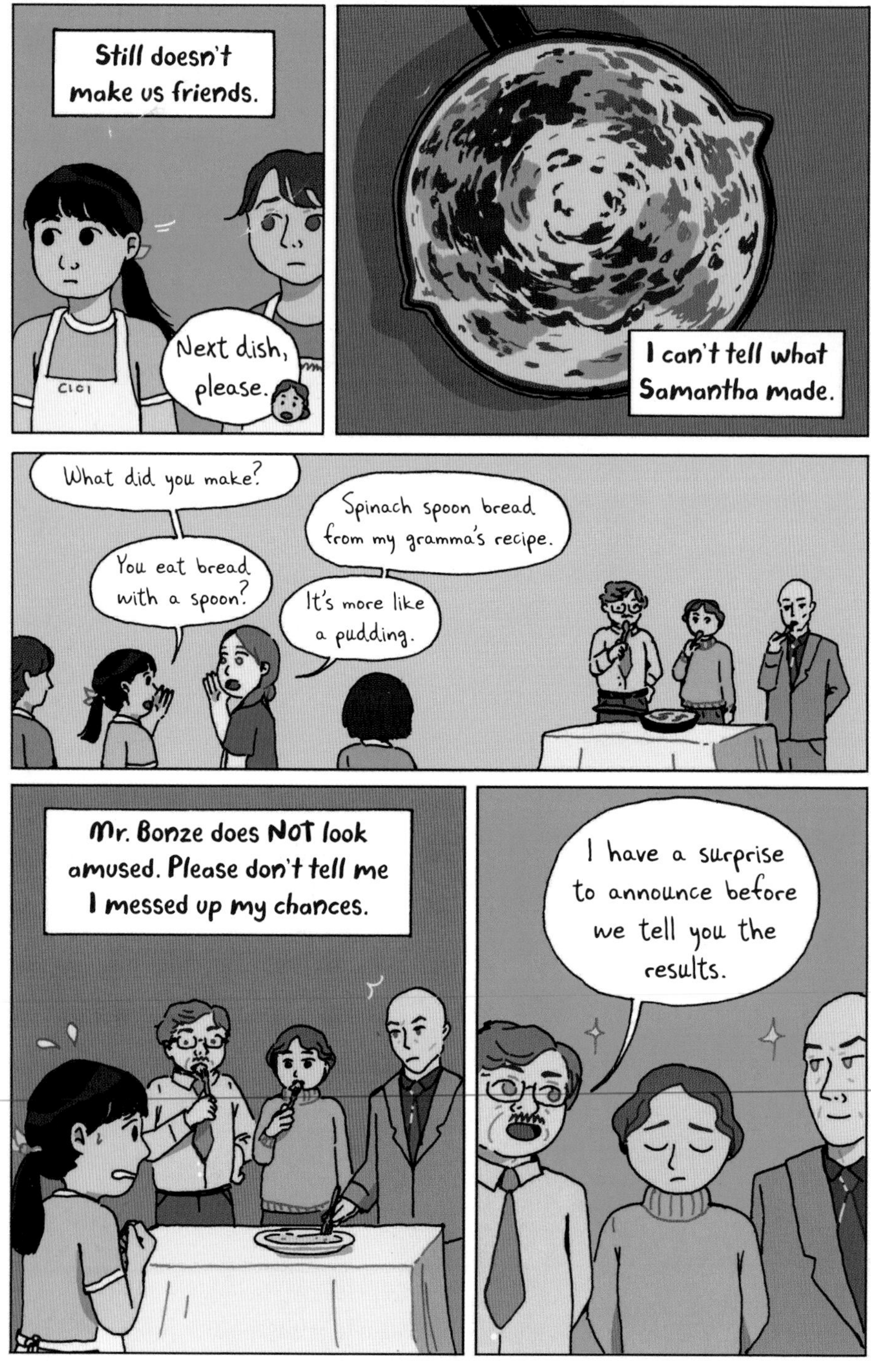
Still doesn't make us friends.
CICI
Next dish, please.
I can't tell what Samantha made.
What did you make?
You eat bread with a spoon?
Spinach spoon bread from my gramma's recipe.
It's more like a pudding.
Mr. Bonze does NOT look amused. Please don't tell me I messed up my chances.
I have a surprise to announce before we tell you the results.

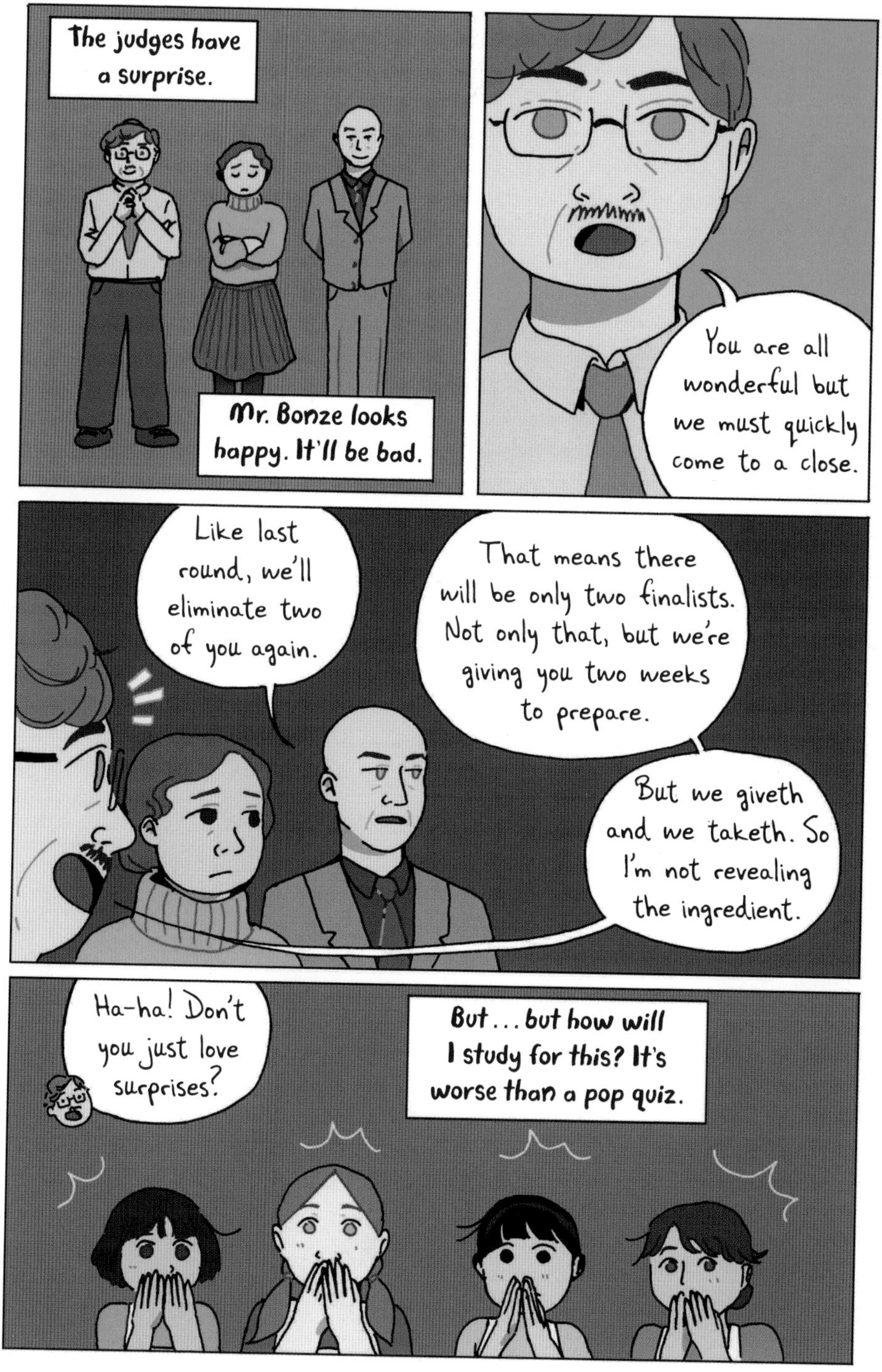
The judges have a surprise.
Mr. Bonze looks happy. It'll be bad.
You are all wonderful but we must quickly come to a close.
Like last round, we'll eliminate two of you again.
That means there will be only two finalists. Not only that, but we're giving you two weeks to prepare.
But we giveth and we taketh. So I'm not revealing the ingredient.
Ha-ha! Don't you just love surprises?
But . . . but how will I study for this? It's worse than a pop quiz.

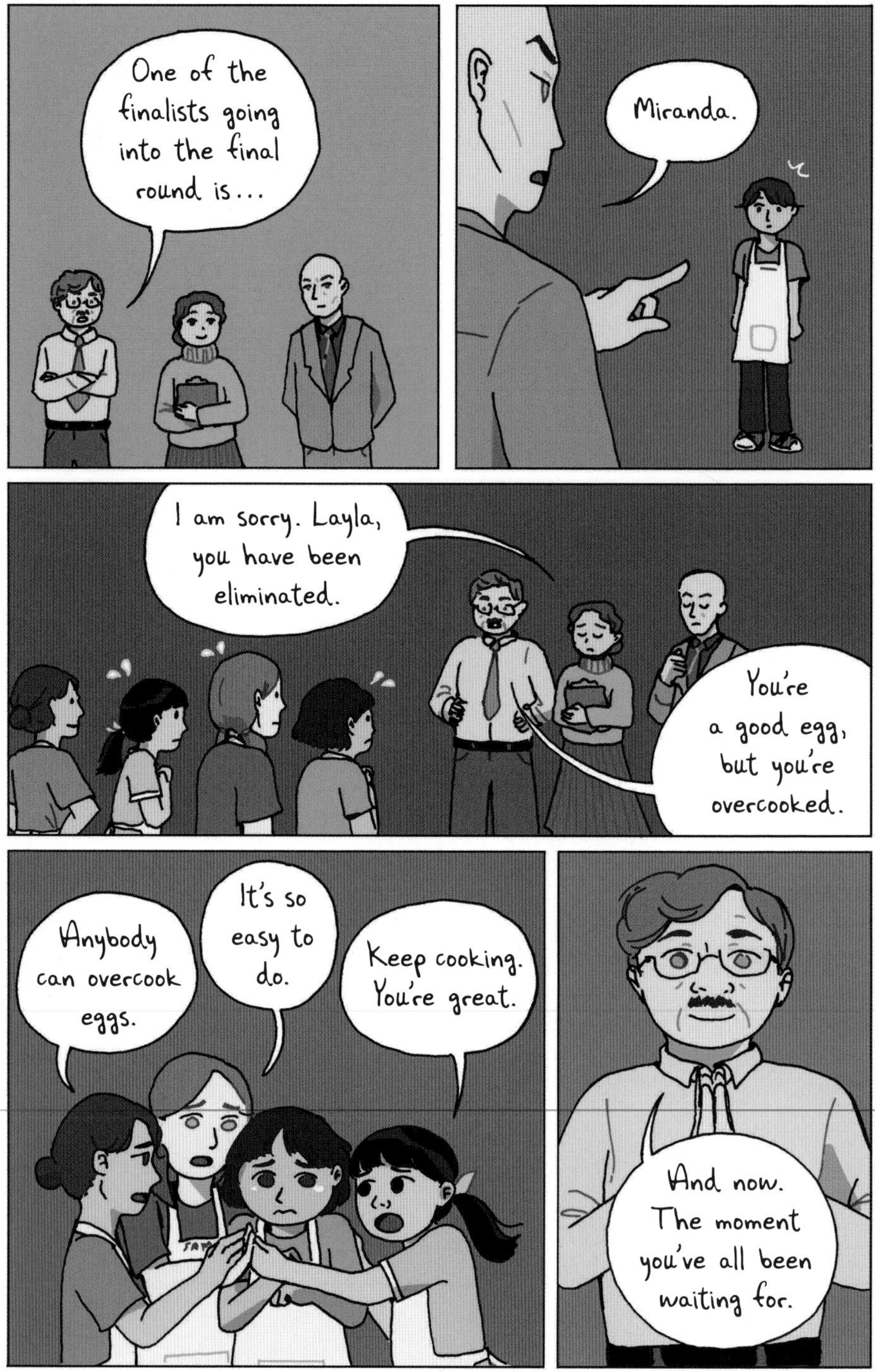
One of the finalists going into the final round is...
Miranda.
I am sorry. Layla, you have been eliminated.
You're a good egg, but you're overcooked.
Anybody can overcook eggs.
It's so easy to do.
Keep cooking. You're great.
And now. The moment you've all been waiting for.

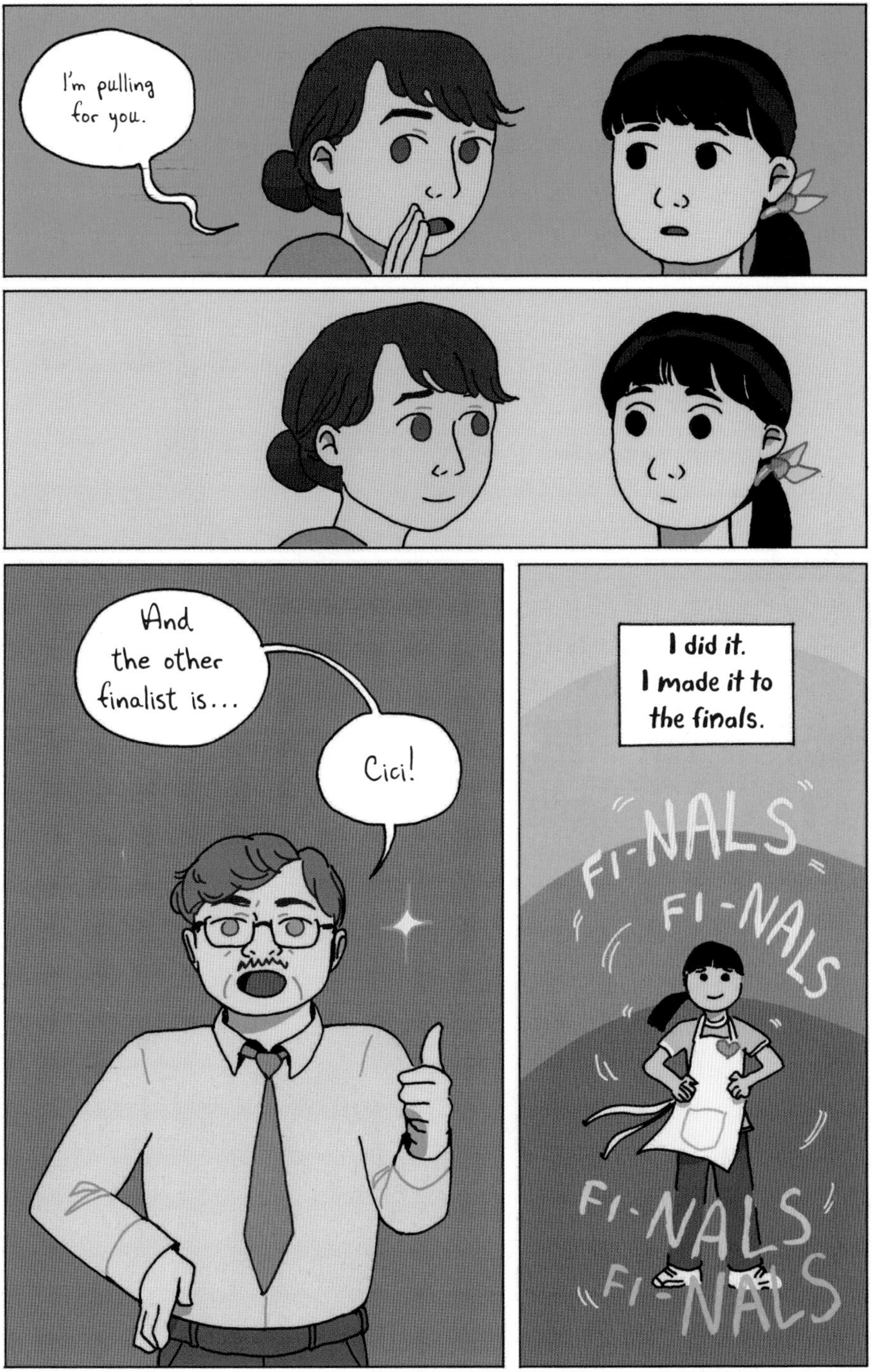
I'm pulling for you.
And the other finalist is...
Cici!
I did it. I made it to the finals.
FI-NALS
FI-NALS
FI-NALS
FI-NALS

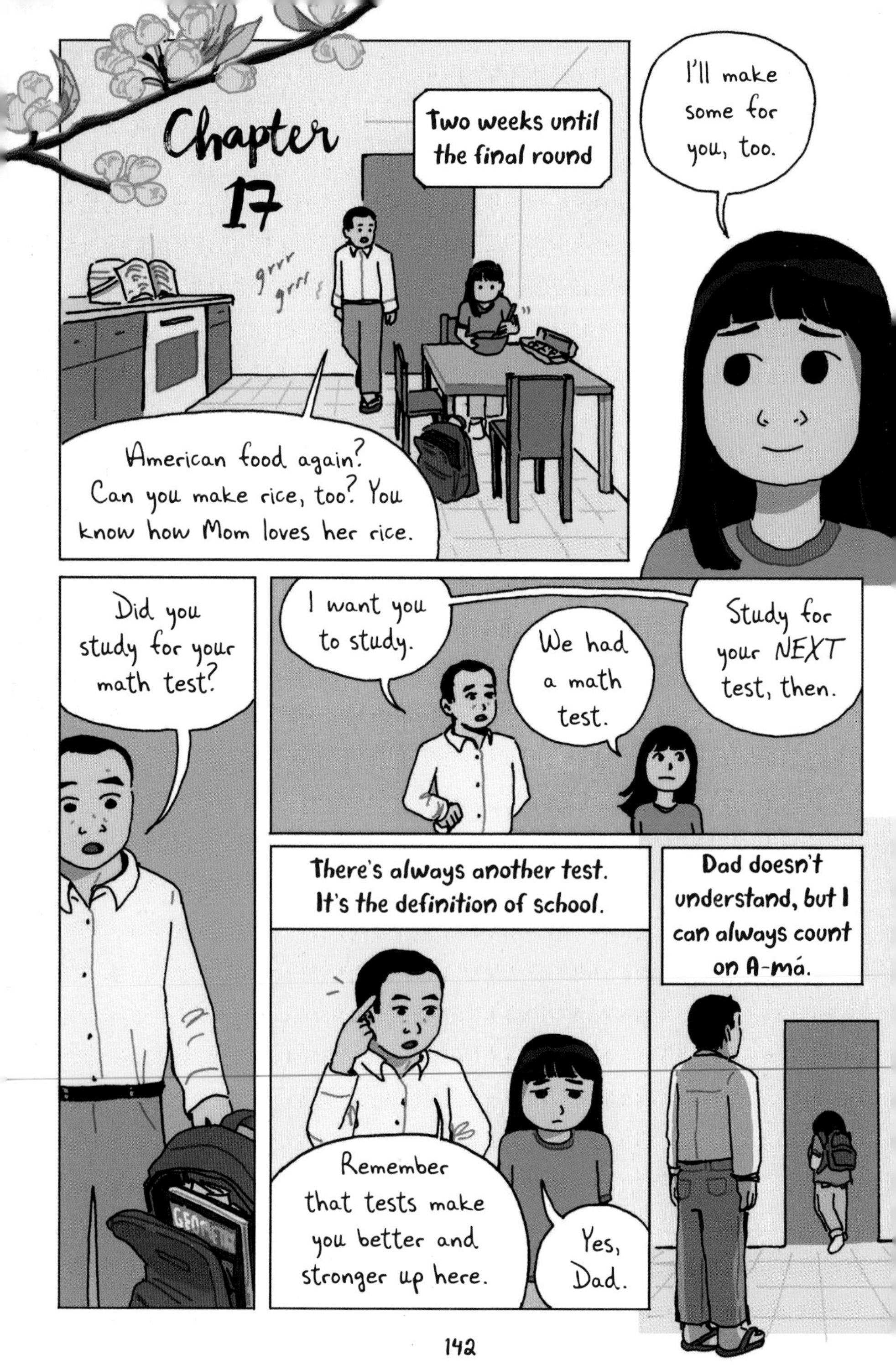
Chapter 17
Two weeks until the final round
grrr grrr
American food again? Can you make rice, too? You know how Mom loves her rice.
I'll make some for you, too.
Did you study for your math test?
I want you to study.
We had a math test.
Study for your NEXT test, then.
There's always another test. It's the definition of school.
Remember that tests make you better and stronger up here.
Yes, Dad.
Dad doesn't understand, but I can always count on A-má.

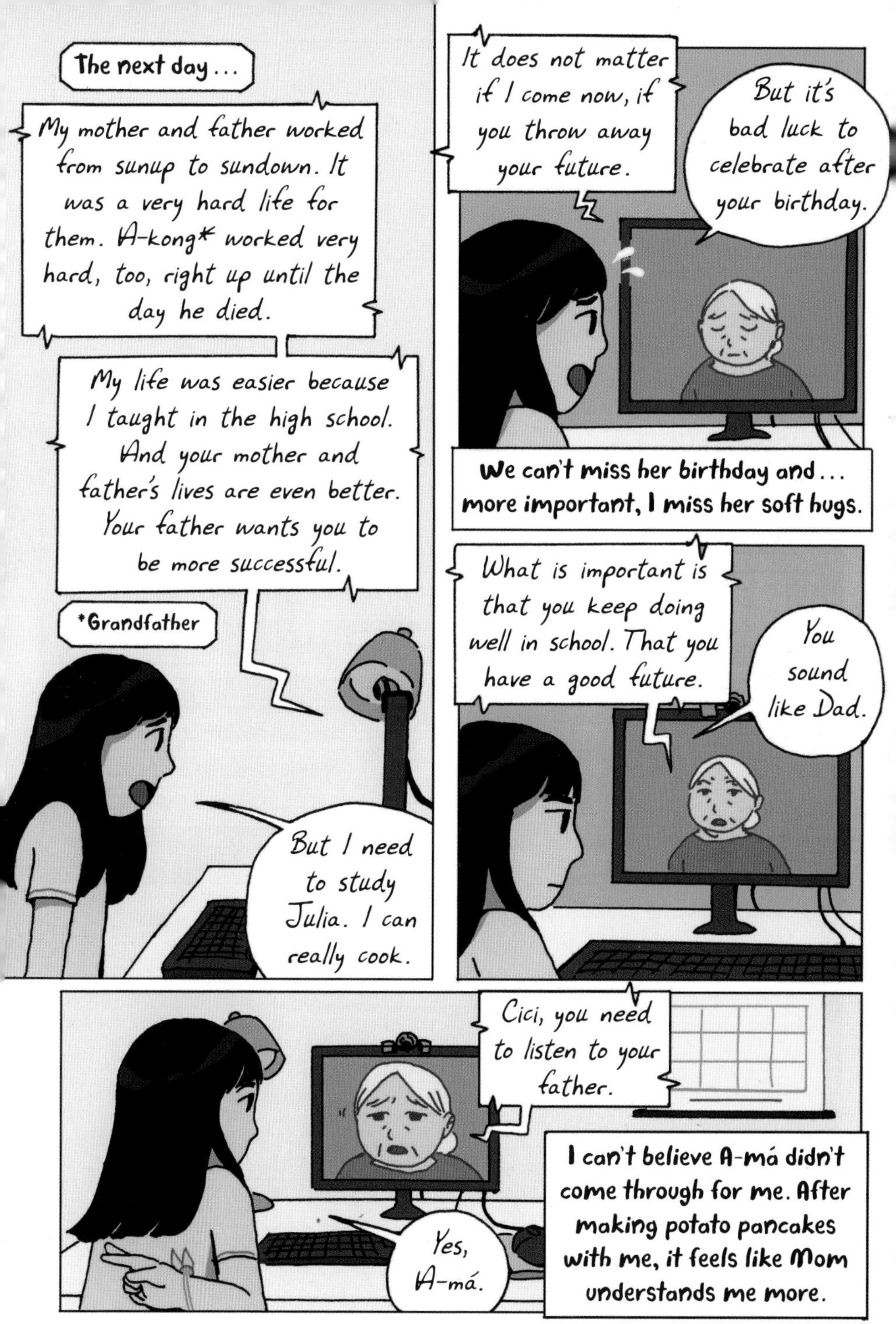
The next day . . .
My mother and father worked from sunup to sundown. It was a very hard life for them. A-kong* worked very hard, too, right up until the day he died.
My life was easier because I taught in the high school. And your mother and father's lives are even better. Your father wants you to be more successful.
*Grandfather
But I need to study Julia. I can really cook.
It does not matter if I come now, if you throw away your future.
But it's bad luck to celebrate after your birthday.
We can't miss her birthday and . . . more important, I miss her soft hugs.
What is important is that you keep doing well in school. That you have a good future.
You sound like Dad.
Cici, you need to listen to your father.
Yes, A-má.
I can't believe A-má didn't come through for me. After making potato pancakes with me, it feels like Mom understands me more.

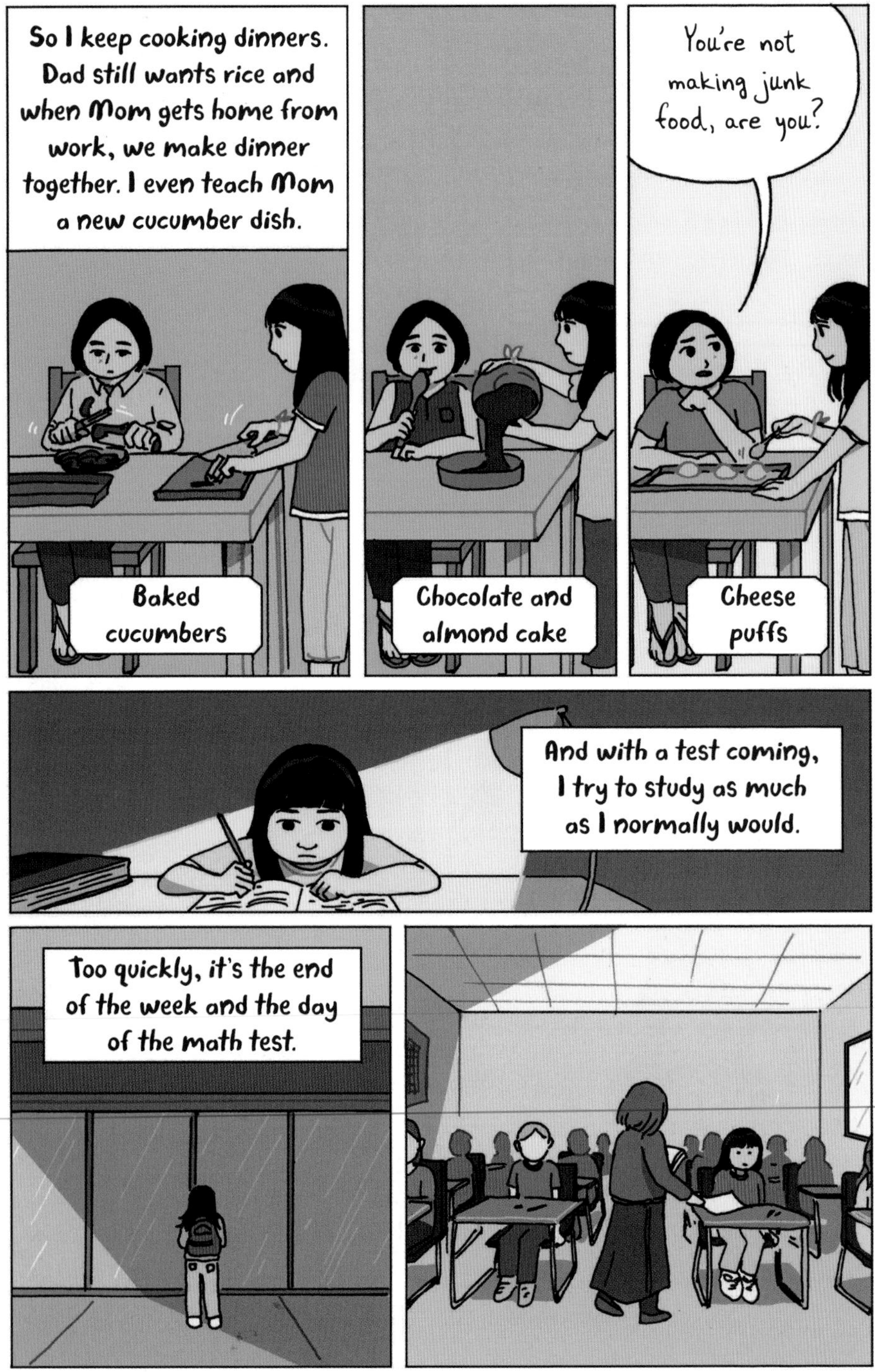

So I keep cooking dinners. Dad still wants rice and when Mom gets home from work, we make dinner together. I even teach Mom a new cucumber dish.
Baked cucumbers
Chocolate and almond cake
You're not making junk food, are you?
Cheese puffs
And with a test coming, I try to study as much as I normally would.
Too quickly, it's the end of the week and the day of the math test.

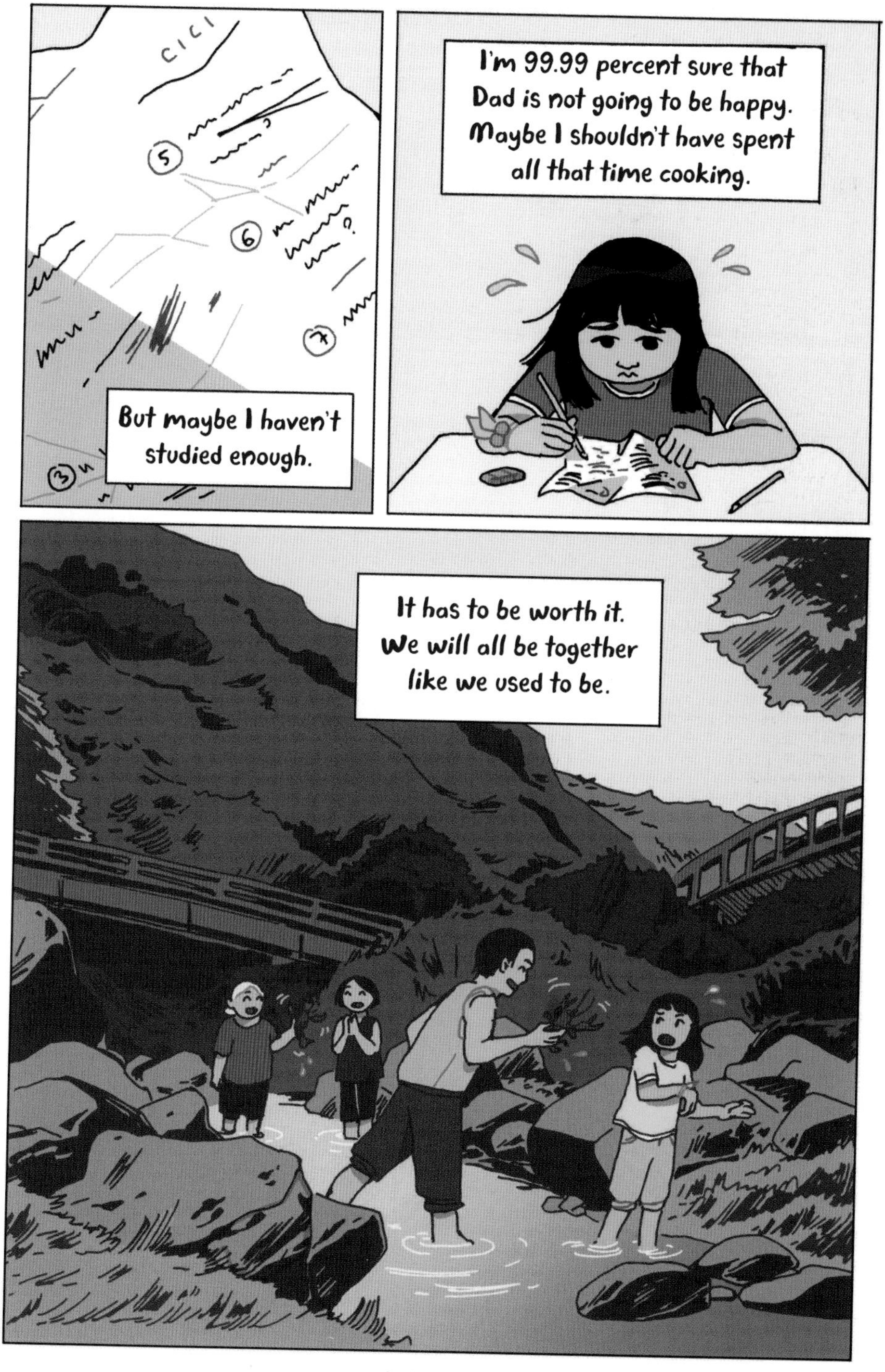
CICI
But maybe I haven't studied enough.
I'm 99.99 percent sure that Dad is not going to be happy. Maybe I shouldn't have spent all that time cooking.
It has to be worth it. We will all be together like we used to be.

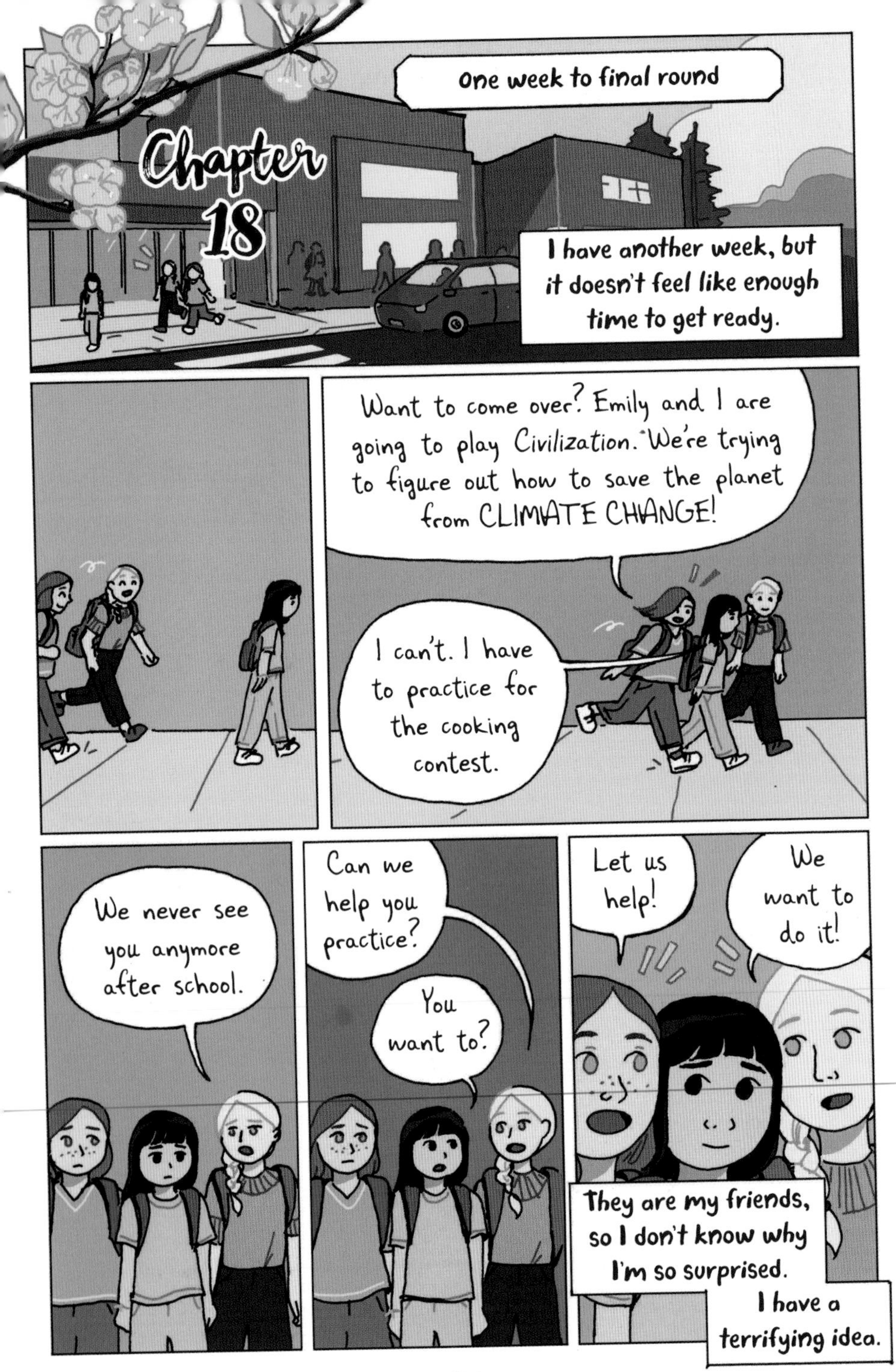
One week to final round
Chapter 18
I have another week, but it doesn't feel like enough time to get ready.
Want to come over? Emily and I are going to play Civilization. We're trying to figure out how to save the planet from CLIMATE CHANGE!
I can't. I have to practice for the cooking contest.
We never see you anymore after school.
Can we help you practice?
You want to?
Let us help!
We want to do it!
They are my friends, so I don't know why I'm so surprised.
I have a terrifying idea.

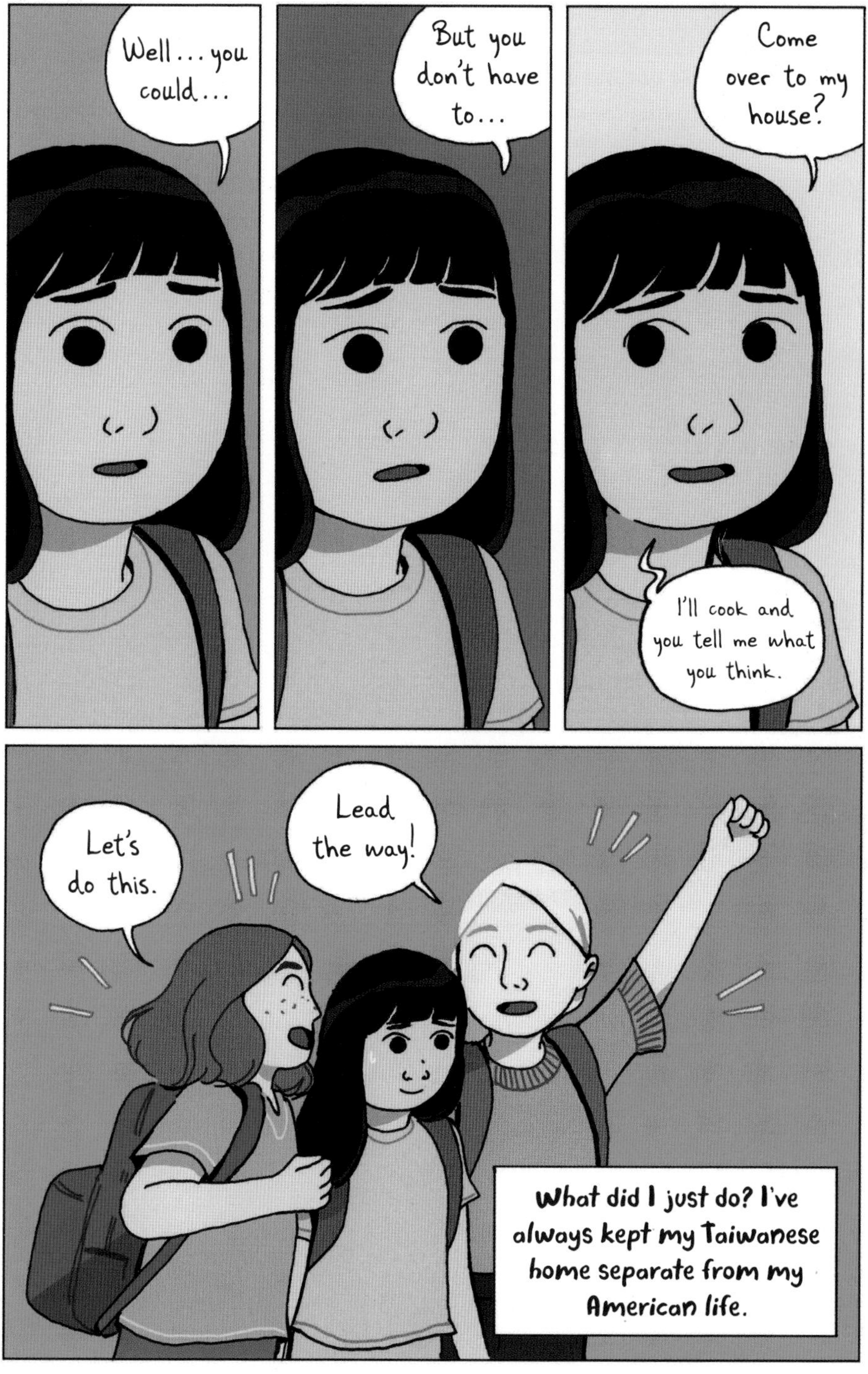
Well... you could...
But you don't have to...
Come over to my house?
I'll cook and you tell me what you think.
Let's do this.
Lead the way!
What did I just do? I've always kept my Taiwanese home separate from my American life.

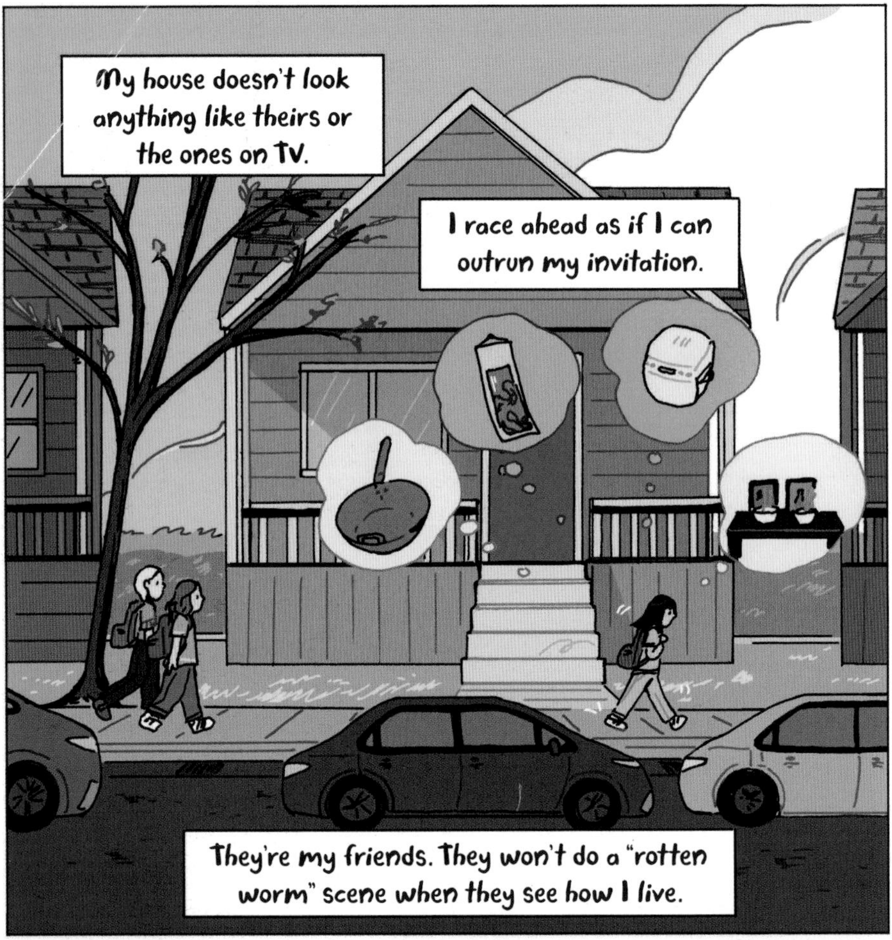
My house doesn't look anything like theirs or the ones on TV.
I race ahead as if I can outrun my invitation.
They're my friends. They won't do a "rotten worm" scene when they see how I live.

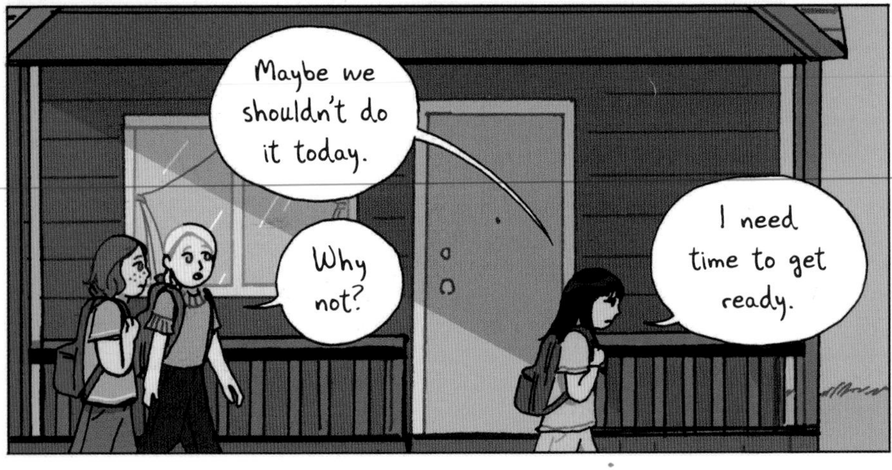
Maybe we shouldn't do it today.
Why not?
I need time to get ready.

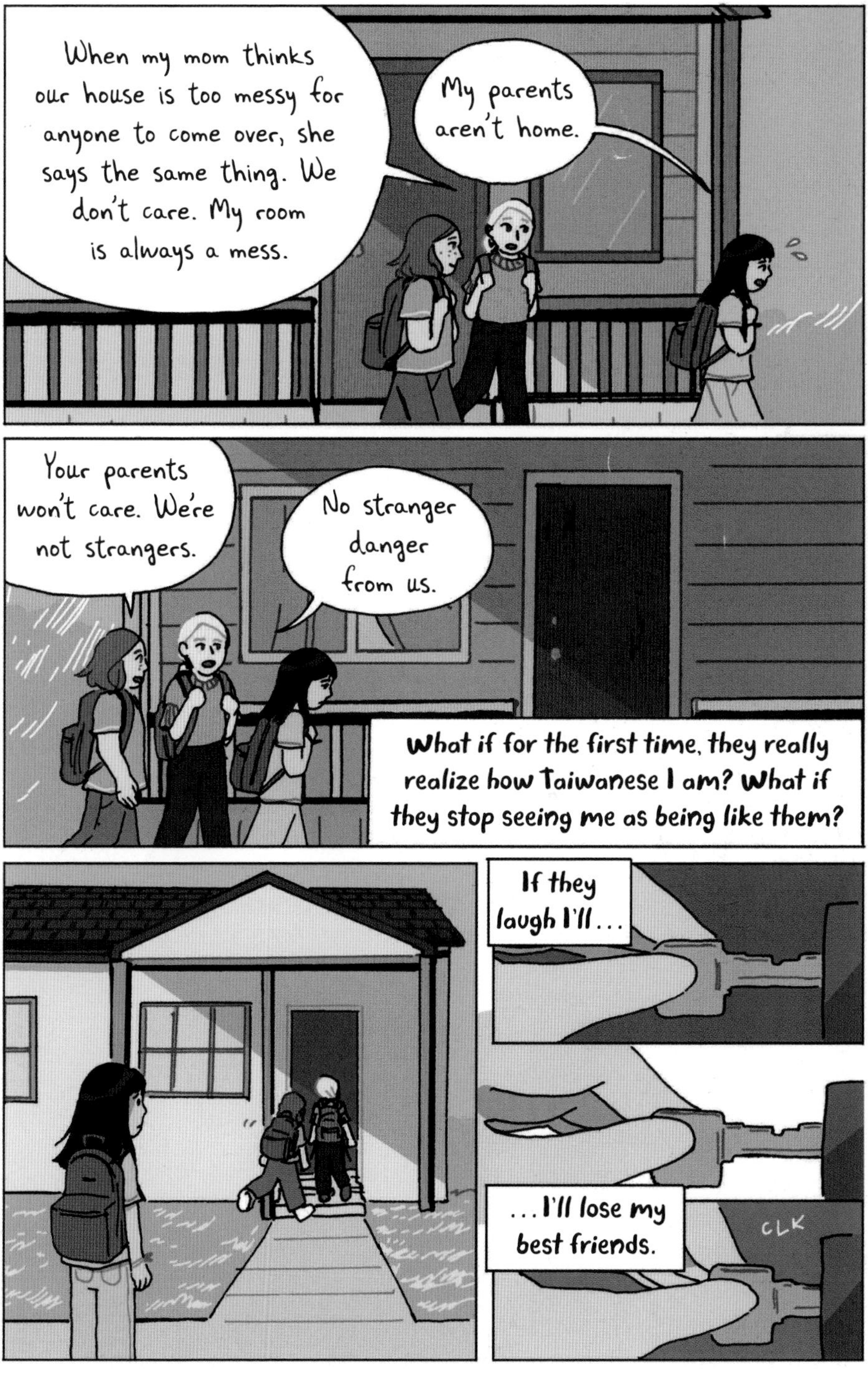
When my mom thinks our house is too messy for anyone to come over, she says the same thing. We don't care. My room is always a mess.
My parents aren't home.
Your parents won't care. We're not strangers.
No stranger danger from us.
What if for the first time, they really realize how Taiwanese I am? What if they stop seeing me as being like them?
If they laugh I'll...
...I'll lose my best friends.
CLK

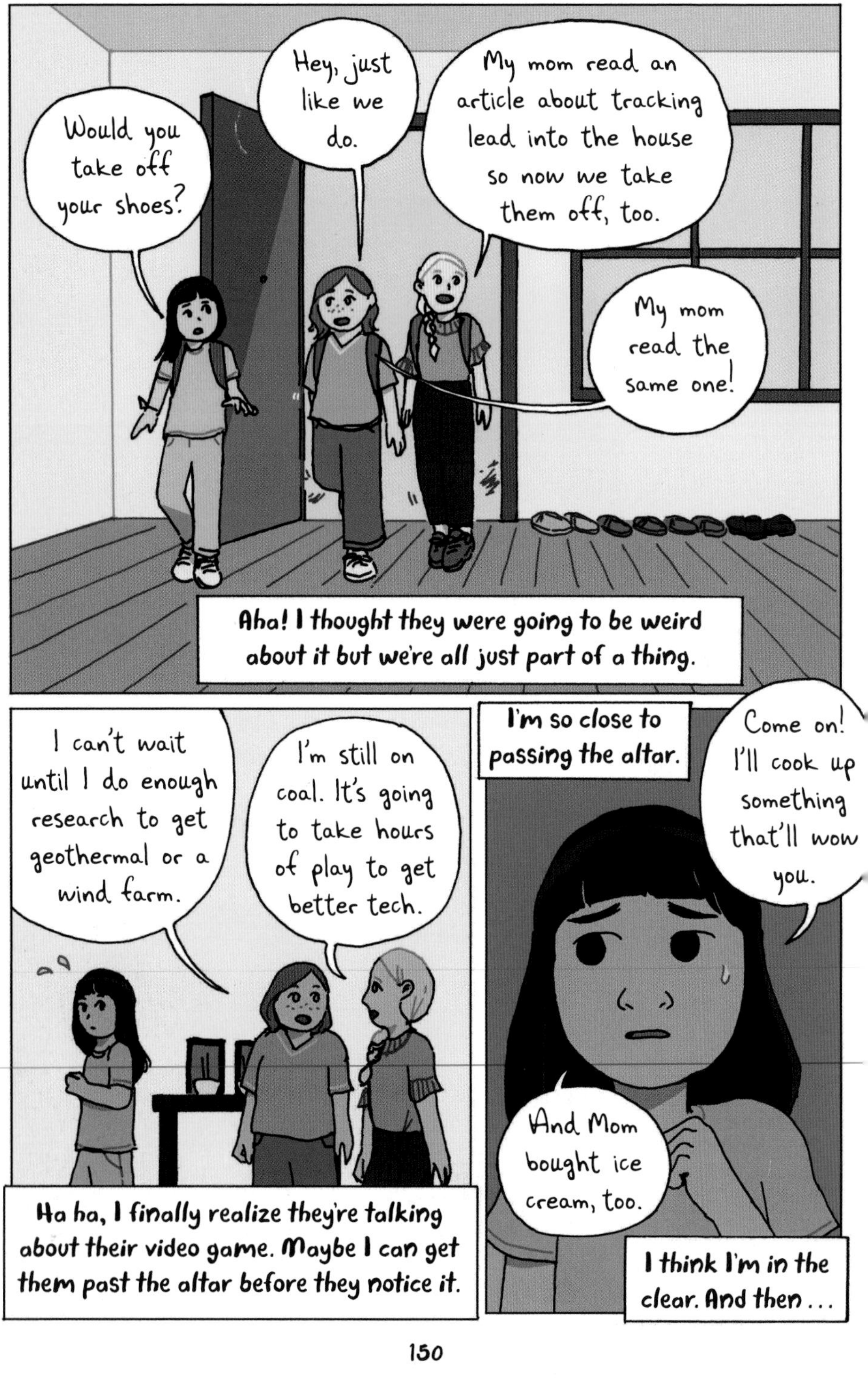

Would you take off your shoes?
Hey, just like we do.
My mom read an article about tracking lead into the house so now we take them off, too.
My mom read the same one!
Aha! I thought they were going to be weird about it but we're all just part of a thing.
I can't wait until I do enough research to get geothermal or a wind farm.
I'm still on coal. It's going to take hours of play to get better tech.
Ha ha, I finally realize they're talking about their video game. Maybe I can get them past the altar before they notice it.
I'm so close to passing the altar.
Come on! I'll cook up something that'll wow you.
And Mom bought ice cream, too.
I think I'm in the clear. And then . . .

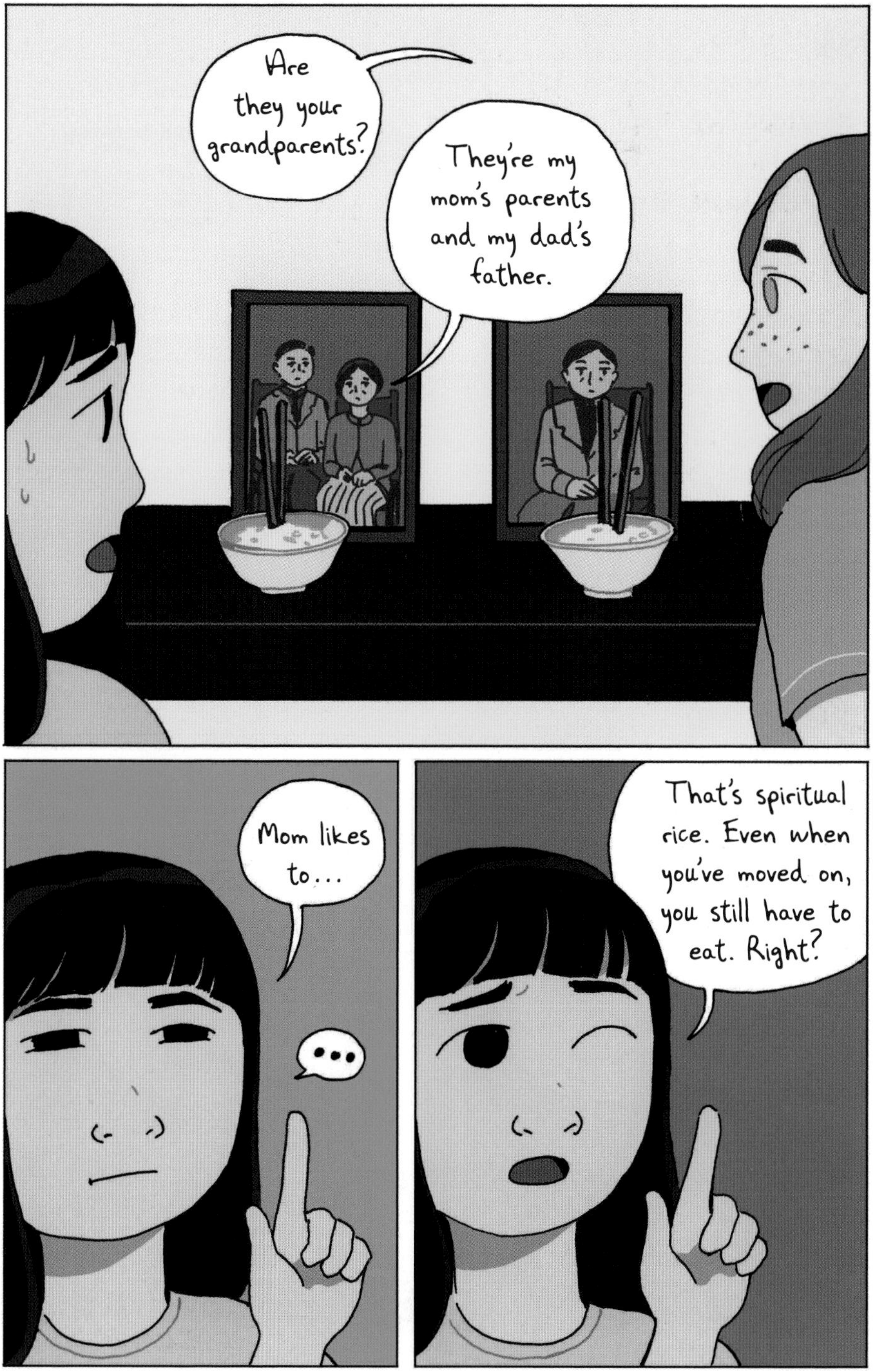
Are they your grandparents?
They're my mom's parents and my dad's father.
Mom likes to...
...
That's spiritual rice. Even when you've moved on, you still have to eat. Right?

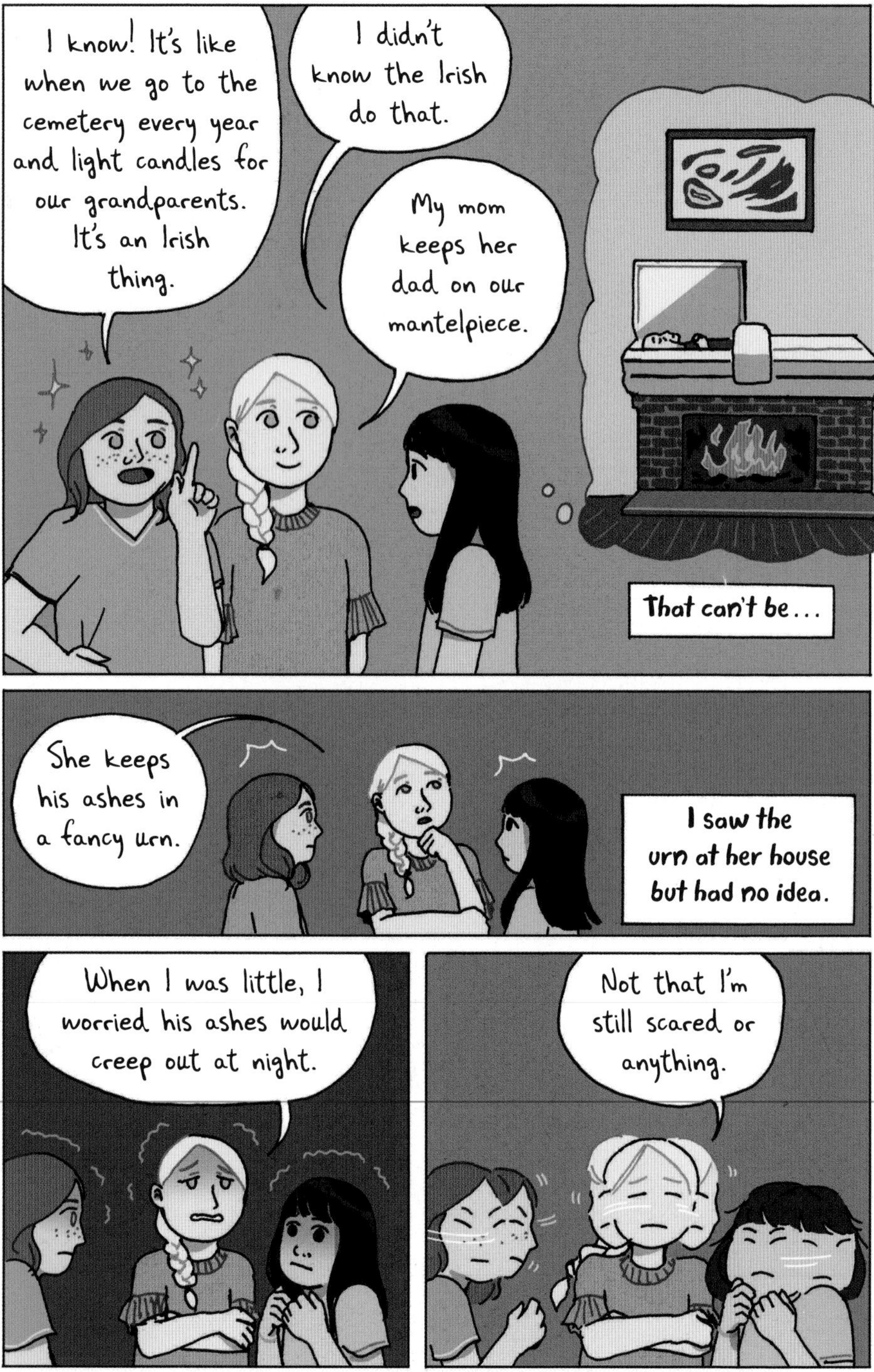

I know! It's like when we go to the cemetery every year and light candles for our grandparents. It's an Irish thing.
I didn't know the Irish do that.
My mom keeps her dad on our mantelpiece.
That can't be...
She keeps his ashes in a fancy urn.
I saw the urn at her house but had no idea.
When I was little, I worried his ashes would creep out at night.
Not that I'm still scared or anything.

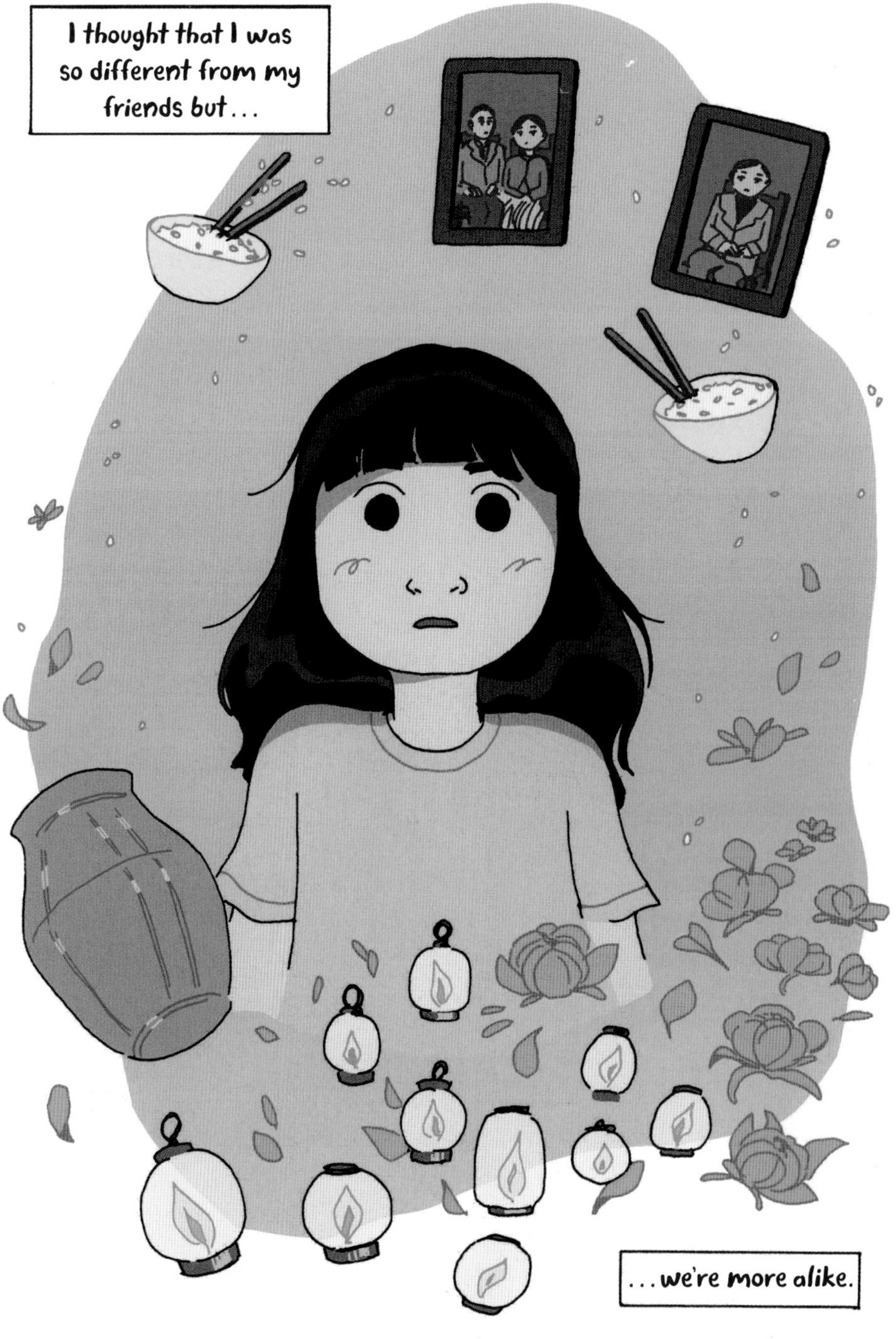
I thought that I was so different from my friends but...
...we're more alike.

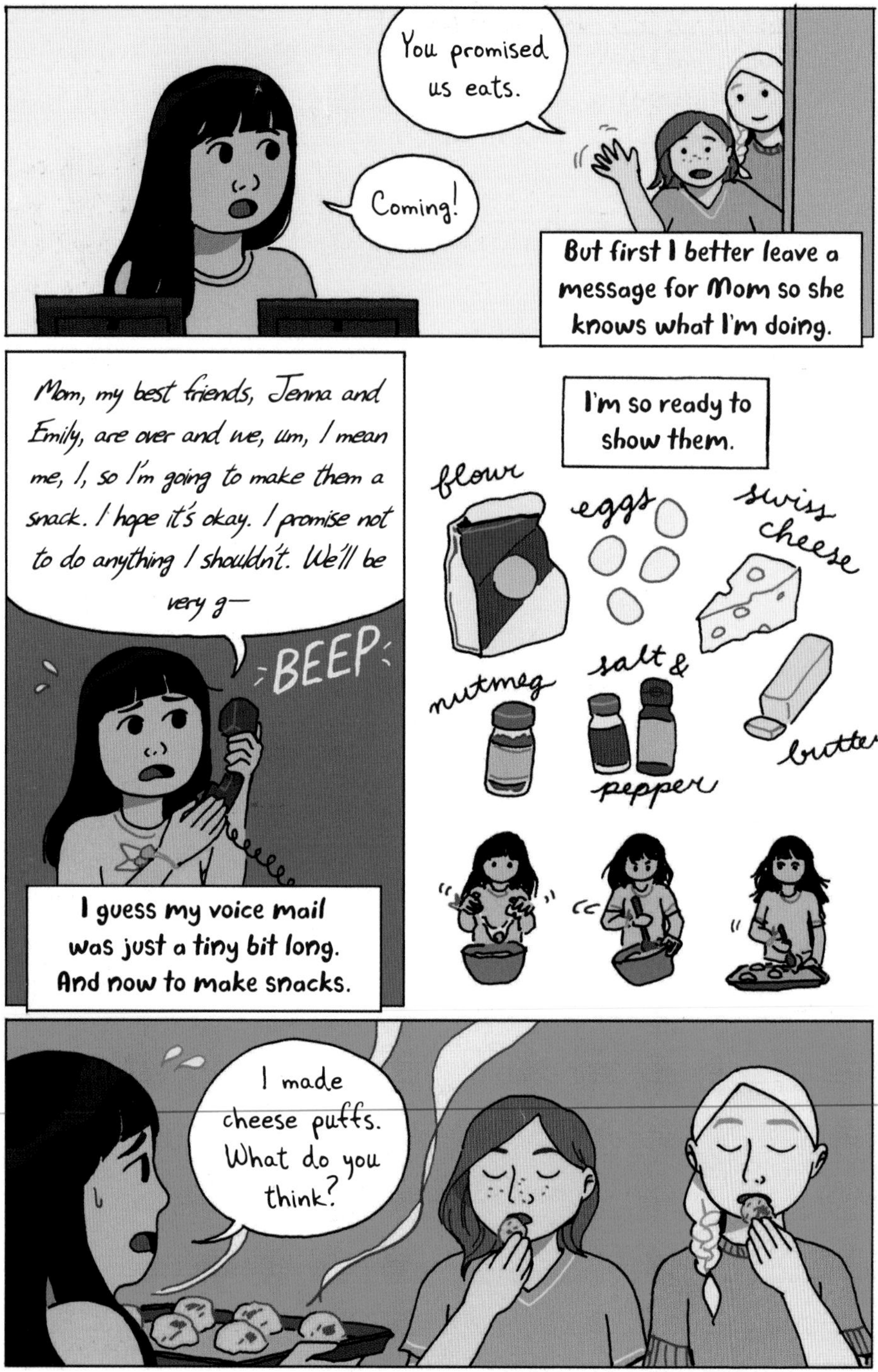
You promised us eats.
Coming!
But first I better leave a message for Mom so she knows what I'm doing.
Mom, my best friends, Jenna and Emily, are over and we, um, I mean me, I, so I'm going to make them a snack. I hope it's okay. I promise not to do anything I shouldn't. We'll be very g—
BEEP
I guess my voice mail was just a tiny bit long. And now to make snacks.
I'm so ready to show them.
flour
eggs
swiss cheese
nutmeg
salt &
pepper
butter
I made cheese puffs. What do you think?

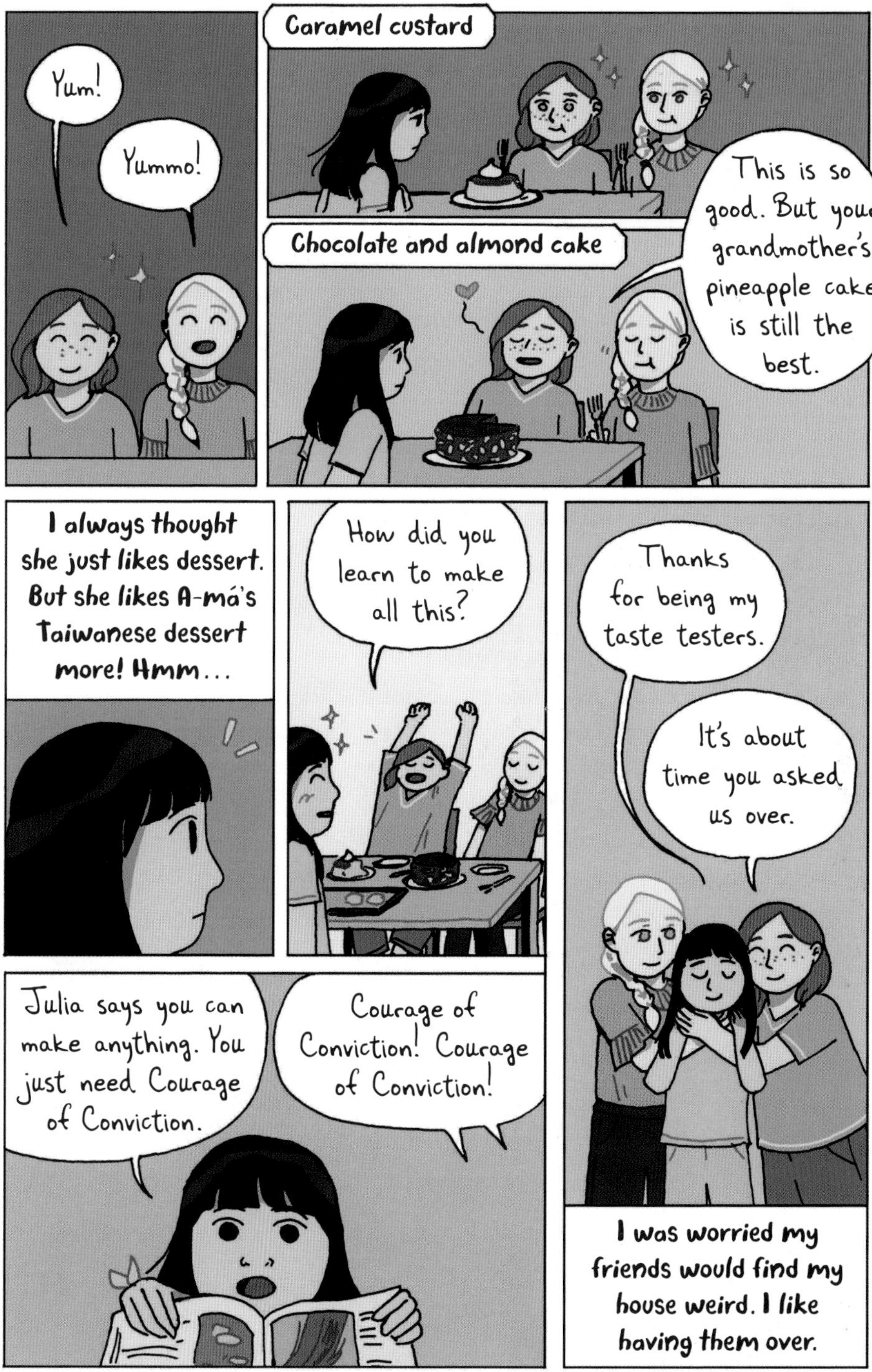
Yum!
Yummo!
Caramel custard
Chocolate and almond cake
This is so good. But your grandmother's pineapple cake is still the best.
I always thought she just likes dessert. But she likes A-má's Taiwanese dessert more! Hmm...
How did you learn to make all this?
Thanks for being my taste testers.
It's about time you asked us over.
Julia says you can make anything. You just need Courage of Conviction.
Courage of Conviction! Courage of Conviction!
I was worried my friends would find my house weird. I like having them over.

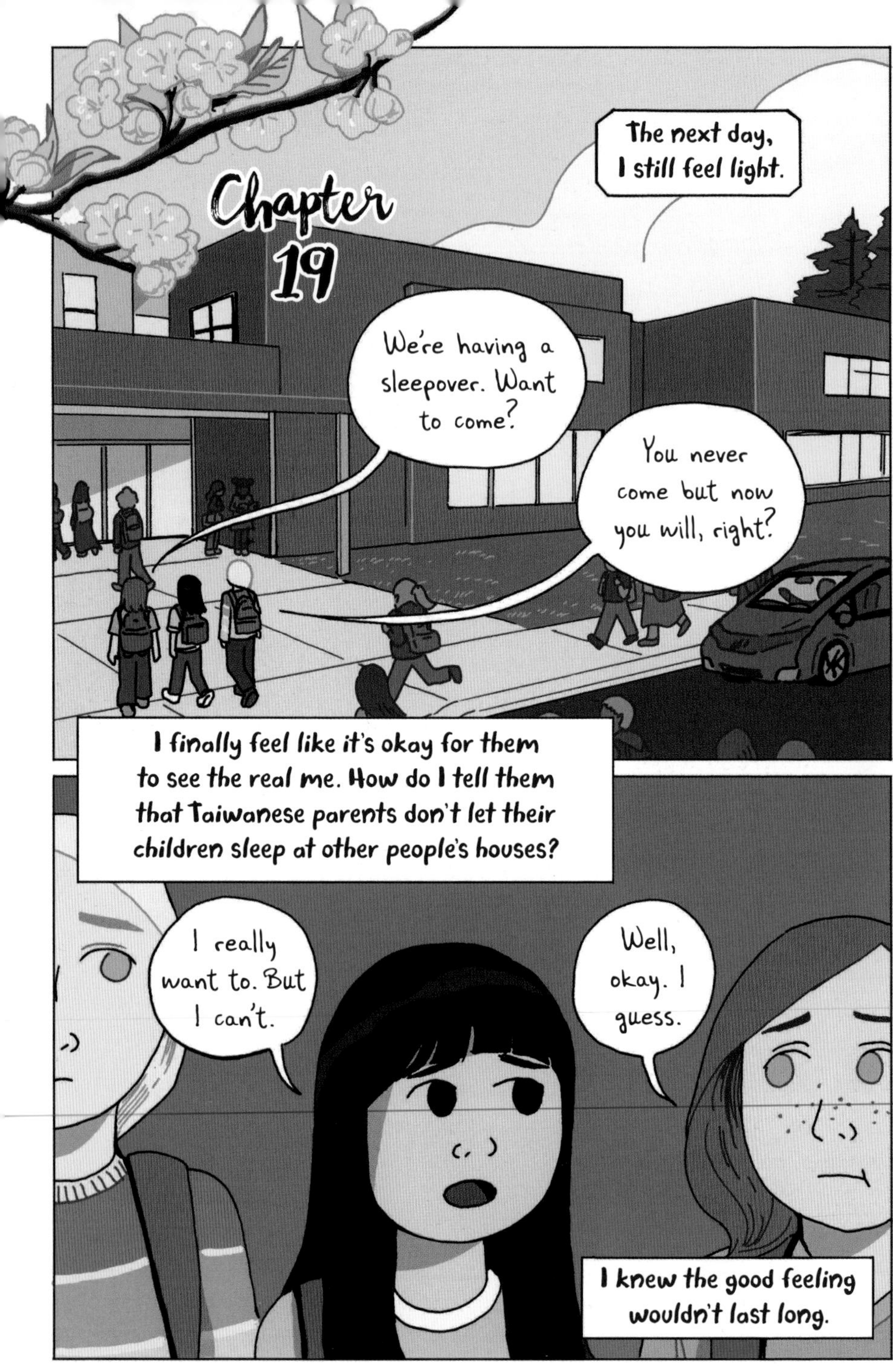
Chapter 19
The next day, I still feel light.
We're having a sleepover. Want to come?
You never come but now you will, right?
I finally feel like it's okay for them to see the real me. How do I tell them that Taiwanese parents don't let their children sleep at other people's houses?
I really want to. But I can't.
Well, okay. I guess.
I knew the good feeling wouldn't last long.

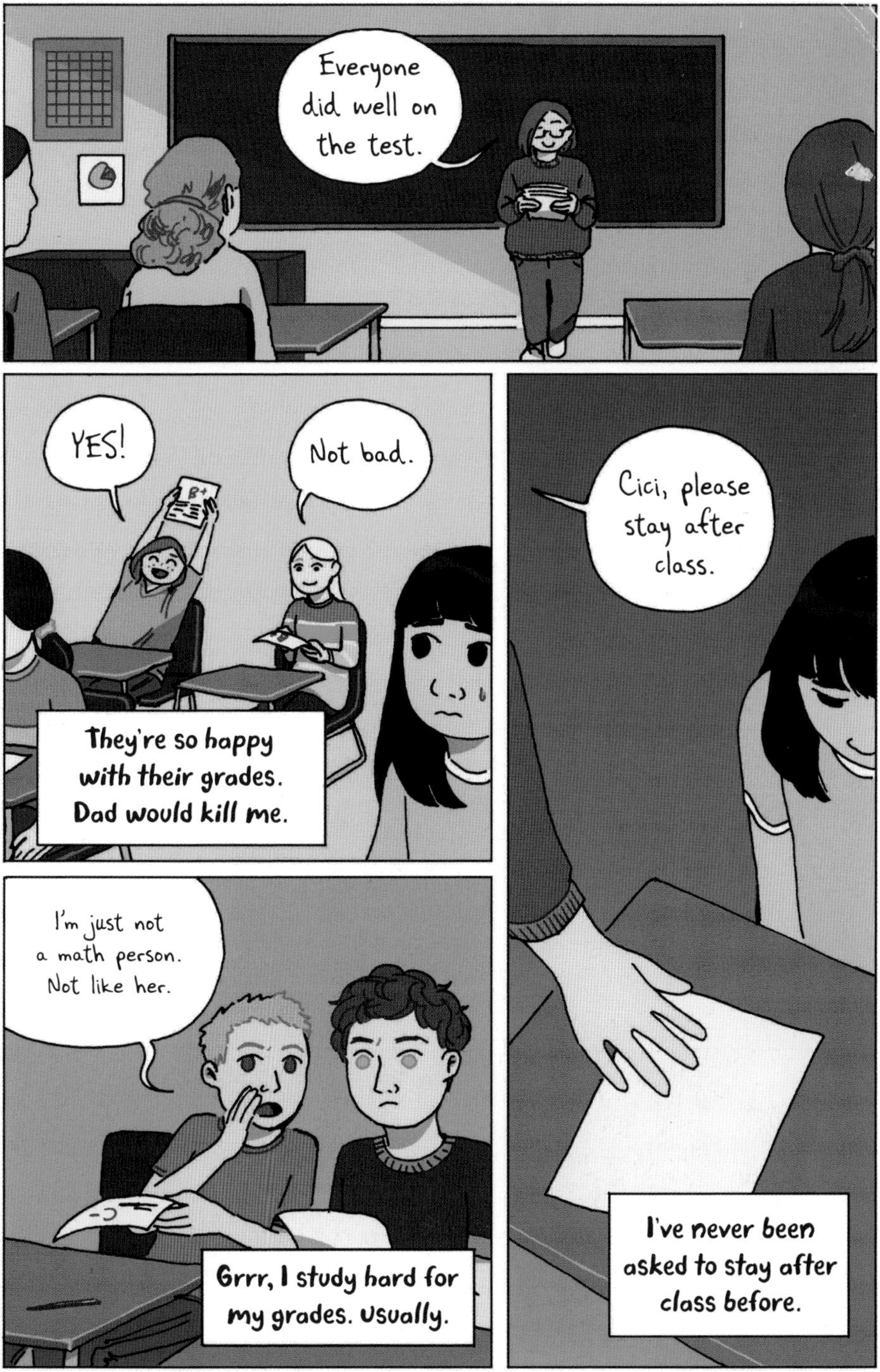
Everyone did well on the test.
YES!
Not bad.
They're so happy with their grades. Dad would kill me.
Cici, please stay after class.
I'm just not a math person. Not like her.
Grrr, I study hard for my grades. Usually.
I've never been asked to stay after class before.

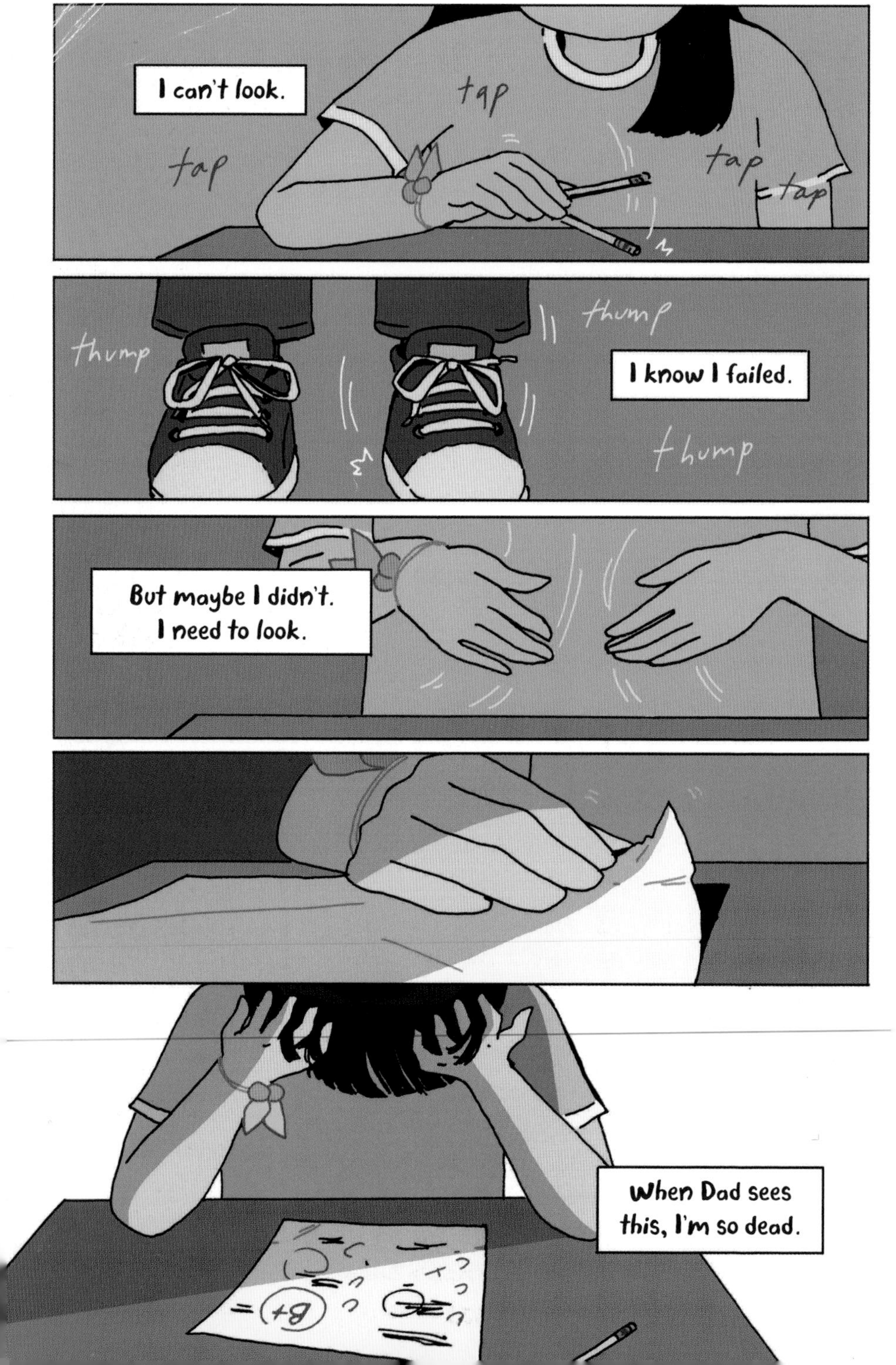
I can't look.
tap
tap
tap
tap
thump
thump
I know I failed.
thump
But maybe I didn't.
I need to look.
When Dad sees this, I'm so dead.
B+

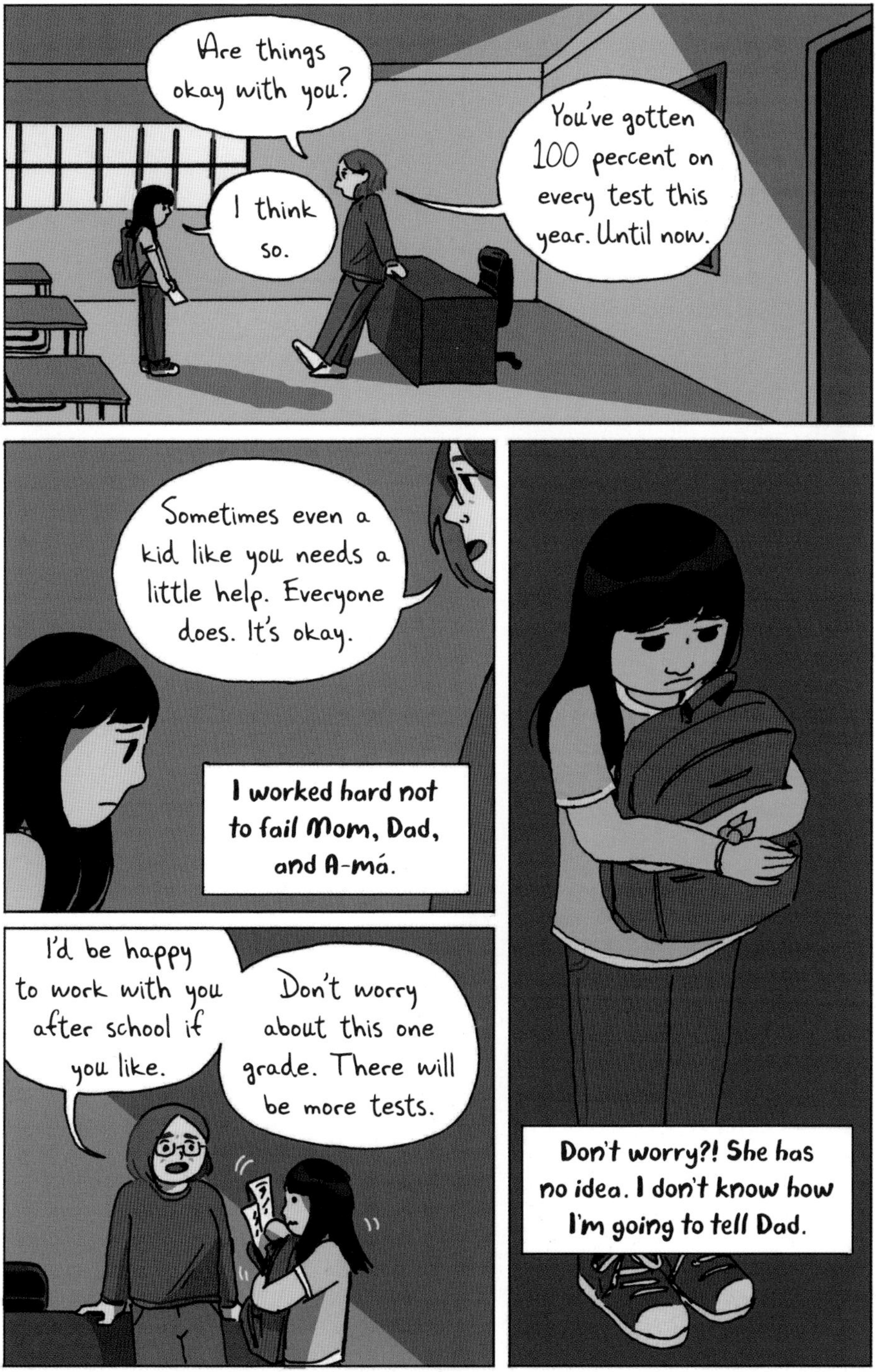
Are things okay with you?
I think so.
You've gotten 100 percent on every test this year. Until now.
Sometimes even a kid like you needs a little help. Everyone does. It's okay.
I worked hard not to fail Mom, Dad, and A-má.
I'd be happy to work with you after school if you like.
Don't worry about this one grade. There will be more tests.
Don't worry?! She has no idea. I don't know how I'm going to tell Dad.

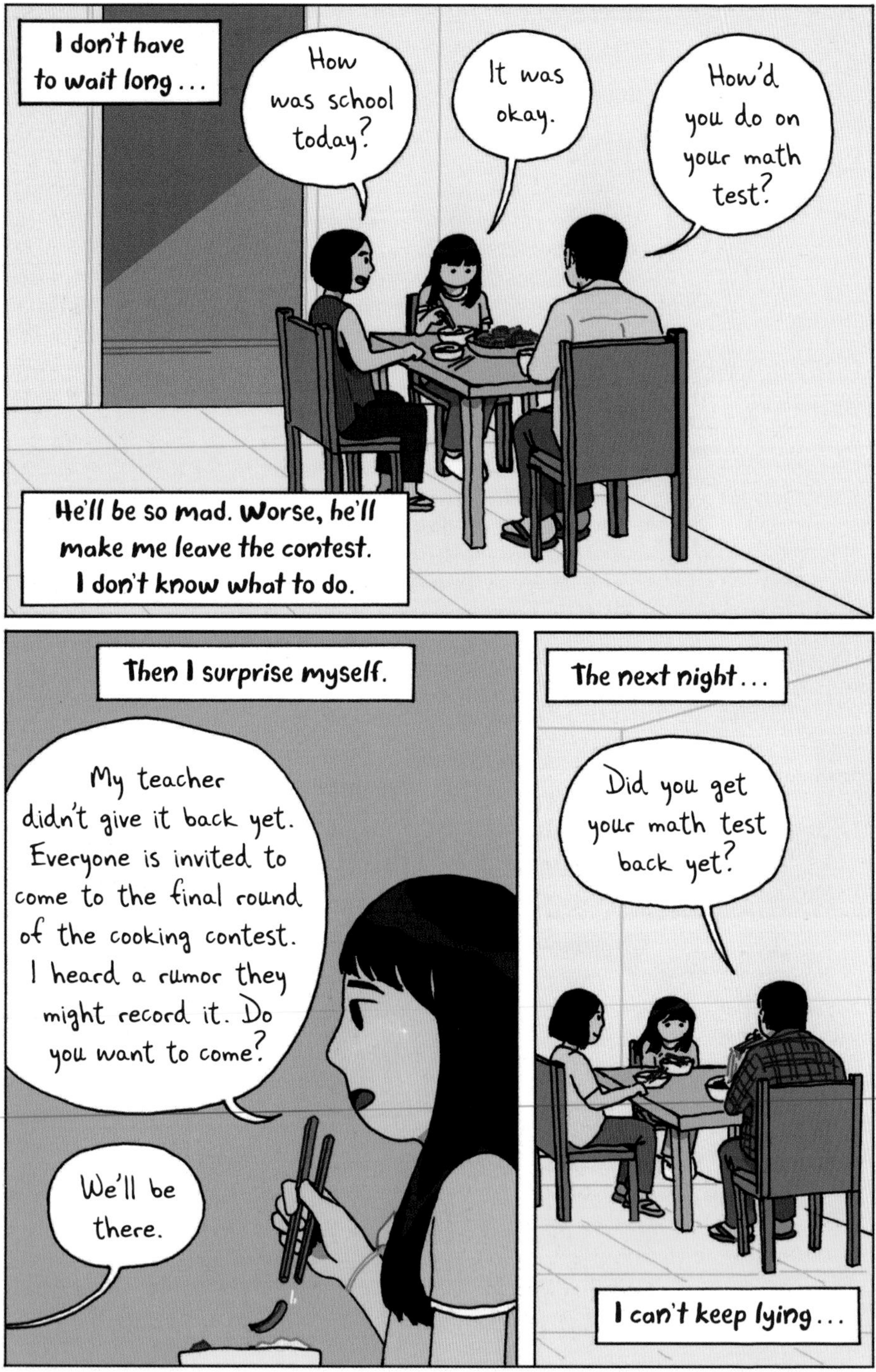
I don't have to wait long . . .
How was school today?
It was okay.
How'd you do on your math test?
He'll be so mad. Worse, he'll make me leave the contest. I don't know what to do.
Then I surprise myself.
My teacher didn't give it back yet. Everyone is invited to come to the final round of the cooking contest. I heard a rumor they might record it. Do you want to come?
We'll be there.
The next night . . .
Did you get your math test back yet?
I can't keep lying . . .

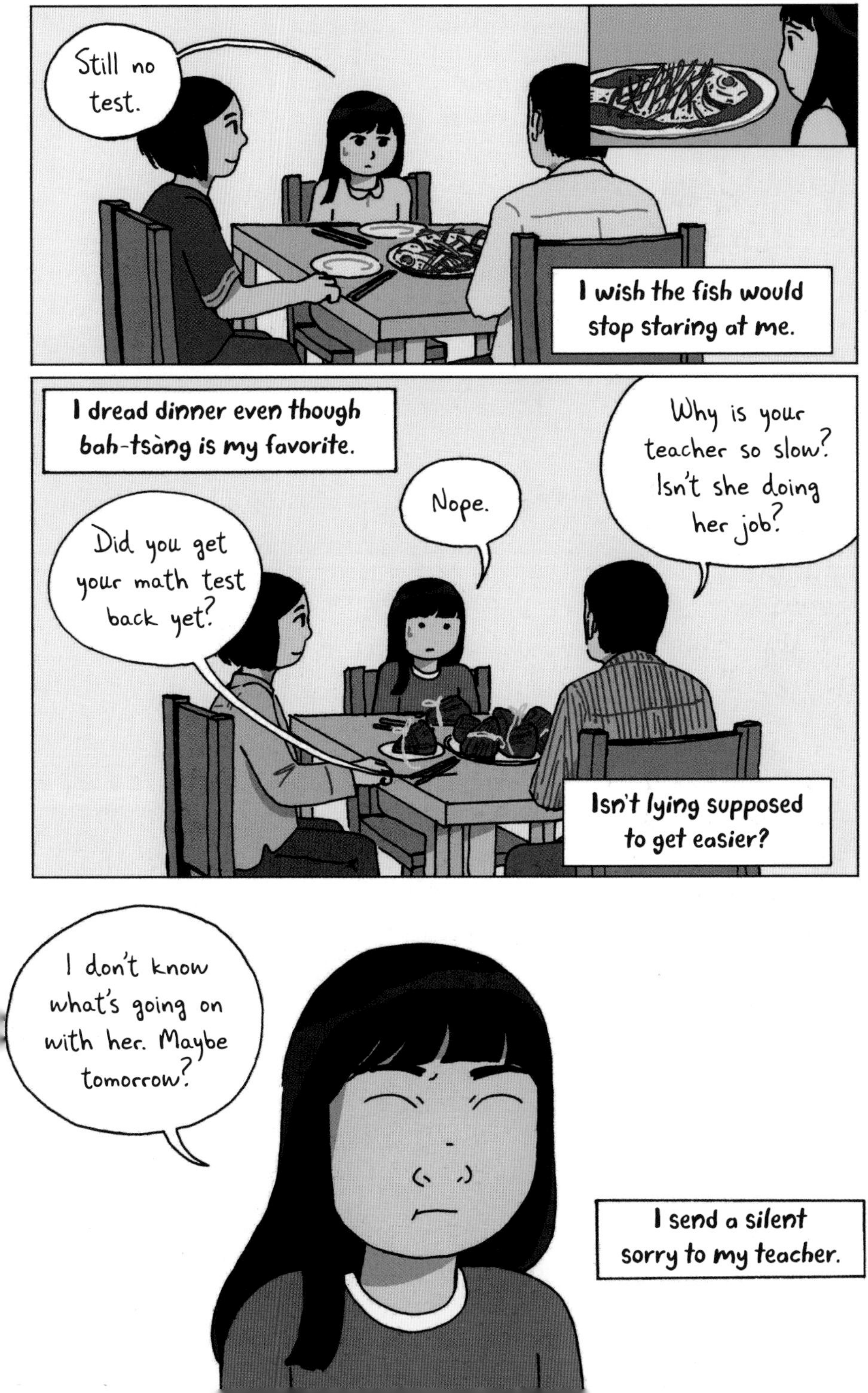
Still no test.
I wish the fish would stop staring at me.
I dread dinner even though bah-tsàng is my favorite.
Did you get your math test back yet?
Nope.
Why is your teacher so slow? Isn't she doing her job?
Isn't lying supposed to get easier?
I don't know what's going on with her. Maybe tomorrow?
I send a silent sorry to my teacher.

I just know Dad will find out, but I won't think of it right now.

Splash splash

Szzzzzzz

chop chop chop chop

BOO—UP
BOO—UP

I forgot to call A-má!

Cici, Cici, you forget to call.

I'm so sorry. I never forget.

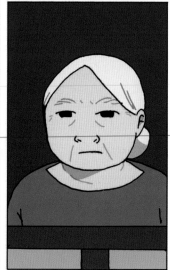

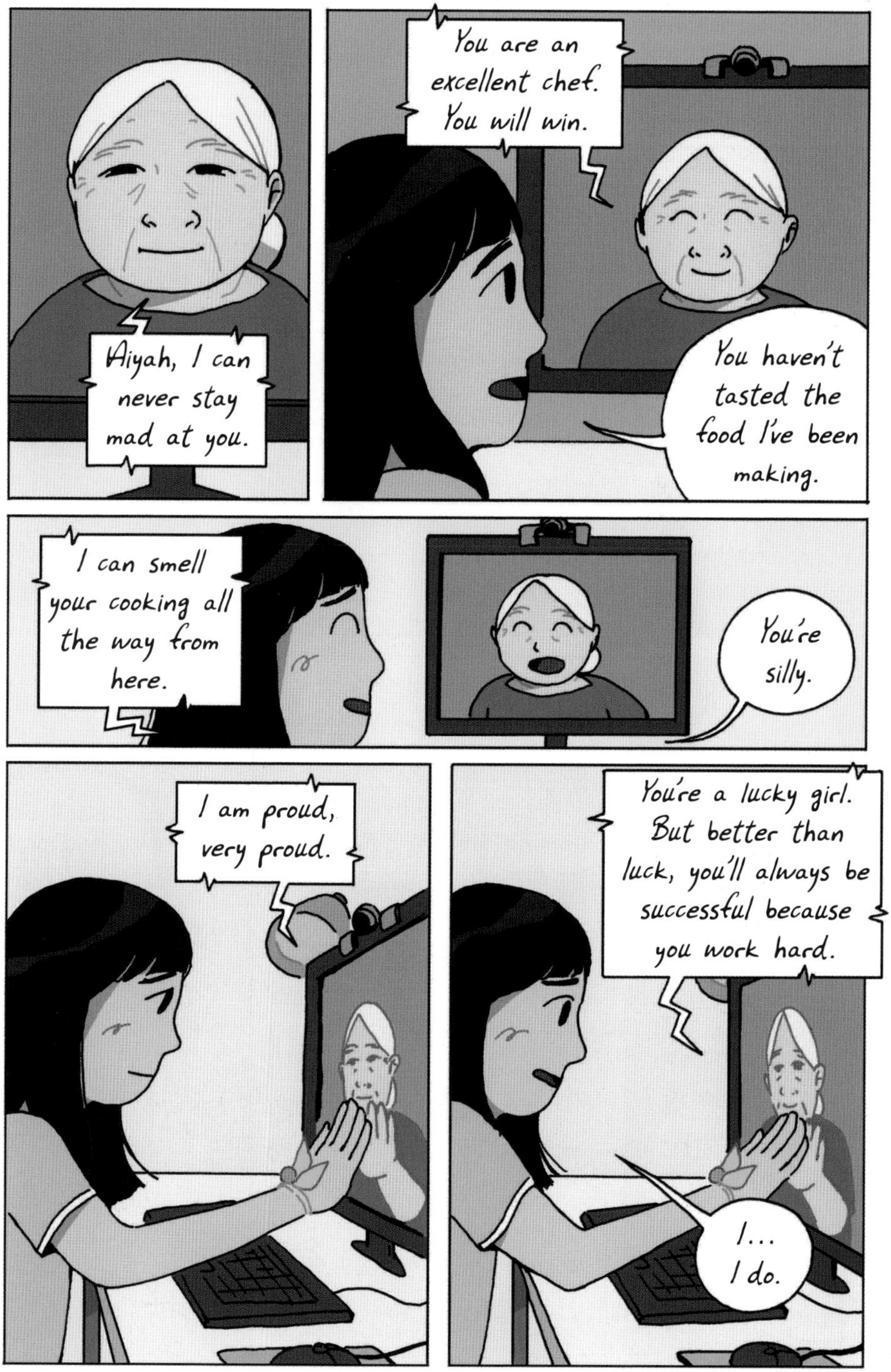
Aiyah, I can never stay mad at you.
You are an excellent chef. You will win.
You haven't tasted the food I've been making.
I can smell your cooking all the way from here.
You're silly.
I am proud, very proud.
You're a lucky girl. But better than luck, you'll always be successful because you work hard.
I... I do.

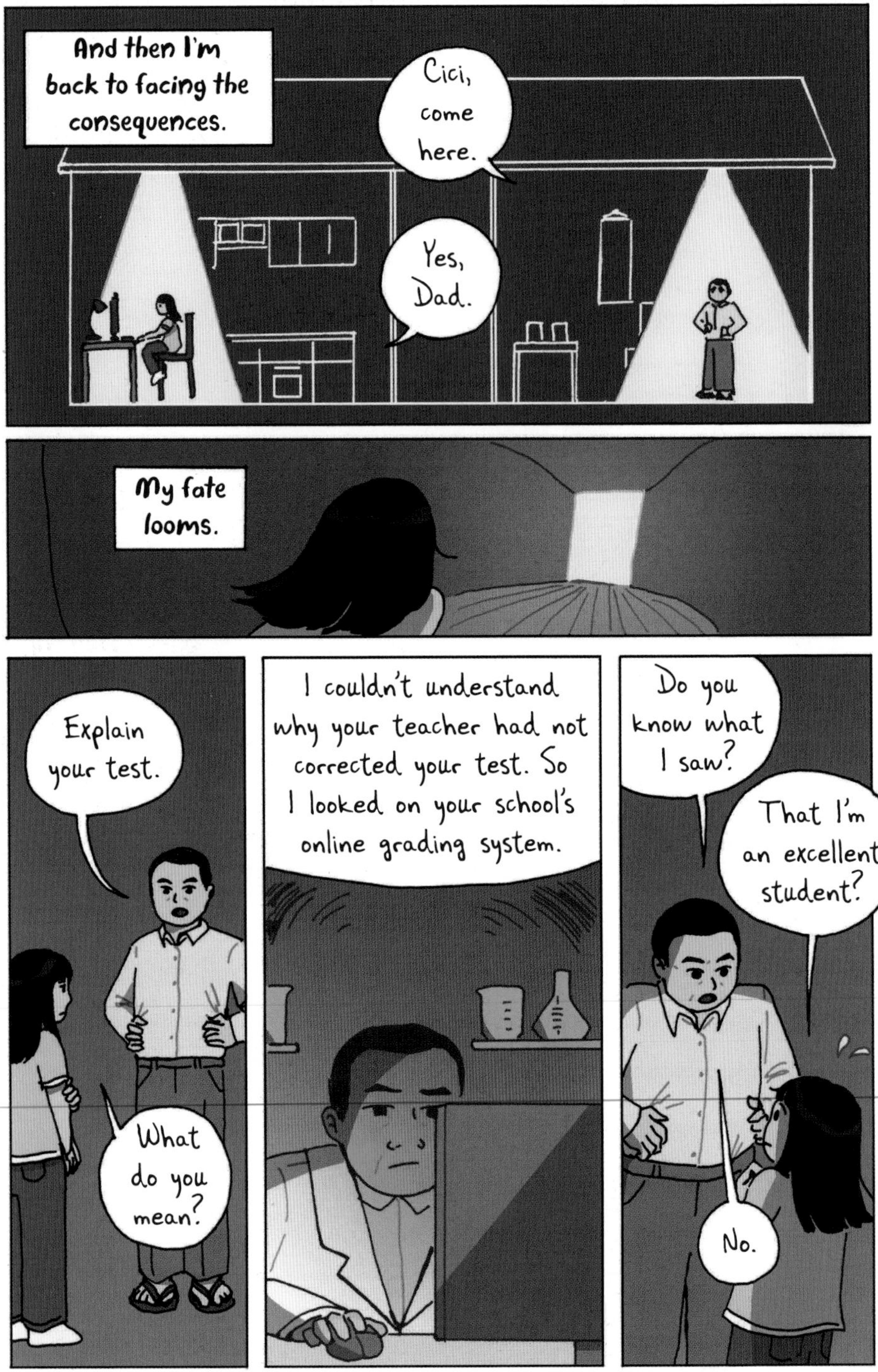
And then I'm back to facing the consequences.
Cici, come here.
Yes, Dad.
My fate looms.
Explain your test.
What do you mean?
I couldn't understand why your teacher had not corrected your test. So I looked on your school's online grading system.
Do you know what I saw?
That I'm an excellent student?
No.

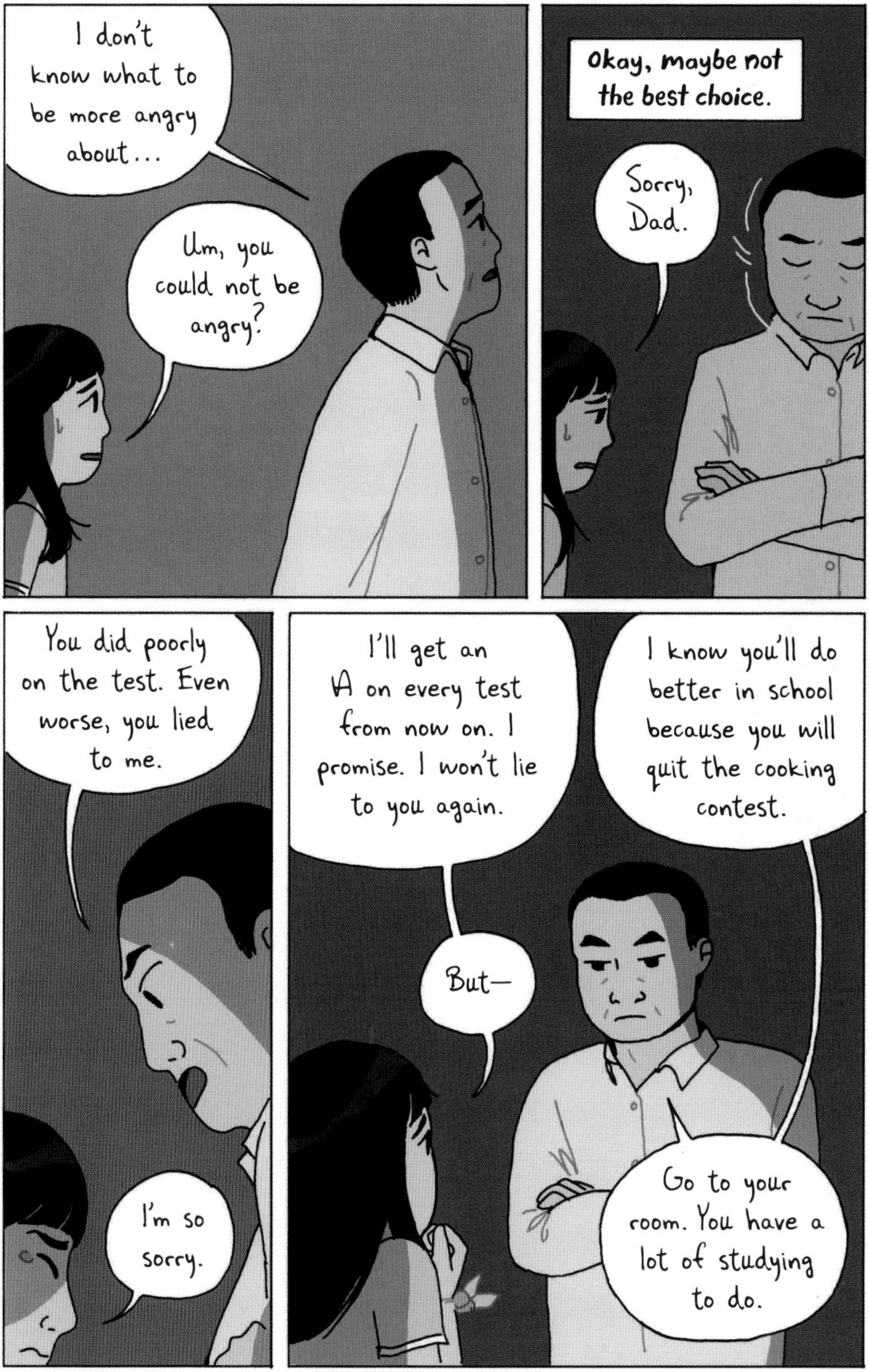
I don't know what to be more angry about...
Um, you could not be angry?
Okay, maybe not the best choice.
Sorry, Dad.
You did poorly on the test. Even worse, you lied to me.
I'm so sorry.
I'll get an A on every test from now on. I promise. I won't lie to you again.
I know you'll do better in school because you will quit the cooking contest.
But—
Go to your room. You have a lot of studying to do.

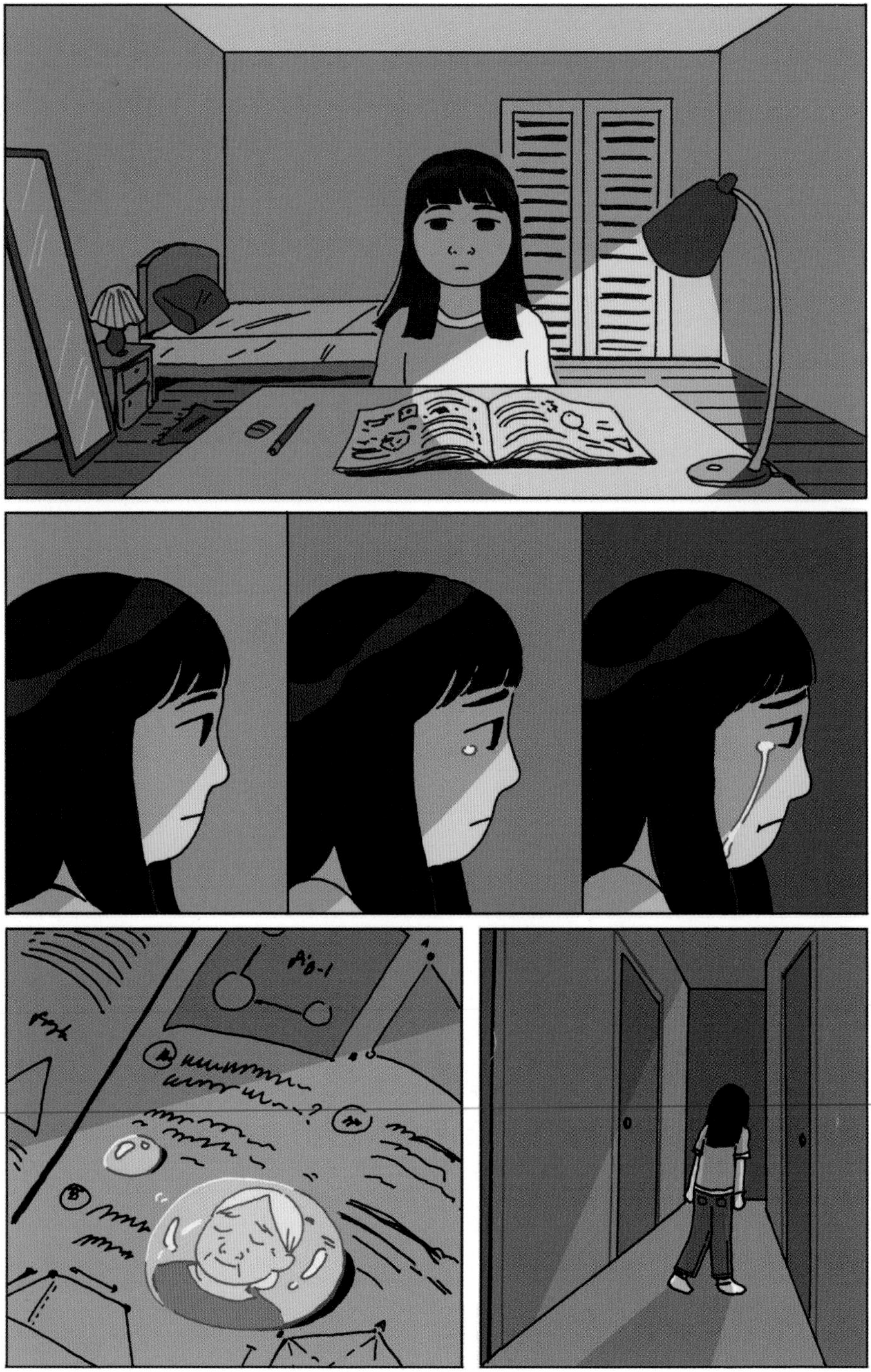

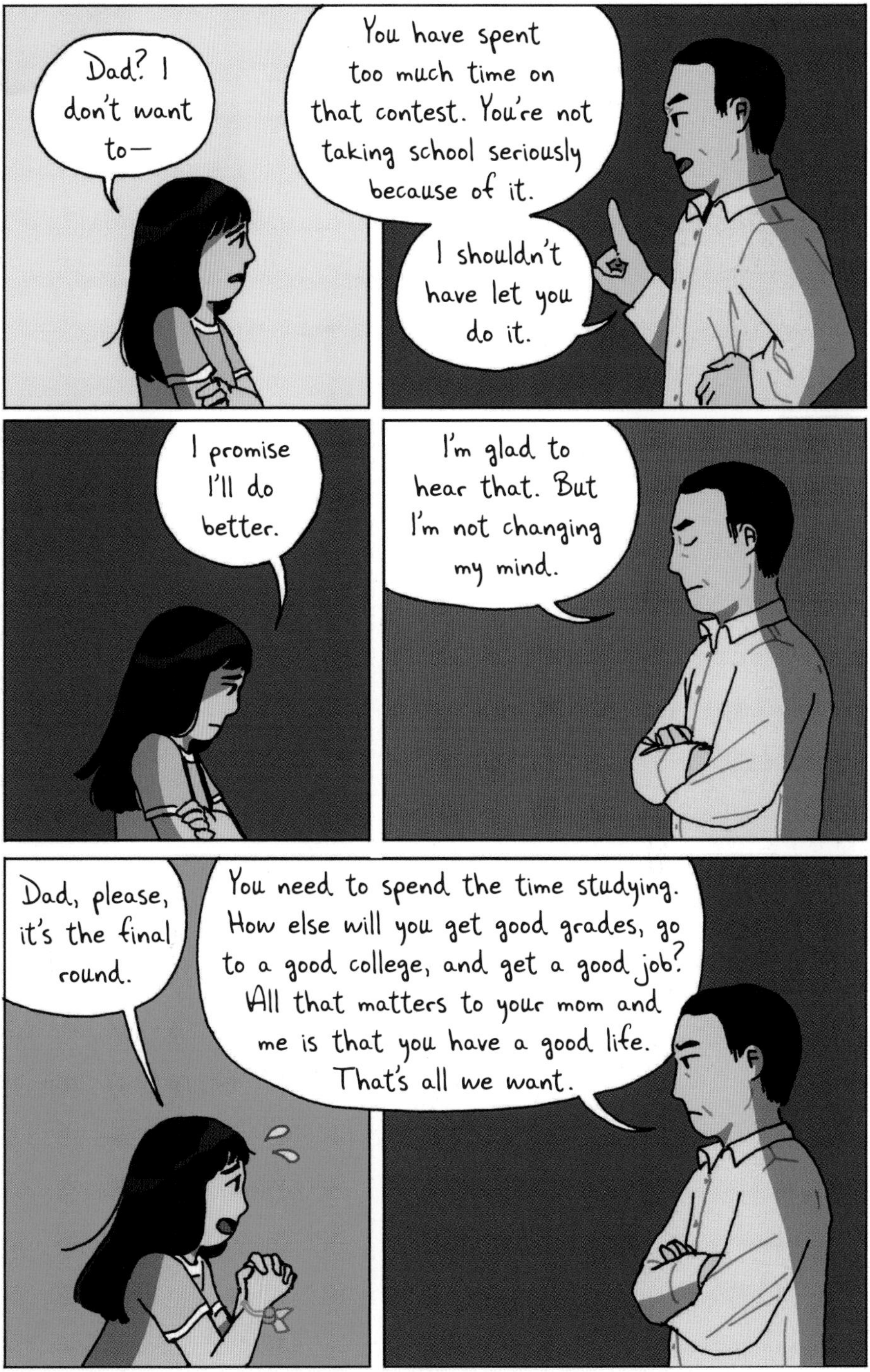
Dad? I don't want to—
You have spent too much time on that contest. You're not taking school seriously because of it.
I shouldn't have let you do it.
I promise I'll do better.
I'm glad to hear that. But I'm not changing my mind.
Dad, please, it's the final round.
You need to spend the time studying. How else will you get good grades, go to a good college, and get a good job? All that matters to your mom and me is that you have a good life. That's all we want.

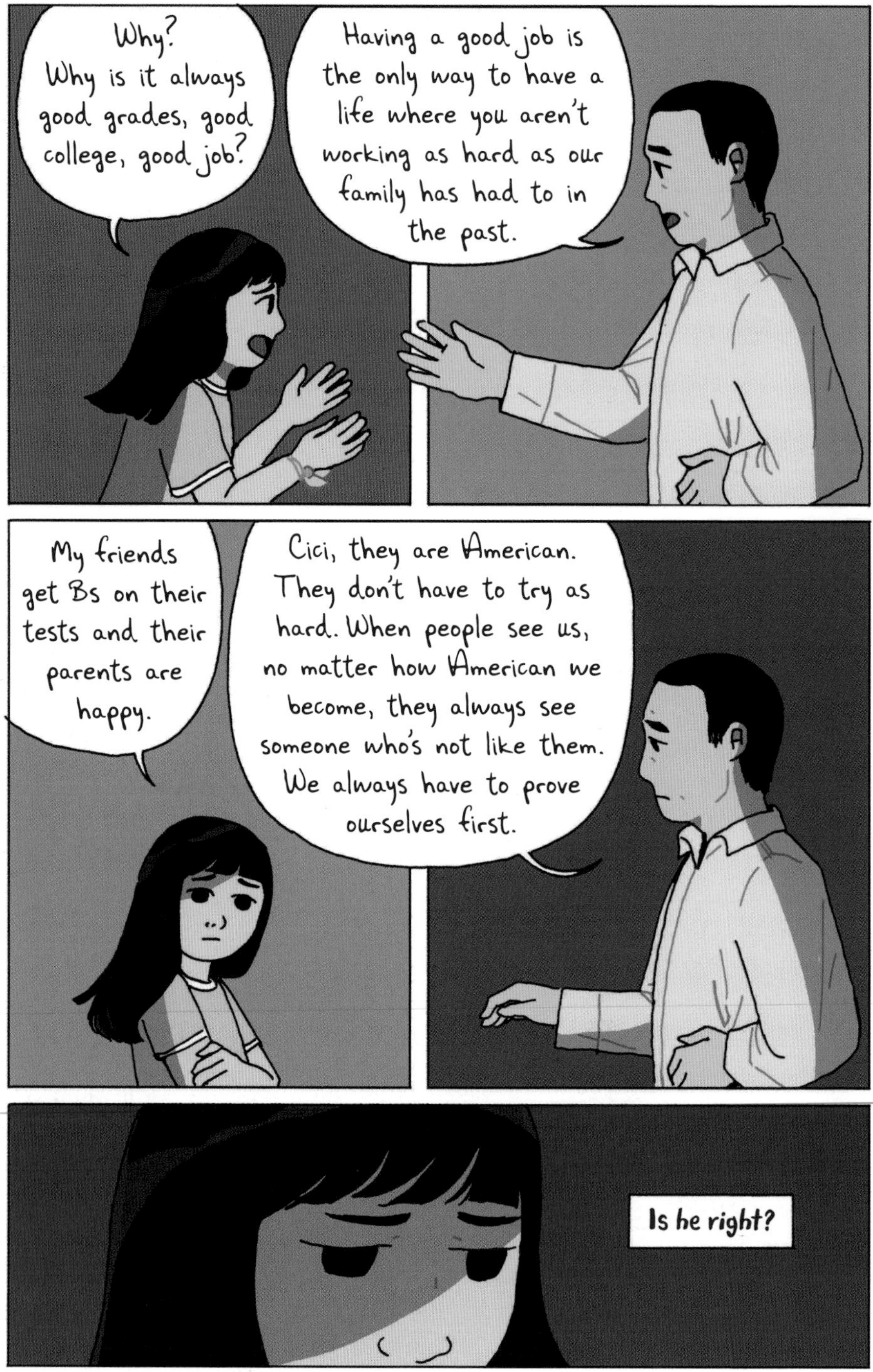
Why? Why is it always good grades, good college, good job?
Having a good job is the only way to have a life where you aren't working as hard as our family has had to in the past.
My friends get Bs on their tests and their parents are happy.
Cici, they are American. They don't have to try as hard. When people see us, no matter how American we become, they always see someone who's not like them. We always have to prove ourselves first.
Is he right?

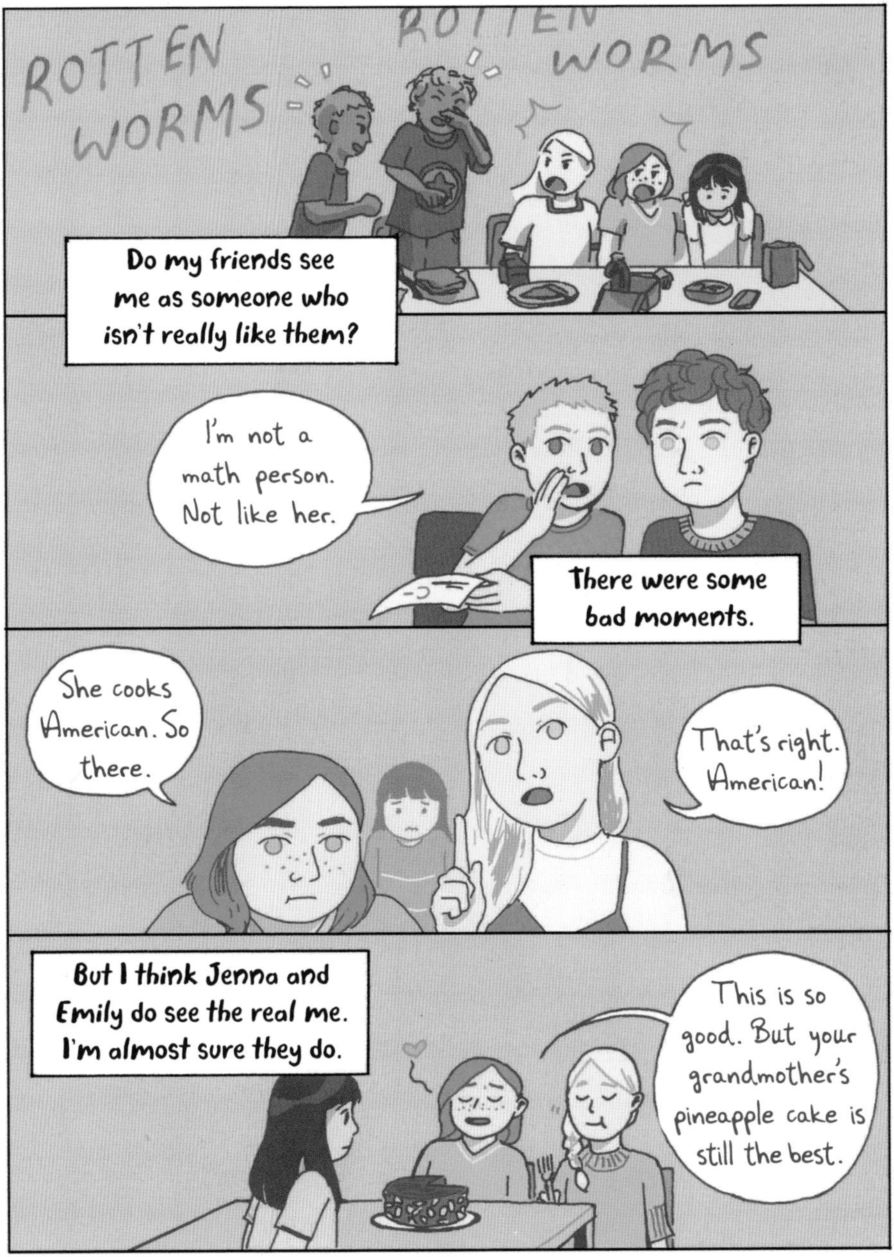
ROTTEN WORMS
ROTTEN WORMS
Do my friends see me as someone who isn't really like them?
I'm not a math person. Not like her.
There were some bad moments.
She cooks American. So there.
That's right. American!
But I think Jenna and Emily do see the real me. I'm almost sure they do.
This is so good. But your grandmother's pineapple cake is still the best.

I need to convince Dad to let me finish the contest. I need to bring A-má here. I need her.

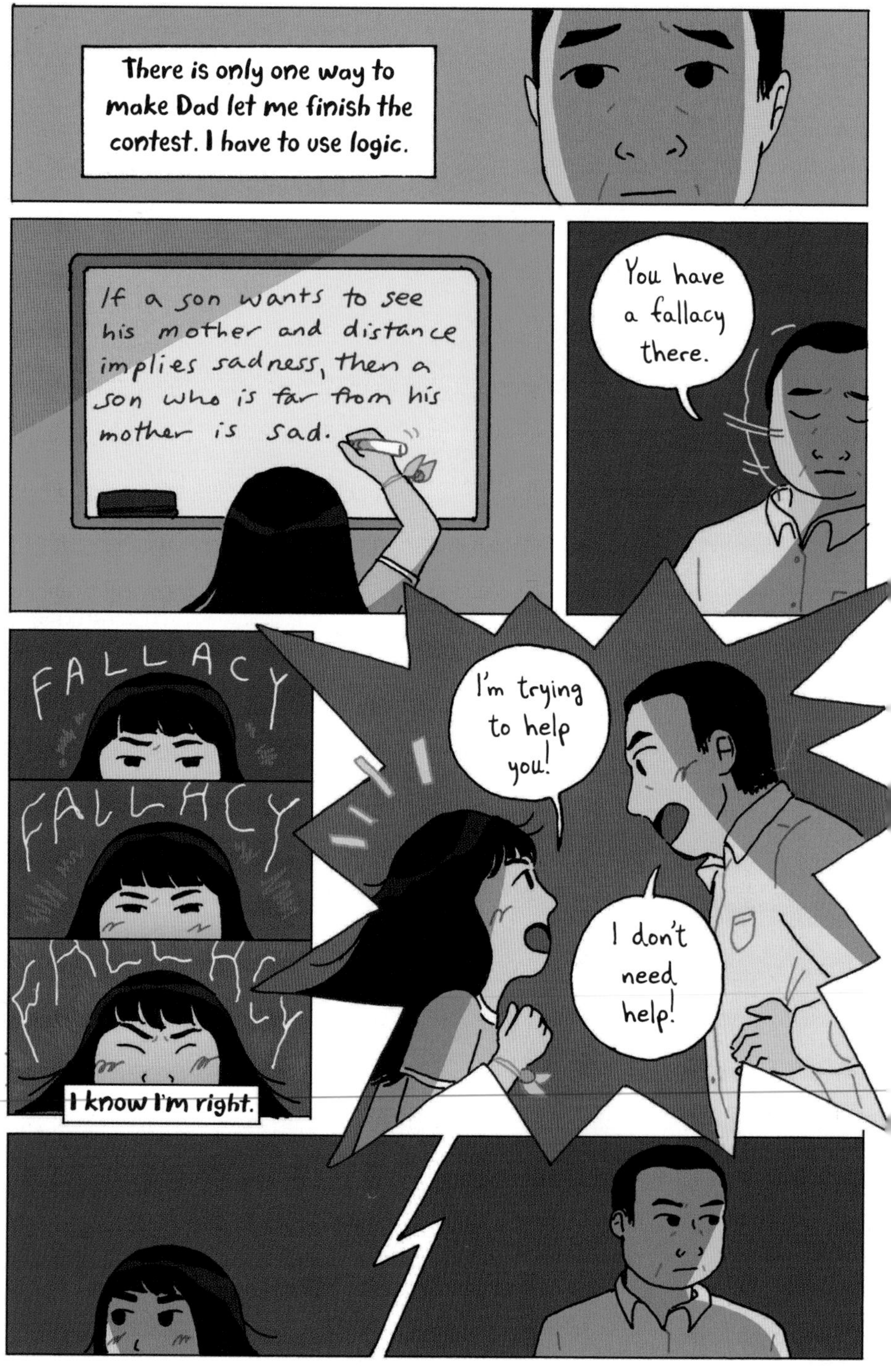

There is only one way to make Dad let me finish the contest. I have to use logic.
If a son wants to see his mother and distance implies sadness, then a son who is far from his mother is sad.
You have a fallacy there.
FALLACY
FALLACY
FALLACY
I know I'm right.
I'm trying to help you!
I don't need help!

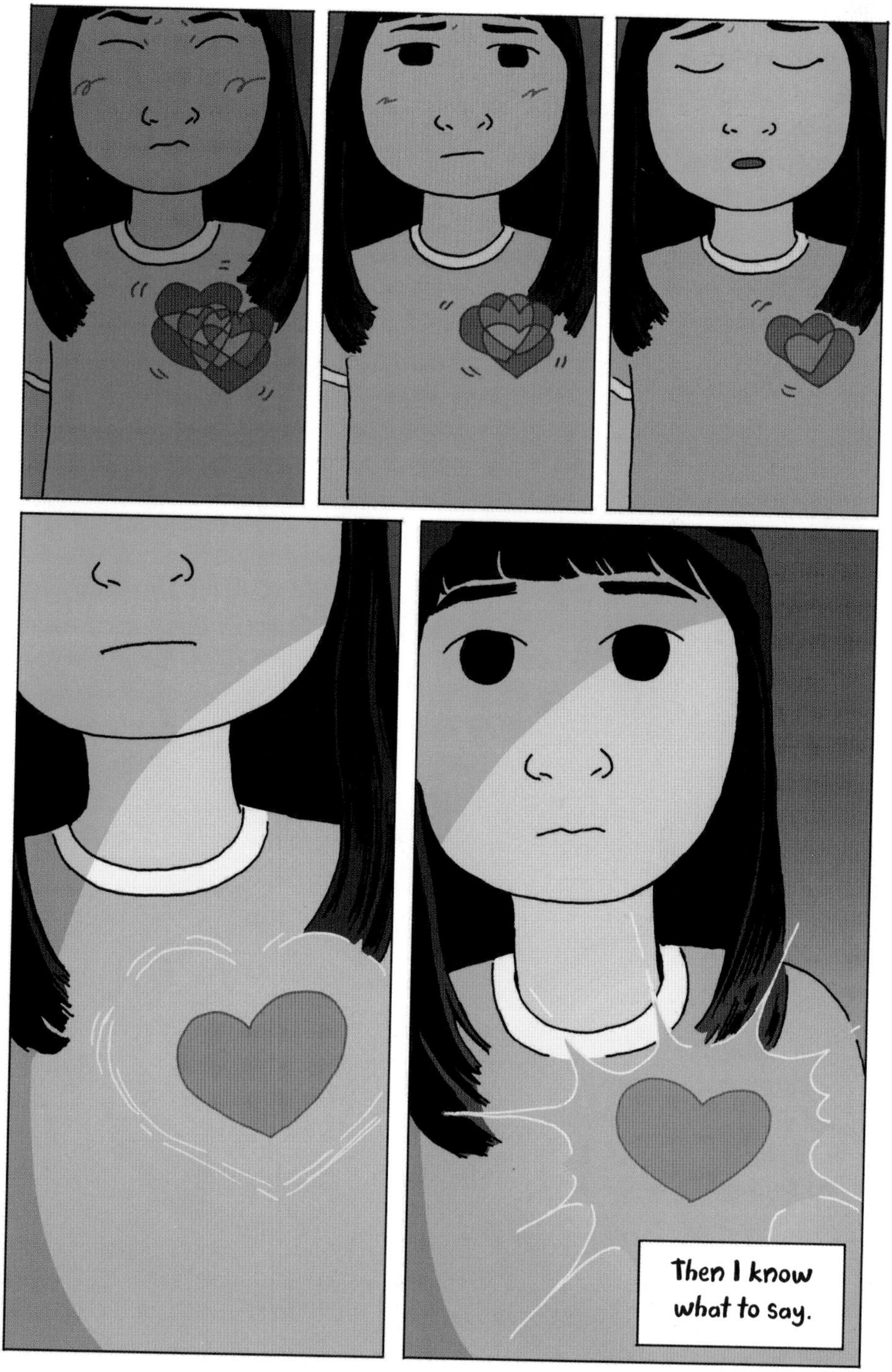
Then I know what to say.

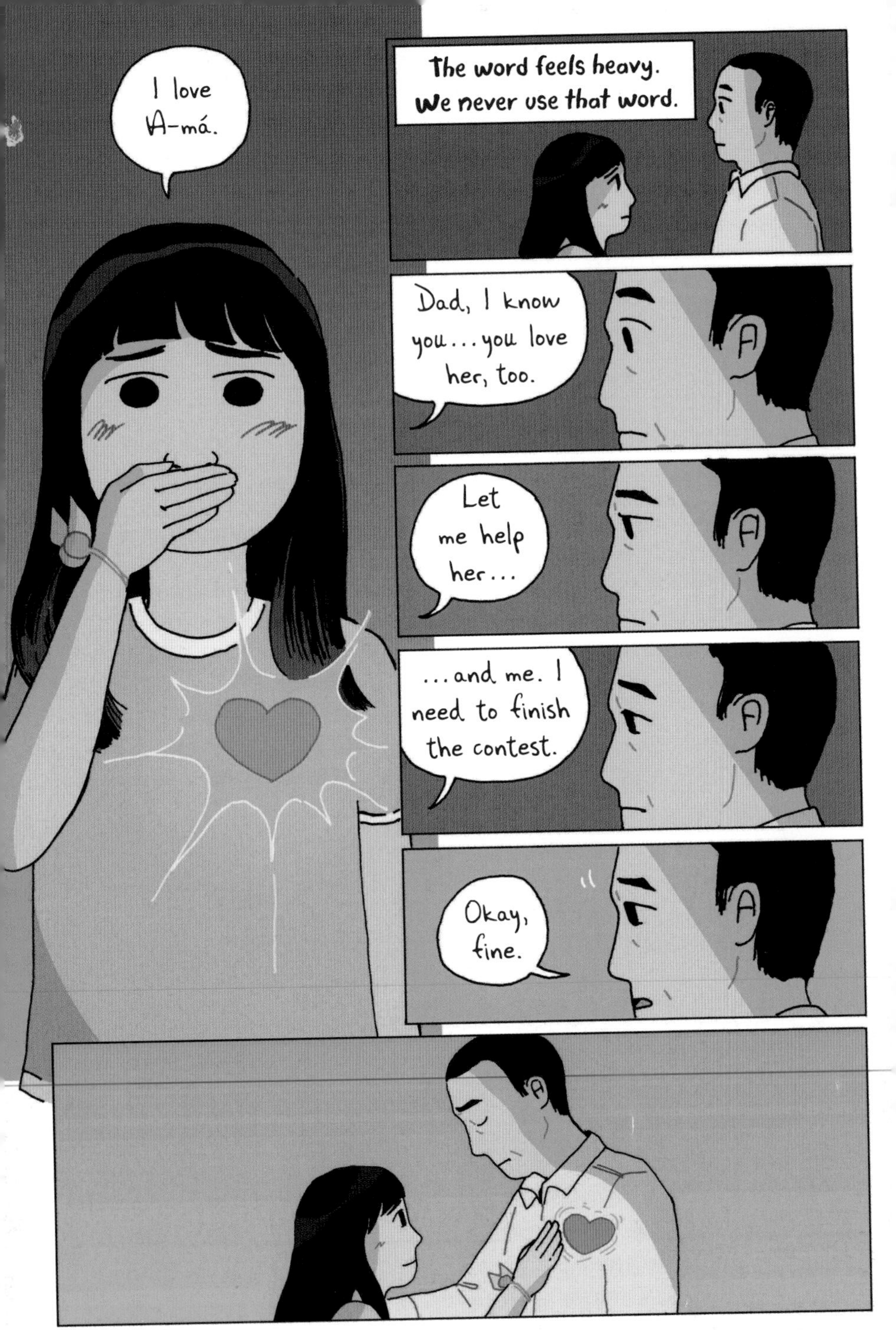
I love A-má.
The word feels heavy. We never use that word.
Dad, I know you... you love her, too.
Let me help her...
...and me. I need to finish the contest.
Okay, fine.

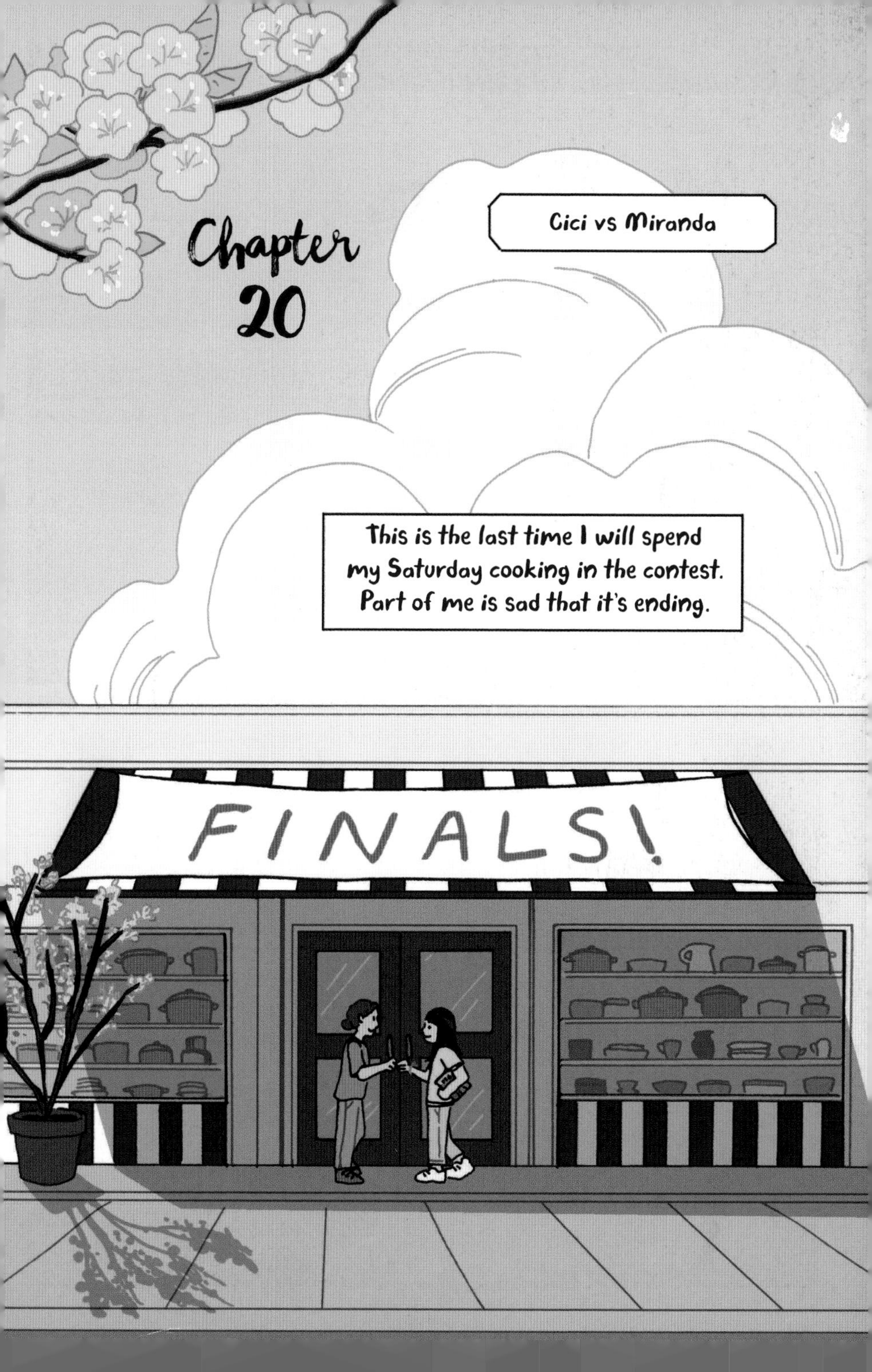
Chapter 20
Cici vs Miranda
This is the last time I will spend my Saturday cooking in the contest. Part of me is sad that it's ending.
FINALS!

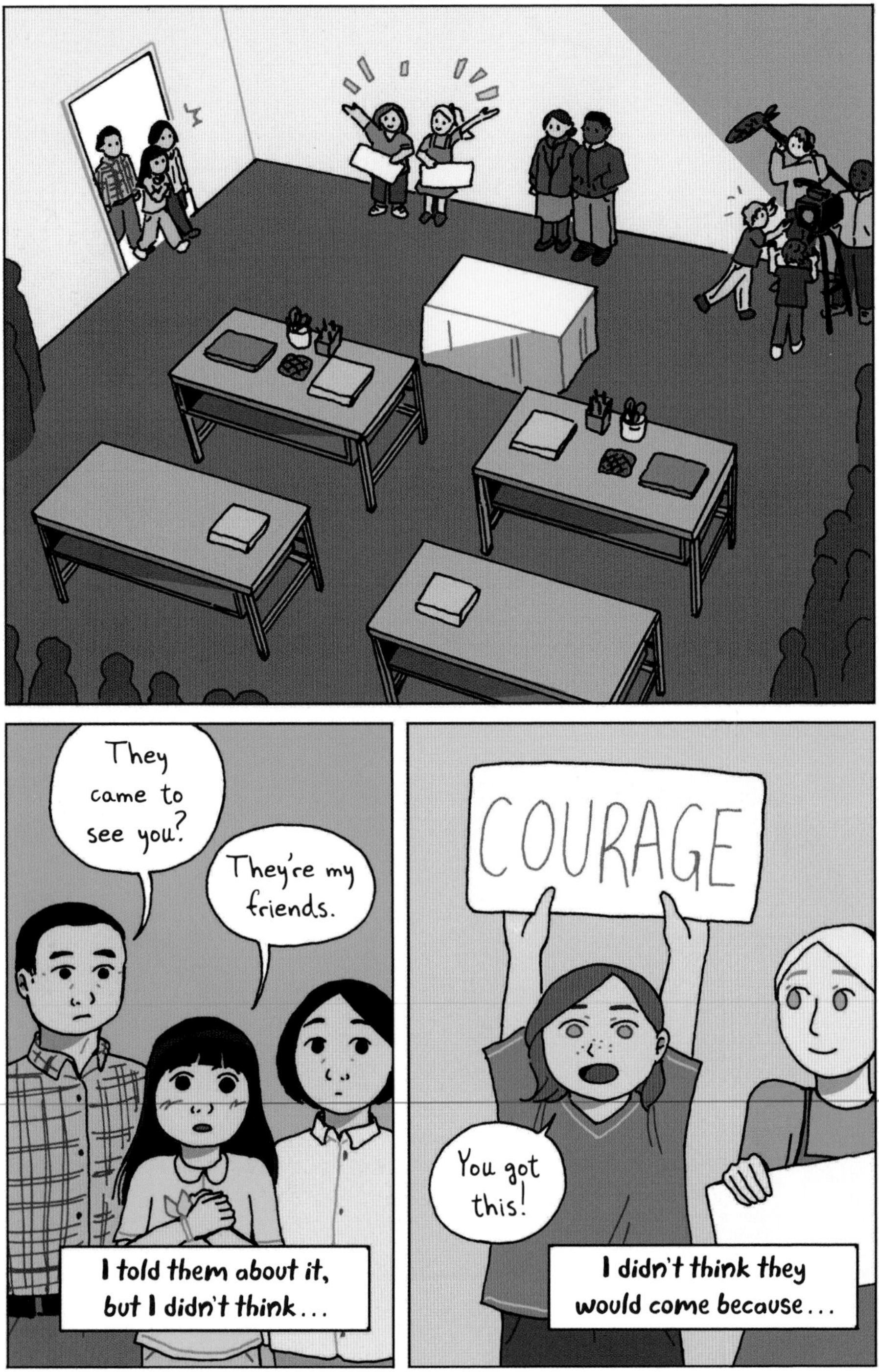
They came to see you?
They're my friends.
I told them about it, but I didn't think...
COURAGE
You got this!
I didn't think they would come because...

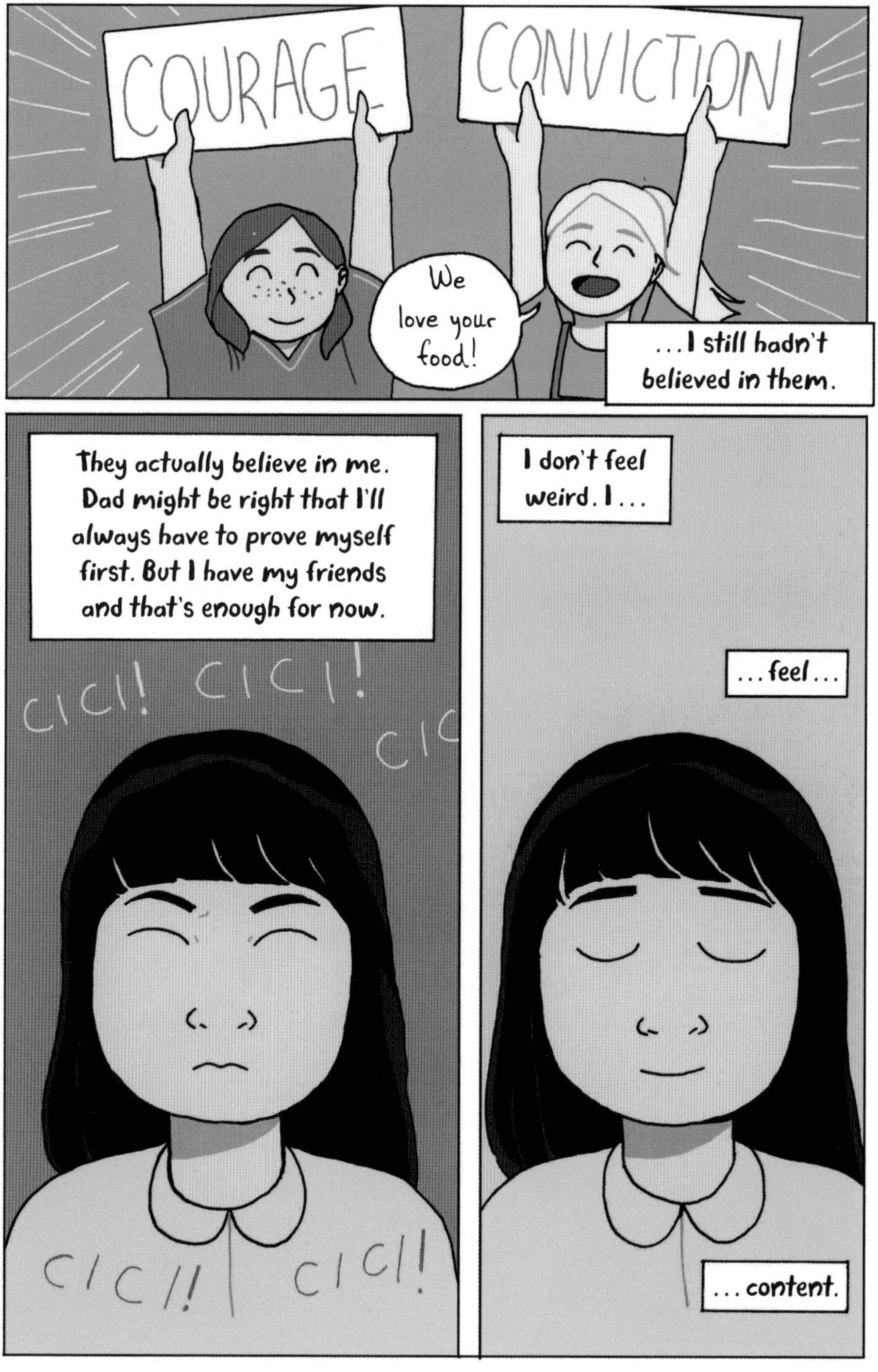
COURAGE
CONVICTION
We love your food!
...I still hadn't believed in them.
They actually believe in me. Dad might be right that I'll always have to prove myself first. But I have my friends and that's enough for now.
CICI! CICI!
CIC
CICI! CICI!
I don't feel weird. I...
...feel...
...content.

Cici is changing.

It's good.

Yes... it is.

Good luck, Cici.

Thanks, Amy. I hear you're moving back to England.

This is my fiancé, George. I wish...

You don't need me anymore. I know you'll be fine.

I...I...I want you to be happy.

I will be. And you will come visit. Anytime you want to talk, I'll be there for you.

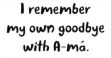

I remember my own goodbye with A-má.

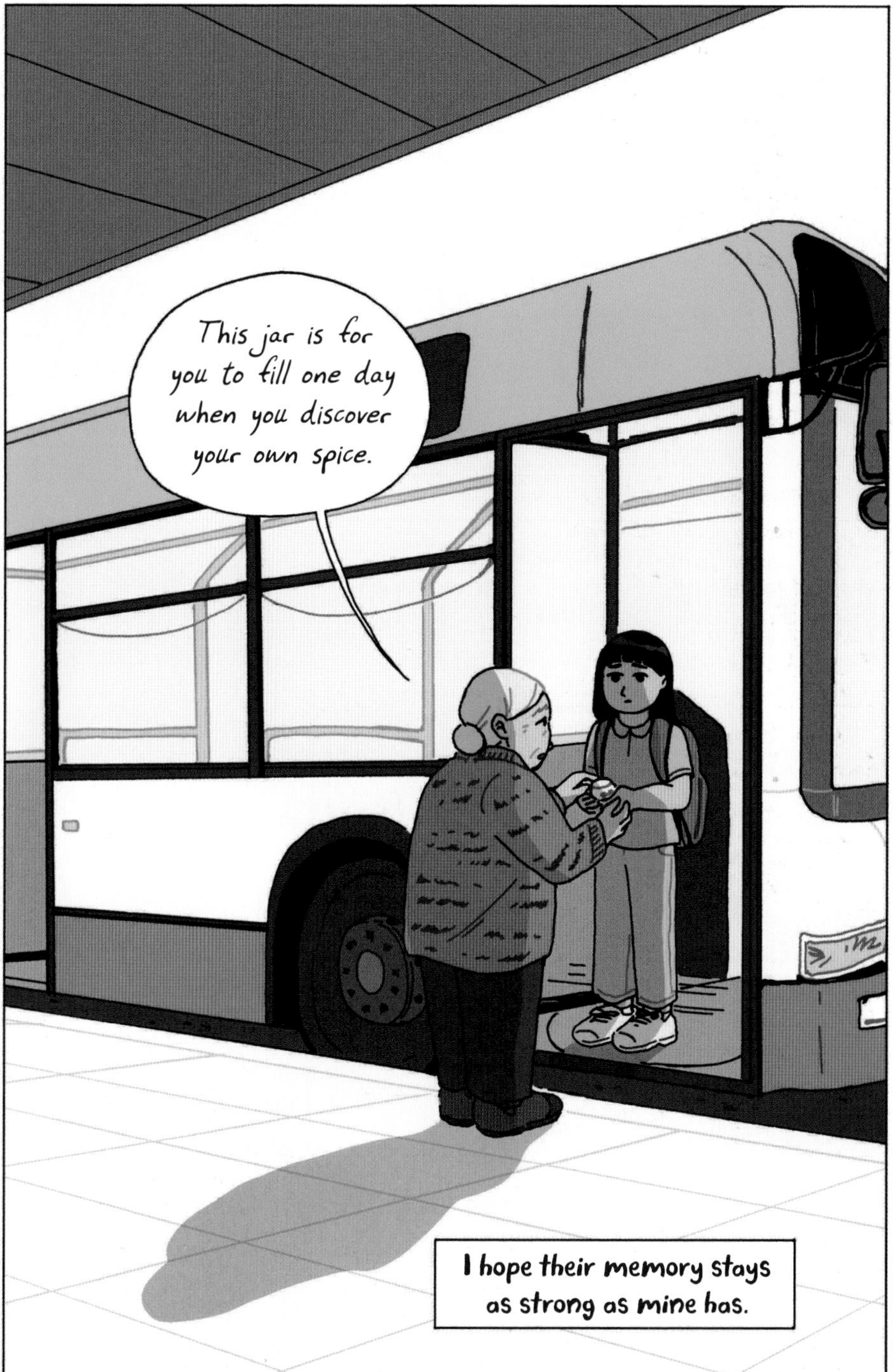
This jar is for you to fill one day when you discover your own spice.
I hope their memory stays as strong as mine has.

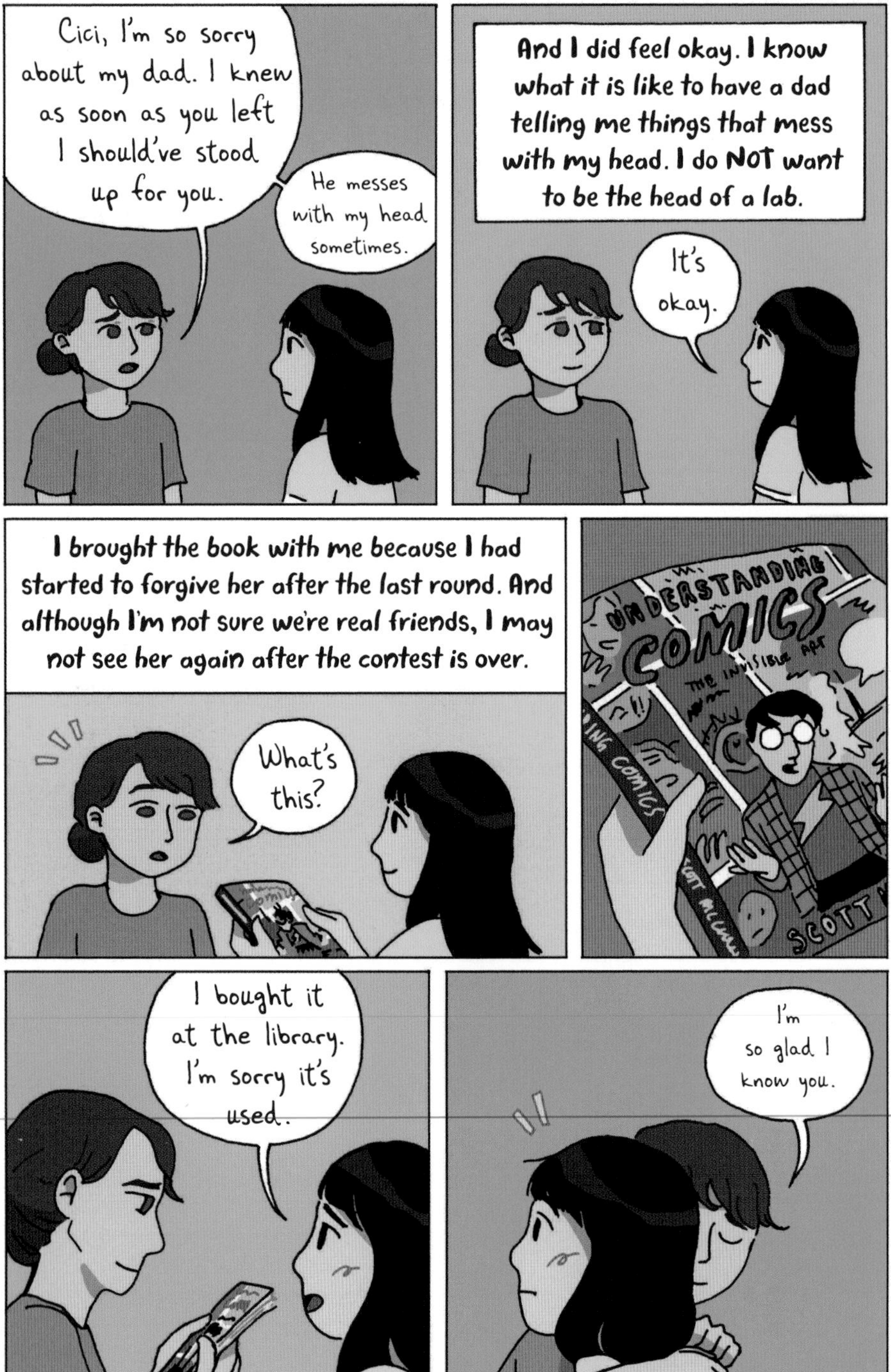
Cici, I'm so sorry about my dad. I knew as soon as you left I should've stood up for you.
He messes with my head sometimes.
And I did feel okay. I know what it is like to have a dad telling me things that mess with my head. I do NOT want to be the head of a lab.
It's okay.
I brought the book with me because I had started to forgive her after the last round. And although I'm not sure we're real friends, I may not see her again after the contest is over.
What's this?
UNDERSTANDING COMICS
THE INVISIBLE ART
SCOTT
I bought it at the library. I'm sorry it's used.
I'm so glad I know you.

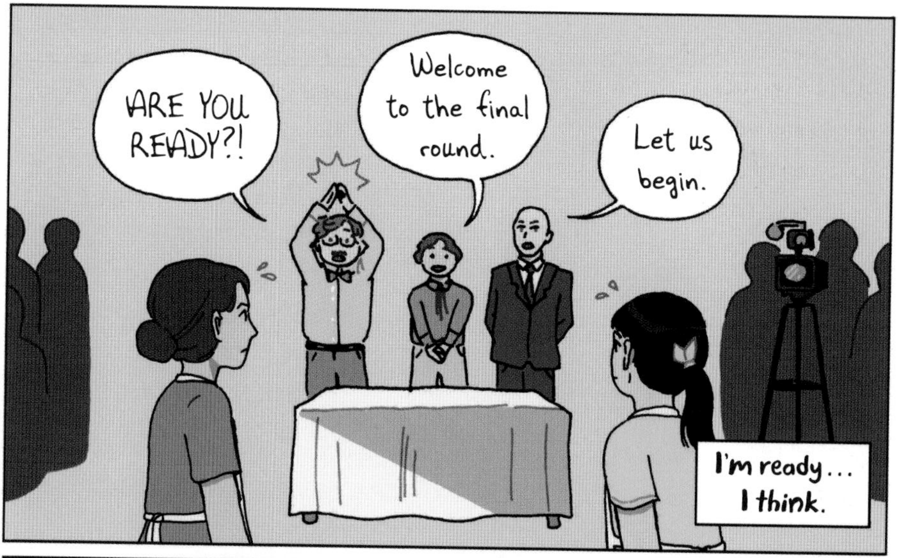
ARE YOU READY?!
Welcome to the final round.
Let us begin.
I'm ready... I think.

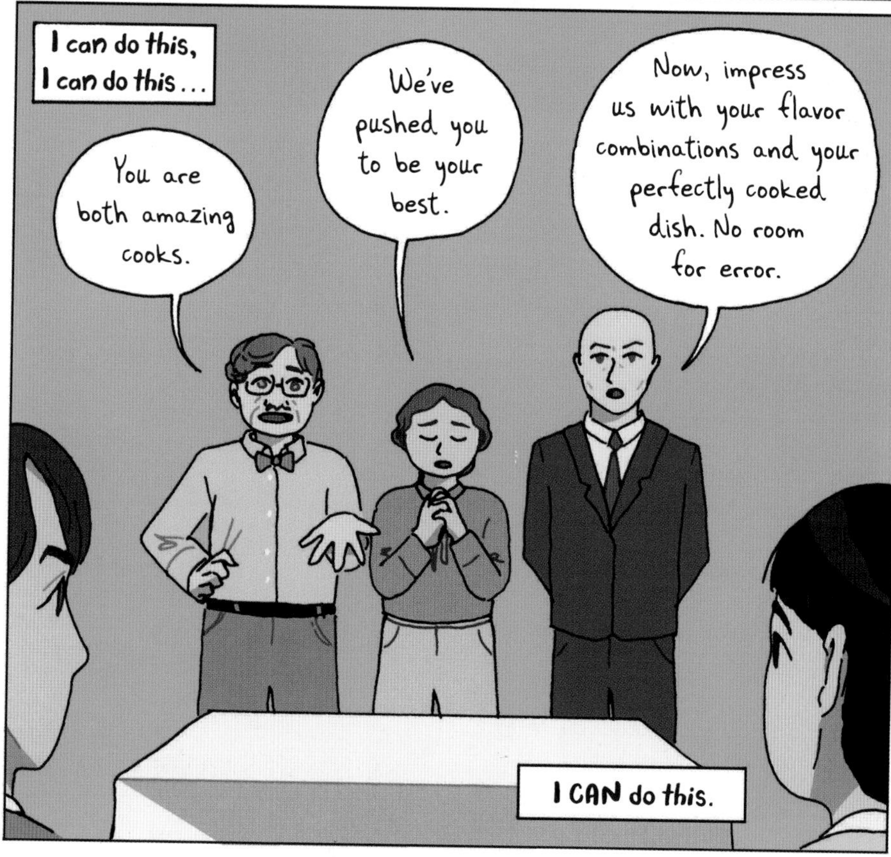
I can do this, I can do this...
You are both amazing cooks.
We've pushed you to be your best.
Now, impress us with your flavor combinations and your perfectly cooked dish. No room for error.
I CAN do this.

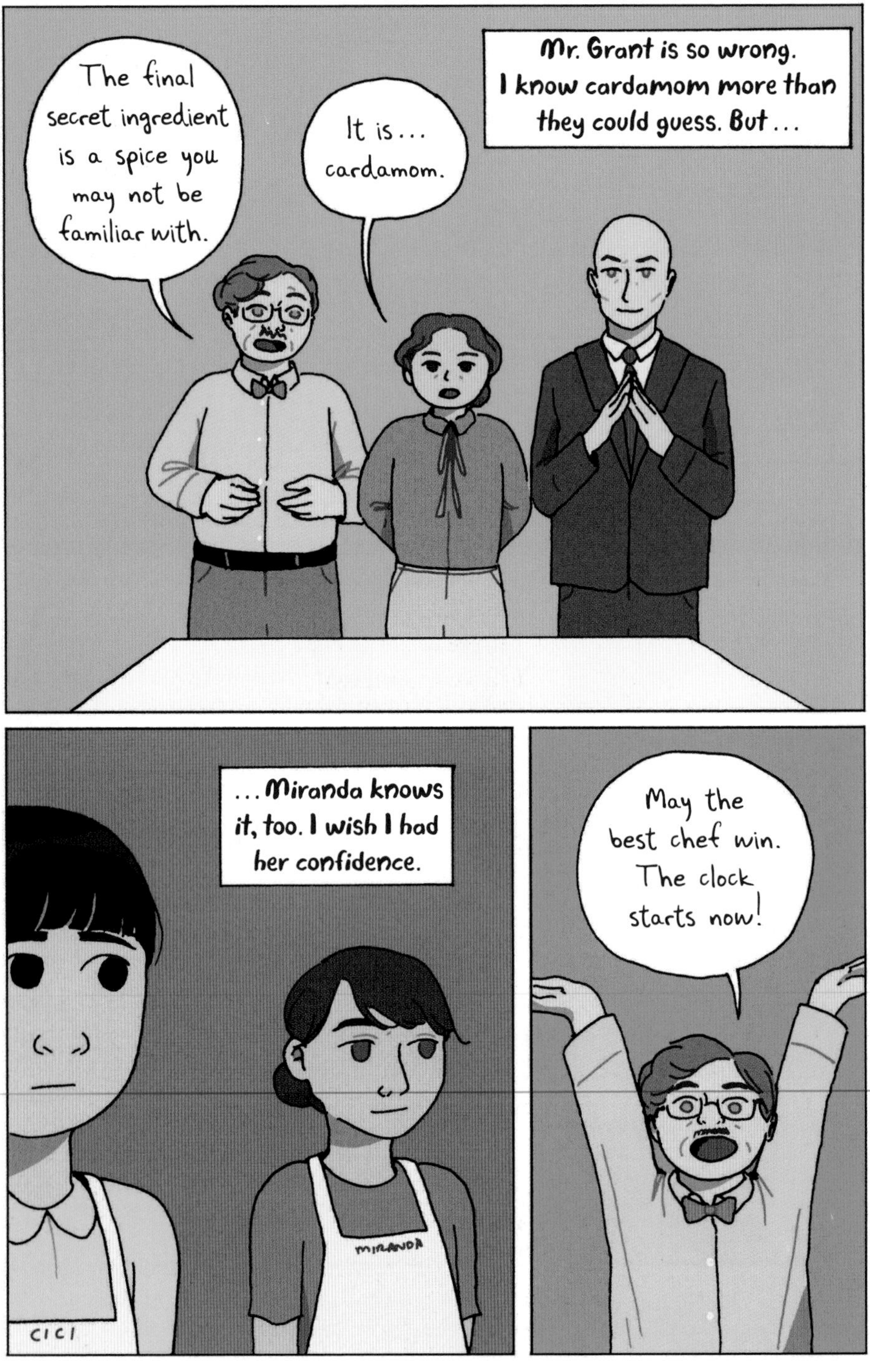
The final secret ingredient is a spice you may not be familiar with.
It is... cardamom.
Mr. Grant is so wrong. I know cardamom more than they could guess. But...
...Miranda knows it, too. I wish I had her confidence.
MIRANDA
CICI
May the best chef win. The clock starts now!

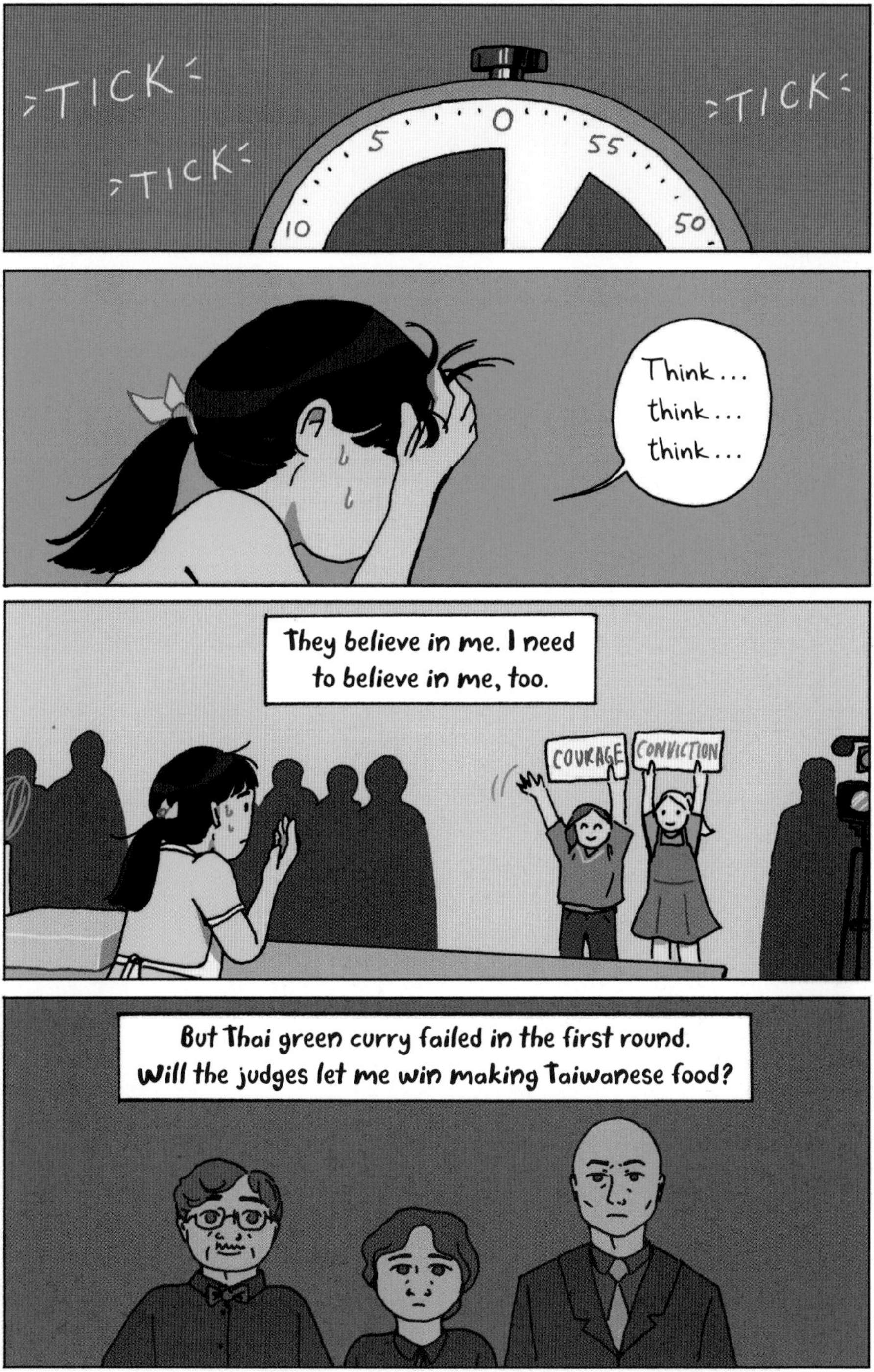
TICK
TICK
TICK
5
0
55
10
50
Think... think... think...
They believe in me. I need to believe in me, too.
COURAGE
CONVICTION
But Thai green curry failed in the first round. Will the judges let me win making Taiwanese food?

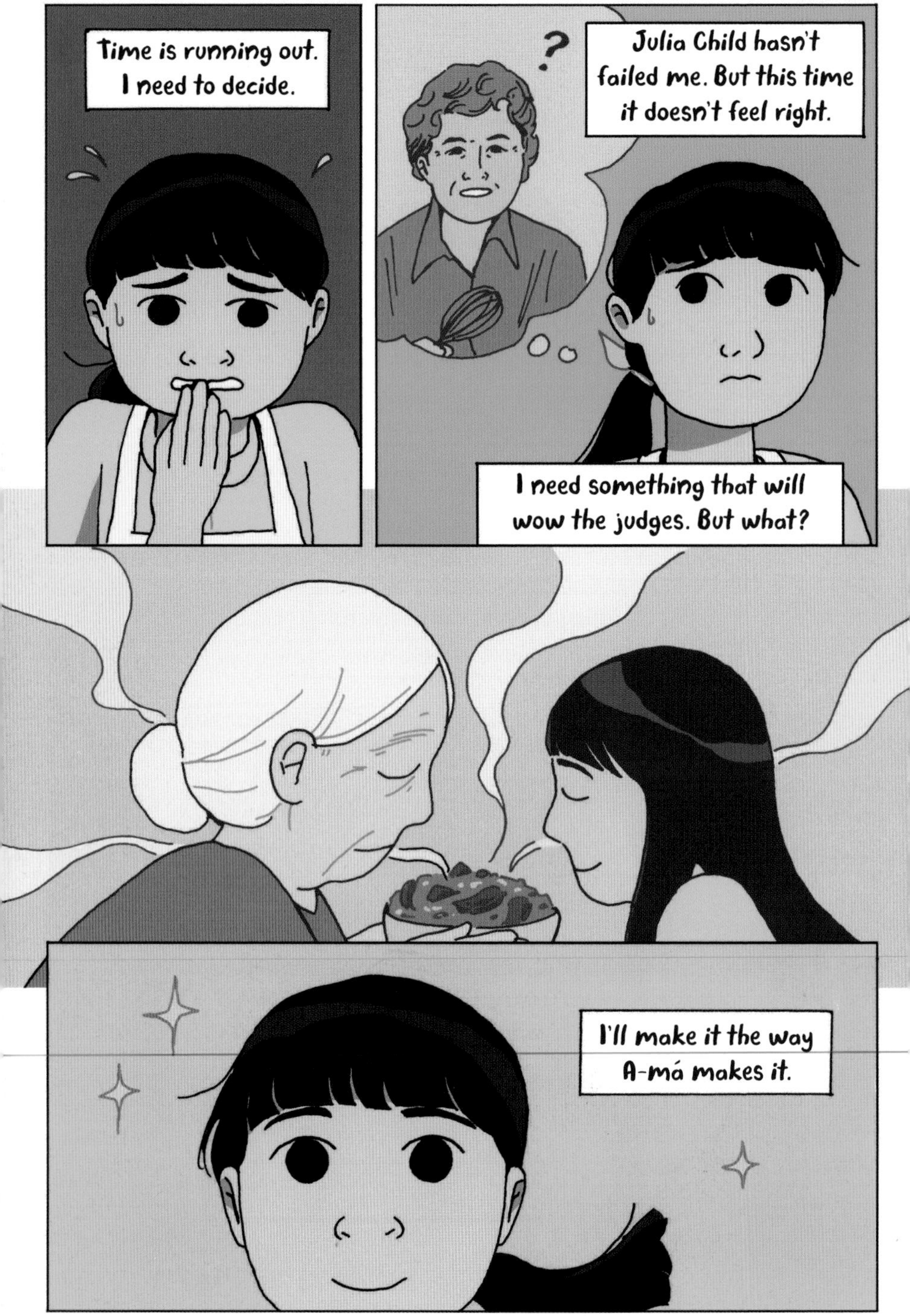
Time is running out. I need to decide.
Julia Child hasn't failed me. But this time it doesn't feel right.
?
I need something that will wow the judges. But what?
I'll make it the way A-má makes it.

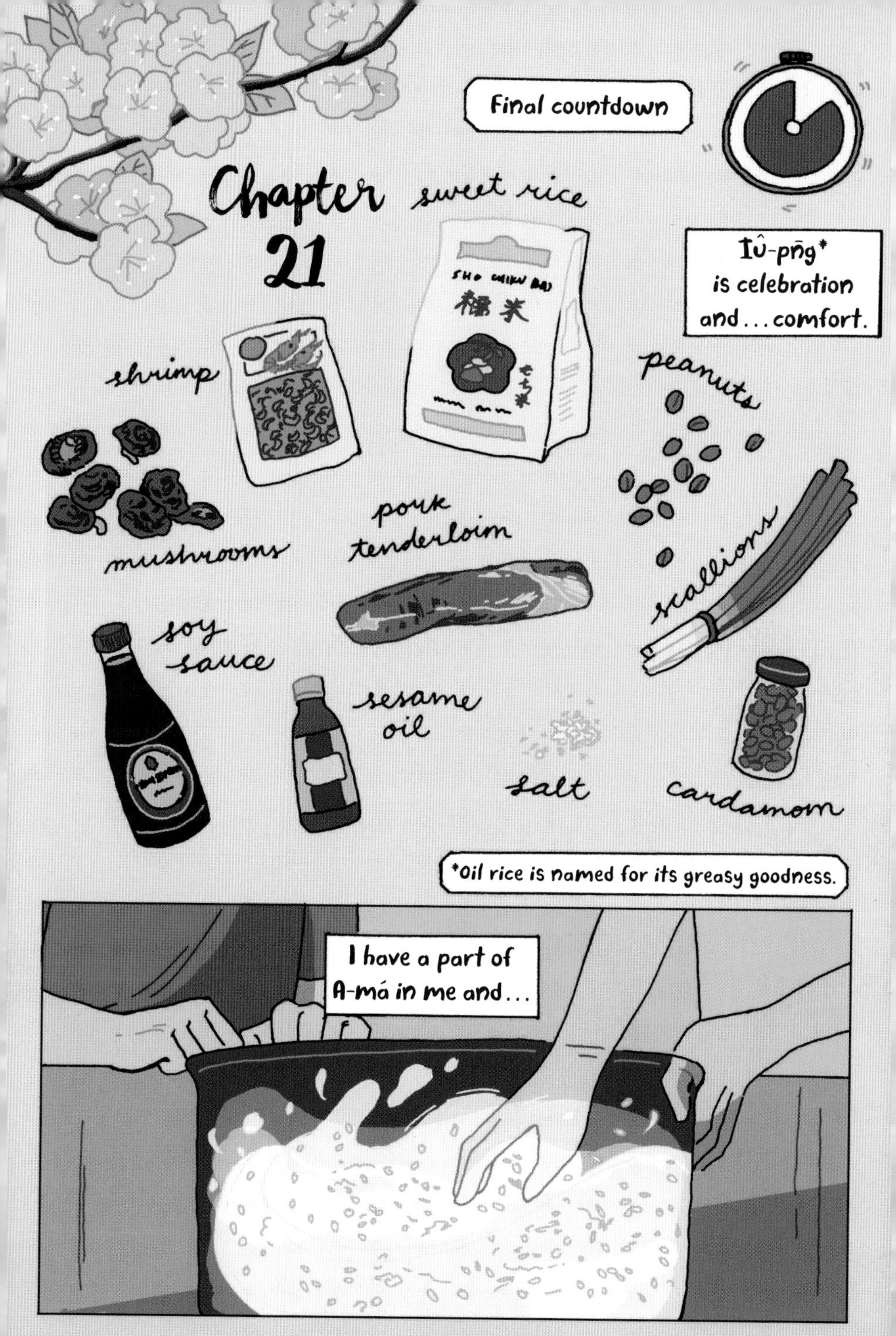
Final countdown
Chapter 21
sweet rice
SHO CHIKU BAI
糯米
もち米
Iû-pn̄g*
is celebration
and... comfort.
shrimp
peanuts
mushrooms
pork tenderloin
scallions
soy sauce
sesame oil
salt
cardamom
*Oil rice is named for its greasy goodness.
I have a part of
A-má in me and...

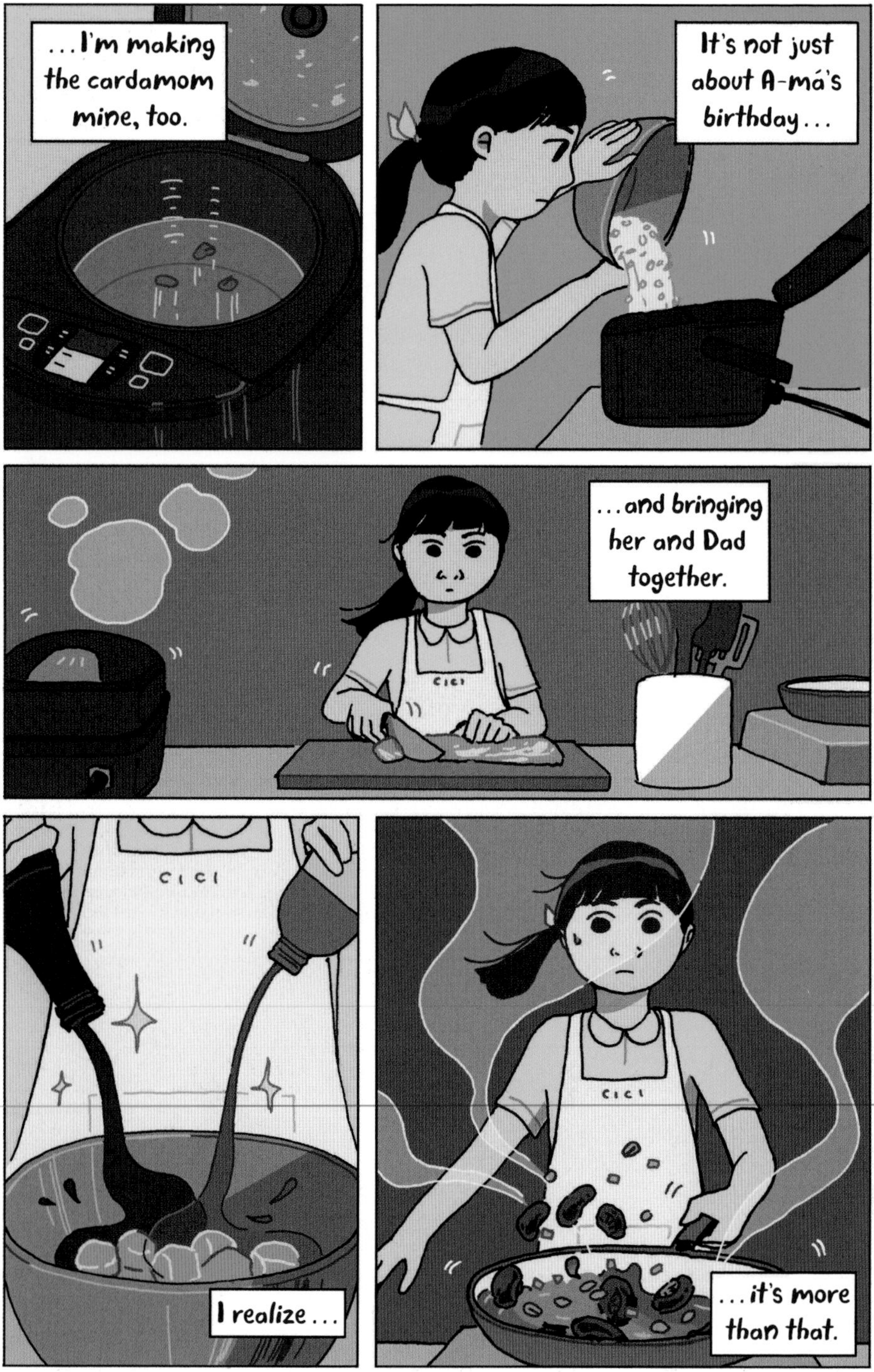
...I'm making the cardamom mine, too.
It's not just about A-má's birthday...
...and bringing her and Dad together.
CICI
CICI
I realize...
CICI
...it's more than that.

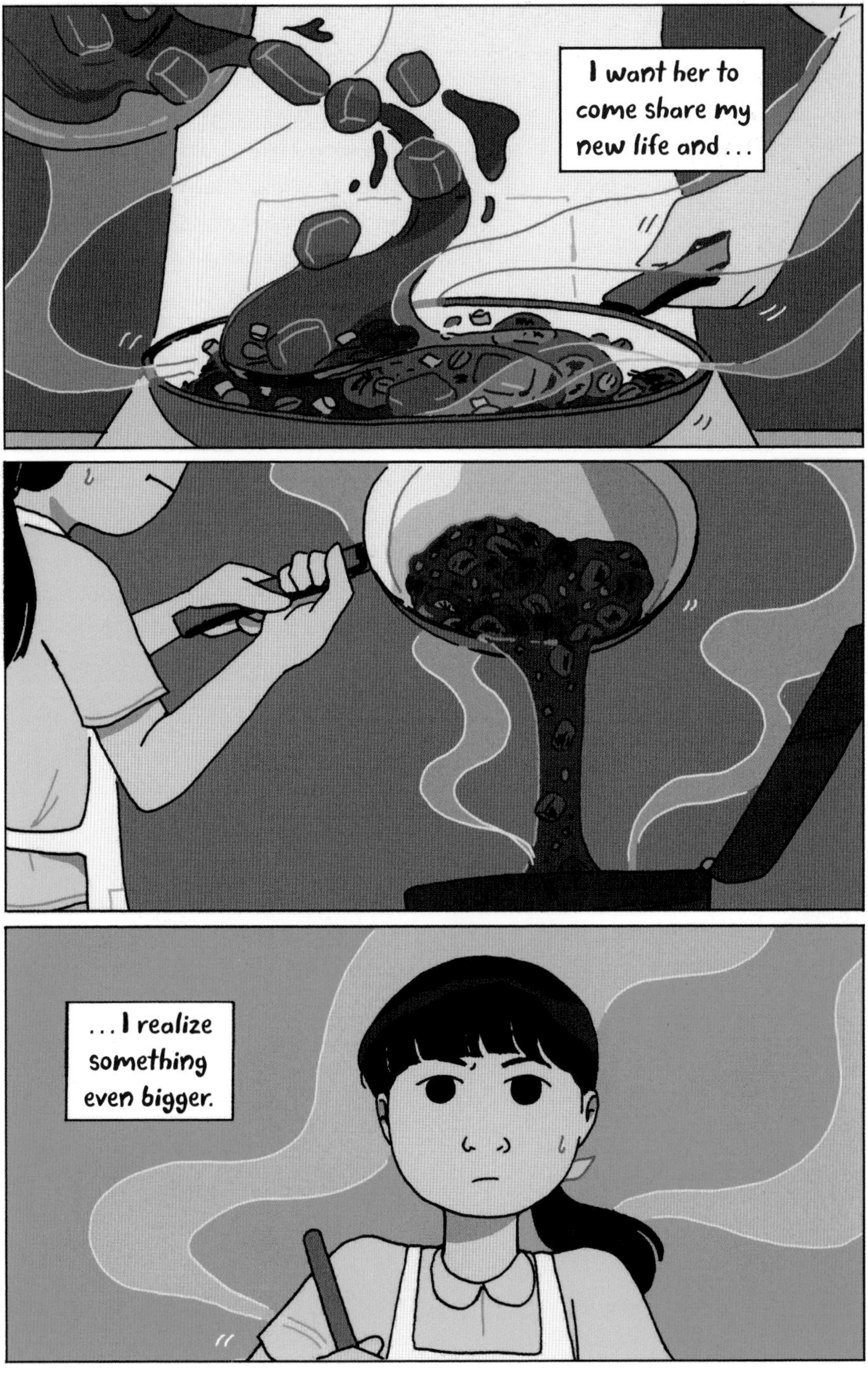
I want her to come share my new life and . . .
. . . I realize something even bigger.

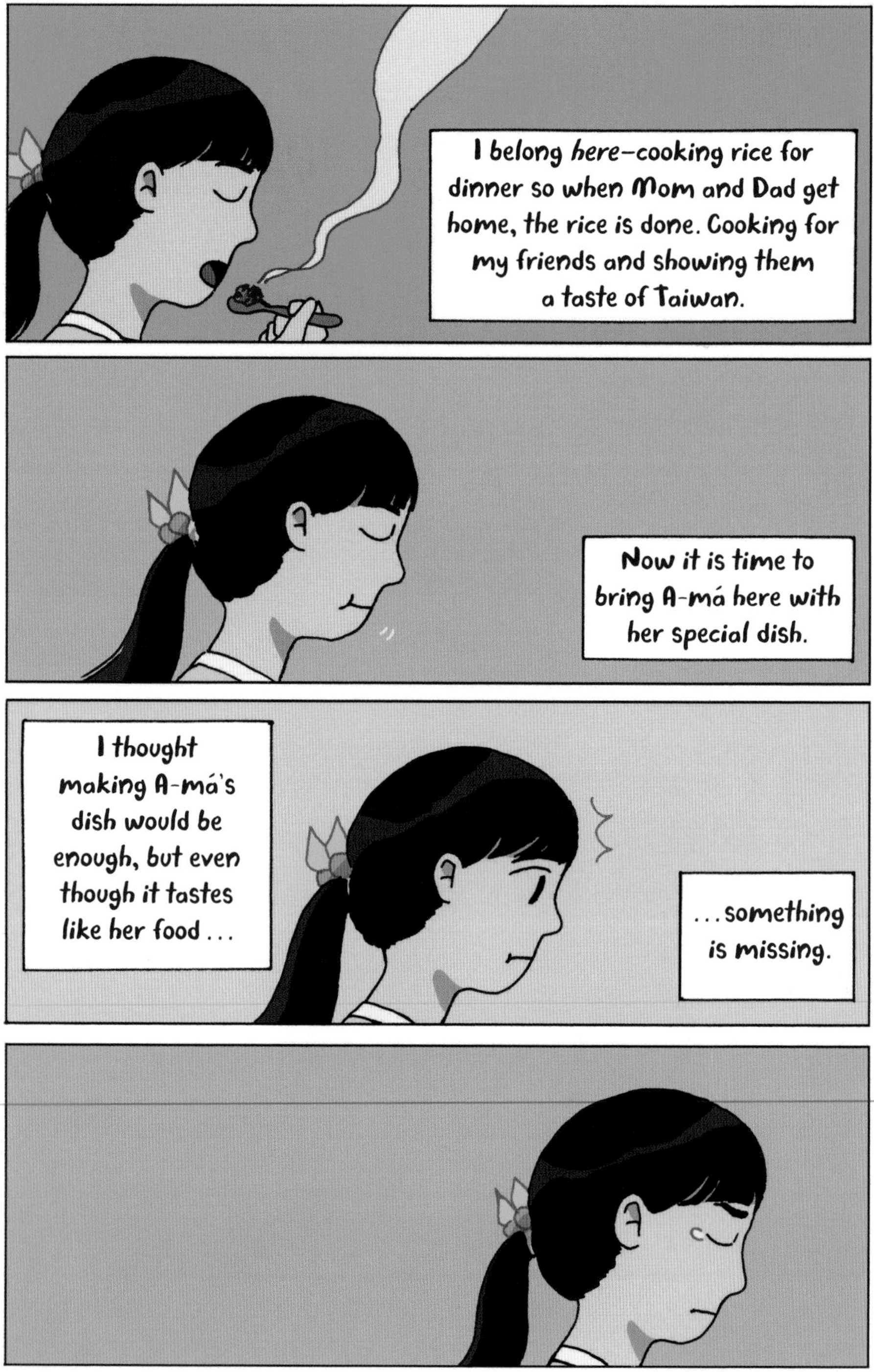
I belong *here*—cooking rice for dinner so when Mom and Dad get home, the rice is done. Cooking for my friends and showing them a taste of Taiwan.
Now it is time to bring A-má here with her special dish.
I thought making A-má's dish would be enough, but even though it tastes like her food . . .
. . . something is missing.

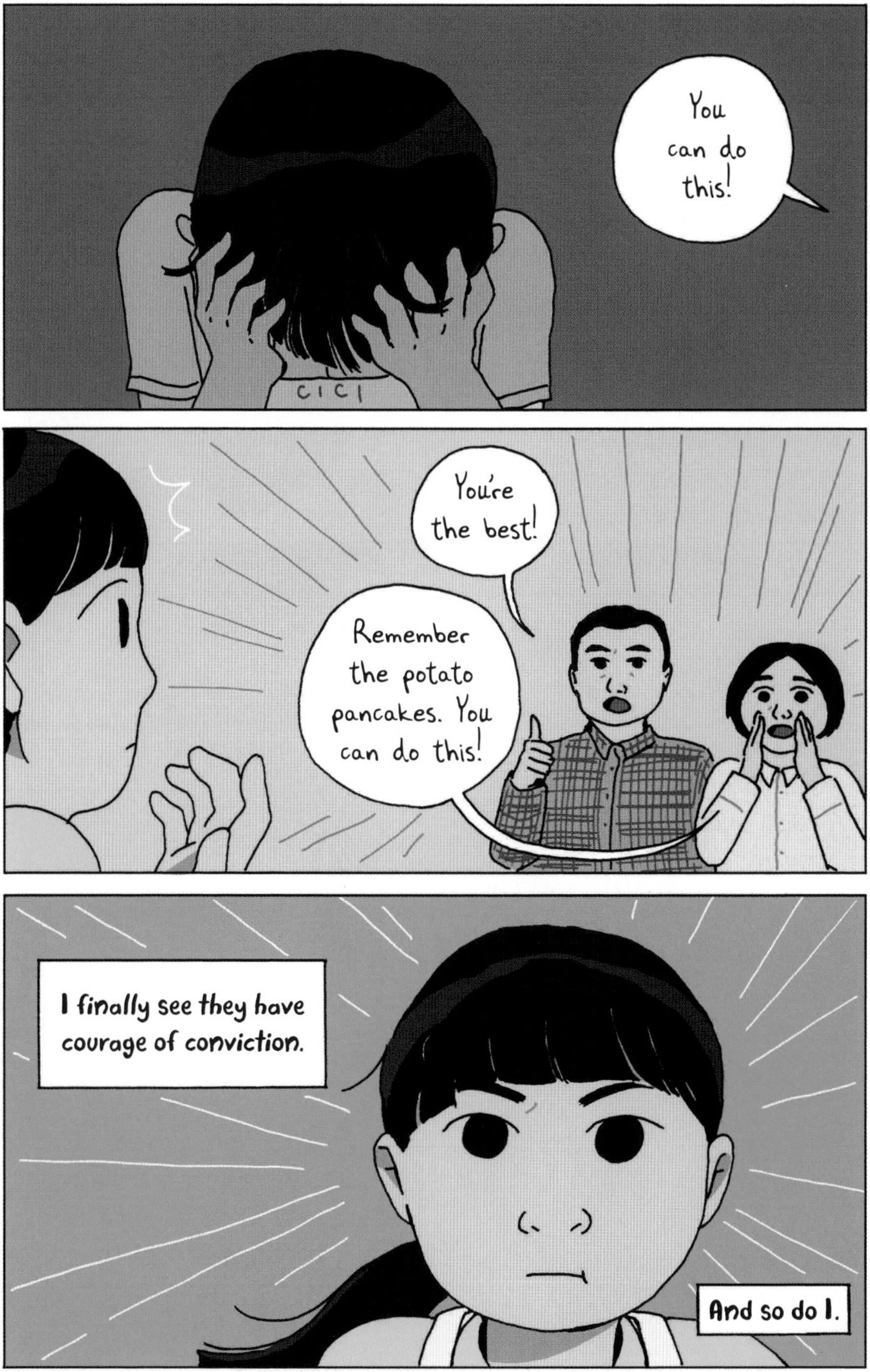
You can do this!
CICI
You're the best!
Remember the potato pancakes. You can do this!
I finally see they have courage of conviction.
And so do I.

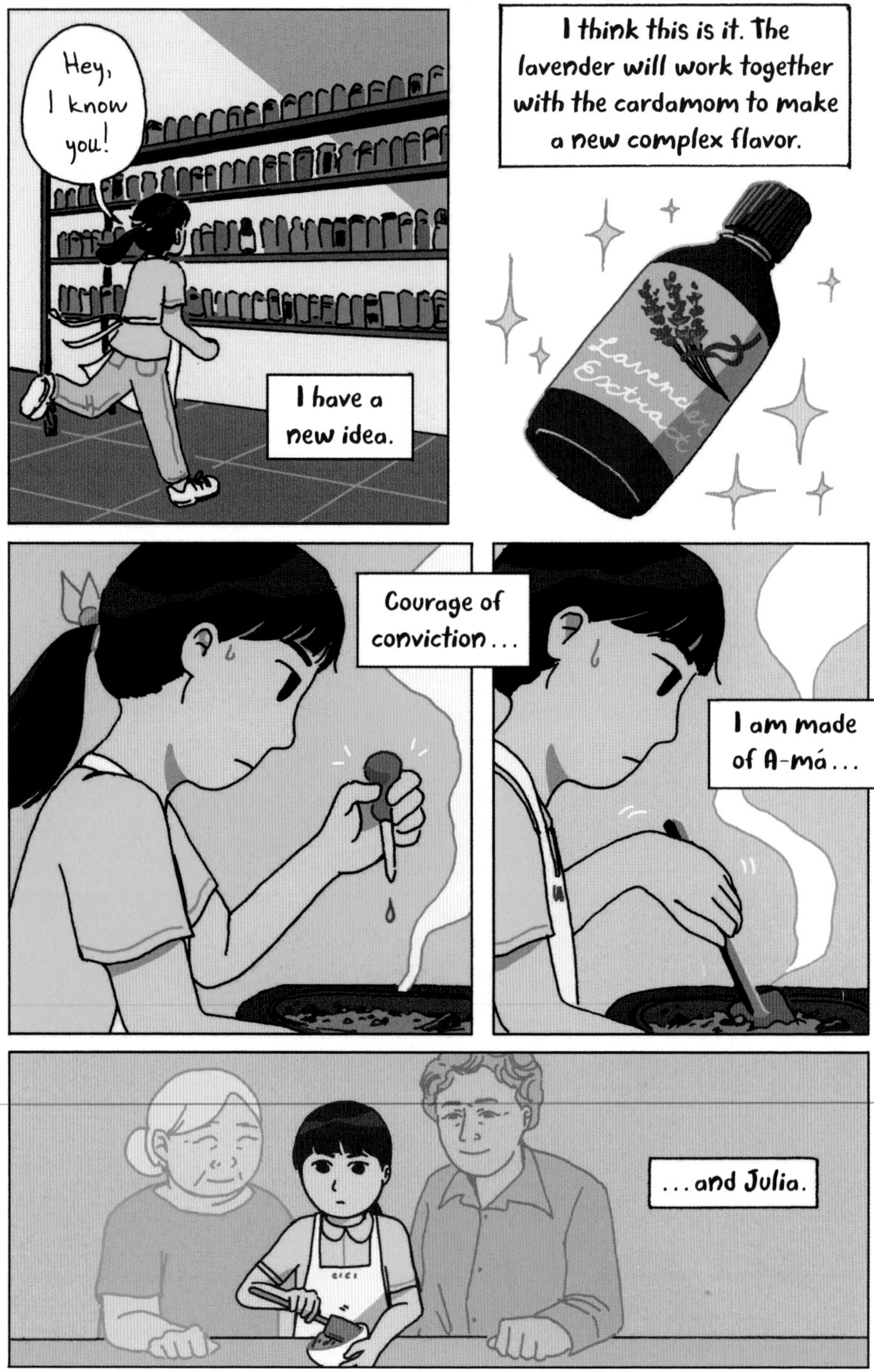
Hey, I know you!
I have a new idea.
I think this is it. The lavender will work together with the cardamom to make a new complex flavor.
Lavender Extract
Courage of conviction...
I am made of A-má...
...and Julia.

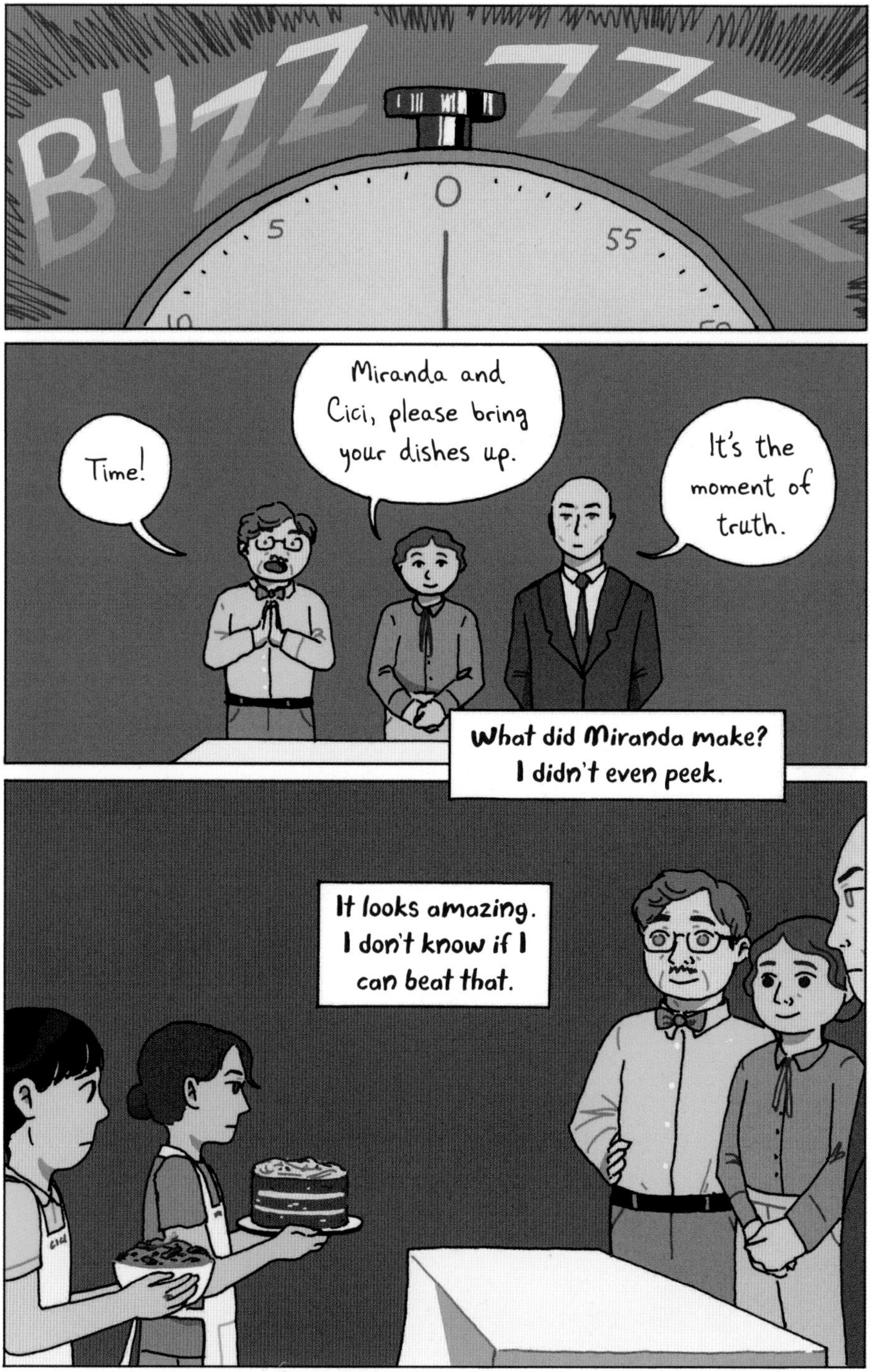
BUZZZZZ
5
0
55
Time!
Miranda and Cici, please bring your dishes up.
It's the moment of truth.
What did Miranda make? I didn't even peek.
It looks amazing. I don't know if I can beat that.

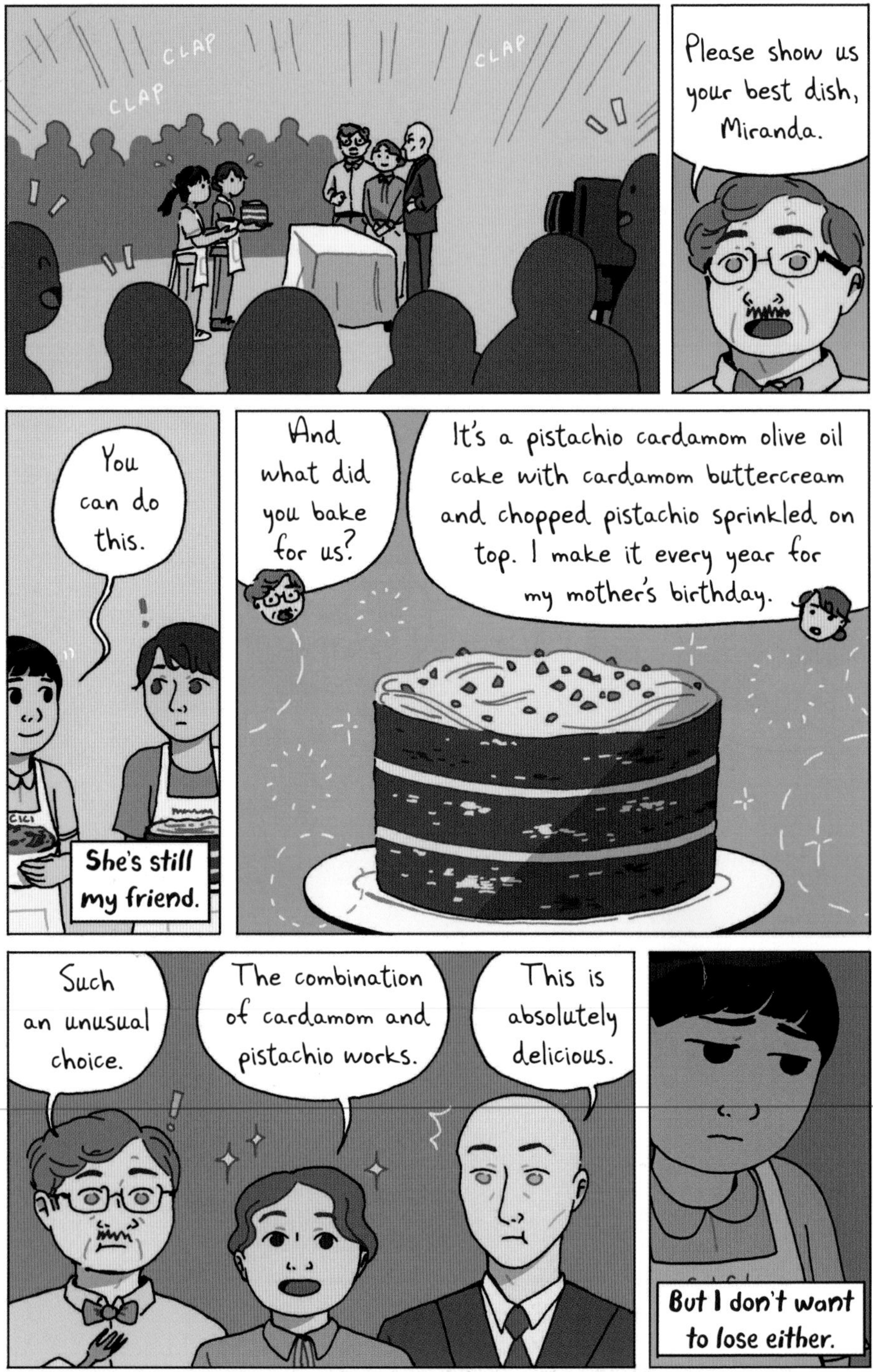
CLAP
CLAP
CLAP
Please show us your best dish, Miranda.
You can do this.
She's still my friend.
And what did you bake for us?
It's a pistachio cardamom olive oil cake with cardamom buttercream and chopped pistachio sprinkled on top. I make it every year for my mother's birthday.
Such an unusual choice.
The combination of cardamom and pistachio works.
This is absolutely delicious.
But I don't want to lose either.

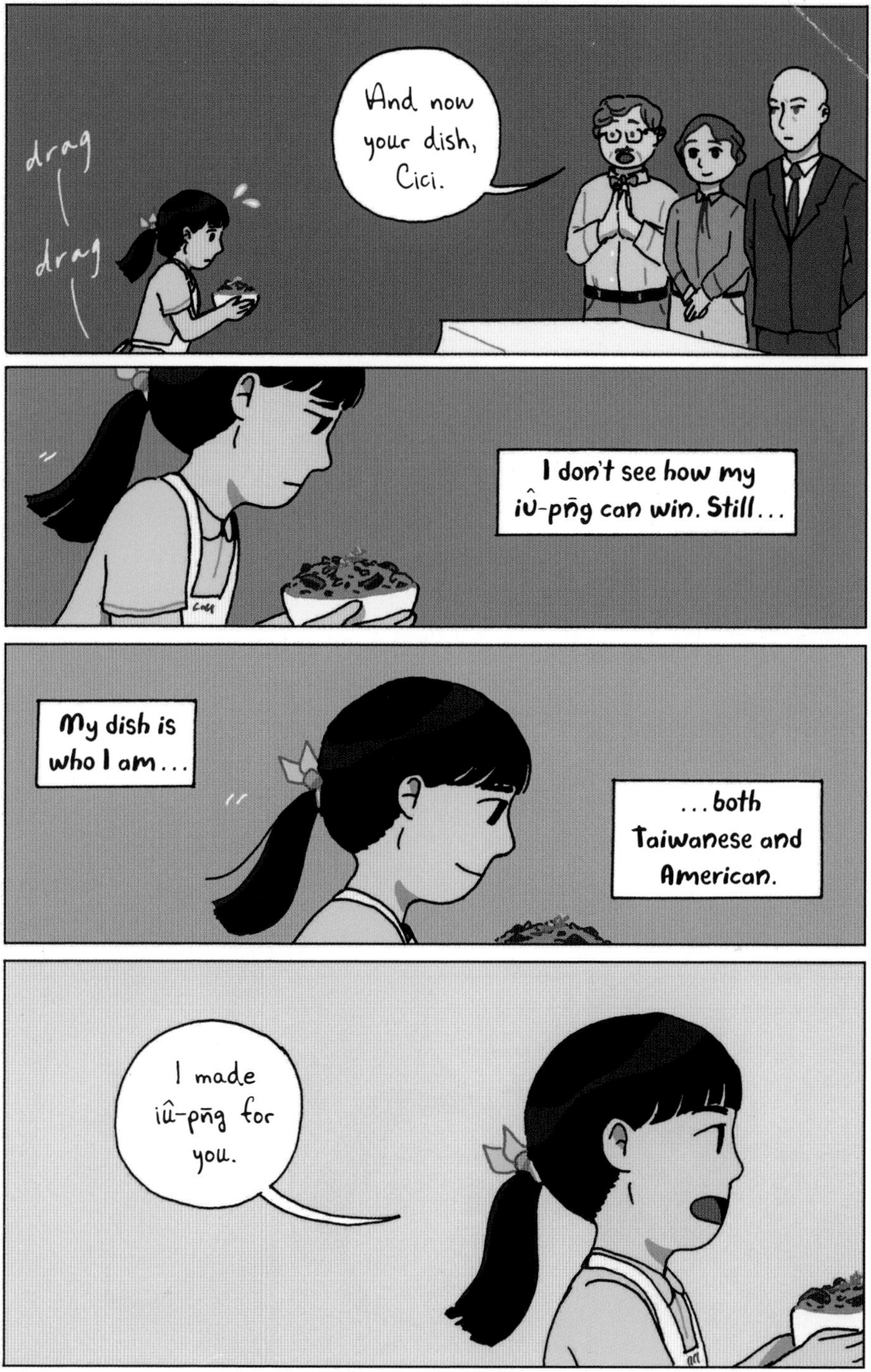
drag
drag
And now your dish, Cici.
I don't see how my iû-pn̄g can win. Still...
My dish is who I am...
...both Taiwanese and American.
I made iû-pn̄g for you.

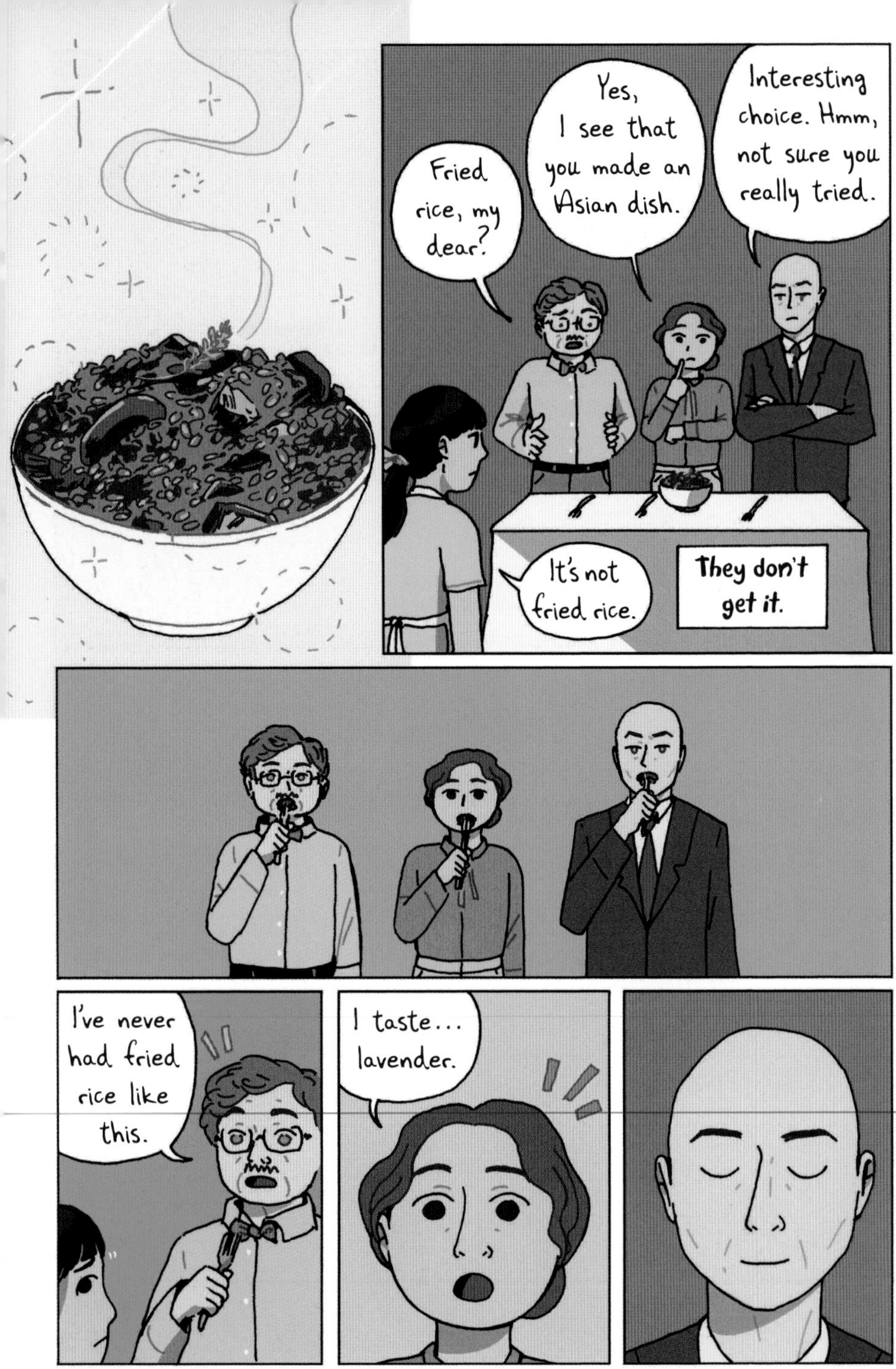
Fried rice, my dear?
Yes, I see that you made an Asian dish.
Interesting choice. Hmm, not sure you really tried.
It's not fried rice.
They don't get it.
I've never had fried rice like this.
I taste... lavender.

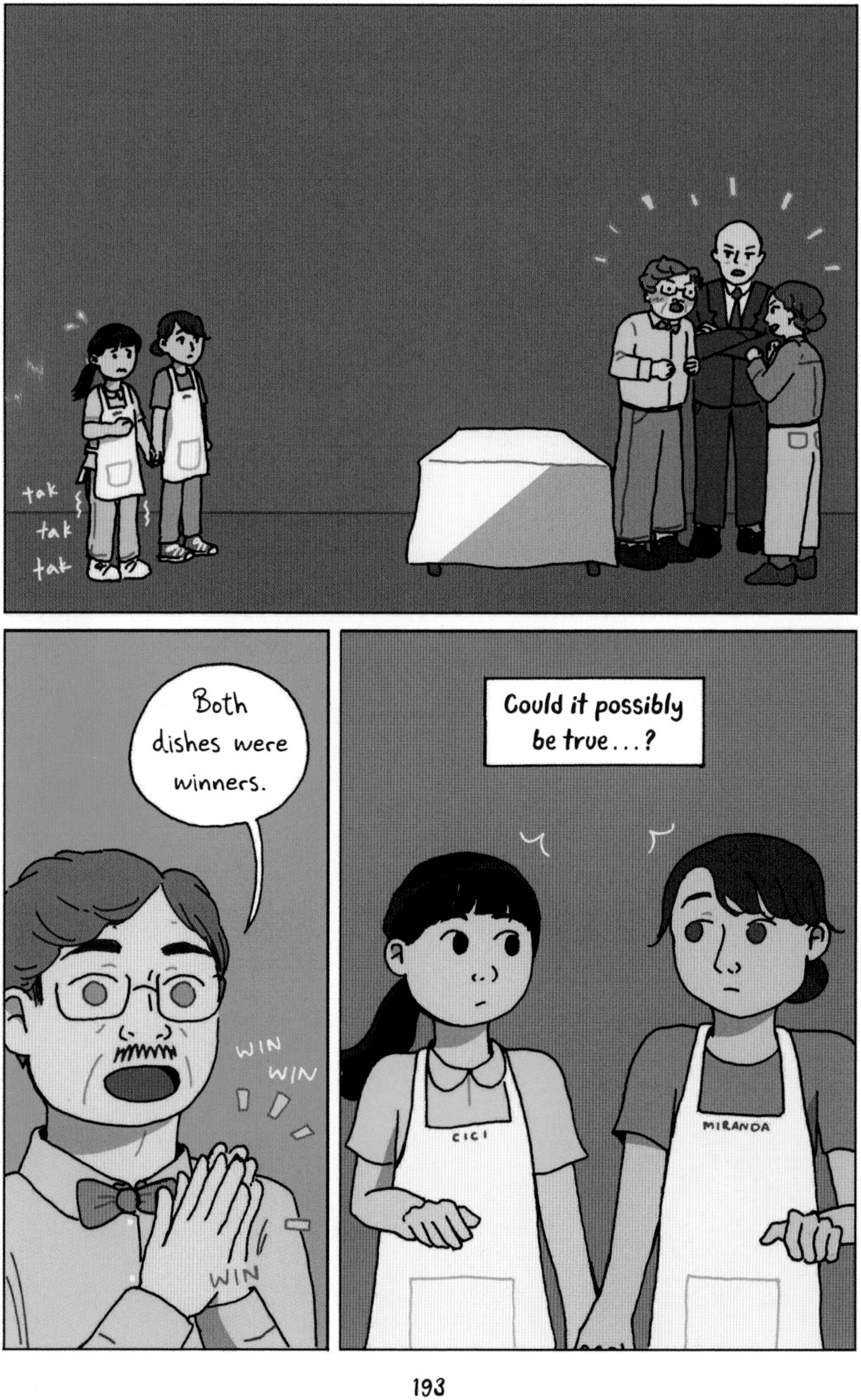
tak
tak
tak
Both dishes were winners.
WIN
WIN
WIN
Could it possibly be true...?
CICI
MIRANDA

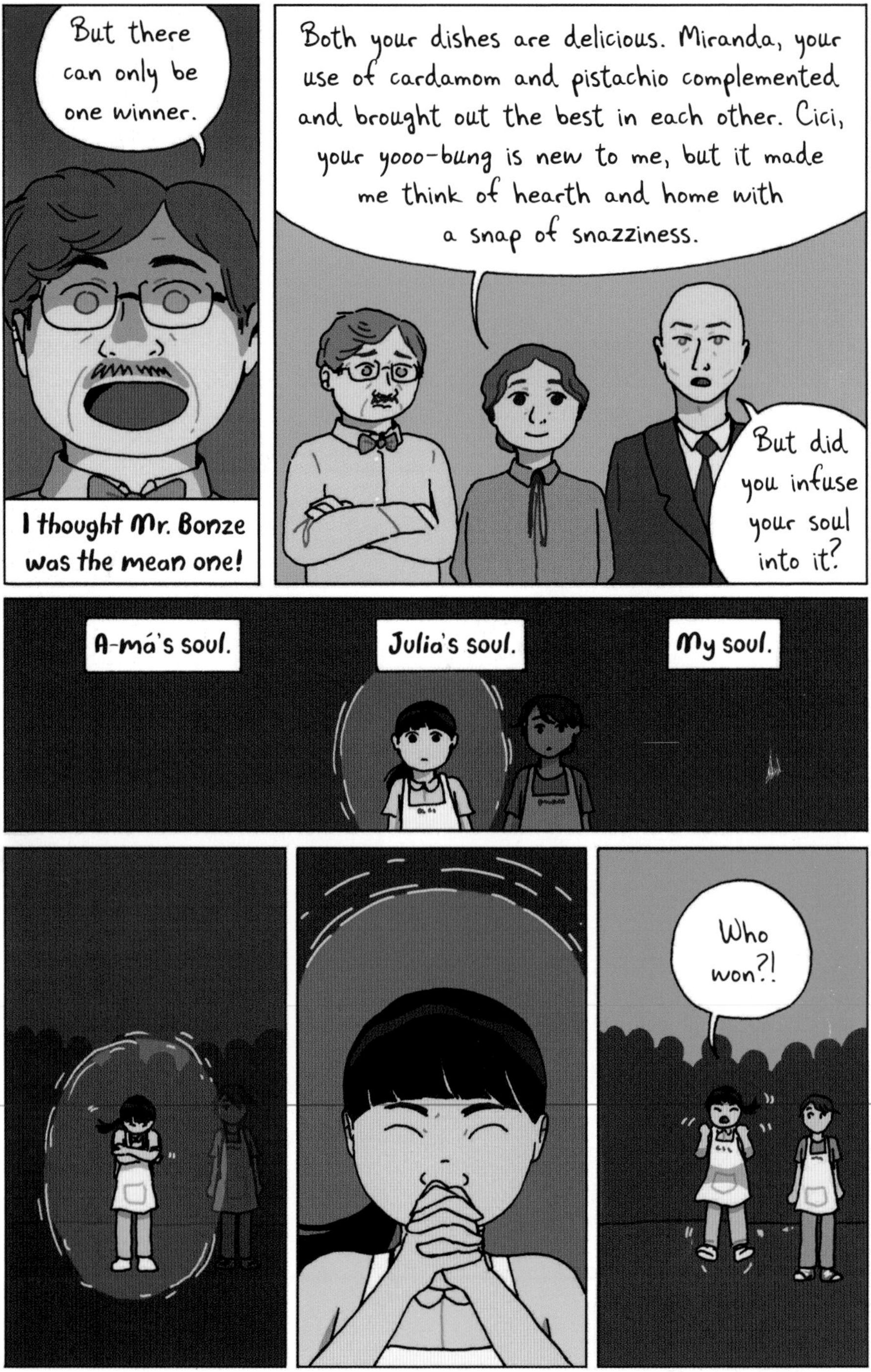

But there can only be one winner.
I thought Mr. Bonze was the mean one!
Both your dishes are delicious. Miranda, your use of cardamom and pistachio complemented and brought out the best in each other. Cici, your yooo-bung is new to me, but it made me think of hearth and home with a snap of snazziness.
But did you infuse your soul into it?
A-má's soul.
Julia's soul.
My soul.
Who won?!

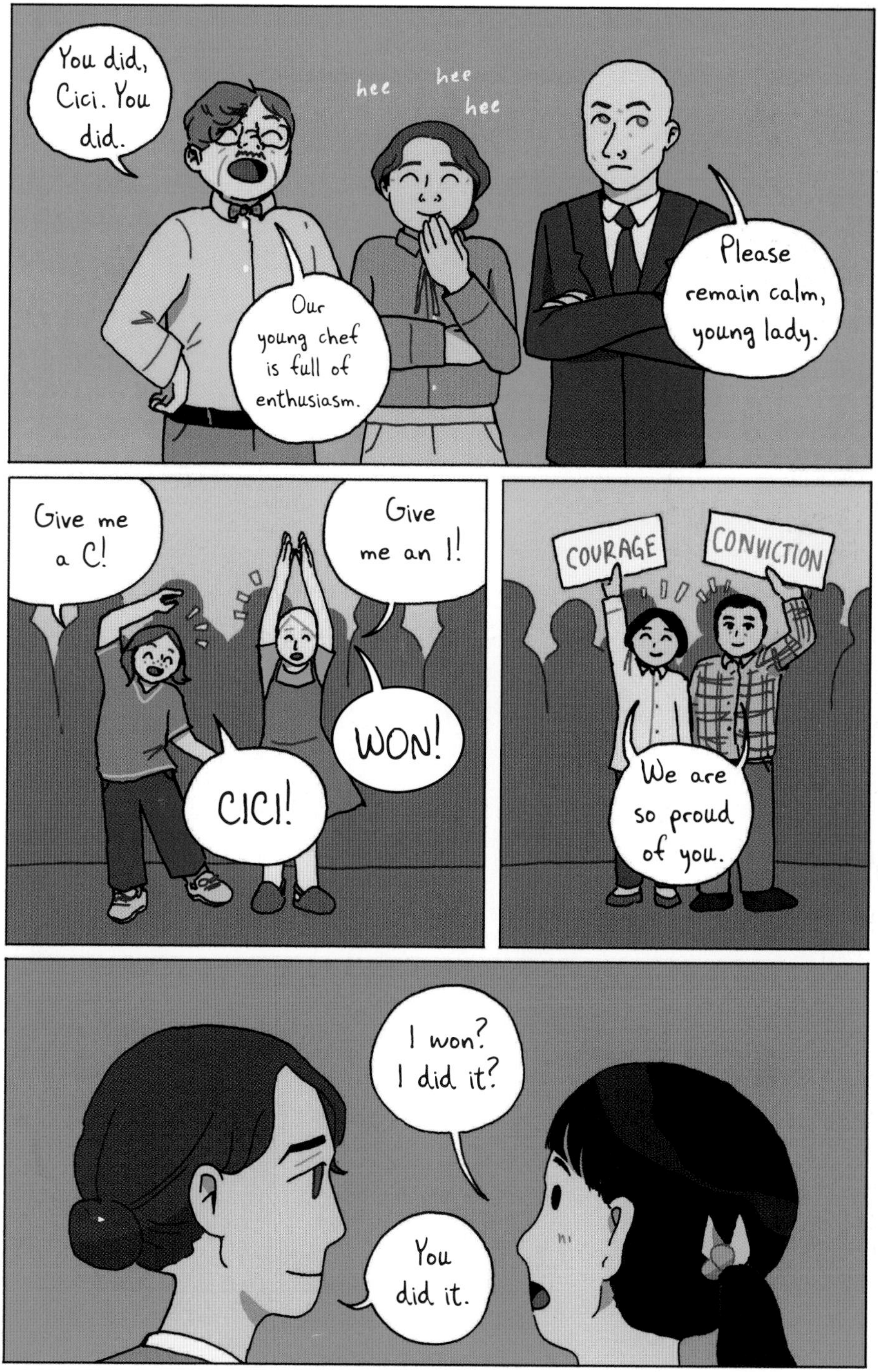
You did, Cici. You did.
hee hee hee
Our young chef is full of enthusiasm.
Please remain calm, young lady.
Give me a C!
Give me an I!
CICI!
WON!
COURAGE
CONVICTION
We are so proud of you.
I won? I did it?
You did it.

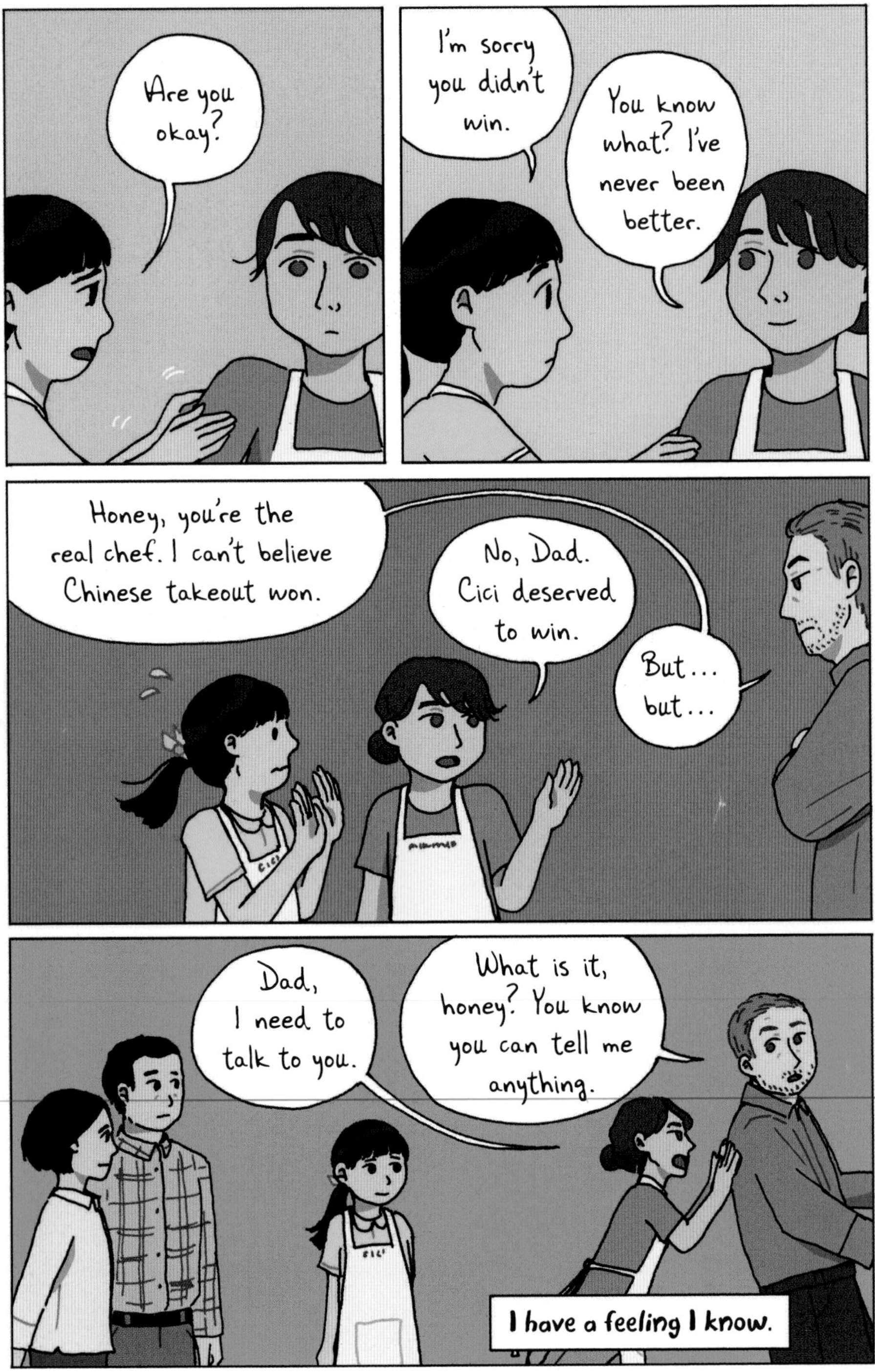
Are you okay?
I'm sorry you didn't win.
You know what? I've never been better.
Honey, you're the real chef. I can't believe Chinese takeout won.
No, Dad. Cici deserved to win.
But... but...
Dad, I need to talk to you.
What is it, honey? You know you can tell me anything.
I have a feeling I know.

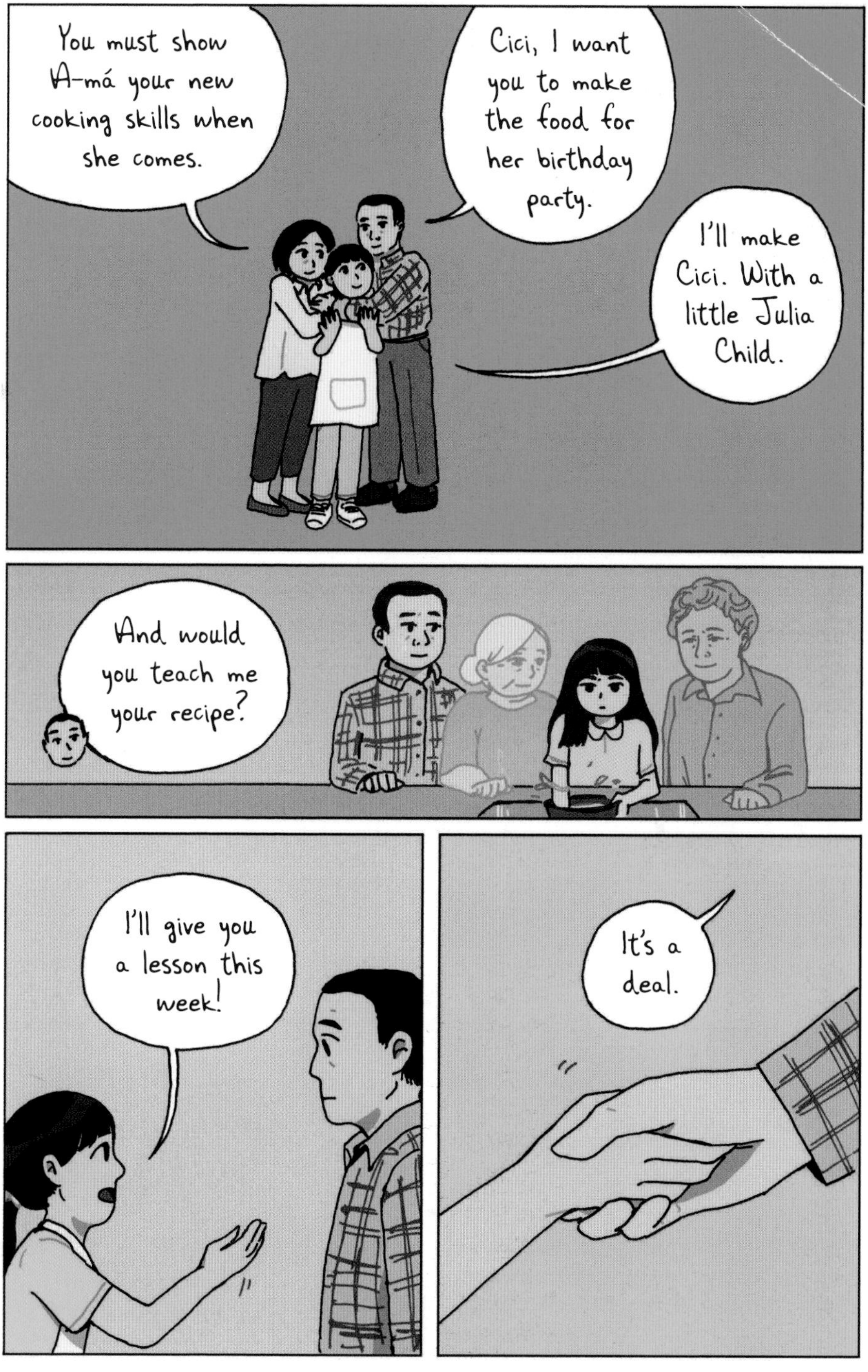
You must show A-má your new cooking skills when she comes.
Cici, I want you to make the food for her birthday party.
I'll make Cici. With a little Julia Child.
And would you teach me your recipe?
I'll give you a lesson this week!
It's a deal.

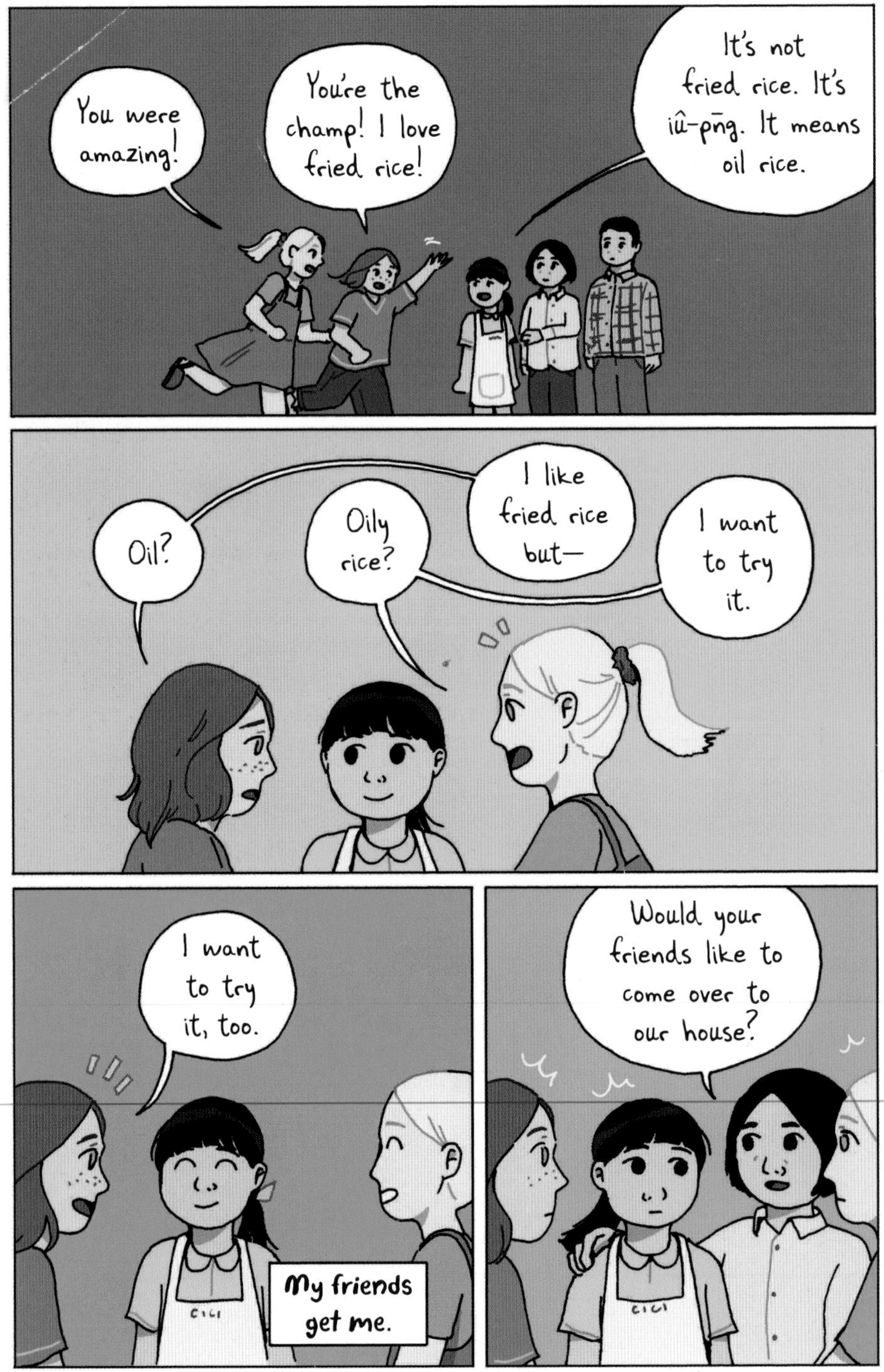
You were amazing!
You're the champ! I love fried rice!
It's not fried rice. It's iû-pn̄g. It means oil rice.
Oil?
Oily rice?
I like fried rice but—
I want to try it.
I want to try it, too.
CICI
My friends get me.
Would your friends like to come over to our house?
CICI

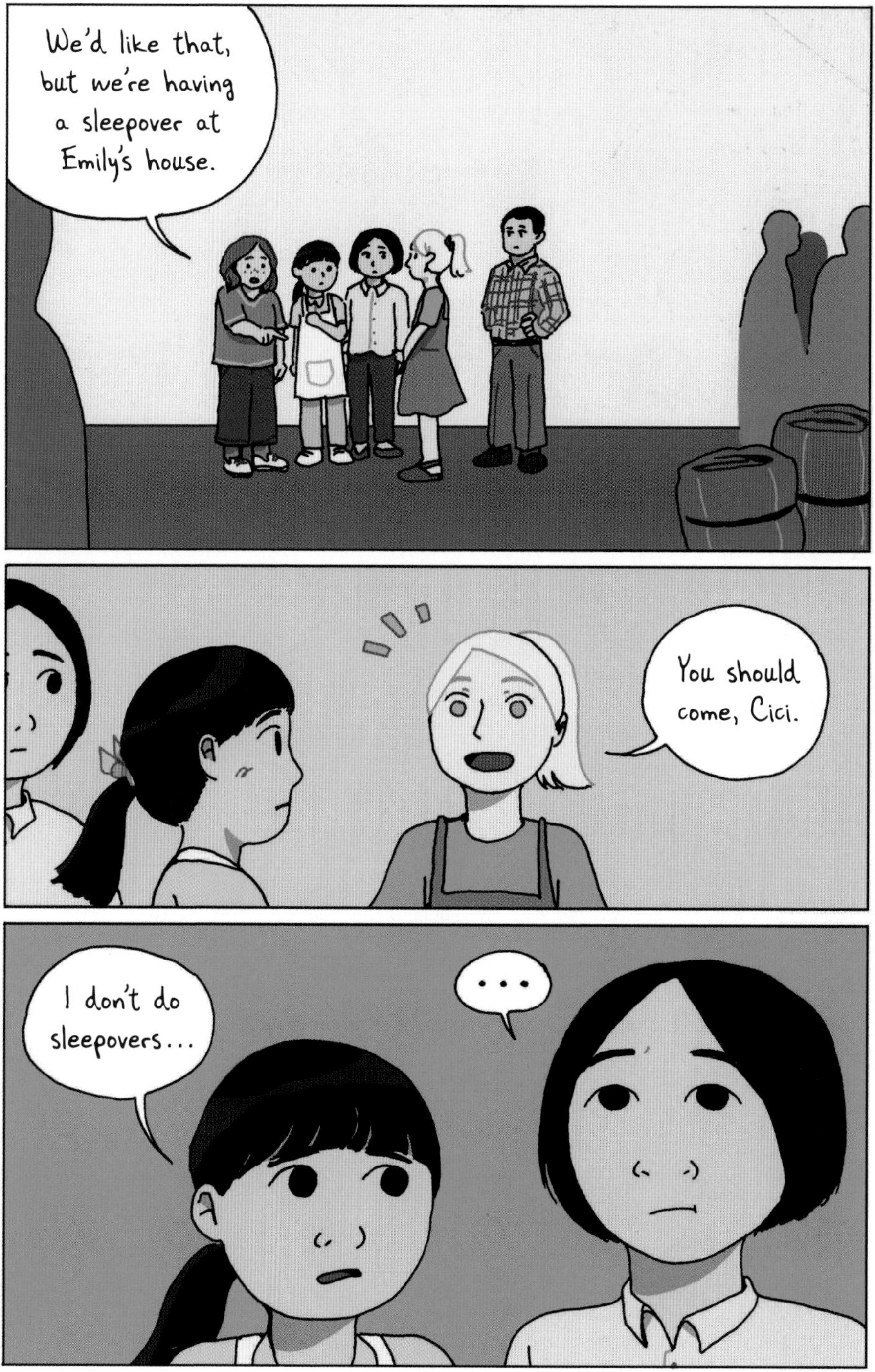
We'd like that, but we're having a sleepover at Emily's house.
You should come, Cici.
I don't do sleepovers...
...

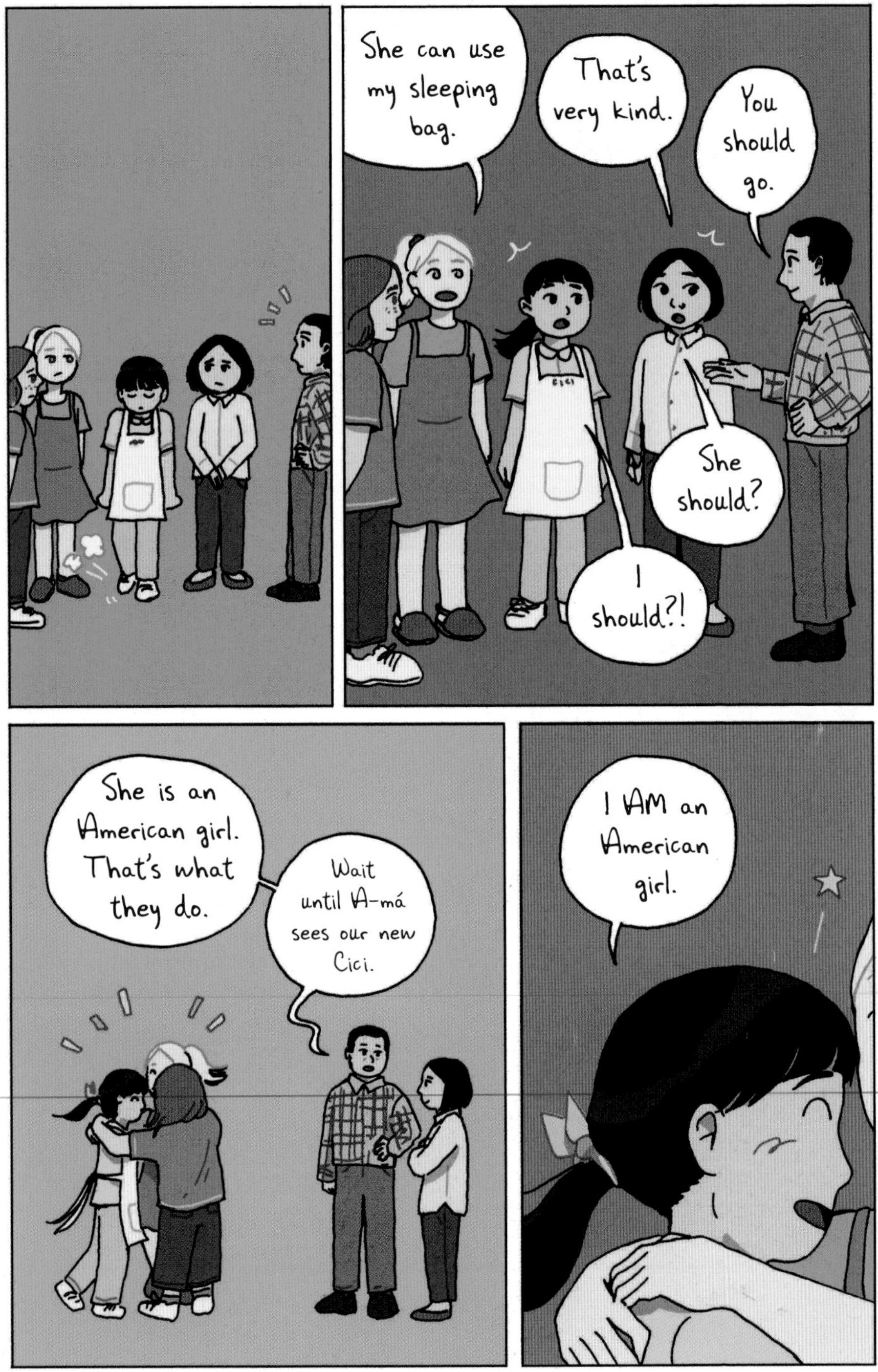
She can use my sleeping bag.
That's very kind.
You should go.
She should?
I should?!
She is an American girl. That's what they do.
Wait until A-má sees our new Cici.
I AM an American girl.

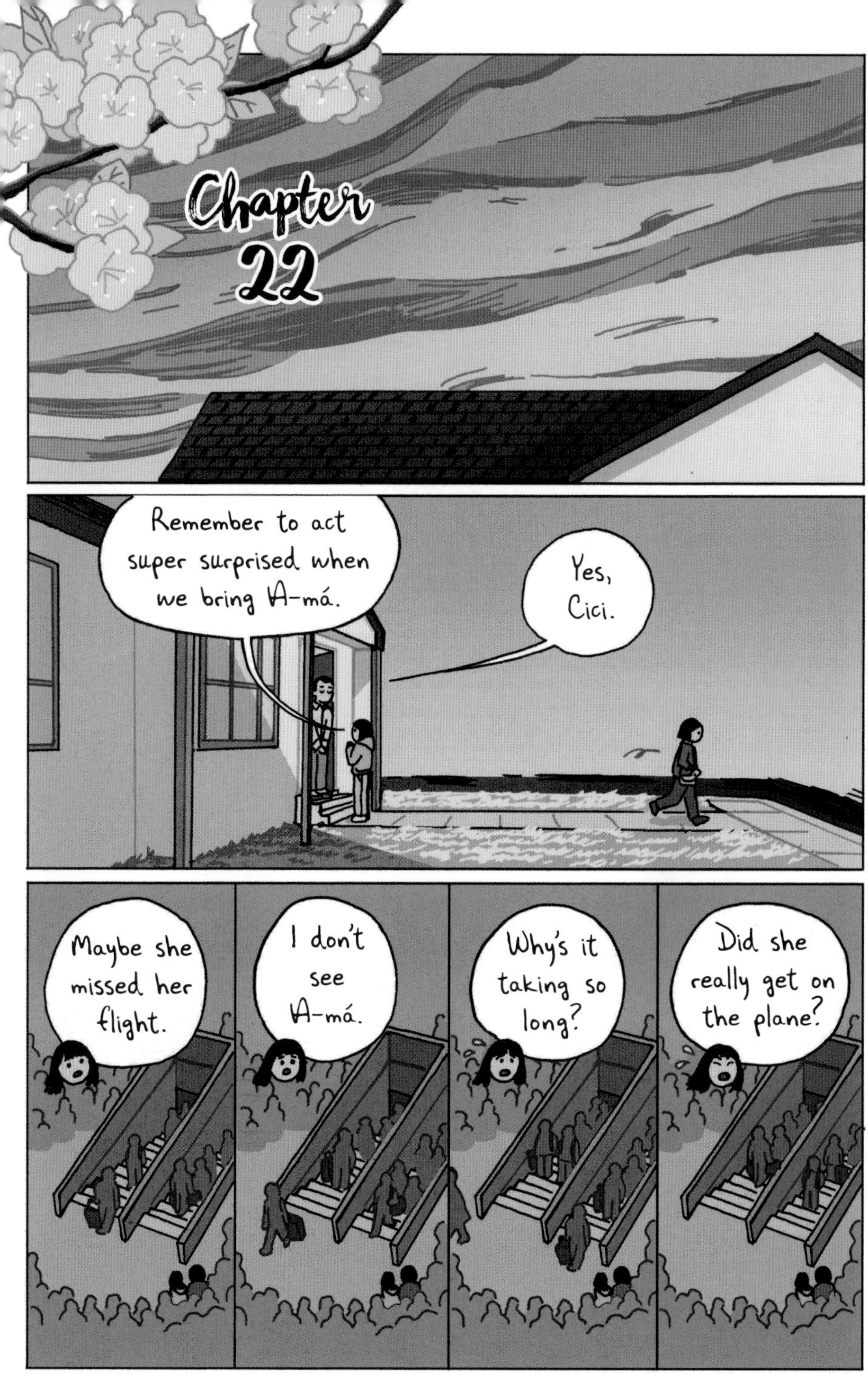
Chapter 22
Remember to act super surprised when we bring A-má.
Yes, Cici.
Maybe she missed her flight.
I don't see A-má.
Why's it taking so long?
Did she really get on the plane?

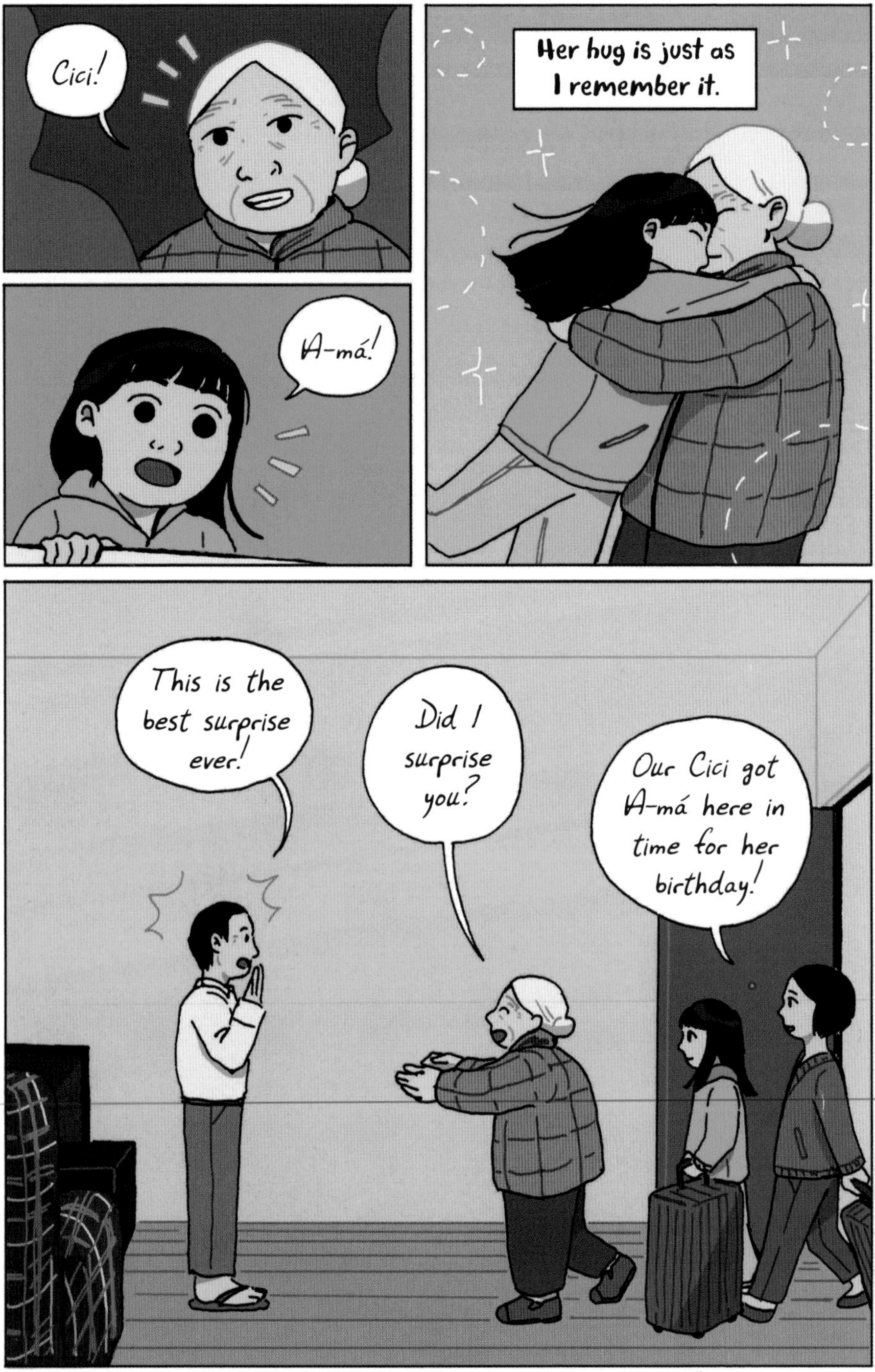

Cici!
A-má!
Her hug is just as I remember it.
This is the best surprise ever!
Did I surprise you?
Our Cici got A-má here in time for her birthday!

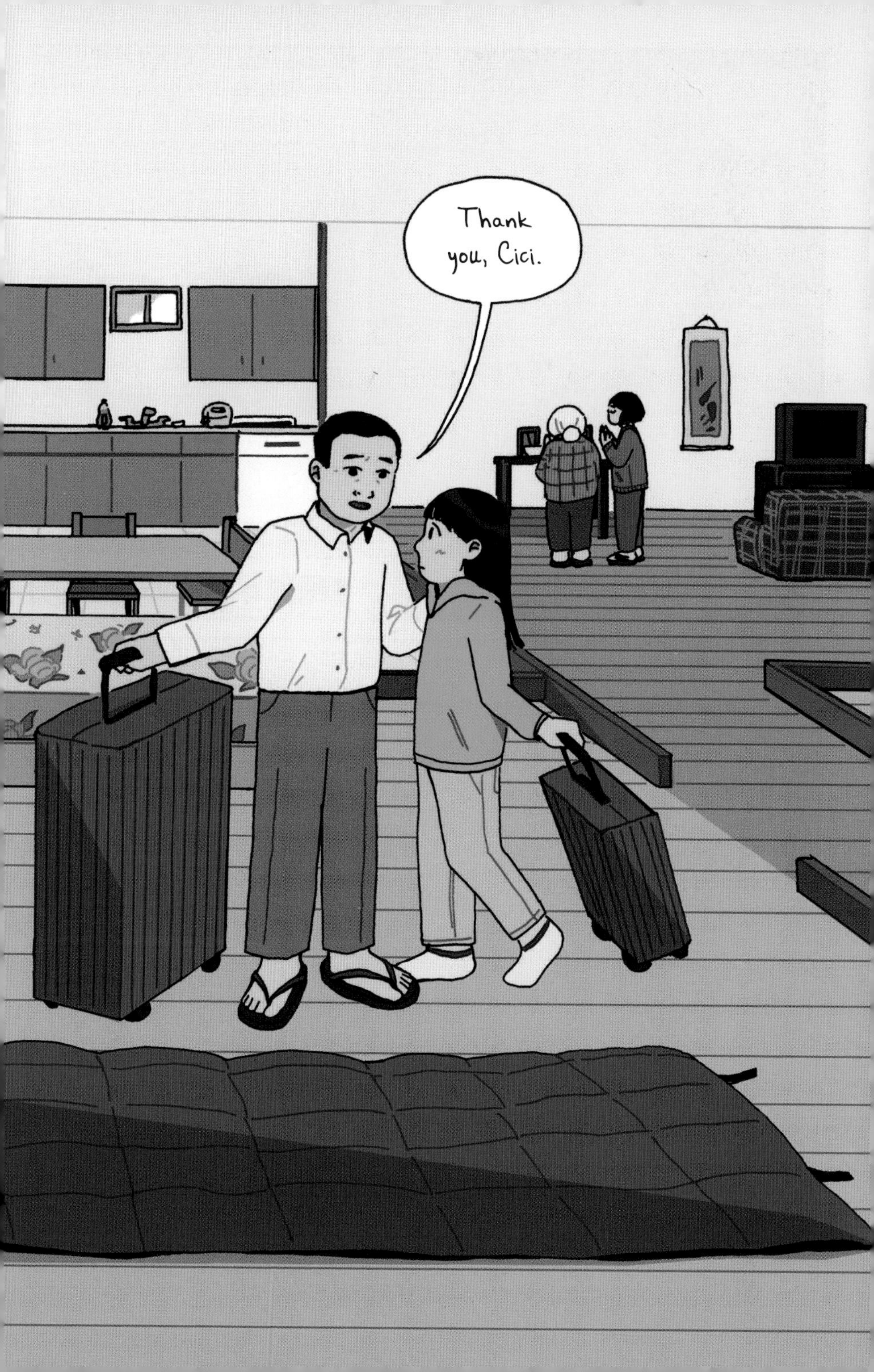
Thank you, Cici.

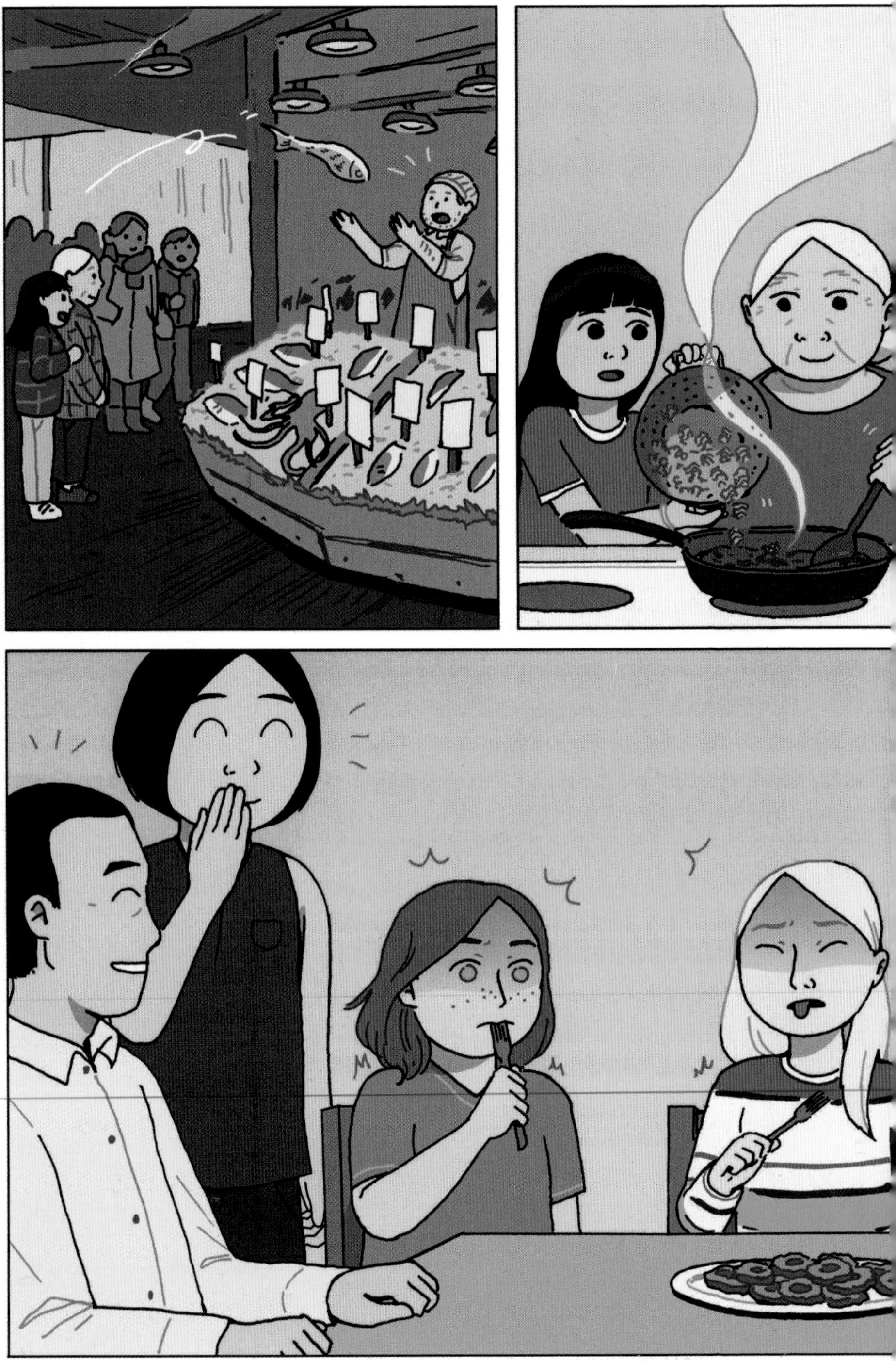

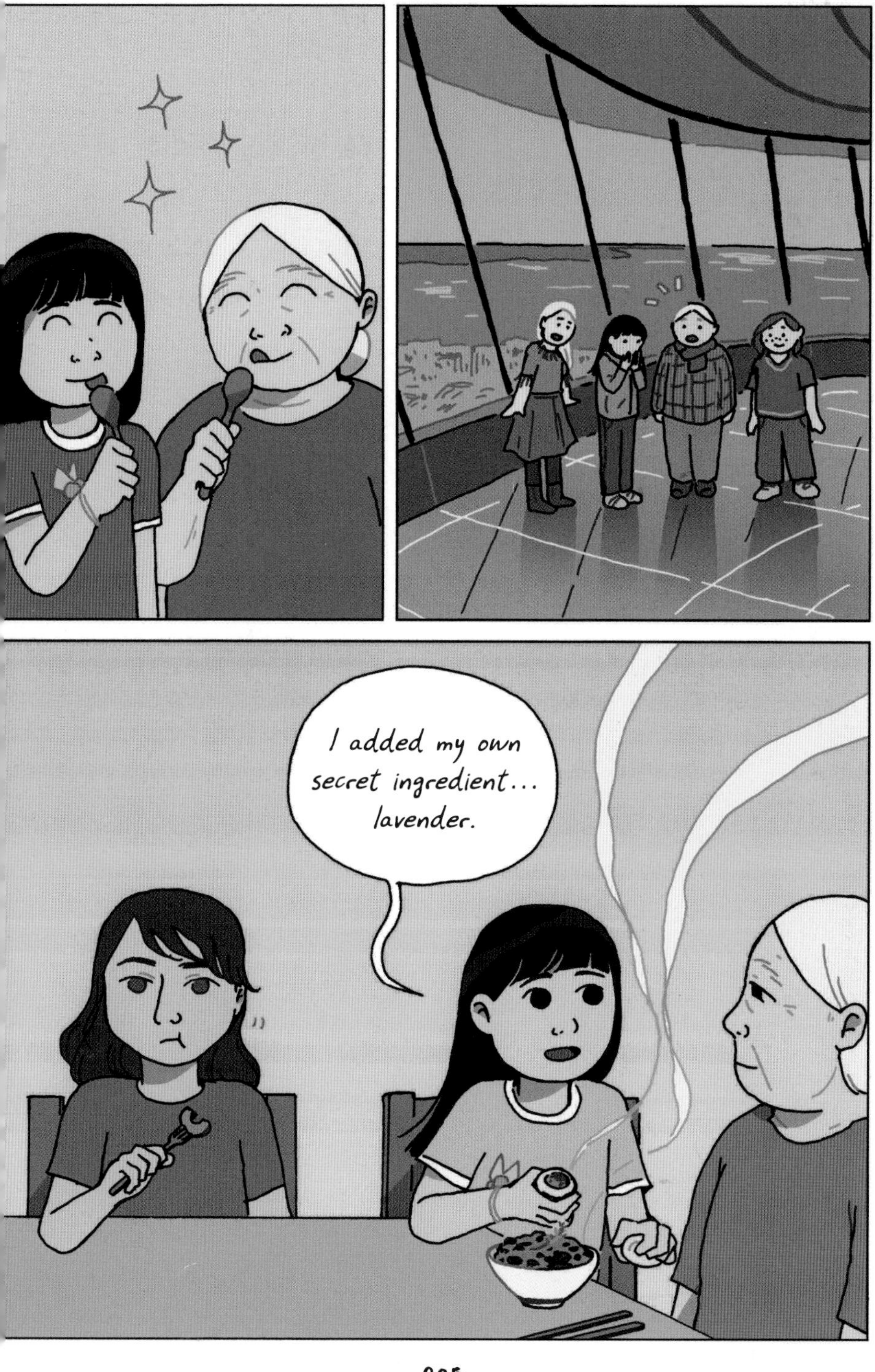
I added my own secret ingredient... lavender.

For Lucien, Terry, and Schuyler—L.L.M.

To friends who kept me uplifted
and encouraged every step of the way—A.X.

HarperAlley is an imprint of HarperCollins Publishers.

Measuring Up
Text copyright © 2020 by Lily LaMotte
Illustrations copyright © 2020 by Ann Xu
Colors by Sunmi. Flats by Cynthia Yuan Cheng and Ashanti Fortson.
All rights reserved. Printed in Slovenia.

Library of Congress Control Number: 2020938942
ISBN 978-0-06-297387-0 — ISBN 978-0-06-297386-3 (pbk.)

The artist used ink on paper and Adobe Photoshop to create the digital illustrations for this book.
Typography by Erica De Chavez
20 21 22 23 24   GPS   10 9 8 7 6 5 4 3 2

First Edition